I0618223

BETRAYAL IN THE LOUVRE

Copyright by Henry J. Gaudreau

This book is a work of fiction. Names, characters, places, and incidents are the product of the author's imagination or are used fictitiously.

All rights reserved. No part of this book may be used or reproduced in any manner whatsoever without the written permission of the publisher.

ISBN: 0989403408
ISBN-13: 978-0-9894034-0-5

Cover design by Margie Schramke

Cover Photograph by Moyan Brenn

Excerpt from THE COLLINGWOOD LEGACY copyright 2013. All rights reserved. No part of this book may be used or reproduced in any manner whatsoever without the written permission of the publisher.

DEDICATION

For Eve – The best is yet to come.

Thomas – I'm so proud.

Mom – I can't thank you enough.

A simple trip to an antique show leads to a fight for their life

Jim and Eve Crenshaw live on a small farm in mid-Michigan. It's a peaceful life. But when they find an ivory tube containing one of the four pieces of French Royal Regalia they are dragged into an international hunt for the remaining three pieces.

Marie Antoinette's heart breaks as her child is ripped from her arms while the French Revolution convulses France. A WWI doughboy is caught in the horror of war.

Chased by Europe's most dangerous killers, only Jim's cunning and Eve's bravery can save them.

Fast paced, non-stop suspense pushes this story through the French Revolution, World War One, Montreal, Paris and the French countryside.

BETRAYAL IN THE LOUVRE

H J Gaudreau

Copyright © 2013 Henry J. Gaudreau
All rights reserved.
ISBN: 0989403408
ISBN-13: 978-0-9894034-0-5

ACKNOWLEDGMENTS

I live with a school teacher. She dreams about children. She is what every teacher should be. I was blessed to have two high school teachers who were, in their own way, equally dedicated. Mr. Glen Davis and Mr. Thomas Carstensen. They taught me to write.

Every novel needs an editor. I have the best.

My wonderful wife was forced to endure countless passages which were modified, deleted or kept as the process wore on. Friends and family were wonderful test subjects and provided extremely helpful and honest feedback.

Special thanks to my SIL. Sherrie your constant, unwavering enthusiasm was, and is, much appreciated.

Many thanks to Margie Schramke, a wonderful talent!

Please Support:
SAVE THE CHILDREN
54 Wilton Road
Westport, CT 06880
www.savethechildren.org

Betrayal in the Louvre

H J GAUDREAU

Prologue

The notice that would forever change their lives was not found in a local, big city newspaper; rather it was in a weekly crier called the "Michigan Voice". That Eve saw it at all was a bit of a surprise. They rarely, if ever picked up the Voice. But for some reason fate intervened, and Jim had grabbed the paper as he left the town's only hardware store. Now, sitting on the back porch, drinking her coffee, waiting for Jim to finish in the barn, Eve thumbed through the only reading material available. And there it was, third page, lower left: "Antique Show and Charity Auction Returns to Detroit." Jim, more than Eve, enjoyed the show. Rarely could they afford the items for sale; this was not a "clean out the garage" kind of antique show. This show was hosted by some of the country's finest auction houses. They didn't attend as buyers. Jim was a collector of arcane bits of trivia and simply found the auction to be a treasure trove of "interesting stuff".

Suddenly, the baying of a beagle could be heard behind the equipment shed, a gray ghost raced around the building and headed for the pasture. Molly had picked up the scent and was close behind the rabbit.

Jim stepped from the barn, slid the door shut and walked to the house. "Your antique auction is next week," she said as he climbed the porch steps. Jim washed his hands at the outdoor sink then sat in a deep wicker chair next to his wife.

"Great! That thing is always so interesting. And this year I've got something I want to take."

Eve started to laugh, "You really are a nerd. You know that don't you?"

Jim just grinned.

"What do you want to sell?"

"Well, I'm not really sure. Remember that stuff my great grandfather brought back from World War One? I'm hoping someone at the show will recognize it and be able to tell me a little bit more."

"Like if we've been hauling junk around the world for the past thirty years or not?" Eve asked in a gentle dig.

"Well, yeah," he grinned. "In any case, I thought this was

a good chance to have it appraised. At least someone might be able to tell me what it is. And if not, maybe the Tigers are playing."

"I knew there was more to this than an antique auction! C'mon, call your dog and let's go in. I'm hungry."

Chapter 1

Paris

3 June 1789

General Nicolas Luckner was out of bed before the man, for a man it surely was, on the other side of the door pounded a second time. In a moment he had a brace of .60 caliber holster pistols in his hands and was standing, naked, back to the wall, next to the door. The woman in the bed felt a wave of fear wash over her. The wave crested, then, human nature what it is, she admired the view.

From outside the door a young man's voice called, "Mon General, it is urgent."

Luckner recognized the voice of his new adjutant and relaxed. The man, boy really, had been with him for only the past two weeks. This was the first time he'd been to the General's room after their morning drill. Luckner opened the door and let the man-boy in. The adjutant instinctively began a salute, saw the General was naked and attempted to look away. He turned his right shoulder to the General and found himself facing a young, naked, red-haired woman sitting cross-legged on the bed. His surprise evident he involuntarily took a step backward, whereupon he collided with the General. Shaken he spun around to meet the now angry glare of the man he feared more than anything in this life and, he was convinced, the next as well.

He stammered once, cleared his throat and before the General had finished inhaling in preparation for what surely would be one of history's great tongue-lashings he managed to stammer out the news he had been sent to deliver. "Sir, ah...Col DeAubry asked that...you have...you are supposed to..." The Adjutant's young eyes couldn't overcome the powerful draw of the woman's naked body. Like a bee to honey his eyes, without command, turned to her. The woman caught the glance, and vixen that she was, instantly decided to toy with the man-boy. She went into an exaggerated yawn, stretching her arms over her head, thrusting her bare breasts at the Adjutant. Then, like a cherry on top of a banana split, she smiled. The Adjutant's slim hold on his composure cracked.

The breach only lasted a moment as a thick hand slapped him on his left ear. The General stared down a long pointed nose, suppressed a smile and waited. The young officer regained his composure, stiffened, looked directly at the General and said, "Sir, Col DeAubry has asked that I relay a message."

"Well?" General Luckner's expression was stern, as befit a General. He was enjoying this little game. The man-boy tried again, "The King has summoned you." Luckner's brain instantly went to full attention.

"For what purpose? When and where? These things should have been said already." Luckner did not suffer fools gladly, the game was over, the humor gone. The young man was now angering the General. Had he never seen a naked woman before?

"Le Château de Versailles. Immediately."

"Tell the Colonel 'thank you' and I shall be with him in five minutes," Luckner said. The Adjutant, from sheer habit, saluted; stole another glance at the naked woman and fled the room. The General closed the door behind him. "No, he probably hasn't," he thought. Then his mind snapped back to the summons.

It was time, he was sure of it. This was necessary. There had been enough of patience, negotiations, maneuvering, politics and talk, talk, talk. Now, he was going to be told to round up the rabble and stuff them into the Bastille like so much sausage. Or, better yet, he'd put them to the sword tonight. He began to assemble his uniform. In a few short minutes he was dressed; except for the boots. He could not find his boot hooks. His frustration grew as he looked under the bed, under the rug, behind the door…then he remembered. Reaching into the pile of woman's clothing on the floor he found them. The woman smiled at him. In a moment his boots had been pulled on and he was out the door.

Outside the tavern Col DeAubry sat comfortably astride his horse, his attention focused on the hard piece of bread and moldy cheese which constituted his breakfast. A tall, rather lanky man, DeAubry had been born to a shoe cobbler. He had run from his apprenticeship at the first chance. At the age of twelve he'd taken a job as an assistant to a farrier and developed considerable expertise with horses. Five years later the man who had become more a father than employer was killed when a horse with an abscessed foot kicked him in the head. DeAubry found himself without means, a great deal of expertise in horses and a perfect fit for the cavalry.

The Colonel was known as a calm, sensible officer who could make things happen. He'd been with the General his entire career. Except, of course, for the three years he'd spent, at Luckner's insistence, with Rochambeau. He had survived a fever in the West Indies and distinguished himself on more than one occasion while fighting the British in their war with the American colonialists. His study and knowledge of siege warfare had been particularly useful in the later part of that campaign.

Under Luckner's sponsorship he'd risen to an almost unheard of rank for a man so low born. He was a trusted second to the General and the men feared and respected DeAubry as much as they feared and respected the General.

A few moments after DeAubry received the message a smartly dressed, fully alert General Nicolas Luckner exploded from the tavern's front door and mounted the horse held by the Adjutant. DeAubry relayed what little information he had, took up his position on the General's left and they began the short ride to the Château de Versailles. It was mid-afternoon, a light rain fell from a gray sky. The rain was welcome in Luckner's mind. It kept the rabble in their houses and it washed the sewage and animal droppings from the streets.

As they approached Le Potager du Roi the General noticed several handbills tacked to the trees outside of the royal garden's tall fence. Before he could pull one from its posting he spotted several men running across the road into the buildings and fields to his right. Instinctively his hand went to his pistol and he surveyed the doors, windows, alleys and bushes along his route. He wished he'd taken an escort; two men and a man-child would not do. He was not afraid of these traitorous fools, but he did not wish to be delayed. He would speak to DeAubry later about this.

Not knowing what the handbills were all about but feeling they may play a part in the upcoming meeting with the King he stopped, dismounted and ripped one from the trunk of a large oak tree. The Colonel did the same. DeAubry was shocked by what he read, the author accused the Queen of being a lesbian and whore.

"More attacks on the Queen's reputation." DeAubry muttered as he shook his head. Luckner read the paper in his hand. It railed against the King's treasurer Monsieur de Barentin, incompetent government and the King's intelligence. He snarled, crumpled the paper and tossed it to the ground. Other bills peppered the trees and buildings for the next several hundred yards. They walked their horses for a few moments, silently reading the posters.

DeAubry examined the fields and buildings. A boy appeared from behind a cottage. He yelled something and threw a rotten apple in their direction. The apple landed well short. What were these people about? There had been a time, not so long ago when the French military had faced down the British across the globe. People had looked at him with pride. Now? Well, now things were different weren't they? DeAubry couldn't put his finger on it, something was happening. He was looked at with contempt, sometimes hate. He didn't understand it, he didn't know what it was, but he knew change was coming. And, from all he had seen, it wasn't change for the better.

Luckner was mounting his horse. The rain was thicker now; the sky seemed a darker shade of gray. Settling into the saddle the General pulled his collar up against the wind and the rain. He pulled his sword, indicated to the Adjutant to do the same, then leaning toward the still dismounted DeAubry he said, "Have as many men as possible, with good horses, at the palace in an hour. I suspect we're going to be busy tonight." Luckner then turned his horse in the direction of the château, kicked the animal with his heels and cantered away. DeAubry would do his best, but horses were becoming scarce.

Chapter 2

"The Detroit Antiques Show is the biggest in the mid-west and I'm not going to miss it. Who knows, we could have something worth bizzillions of dollars." Herman James Crenshaw, retired Air Force Colonel, now proud co-owner with his wife of a sixty acre farm called from the attic of his cottage styled log home. "Hey, do you know where that box of my great grandfather's stuff is?" The sound of boxes being moved and old furniture banging could clearly be heard above Eve Crenshaw's head. "Damn..." More thumping of boxes. "Eve could you bring up a flashlight please? I forgot to turn on the light."

She stood at the bottom of the attic ladder, face turned up to the dark void overhead and smiled. "Yes Jim, I'll get you a flashlight." Eve walked into the kitchen and retrieved one from the pantry. "Hon, here's the flashlight." She climbed the ladder, flicking on the light switch next to the attic door and pulling a cobweb from her shoulder length honey auburn hair. Light filled the room, making the flashlight superfluous. "Did you find it?" she asked, doing her best to suppress a grin and failing.

"No, but I did find that lamp you bought in North Dakota." They both laughed. It was the worst lamp they'd ever seen. They bought the lamp to use as a gift in their squadron's dirty Santa Christmas gift exchange; the object of which was to find the ugliest, funniest gift possible. Unfortunately, Jim had received orders before the party and they'd spent that Christmas moving into another house at another Air Force base. Now, here they were nearly thirty years later, retired from the Air Force and they still had it. She laughed at the absurdity of the thing. Jim smiled at his wife, he loved how her golden eyes sparkled when she laughed.

"Hey, here it is!" Jim triumphantly held up a wooden Boraxo soapbox. He sat the box on the floor, knelt beside it and opened the top. Inside was a mess kit, with his Great grandfather's name crudely etched onto the back of the pan. Jim held up the mess kit, showed it to Eve, still standing on the ladder, and then placed it on the attic floor. Next he held up a cigarette lighter with "Ardennes 1918 – Crenshaw" carved into the side. "Can you believe these things were used in the mud and trenches of World

War One? It's amazing." Jim was an unabashed history nut. In rapid succession the lighter was followed by a knife, a badly aged book with a faded cover, a handful of uniform decorations, none of which Jim recognized, a patch with a red arrow pierced by a small line and a dirty light coffee brown coloured tube with dirty brass ends.

"What's that?" Eve asked.

"I don't know," said Jim "but this is what I've been looking for. I've been wondering about this thing since we found it when we went through Mom's stuff. I'm betting it's a map case, maybe German. I'm hoping someone can tell me at the show. But maybe it was used to carry something like a unit flag or maybe it was a spacer of some sort."

"Let's open it and see what's inside."

"I've tried. I can't unscrew the damn thing and these lids don't pop off. I'm afraid of breaking it if I put too much pressure on it," Jim replied. Studying the tube for a moment Jim looked at Eve and said, "It just seems like it's pretty well made, it's a quality piece; but what it is I'm totally blank on. I've tried looking in museums and on-line and I've never seen anything remotely like it. So, this is my last hope at solving the great Crenshaw mystery."

"Well, let's hope the mystery is solved then," she said.

They examined the tube. It seemed fairly stained and dirty. It had some markings on the side but they couldn't make out what they were. The ends were metal and appeared as if they would polish nicely.

"This thing's filthy. I'll get a couple of rags and some soap and water." Eve started for the workbench.

"No, no, we can't do that. They say you shouldn't clean an antique; it makes it less valuable. We better wait. I want an expert to see this thing."

"Jim, that's nuts."

"No it's not, any expert will tell you that."

"Name one."

"That fat guy on TV, he says that all the time," Jim began to grin.

"You're making that up…but okay." She looked at Jim and smiled back. "Just wrap that thing up before you put it on my car's carpet."

"Okay, okay, you've got a deal," Jim said as he began

putting the various items on the attic floor back in the box.

"That's all you're taking? It's a forty dollar ticket! We've got to take more than just that," she exclaimed.

"Well, I've got a couple of tools that I could get rid of. And, we could take this lamp," Jim smiled.

"The lamp? No, that's special." Eve laughed and backed down the ladder.

Chapter 3

Louis XVI studied the scene outside the rain-streaked window. The lead lined windowpanes distorted the view of the ornate gardens of the Château de Versailles. He didn't see the distortion, he didn't see the gardens. He simply stared in the direction of the Hotel des Menus Plaisiers. The afternoon was cold, gray, wet. It seemed as if a dark cloud simply grew from the horizon, centered on that damned hotel. The cloud expanded up and over him. It closed in around him, through him and squeezed his heart so that it was hard to breath; even harder to think. And now, more than ever he needed to think.

Things were going badly and he knew it. It was a slow, rumbling avalanche and it was coming right at him. Insults had been shouted. Shouted at him! Things were said in the newspapers and on handbills. Most of France had suffered poor harvests, the Treasury was empty, and his wife was making a mess of things. A raucous group of Parliaments, the councils in each region, had demanded action. That fool, François de Paule de Barentin, had encouraged a general meeting with the nobility, the clergy and the people, an Estates-General. It was a rarely used thing, it would be the first since 1619. And now, there they were, assembled in that damned hotel. Things were not calmer; they were worse. The Estates-General was a disaster. The whole thing was a mockery to his reign.

He had lost control from the beginning. His advisers had no advice of course, worthless fools. They simply made matters worse. The commoners had not understood their role. They even tried to sit in the front of the theater! These uncultured fools didn't even recognize the protocol of such a meeting. The rules for the conduct and proceedings were clearly established in L'Etiquette of 1614. The clergy and nobility were to sit in the front, dressed in the formal regalia defined by their station in the nobility. The representatives of the Third Estate; landsmen, tradesmen and minor members of the nobility were to sit at the back; far away from the throne as befit their standing. It was simply the way things were done.

That had been the first issue, harangued and argued with

but finally overcome. It had been, well…uncomfortable.

Then Barentin began with a procedural process formalizing the rules for the conduct of the assembly. The fool completely misread the crowd. He talked for hours, forgot what he was about and tried to get right to the financial situation of the country and address taxes. It resulted in a near riot. They wanted to talk about procedures. Louie had already agreed to double representation for the commoners. He had made a major concession. Was that not enough? Surely that had no impact on the procedures for votes on issues before the Estates-General. Each estate would vote by orders – thus each estate had an equal voice. That was certainly fair; he did not see an issue. Individual votes would apply only insofar as how the total order voted. To do otherwise, was contrary to the rules. Besides that, well, damn-it, he was the King.

Last week these fools had formed the Communes. What the hell was that? Worse, they had invited him to participate! Participate! Of course he had refused, what choice did he have? This was an action against God! He was King and a representative of God. It could not stand!

Finally, his Councilors understood; military force would be necessary. He didn't want to do that to his own people. Yes, it might work. No, he couldn't do that. He vacillated. He couldn't decide. Now even that seemed to be slipping away. What was happening?

He could sense a growing danger. It was out there, perhaps in this black cloud of mist sweeping up from the river Somme. It pushed down on him and his Palace. It crept in, hidden on the back of that mist. He could not stop it; he didn't know how to fight it. But he knew, he knew that change, danger and, perhaps death itself was stalking him. He could feel it, sense it and it chilled him. His stomach had tightened; a taste of bile had risen in his throat and was with him day and night. He had waited long enough; he would not be irresolute about this, now was the time. Now he needed to protect the throne and his son.

And that was the purpose of this afternoon's meeting. Was he being prudent? A coward? Or, realist? He hadn't decided, and he no longer had time to think of it. The heavy clap of boots on stone echoed behind him. He glanced one more time in the direction of that hateful hotel, noticed the rain had increased. An omen? He turned to face Lieutenant General Nikolaus Luckner. Luckner was a German. And, as such he couldn't rid himself of his German accent. He was one of the few men Louis had ever heard who could make the beautiful French language sound hard and rough. He was tall and weathered having spent his life under saddle. Louis supposed he could be called a good-looking man. Those looks and the size of his purse assured him of a warm bed each night. His military expertise was without question though in a few short years he would, not for the first time, change his loyalties. He was well educated, having studied with the Jesuits of Passau. His military experience was extensive, and to say varied understated it. He had served with the Bavarian, Dutch and Hanoverian armies. He had fought as a commander of Hussars during the Seven Years War against Louis' father. Now however, he seemed to have found a home in the French army. He was a strange pick for the task at hand the King thought. But, the two had an odd closeness that seemed more a function of nature than of their personalities. Was he a friend? Louis thought not, but he was no enemy. In any case, here he stood, looking directly at the King.

Luckner hadn't yet made his obedience; no sign of acknowledgment, he simply stared at the King. It irritated Louis, but he didn't have time to make a point of it. After a moment's pause, Louis spoke, "Nikolaus, I have a most delicate task for you."

"At your command sire," Luckner said.

The king smiled in spite of himself. Luckner never used the honorarium "Sire", it sounded ironic, fake and contrived coming from him. Yet, perhaps the seriousness of the day had made itself known to him. Who could know? He looked hard at his General. What was in the man's soul? Could he be trusted? The choice had been made, he continued.

"I believe there is some danger on the horizon. The communes seem to reject the authority of the King and it will take some time to reassert that understanding."

"Have you considered simply putting them to the sword?" Luckner asked fully expecting to be sent out to do just that.

"I have. Yet the countryside would not bear it. The people would rise up against me. No, it is better to work this out. But, there are some…" He paused, his face grew dark. No, not dark. Something else, Luckner couldn't put his finger on it. "I

14

think we will have some difficult days," the king said more to himself than to his General.

Louis turned to the window. The dusk was deepening into night. The rain had steadied and except for the pattern inlaid in the marble courtyard, the Cour de Marbre, he couldn't see anything. He thought about that, yes, the scene was blurred outside as well as in. He was quiet for a long moment. Luckner became uncomfortable. What was happening to this King? The man needed to stiffen his spine, put the leaders of this crisis to the block and be done with it. He was about to interrupt the silence when the King turned. He seemed to have found a bit of strength.

"My son, Louis-Joseph, will die tonight. An announcement will be made at dawn. His death will be attributed to tuberculosis. It will fit well with his illness of last year. You are to take the Dauphin, along with a woman of the Queen's choosing away from Paris. My suggestion is to Montmedy or Sedan Castle, but you may have better knowledge. He must not be recognized or his very existence known until the Estates-General is successfully closed."

General Luckner knew what this meant, but remained silent. Instead he nodded his head in agreement, but inwardly he wondered if it ever would be "successfully closed." Nevertheless, this was a prudent decision and a minor ruse that could be explained in due course. "Of course, it shall be done my friend," he said.

The King again turned to the window. Over his shoulder he said, "Things will never be the same…" He grew thoughtful. Luckner stood in silence.

"Sire?" The irony was gone.

Louis turned, looked directly into Luckner's eyes and said, "Take my son's Letters of Royal Patent and funds for a long stay."

The King looked past his General. Silence filled the room. Luckner knew this was not the time to interrupt the King, he focused on the man's eyes. They were heavy; he looked tired. No, not tired…they were, what? Dead?

"And, Nicolas, I need you to take some other things. Remove "La Joyeuse", the Coronation Crown, and the Holy Ampulla with my son. Ensure only your most trusted men accompany you…tell no one, save, in good time, the Dauphin."

Luckner's face hardened; his grey eyes narrowed. He knew

now what was in the King's mind. "Sire, I'm sure it will not come to that. The crown is safe with the House of Bourbon."

"I'm not so sure. In any case, do this for me."

Lieutenant General Nikolaus Luckner, for the first time, took his adopted King's hand and kissed the royal ring. He bowed, walked backward for five paces, turned and with crisp military bearing, walked out of the room.

Louis the sixteenth slumped. A wave of sadness; the sadness of a parent losing a child, not a King losing a kingdom, swept over him. He turned to the window once more. He knew. He knew deep in his soul that he would never see his son again.

Chapter 4

Waco, Texas

10 August 1917

The 32nd Infantry Division under Major General James Parker had been assembled from the National Guard units of Wisconsin and Michigan. Some of its elements had deployed with General John "Black Jack" Pershing in his pursuit of the Mexican border raider, Poncho Villa. Thus, the Division was experienced in large troop movements and the issues associated with supplying a large, mobile group of men and machines.

Commanding General Parker was an experienced and intelligent soldier. Unlike many military men of his generation he paid close attention to world politics and technological innovations in addition to the more traditional study of military history. As early as 1915 he felt certain the United States would be drawn into the conflict just starting in France and spreading across the Western Hemisphere. His estimations proved prophetic. When a German diplomatic message, the 'Zimmermann note,' fell into United States hands exposing Germany's attempted alliance with Mexico against the United States the country quickly abandoned its neutral policies. The United States declared war in April 1917.

Parker had been certain his division would be one of the first sent into action. He had already set his mind to the issues of moving this huge organization from here to there and keeping it in action once assembled on foreign soil.

In his youth, Parker had been taught that an Army was dependent on hay and the feed bag. That was nearly true today, only hay and the feed bag had been replaced with gasoline and spare parts. And, now one more item had been added to the list, mechanics.

Mechanics were few and far between, so General Parker decided to teach his own. And, he knew that moving a Division was difficult and slow. He wanted it fast and easy; so beginning in the summer of 1916 he had his men pack and unpack trucks, tear down and rebuild engines, change tires, overhaul weapons, move, shoot and do it all again. They marched, they exercised, and they attended classes. They could strip and reassemble their new 1903 Springfield rifles blindfolded. They could disassemble their trucks and reassemble them.

The training in the heat of west Texas was brutal. The men from Wisconsin and Michigan suffered. Most had been struck down with heat exhaustion at least once, several more than once. One man had died of heat stress. But the training never let up.

Corporal John Turner rolled over in his bunk and looked over the side. "Oushel, I'm telling you, this is the hottest summer I ever been through. I ain't never been this hot; I swear Hades itself ain't this hot, nooo, it ain't."

Turner had joined the Army after a fight with his father. "Pup" as his father had called him had accompanied his Uncle on a trip to Chicago when he was thirteen. He had seen the big city and wanted no part of being a dairy farmer after that. By the time he was sixteen he'd quit school and was planning his escape. The next year he announced he was leaving and his father had erupted. Six months later he was in Chicago, penniless and, when he could sneak past the owner, sleeping in a barn. It only took a week of Chicago winter to convince him that he could crawl back to his father and admit he was beaten or join the Army. The Army looked like the better option.

"I swear if I take apart another truck engine I'll go crazy. I'm telling you John, I've seen the insides of every motor in the division!" Oushel Crenshaw replied.

Oushel and John had become good friends over the past several months. Oushel admired John; he was older, had been in the Army six months longer and knew how everything worked. John was where someone went to find out the latest news. John was someone who knew about things, he was smart. Oushel was an only child. His mother had died of measles when he was four. His father worked as a lumberjack and they followed the tree line around northern Michigan. It couldn't last, eventually the trees were all gone and his father went to Detroit hoping to land a job with Mr. Ford. The day Oushel turned seventeen, he told his father that he didn't want to work in the factory and he was joining the Army. Six weeks later he was on a train for the first time in his life, headed to Waco, Texas.

In early November John announced that they were "on the list." Oushel wasn't sure exactly what that meant, but didn't want his friend to think him stupid so he didn't ask. A day and two trips through the chow line later he had it figured out, they were going to France. Everyone wanted one last leave.

"Think the General will let us take leave before we go? I'd like to see my Dad," Oushel asked John that evening. He was a little embarrassed about asking, but he did want to see his father. They'd been close for his entire life. Now he was afraid he'd never see him again.

"Ain't no way. He can't have us trying to git home and back. Suppose orders come down for us to move right now. No, I seen this before, we ain't gettin' no leave." Turner rolled a cigarette, licked the paper and twisted the ends.

"Well, I'm asking the Captain anyway."

"Ask all you want, he ain't gonna let you go."

Oushel thought about that. John was probably right; at least what he said made sense.

"I could take the train. It would only be a week, maybe ten days."

"Oush, it ain't possible. The Captain got his orders and they say no leave for nobody. You ain't goin'."

A day later Oushel tried anyway. John was right, no leave was granted. The 32nd Infantry Division began to move to Europe in December. In January they suffered their first casualties when a German U-boat sank a troop ship carrying elements of the transportation section. By February the Division was scattered across the ports and bases of England and southern France. It took three weeks for the Division to reform. Several of the more junior officers complained the war would be over before they saw action.

The Germans launched a major offensive, with a hundred thousand men in March. In April the Division went into action. The majority of the officers didn't live to see the summer.

Chapter 5

I

Most would believe the items that marked and inferred royalty would be kept in a throne room or a vault somewhere in the Palace. They would be wrong. The Regalia of the French crown were kept in the newest and largest of the chapels of the Château de Versailles. Begun in 1689 and consecrated in 1710 the fifth chapel was an engineering and artistic masterpiece. It was here where Louis had married Marie Antoinette. Its architecture, inlaid floors and bas-relief sculpture of Louis XIV Crossing the Rhine, made it a favorite of the Chateau's residents.

Luckner left the protection of the palace and stepped into the night. His adjutant quickly took up position on his left. Luckner gave him his instructions as they walked. The man-child answered "Oui, mon Général," gave Luckner his knapsack and was off. It was still chilly; summer hadn't yet taken hold of the continent. The General crossed the Cour de Marbre and descended the steps to the Royal Courtyard. As he walked, he pulled his collar up. His felt hat, not dried from this afternoon's ride was becoming even heavier from the rain.

Crossing the yard he turned to his left, rounded the building and continued to the Chapel. Its exterior was truly a remarkable, beautiful structure. Sadly, some complained its roofline, thrusting high above the rest of the Palace, clashed with the architectural beauty of the building. Had it occurred to Luckner to think of these things his classical training would have prohibited him from agreeing.

He ascended the steps, pushed open the doors and entered the narthex. Here, he paused to gain his bearings. Examining the walls in the flickering candlelight, he quickly found what he was looking for. A pair of ancient and ornate swords were crossed over a large cross, the insignia of the L'Ordre des Chevaliers du Saint-Esprit. He removed one, tested its heft and continued. Entering the nave he crossed himself as he marched its length. At the far end stood the altar, its golden carvings of angels standing out against the white marble behind. Having reached the altar steps, not glancing at the masterwork of Coypel, he crossed himself once more and ascended the high altar. Here, he opened the ambry and removed the Bishops crown and a small bottle of Holy Water. These were quickly wrapped in a cloth and placed gently in the knapsack.

He paused to regain his bearings as he retreated to the narthex. Unlike most cathedrals of Europe, this one had a Tribune Royale, a sort of second story, from which the royal family could view the holy altar, be seen by those in attendance in the apse and still maintain the proper distance from their subjects. The Tribune Royale also contained a small altar; it was there that he needed to be.

Finding the proper staircase, he ascended. As he approached the top steps he was forced to look at the ceiling. It was painted with Jean Jouvenet's "The Descent of the Holy Ghost upon the Virgin and the Apostles", truly a masterpiece and, another time he would have spent considerable time examining its many nuances. Now, though he was forced to look at it, he didn't see it.

His intended destination was behind the traditional seating area for the royal family and guests. It served as a private altar and was not visible from the nave. Two guards stood in front of the communion table.

"Leave", he said.

"Mon General, we cannot leave, we are representatives of the King. It is our duty, I must ask you your business." The Sergeant stood at attention; fear streaked across the man's face.

Luckner sympathized with the man. The Sergeant was in an awkward position. But he didn't have the time. Raising the sword he had taken from the shrine to the Knights of the Holy Spirit he placed the point at the man's throat. The Sergeant's eyes met his. "In the name of the King remove yourselves from this place," Luckner said. His eyes locked on those of the Sergeant; this was a good man Luckner thought, there were too few like him. Few would have questioned a General, orders or no. He could see a fire in the man's eyes. Luckner sensed the man's confusion. The Sergeant decided there was no doubt a sword would be driven through his neck if he objected further. He lowered his eyes, glanced at his man and acquiesced.

"Oui, Mon General, I intended no offense," said the Sergeant. He and the Private hurried off.

The small altar was made of marble, with a simple gold cross standing in the middle of the communion table. Behind it, recessed into the wall was an ambry. To this storage area General Luckner proceeded. In front of, and level with the lower edge of the ambry was another communion table, this one also made of white marble. The ambry itself was made up of five wooden doors forming the shape of a U; one central door nearly four feet long and hinged at the bottom and, on each side two square doors of similar construction, one over the other. In the center of the U was a painting of King Solomon holding a sword and a baby, one woman crying, another simply watching. He did not know the artist. The structure was of a beautiful dark Lebanon cedar, with a carved scene of the Archangel Gabriel slaying a demon. The sword of Christ poised above the demon's heart as its central motif. The four smaller doors had similar scenes of holy triumph over evil.

He opened the small door on the bottom right. This compartment held the Patents of the extended family of the House of Bourbon. Inside was a stack of wooden cylinders, butt ends facing outward. A Patent was actually a vellum document, in this case made of calf's leather, attesting to the family tree of a royal. Each of the individual's ancestors and blood relatives were identified. Their portraits painted onto the leather in painstaking detail. It documented the how and why of the bearer's claim to royalty. He closed that door and opened the one above it. Inside this door were only six cylinders; these were the Patents of the King, his Queen, and their three surviving children and one dead child. The cylinders, twenty inches long, were actually hollow elephant tusks. Each end was covered with a gold cap. Engraved into each cylinder was a name. He quickly examined one, then the next, until he finally found the one labeled "Louis-Joseph". Withdrawing the cylinder he secured it in the small knapsack he carried.

Luckner went to the other end of the ambry and opened the top door. Inside was a square box, of Lebanon cedar, a fleur-de-lis inlaid in ivory and the words "The House of Bourbon" inlaid in gold and mother of pearl decorating the top. He removed the box and put it on the altar. Carefully he felt for the small clasp hidden in a relief carved on the front. Finding it, he opened the box. There, cushioned in a purple pillow was a Crown. Certain he had the correct crown Luckner stood to his full height, and listened intently. All the while carefully studying the walls, nooks and shadows of his surroundings. Convinced he was alone, he removed the crown and placed it on the altar. Next, he removed the Holy Ampule from its bed below and carefully sat it next to the crown.

Retrieving the knapsack he removed the crown and bottle of holy water he had taken from the altar below and placed them in the box. The deception complete he replaced the box in the ambry.

Opening the lower door he removed a similar box. Inside he found a purple pillow with a crown sparkling of diamonds, rubies and jewels. He quickly estimated its worth. It was more than enough for his purposes. This was a personal crown, worn at state functions after the coronation. He removed this crown and stuffed it into his knapsack. This he could use to pay for the Dauphin's expenses...and maybe a small reward for his services.

Next, he examined the central door. Quickly finding the latch he released it and lowered the door. Inside, a shelf, covered with purple velvet, held a box, also of Lebanon cedar and more or less fitting the dimensions of the shelf holding it. He removed the box. Its cover also had the fleur-de-lis inlaid in ivory. The words "The House of Bourbon" were inlaid in gold and mother of pearl above the seal. Below the seal were the words "The Final Argument Of The King".

He lifted the box out of the compartment and also placed it on the table-altar. He then placed the sword he'd removed from the wall in its place and closed the door. Preparing to open the box he paused, knowing exactly what was inside. He sucked a breath between clenched teeth and opened the box. Held in place by simple leather straps over a purple pillow lay the sword "La Joyeuse'. Luckner was a man not easily impressed; this weapon impressed him. The blade was clearly made for its work. It shown brightly; the edge sparkled in the candlelight. The pommel was large, gold and intricately carved. The handle was wrapped in sweat and blood stained leather. The hilt had more than a few nicks, this sword had been used in battle and had done its work well. The sword had instilled fear across the entirety of Europe. It was said to possess powers that made its holder unbeatable in battle. That had certainly been the case as it had slashed its way across all of Europe and Italy. This sword had been sung about since the eleventh century. The song of Roland exclaimed that it changed colour thirty times a day. It had been forged to contain the Spear of Destiny within its pommel; and forged from the same unearthly metal as Roland's Durendal and Ogier's Curtana. Before him lay the sword of the King of the Franks, the King of the Lombards, and the Emperor of the Romans. This was the Sword of Charlemagne.

Spending only a moment to honor the sword, he slung the small knapsack over his shoulder, stuffed the box containing La Joyeuse under his arm and left the chapel.

II

The Chateau de Versailles contains over 700 rooms and 67 staircases. Only a small portion of the palace is devoted to the living quarters of royalty. The remainder of the rooms are devoted to official functions, offices, museums, apartments for members of the court, servants' quarters, kitchens, canning rooms, slaughter rooms, wine cellars, guards' quarters, armories, store rooms and similar rooms devoted to the support of the king and his palace.

Wishing to avoid this maze of hallways and rooms, Luckner again elected to walk outside. He left the chapel by the way he had entered, descending the stairs, turning to his right and rounding the corner of the building. The rain was no more than a drizzle. Unfortunately, the box was awkward and difficult to carry. He needed assistance from his men. Fortunately, they were now here. He entered the Cour Royale. There, fifty of his best men sat patiently upon their horses, the rain not bothering them in the least.

"Colonel DeAubry" Luckner called.

"Oui, Mon General" a voice from the dark edge of the group sang out.

"Colonel, take this box and knapsack, secure them in a coach." He paused then added, "A traveler's coach, not a royal coach. Do you understand?"

"Oui."

"Good, have the turn-out ready in fifteen minutes. I'll meet you at the stables. Keep the coach out of sight as much as possible." With that he turned and walked toward the Cour de Marbre. Stopping briefly, he pointed at a Sergeant and a Private then said, "You and you, come with me, hurry."

The men dismounted, handed the reins of their respective mounts to their comrades and hurried after the General.

Luckner marched across the Cour de Marbre and entered the Dauphin's guardroom. From there he moved to the anteroom. As he entered the anteroom a woman wearing a green dress with purple trim was surprised as she relaxed on a chaise, she immediately stood. Luckner examined her. Not a woman, in fact, she was a mere child. She must be one of the Dauphin's governesses. She hadn't said a word; fear streaked her face.

"Where is he?" he asked. The girl began to stammer.

"Do not delay me young lady," Luckner said in his commanding, harsh French.

The girl simply pointed at the bedchamber door.

Luckner and the two men crossed the room and entered the Dauphin's bedchamber. Marie Antoinette, Queen of France, looked up from a couch in the center of the room. A young boy sat next to her. A picture book lay across their legs. Her eyes met Luckner's.

"Madame, I am sent by the King to take the boy. We must leave at once." Luckner tried to sound warm and understanding. In his German accented French he did not succeed.

Marie Antoinette looked at the General. She thought how unfair life had been for her. Selected to marry the future King of France at the age of 13, it had taken painful dental surgery to correct her crooked teeth before the Dauphin had agreed to the wedding. They had married the next year and she had left her home in Austria, never to see it again. Her husband, sexually inept, did not come to her bed for seven years. When he did it was rare, and his sole purpose was to ensure an heir. There was little love in the act. Now that four children had come of the union, his visits were even more rare. In fact, it had been nearly two years since he had last bedded her. Marie, feeling very lonely, had taken to a small set of cottages on the grounds, the Hameau de la Reine, filling her days with gardening, gambling and shopping.

The latter two vices drew unwanted attention from the treasury and eventually her King. It fed the already not insignificant distrust of her at court. She was called "the Austrian" and, it seemed these little vices had cost her early popularity with the people of France. Eventually, she found love in the arms of another woman. Her first consort being the Princesse de Lambelle. That affair did not last long, ended amiably and the Queen moved on. Soon, a new lover entered her life, the duchesse de Polignac; Yolande de Polastron. This woman became her constant companion, at her side as she shopped, played the horses, gambled and gardened. Yolande filled the void an even half-attentive husband should have filled. She also grew to love the children as much as Marie.

The Queen of course knew the purpose of Luckner's visit. She knew, she understood, but she did not believe it necessary. Events would eventually prove her wrong. "Where do you intend to take my child?" she asked. Already tears were forming in her eyes.

"I do not believe it wise to tell you Madame, just know that he will be safe." The General saw her distress. He tried to soften his voice even more, "I am to bring a governess of your choosing."

The Queen held the boy tightly. She sobbed silently. This was too fast, too abrupt. Finally, she whispered, "No, no, mon General." Marie, knowing her pleading would do no good, finally gathered herself. "Take Yolande".

Luckner turned to the Sergeant, "Gather up the Duchesse, no luggage."

"You," he said pointing at the Private, "Assist the young girl outside, pack one small trunk for the Dauphin. You must be able to carry it yourself."

He took the boy from the Queen's arms. The child began to cry, just small convulsions. Luckner could feel the shudders as he held the child. She simply stared at him, locking his eyes with an emotion he could not identify, hate, gratitude, confusion, he didn't know. He felt a bit of pity for the woman, but only a small amount. He was a soldier; he had his orders.

He lifted the boy to his shoulder, turned and walked out of the room. Marie Antoinette sat and sobbed. She was a mother who would never see her son again.

Chapter 6

Colonel DeAubry had had some difficulty finding a simple four poster carriage for the General's use. Eventually, one of the men discovered a sadly used, shabby example in a small shed near the quarters of one of the many bureaucrats which staffed the palace. It was perfect, exactly like the many that clogged the streets of Paris day and night. They harnessed four horses from the King's stables and were ready for the General shortly thereafter.

They did not have long to wait. The General came hurrying into the stables holding a young boy, closely followed by the Private carrying a trunk. The child looked about the stables, did not find his mother, or for that matter anyone he knew, and began to cry again. At this the General looked exceedingly uncomfortable. His discomfort did not last long as soon thereafter the Sergeant appeared with the handsome duchesse de Polignac. She immediately went to the child and calmed him.

The General then examined the turn out. He did not like the horses. They were much too fine for the carriage and would draw unwanted attention. A sharp word to the Colonel and soon they found a less well muscled set of horses, unmatched in any way and quickly had them reharnessed to the carriage. This detail attended to the General then directed the Sergeant and the Private to remove their uniform coats and replace them with plain cloaks from the stable tack room. He did the same. Satisfied, he returned to the courtyard. Watching the men as they completed last minute details he frowned. Their uniforms would stand out, but there was nothing for that now.

Taking Colonel DeAubry by the arm he spoke in a low tone. "We must pass unnoticed. We shall proceed in three groups. Our advance guard must be at least a mile in front of the carriage. The distance will disassociate the carriage from the troops. They will appear as a company simply moving through the countryside on some urgent business. Our rear guard must be at least a half-mile behind. Is that understood?"

DeAubry did not like this arrangement and shook his head. "Oui, Mon General, but our defense will be slow to react should anything threaten the carriage."

Luckner thought about this then said, "I know, but we cannot risk being noticed. We shall make for the castle at Sedan. It is heavily fortified and the troops are loyal to the King there. We will travel through this night and tomorrow. I believe we can make Reims before we need rest. We'll find someplace outside of the town and spend tomorrow night there." The Colonel nodded his agreement and soon they had settled on the route of march. In moments the advance guard was sent on their way.

Luckner now turned his attention back to the coach. The duchesse and Dauphin were inside. The boy was peeking out of the window at the General and Colonel. Luckner went to the coach, opened the door and closed all the window curtains.

Stepping to the previously selected Sergeant and Private he asked if either had experience driving a four-in-hand. The Private brightened and said he had driven the hearse in his village from the time he was twelve. Luckner examined the man.....no, boy. How could there be so many children in the Army? The boy couldn't be older than fifteen. "Alright, you drive." "You," he said, indicating the Sergeant, "Ride as the rear coachman". He then examined two coachmen's blunderbusses his Adjutant had removed from another four-poster and placed on the seats of the driver and coachman. They were already loaded, but Luckner reprimed them himself and handed one to the Sergeant. The other he tucked under his arm.

Luckner then surveyed his small band, it would have to do. With a wave he sent the advance guard ahead. Then, he inspected the coach and tack one last time, a small shove sent the Private to the driver's box. He waited a few moments to ensure the advance guard had achieved their separation and, with a quick glance at the Colonel, a shouted "*Bonne chance*" he took his position atop the carriage. One more glance around his small party, a nudge of the Private's shoulder, and they were rolling out of the stables. Ten minutes later the rear guard also left the palace grounds.

They did not stop that night. They did switch teams in the morning, and by the next evening they were nearing Reims. Colonel DeAubry sent word to his advance guard and soon they had discovered a small roadhouse hidden from view by trees and shrubs and considerably off the main road. The men set up camp behind the roadhouse barn. The General and duchesse took rooms above the small tavern. Colonel DeAubry had the few patrons removed and kept in a small shed behind the tavern for the night. He then posted several men inside the tavern itself. He ensured his men stayed alert by paying the keeper to place all alcohol under lock and key. He stressed the importance of this arrangement by thrusting the barrel of his pistol into the right nostril of the man as he set out his terms. Should any traveler find his way to this roadhouse during the upcoming evening he would be told there was no room.

Colonel DeAubry had begun this march with forty-eight men on horseback and two riding the carriage. But they had moved quickly, only stopping to change the carriage horses that morning. Even the best cavalry unit could not sustain that kind of pace for that distance without men being lost or horses throwing shoes, especially when a substantial portion of that march is at night. This was not the best of times. They had lost twelve men to poor horses, a desertion or two, and other issues. He now had thirty-six men on horseback. He hoped several would regain the column by morning but, knowing the terrible lack of food throughout the countryside, he knew their chances of finding fit horses were very slim.

At first light the advance group, now down to twenty men, decamped and rode away from the roadhouse to the woods nearly a hundred yards behind. Once hidden in the woods they turned north-northeast and paralleled the road. After thirty minutes they found a small stream, really no more than a ditch, with brush on both sides leading back to the road. Thus they were able to reenter the road and proceed on their way. At the same time two men from the rear guard departed the roadhouse via the long drive. They were sent ahead for a half-mile, then turned and rode back to the roadhouse, giving the all clear. The General's coach left the roadhouse immediately thereafter with the rear guard taking up their normal half-mile position behind.

The day passed routinely until they reached the center of the small village of Rethal. There, in a gentle sweeping curve of the road to the right, for no apparent reason, Colonel DeAubry's horse slipped on the wet cobblestone. DeAubry, having spent a lifetime on horseback, had his left leg over the neck of the horse and had begun to jump to the ground even before the horse landed on its side. DeAubry landed on his feet, but squarely in the middle of a small pool of liquid, impolitely put there by chamber pot of the occupant of the overhanging second floor. Not able to retain his footing he went to the ground and ended up sitting squarely in the foul liquid. To say he was not amused was an understatement.

Finding his horse now lame, he looked for a replacement. His adjutant offered his, but the two had been together for over a year and DeAubry respected that bond. His problem was resolved shortly thereafter as the men found the local Priest maintained a fine saddle horse. DeAubry, having had a poor experience with a Priest in his youth didn't mind taking the horse at all. He promised to pay a fair price for the horse the next time he passed through the town; all the while knowing the odds of seeing this place again were slim and none.

The delay infuriated the Colonel but did provide some sound intelligence. In the center of the village stood a small kiosk. On it, a poster, crudely printed, described a rally to take place this day in the town of Poix-Terron. The rally was to protest against the ancient regime. It appeared to be led by one Claude Moen the local representative to the commune in Paris. Monsieur Moen had become fired with his democratic zeal during his adventures in the Americas with Rochambeau during the late war with England. Those democratic feelings, combined with a self-serving and violent personality, made Moen an unusually dangerous man. DeAubry didn't know any of this, but he did recognize a threat to their anonymity. Word must be sent to the advance guard and to the General to avoid Poix-Terron at all costs. To this end, he directed one of his men to commandeer a woodsman's cloak and hat, then ride ahead to track down his comrades.

Colonel DeAubry's luck held. His messenger was successful and at Neuvizy both the advance guard and the General altered course for Sauville. This portion of the journey was difficult, the roads oft times degenerating into nothing more than two wagon tracks through the fields. Nevertheless, they pressed on. In a field east of Vendresse they stopped. The Dauphin now thought this to be a great adventure; he had proven to be a good traveler. The duchesse on the other hand, was none too happy with the trip, especially her sleeping arrangements and toilet opportunities for the coming evening. The General made both the Dauphin and the Duchesse sleep inside the coach. He, being perfectly comfortable outside, elected to sleep under the carriage. The rest of the men pitched small tents or slept under their blankets on the ground.

Morning found DeAubry again adjusting his troops, owing to muddy ground, more poorly shod horses and bad roads. He again sent twenty men in the advance guard but was forced to cut the rear guard to ten, including himself. He did not like this situation and suggested to the General that they were close enough to Sedan to simply rejoin the entire troop and march into the castle as a unit. This certainly seemed a more defensible way to move. The General considered this, but owing to Monsieur Moen's activities decided that stealth was a more effective means of protecting their charges and he dismissed the Colonel's suggestion.

The road to Sedan exits Cheehery and turns sharply left, crosses several fields and not much further along enters Cheveuges. From Cheveuges, Sedan is only approximately four miles distant. The road into Cheveuges runs parallel to a long, wooded low ridge. At the end of the ridge and bisecting it flows a small brook, its sides choked with long grasses. The road ran along the ridge to what was once a small woodlot, the wood having found its way to fireplaces throughout Cheveuges many years ago. The road turned sharply right around the now vacant woodlot, and ran hard up along the brook. On the near side of the brook stood a *ferme maconnaise*. The two-story barn had an overhanging roof, with tall pillars, its roof tiles were round and it looked freshly built. Just in front of the barn the road turned back to the left and crossed the brook on a small wooden bridge. From there it ran straight into the southeastern end of the village.

Midday found the advance guard having crossed over this small bridge and passing through Cheveuges. The Lieutenant in charge was tired, and not knowing the town was the home of one Monsieur Claude Moen, was not especially alert as his band rode through the very middle of the hamlet. But then, there was nothing peculiar to alert him. In fact, there was nothing to catch his attention at all. The streets were completely empty, devoid of people, dogs, pigs, or chickens. The Lieutenant exited the village, saw the walls of Sedan in the distance and, just slightly, quickened his pace.

Some fifteen minutes behind the lead group came the coach. General Luckner rode in the coachman's position as did the other guard. The young driver, armed, sat in the box. The Duchesse de Polignac and Dauphin rode inside. The coach slowed considerably to make the hard right hand turn at the phantom woodlot, did not accelerate and then began to turn back to the left to cross the small bridge. At that point, gunfire erupted from the far side of the brook. The horse in the near wheeler position was shot through the head and instantly collapsed in harness. Its lifeless body immediately stopped the coach. General Luckner, who had caught sight of a musket barrel stretching above the long grass as its owner took aim, had begun to stand when a ball struck him in the thigh, its force knocking him off the coach.

Screams erupted from inside the four-poster. In the momentary lull that always occurs after a volley of musket fire, occasioned by the time necessary to reload, rod, prime and aim the weapon, General Luckner picked himself up from the ground, opened the door of the coach and pulled the Dauphin to the ground. He then began a quick, limping trot to the new barn standing beside the road. Immediately behind him came his two men and the Duchesse de Polignac. A second volley erupted before they had taken more than a few steps but the coach and remaining horses blocked their assailant's aim and the rounds passed near them without effect.

Colonel DeAubry, hearing the gunshots urged his horse to a gallop. He and his men were at the scene within minutes. The slight breeze, and the time necessary for the horses to cover the half-mile to the scene had completely dissipated the musket smoke and Colonel DeAubry's troops were thus at the considerable disadvantage of not knowing from where the gunfire had come. Additionally, they had not seen the General and his party take refuge in the barn. Therefore, the normal and natural thing to do was proceed immediately to the now riddled coach. As they surrounded the turn-out another volley of gunfire blasted from the far bank of the brook. Three of DeAubry's men fell to the ground, one dead before impact. The Colonel dropped from his horse, examined the inside of the coach and, finding no one inside turned his attention to his antagonists. "Kill those pigs" he shouted sending his remaining five men across the bridge.

Fortunately for DeAubry's men, only fifteen peasants had set the ambush. Of those, only half had firearms and none of those were, as of yet, reloaded. Their owners did not possess the skill and speed of a trained military man in that particular art. The soldiers were on them in seconds. The work was quickly and efficiently done. Muskets were fired, then pistols, then swords finished the gruesome task.

General Luckner watched with a small bit of satisfaction as his men dispatched the rabble. Unfortunately, he was now presented with a problem. A coach shot full of holes and only a partial team would not pass unobserved through the village in front of them. And, there was the time issue associated with unhitching a dead horse. If ever there was a need to hurry it was now. He would have to carry all the royal trappings and his two guests with the limited number of horses and men available.

Luckner directed the men to remove La Joyeuse and his knapsack from the coach and bring the items to the barn. Turning to Colonel DeAubry he placed him in charge of the artifacts. He then directed the Duchesse aboard the Adjutant's horse, selected another and readied himself for a painful ride the remaining few miles to Sedan. Before mounting the horse the General glanced at Colonel DeAubry who had begun assigning baggage to each of the men, seeing to the wounded, gathering horses and readying for the short ride remaining. This Colonel knew his business.

It was at that critical moment that fate turned against the General. One of the Privates had chased a peculiarly large and burly fellow down on foot. The man had struggled mightily and taken several slashes of the sword, the final blow being to the neck, severing the external carotid artery and causing blood to spurt forth. In the process the Privates' uniform had become soaked with the man's blood. Owing to the distance the man had run the Private had been slow to return. He now entered the barn and rejoined the troop.

There are two rules to remember when working with horses. The first is that they are a herd animal. A horse is not comfortable alone. It wishes to be near other horses. When one horse runs or panics the surrounding horses do as well, assuming the first had good reason. It's purely a survival instinct, present in the animal as a result of evolution. The horse that stood to see why the first was running usually ended up as a meal to some predator.

The second rule goes hand in hand with the first. The horse is a prey animal. Evolution has taught them to be wary. They are extremely alert to any new object or smell in their customary environment. Men have understood these equine idiosyncrasies for thousands of years. Hence, horses are trained to accept different stimuli. Draft horses pulling a carriage are typically trained to be very stoical; children, loud noises, traffic, the hustle and bustle of a street do not disturb them. However, put a snake at their feet and panic ensues. Plow horses on the other hand simply step on the snake and go about their business but do not like the chaos of a village street. Similarly, cavalry horses accept the smell of blood as another part of the environment; most horses however, do not. Colonel DeAubry's commandeered horse, coming as it did from a Priest, was one who did not. The horse smelled the blood soaked jacket of the victorious Private, reared on his hind legs in a panic and backed into the horse behind him. That horse, not knowing what the problem was, but sensing the panic in the first, followed suit. Both horses threw their riders and escaped from the barn, running some fifty yards before stopping.

General Luckner felt time slipping away. He grabbed DeAubry's arm. "DeAubry, we do not have time for this," he hissed.

"I'm sorry Mon General," DeAubry said. What could he do? The horses, as it were, were out of the barn.

"I will take six men, the Duchesse and the Dauphin and make for the fort as fast as possible. We will try to catch up with the advance guard. Once there we will be safe. You gather your damn horses, and catch up as quickly as possible."

The Colonel did not like being separated and having so few men but he could not argue. "Oui, Mon General," was all he could say. With that, the General painfully mounted his horse and the little group trotted across the bridge.

DeAubry and his four men slowly approached the skittish horses. The horse's nostrils flared; they snorted but they did not run. The Adjutant, a bright man-child it turned out, had found a barrel of apples in the barn. The horses couldn't resist the fresh smell of apples and were soon under control, back to the barn and ready to leave. It was at that moment the second wave of peasants found them. They swept out of the woods, jumped the stream and filled the road. Escape was impossible. The five men made it back to the barn where they put up a heroic fight. It did not matter; the peasants were not good shots but what they lacked in skill they made up for in volume. Slowly the Colonel's men died. When it was over there was no sign of la Jeyeuse or the knapsack.

Chapter 7

Cheveuges, like its neighbors, and unknown to the King, and by extension to Lieutenant General Luckner, had become engulfed in politics. The residents had formed their own Commune. Their national Commune representative was more radical than most and he had advocated, and convinced most of the people of the village that ridding themselves of the King was the natural and appropriate thing to do. His adventures in the American war for independence playing a large roll in those feelings.

It did not take long for word to filter through the small village that something had happened just at its outskirts. Gunfire that close could not go unnoticed. No one knew the details but they did know that the King's troops had killed several of their fellow citizens. Wives and mothers were already mourning their unconfirmed losses. Fathers and brothers were swearing revenge.

Cheveuges was, in fact, a very small village. Two roads paralleled each other to form the village. They were connected in the center by a cross street to form the letter "H". General Luckner and his group had approached the town at the southeast corner, intending to leave the road, "cap" the H, rejoin the road and exit to the north. They traveled at a steady trot, not being able to break into a cantor because of the Dutchesse and Dauphin were each doubled on a horse. The Dauphin rode with the General and the Duchesse with the Lieutenant. As they completed crossing the top of the H they were forced to round a large brick building to regain the road. There, they met a large crowd of angry women…and armed men.

In Cheveuges, public notices were posted on the large notice board outside the tavern which faced the side road constituting the cross bar of the H. On the board hung a Royal notice. It was bordered in black and read:

Louis-Joseph

26th Dauphin of France

is Dead

4 June 1789

The King's notice was only incorrect by three days.

Chapter 8

Jim didn't normally like visiting downtown Detroit. Not because of the bad reputation of the city; that was fading fast as the city rebounded from terrible economic times. No, Jim's problem was that he tended to get lost in Detroit. He had lived in many different cities, and even different countries during his long Air Force career, but there was something about navigating in downtown Detroit that did him in. Several trips to Lions games at Ford Field or Tigers games at Comerica Park had been highlighted with him somehow taking the Ambassador Bridge Street exit off Fisher Highway and, there not being any exits, finding himself trapped in line to cross the bridge into Canada. A side trip that cost at least an hour and caused considerable swearing when its inevitability was discovered.

But, this Friday he was happily accepting the challenge. After dropping their beagle, Molly, at the vets they packed the Jeep Grand Cherokee and headed for the show. Immediately upon entering I-94 east bound Eve stuck the GPS to the windshield between them. Then, she pulled the written directions to the hotel, the restaurant and the convention center from her purse. Eve was an experienced traveler and she knew her husband's tendency to simply rely on his memory rather than a map to find places. Tonight, she had two priorities; she was going to eat a nice dinner and she wasn't going to Canada. By six-thirty, both goals had been met. They had eaten a very nice meal and, not visited Canada; though Eve had their passports in her purse just in case. As an added bonus, they had checked in at the proper hotel.

At seven o'clock they were departing the ticket window and walking up the ramp into Cobo Hall. The term "Hall" being an understatement on the order of describing the Empire State Building as just another office building. Cobo Hall, located on the precise spot where it is said Antoine de la Mothe Cadillac, a French colonist, first set foot in 1701 and claimed the area for France in the name of King Louis XIV, is a two million four hundred thousand square foot mega center.

The Detroit Antique Show, more formally known as "The Detroit Antique Show and Charity Auction", is held each fall. The show had developed and grown over the years. Now, rather than a garage sale on steroids, it had become one of the premiere springtime outlets for top auction houses from around the country. Detroit's mixture of world-class accommodations and a devoted effort to populate the buying crowd with celebrities guaranteed excitement and valuable and unique auction items.

The antiques show runs four days from nine in the morning to nine at night. It begins on a Wednesday morning and ends on Sunday evening. Saturday and Sunday evenings are what make the show unique. On Saturday, an auction is held of items with an appraised value less than a thousand dollars. That doesn't mean that all items sell for less than a thousand dollars, many times the sales price is higher, sometimes significantly higher. It always seems to be the case that someone simply must have an item, regardless of price and good judgment. Or, a simple case of auction fever strikes some unfortunate novice. Saturday caters to the people that get carried away. Naturally, the show organizers do everything in their power to promote that particular malady.

Sunday is when things really get interesting. All the items have an appraised value greater than one thousand dollars; many items are appraised at several thousand. The Detroit Mayor, sports stars, media stars and other celebrities are recruited with the lure of their name being associated with big dollars going to many of the cities charities. These people are then encouraged to put their star power behind personal invitations to hundreds of high rollers from around the country. A professional marketing firm selects these high-income individuals based upon an in-depth analysis of their buying patterns. Detroit's rich and famous, as well as personalities from around the country, are commonly seen bidding against each other for works of traditional Native American art, Americana, folk art and some of the strangest things ever seen at an auction. It's a spectacular event and raises hundreds of thousands of dollars for charities all over the metro area.

It wasn't the auction that drew Jim. The show had one other high value draw: expertise. And that expertise was free for those who had something interesting enough to make it past the screeners. The entire process had a sort of game show flavor. The concept was fairly simple and logical. Members of the public were encouraged to bring their antiques, have them appraised and, if the owner wished, place them in the Saturday or Sunday auction. What the public was not told was that the initial screening of the antiques was done by antique shop hired help, interns, temporary hires and assistants of the name brand auction house appraisers. These people were not novices. They usually had considerable time in the world of antiquing, but they were not the experts. It wasn't meant to be condescending; it simply had to be that way. There were vast numbers of antiques coming through the door. And, the truth of the matter was, most people were simply bringing a slightly different version of Grandma's broach. There were hundreds of items to be appraised and only a few, true experts.

Jim and Eve showed their tickets at the door and then purchased a show program. Handing Eve the program Jim said, "You can't tell the…" "Players without a program," she finished the phrase. She could predict his sayings and when he'd use them. He grinned at her, kissed her lightly and they made their way to the Detroit Hall of the Cobo Convention center. The room was huge: 200,000 square feet. And, the false wall had been removed to join with the MaComb Hall, another 150,000 square feet. They were stunned. They had expected large, but not this large. It would take an entire weekend just to get an idea of what was here. It was hopeless trying to really see it all.

As they were getting their bearings Jim spotted a sign hanging from the ceiling. The sign read "ANTIQUE REGISTRATION AND APPRAISAL". Pointing it out to Eve he said, "I guess it doesn't get any simpler than that!" They immediately set course through the crowd toward the sign. Red velvet ropes hung from golden stands forming an isle to the registration desk. The line wasn't very long, after all, it was well past 7 P.M. Most show attendees were going home not coming in. A tired, older woman, with blue gray hair asked if they had anything for appraisal. Eve answered that they did and the woman handed her a form and a short golf course pencil. The form asked for a description of the item, country of origin, estimated value and other details. Jim, being a history buff, was annoyed that he had no idea what the odd tube was, but he assumed it came from Europe and had been used in the Great War by his Great grandfather. He simply described the item as a tube with brass caps, age unknown, probably from Europe and used in World War I. Beyond that he left the rest of the form blank.

In short order a young man, wearing a blue blazer with

nametag, a gaudy tie and old, scuffed brown shoes approached them. He was holding their form.

"Good evening, Mr. and Mrs. Crenshaw. I'm John Taylor and I'm your appraiser for tonight."

Jim was slightly taken aback. John Taylor didn't appear to shave. "May I see the tube you've described please?" Jim handed him the tube and watched Taylor's face. Taylor was not a poker player. His surprise and confusion was immediate.

"Well sir, I'm not sure what this is. I think this may be made of ivory and I think, well, I'm not sure but this doesn't look like brass on the ends. It's these markings on the side that I cannot make out. It may be Cambodian." Jim glanced at Eve; she could tell Jim didn't agree but was keeping quiet. "I think we'd better ask Mr. Ito." With that last sentence Jim had achieved his goal of having a professional appraisal done of his great grandfather's tube.

Taylor led them to the far side of the Detroit Hall. There, under a sign which read "Chinese Pottery and Carvings" sat a long table and a large man. Mr. Ito was holding a green vase close to his nose and had a jeweler's monocle in his right eye. Jim and Eve took a few steps back as he addressed the owner of the vase. When he had finished, Jim, Eve and John Taylor stepped forward. Introductions were done all around and Jim gave a brief history of the tube to Mr. Ito.

Ito began to carefully examine the tube. He held it to an ultraviolet light. He turned it and rolled it in his hands, his monocled eye taking in every square inch. Finally, he put the tube down on the table. He then reached into a toolbox behind him and removed a dish, water bottle and a soft cloth. In short order he began to gently clean a portion of the tube.

After several minutes he sat back in his chair, removed the monocle and said, "This is not from the orient. It is a beautiful piece, the caps at the end are done with amazing workmanship and the carving in the middle is an extraordinary piece of scrimshaw. But, no, not from the orient. I think you need to speak to someone more versed in French antiques. This name looks French." He held up the tube and pointed. Under the grime could be seen a carving of a flower, centered in one of the pedals of the flower was the name "Louis".

Jim's surprise was evident. He'd never seen that carving before. He was actually a little embarrassed for not noticing it and he said so. "Not to worry," said Ito. "The grime has filled in the engraving. I nearly missed it myself. To be honest, I was trying to get a better view of the material this tube is made from. I thought for a moment it was plastic, but I am certain it is elephant ivory. This is an extraordinary piece. It's a container of some type I think. Good luck with this. I am curious to know the outcome."

With the last remark he looked at their escort who immediately took the hint. They thanked Mr. Ito for his efforts and then turned to follow John Taylor.

Taylor led them through the floor displays to a central booth. Over the booth hung a sign which read "French Pottery, Jewelry and Statues". There sat a middle-aged woman very thin with too much makeup; next to her sat a distinguished man wearing a double breasted, European suit. A short, stout woman hovered over the man as he examined a porcelain statue.

"Madame I do believe this statute she was made in Orleans," the man with the double breasted suit said. "See here she has the maker's mark? That is the mark of Monsieur Henri Beau, a man who worked in Orleans, he from annee 1725 a 1760. He had une petite small shop, was known for these small statues they in porcelain and their deep colours. He became petite famous him, how do you say...fabrique un peu, making a few of these statues for the Duke of Orleans. I would estimate this would sell at auction for..."

The man paused, tilted his head back and appeared to be doing some computations. Eve and Jim glanced at each other, to their well-traveled eyes this looked more for show than anything else.

"Ahhh...for three to four thousand dollars"

The woman squealed with delight. She thanked the expert profusely and hurried away to tell her friends. At that point John Taylor approached, turned to Jim and Eve and said, "Mr. Crenshaw, Mrs. Crenshaw this is Mr. Raymond LeDuc, deputy curator of the Reims Museum in France."

LeDuc quickly studied Eve, paid no attention to Jim and said, "How may I be of service?"

Jim explained what he knew of the tube, which was essentially a repeat of what Mr. Ito had told him moments ago. Monsieur LeDuc asked to see the tube. He then placed it under his magnifying glass and carefully examined every part of it. He glanced up at Eve. Jim thought he looked more serious than when he had been while playing with the plump lady. Without taking his eye from the tube, LeDuc reached under the table and came out with a spray bottle and a cloth. He sprayed the tube and began to wipe it.

Eve poked Jim in the ribs and whispered, "There goes your theory about keeping the value if you don't clean an antique." Jim winced and nodded.

Finally, LeDuc straightened up. "This is definitely French. If it is what I believe it to be you have a most unique and valuable object here." He continued to clean the tube. Finally, engraving could be seen on the end-caps. LeDuc sat back in his chair. "This is remarkable," he said and looked up at them.

Jim and Eve cast nervous glances at each other, then they turned back to LeDuc. The man had disappeared under his table. Jim fought down a smile, Eve wasn't so successful. The sound of tools being moved about in a toolbox could be heard.

He reappeared, "Monsieur e Madame Crenshaw please observe here." He had a tool that looked like a sharpened wire embedded in a small screwdriver handle. With the sharpened wire he pointed at the side of the tube. "Here we have a decoupage, a…a carving of a bouquet of flowers, yes?"

Jim, Eve and John Taylor all leaned forward and eyed the tube. Yes, it was clear now. LeDuc's cleaning had revealed a bouquet of flowers stretching the length of one side of the tube.

"*Ici…*" he pointed with the tool in his hand, "is a name, no? You see? The name she is Louis, yes?" They studied the tube, yes, there was a name in very ornate script.

"Ah, *voila, ici* she is another name. You see? It is Joseph." He looked at the couple. "You know who is Louis Joseph?" They shook their heads no. Both John Taylor and the woman with too much make-up did the same.

He didn't tell them. He simply returned to the tube. "Now, Monsieur e Madame, we shall see if you are a very wealthy couple no?" He sat down his probe and began to polish the top of the caps. At last he began to examine the surface of each cap very carefully under his magnifying glass. After several moments he picked up his probe and inserted it into a small hole in one end. He pushed, and they heard a small "click". He then began to remove dirt and grime from a crack that had appeared approximately an eighth of an inch below the edge of the cap and circled the tube. At last, he inserted the probe in the crack and gently began to pry upward. With a small amount of force the cap sprang open on a recessed hinge. He stopped and looked at them without saying a word. They looked back and then at each other.

"What does that mean?" Jim asked.

"We shall know it soon," LeDuc said. He then tipped the tube and a rolled scroll, with a purple ribbon around it slid out. He caught it in his left hand and gently sat it on the table. LeDuc then immediately disappeared below his table. Jim and Eve nervously eyed the scroll, then each other, then their gaze returned to the scroll. LeDuc reappeared wearing white cotton gloves and holding a folded piece of black velvet. He sat the tube aside, unfolded the velvet and placed it on the table. Then, he gently placed the scroll on top of the cloth. After a short examination with a magnifying glass he began to gently untie the ribbon. At last it fell free and the scroll began to unroll. It was made of leather, not paper. Around the edge was a gentle painting of flowers, all white lilies. At the top, in the center was the fleur-de-lis. In the center of the scroll was a painting of a tree, its branches intertwined and extending from a thick trunk. On each branch was a miniature portrait with a name below it. At the foot of the tree was a beheaded serpent and a sword. Under the tree were several lines of text in the same ornate script as the names on the tube.

LeDuc sat stunned. His hands began to shake. Jim and Eve could only stare at the beautiful and unusual document. Monsieur LeDuc took his magnifying glass and silently began to read. Finally, he stood, walked around the table and gripped Eve by the shoulders. "Madame" he said, kissing her on each cheek then releasing her and gripping Jim the same way, "Monsieur…you have the Royal Patent of the Dauphin of France."

Jim and Eve looked at each other. Neither understood what LeDuc was saying. The man's excitement couldn't be contained, his voice raising in pitch he said, "Madame, here…" he pointed at the fleur-de-lis in the top center of the scroll, "this is key…this document she is of the royal French family. See here the fleur-de-lis? This is the sign of French royalty since King Clovis the First. And, see here…" he pointed at a portrait of a young boy. "The Dauphin. You have the Royal Patent of the Dauphin himself!"

Eve turned to Jim then back to LeDuc, "I'm fairly certain we're not talking about a fish, so please tell me what a Dauphin is?"

"Madame, yes in a strange way we are referring to the fish. You see, every member of the royal family he has his own coat of arms. The oldest male child of the King, he is next in line for the throne, no? On his coat of arms swim a pair of the dauphins. So, it has always been tradition to refer to him as The Dauphin. You understand now, no?"

Jim looked at Eve. "Hon, I think this is a very big deal. He's saying this is a very historical document. I'll bet this is an important thing." Turning back to LeDuc he said, "Monsieur LeDuc, can you tell us which Dauphin this applies to?"

"Wait, are there more than one?" Eve asked, still confused.

"Ah, oui, of course," LeDuc said immediately. "You see, madame, it is always so. It is always the oldest living son of the living King. When the King dies, his son, the Dauphin, he becomes the King, no? And his son, he becomes the next Dauphin. If the boy dies, and he has a younger brother then the younger brother becomes the Dauphin, you see?"

Eve nodded. She could see the excitement on LeDuc and her husband's face. As she looked around she also could see that LeDuc's initial reaction had not gone unnoticed by the many passersby. A crowd had begun to develop. Already people were leaning over Jim's shoulder trying to get a better look.

John Taylor, being a bright young man, immediately radioed for additional security. In short order two off duty Detroit police officers were at their sides. LeDuc gently put the document in a lay-flat case. The tube went into a separate case. John Taylor, the guards, Monsieur LeDuc, Jim and Eve then made their way to the show offices and a vault.

After securing their treasures they convened in the office of the Cobo Convention Center manager. Mr. David Shilling, the show director, was using this office as his own during the show week. He had never been associated with the find of an antique of this value and he wanted to know more.

Soft drinks and snacks were brought in and the key players convened around the office couch and sitting chairs. Shilling wanted to hear the whole story. Monsieur LeDuc began with an explanation of the significance of a Royal Patent, and how they were used to document royal blood.

"It is not the word 'patent' like your inventor Thomas Edison made. No, the word is…ahhh, ahhhh…." LeDuc searched his excited mind for the correct English translation. "The word she means the 'open book' in Latin. It is a proof. It is the document, the royal, or noble provides to their betters to prove they are a royal or noble. You see?"

Shilling leaned forward, "You mean to keep someone from impersonating a knight or a prince?"

"Exact!" cried LeDuc. "There was no television, no glamour magazine, so when a noble went from city to city no one knew him. Proof must be provided, you understand?"

"Got it," said Jim. "But why would the king, or even the king's son need one? Everyone knew who the king was I'm sure."

LeDuc frowned, "I must confess, I do not know."

Unfazed by this minor setback LeDuc continued with his story. "The Royal Patents were rarely seen and then only by the church. They were never seen by the public," he said.

Then, as if it were not obvious enough, he stressed that French Royal Patents are extremely rare and extremely valuable. There are two reasons for this. The first is the simple fact that not many have survived.

"There are none, all of the known Royal Patents, they were destroyed by the barbarians during the revolution," he cried.

LeDuc explained this was an attempt to destroy the entire concept of royalty in France. Only a few of the Patents belonging to the lesser nobles were still in existence. Remarkably, one Royal Patent from the family of King Louis XVI existed, that of a cousin. It had been stored in a wooden tube, the acids in the wood slightly damaging the leather over time. The owner had been particularly astute in national politics and fled to Germany in time to salvage his fortune before the revolution. He never returned to France.

The second reason a French Royal Patent is so valuable is its sheer beauty. The Patent on display in Berlin is breathtaking for its detail and technical artistry. Portraits of each of the major members of the royal family and the pertinent family branch are rendered with remarkable realism. Art historians and other scholars from throughout Europe have used this particular document as the source document for identifying specific individuals in various artworks across the continent.

The Patent in the Cobo Center's vault was extraordinary in that the entire Royal line was illustrated. Each member of the royal line had their portrait painted in miniature. The historical value, should it prove authentic, was astonishing. The scroll was bordered with a bright, highly detailed painting of lilies and the central family tree was a beautifully done apple tree, a beheaded serpent lay at its roots and a sword dripping of the serpent's blood hovered over the body.

Monsieur LeDuc tended to focus his dissertation on Eve, to the exclusion of the men around the room. He was in his element. The excitement of the original discovery had not dissipated and he was obviously flirting with her.

"The sword, she is important. She represents the beginning of the French monarchy. She is not the Holy Sword of the Redeemer. No, she is the Sword of Charlemagne. This represents the destruction of evil, represented by the serpent. And the tree, it represents the royal line. See how it takes its glow from the sword," LeDuc continued.

Jim and Eve were then pressed to tell how the Patent came into their possession. "There's really not much we know." Jim said. He then explained that his Great grandfather had fought in the First World War and had returned from Europe with the item. It had been kept in a box in his Mother's house for years and after his sister had taken over the home he had moved the box to his own home.

As the evening wound to a close David Shilling leaned forward in his chair and locked eyes with each of them, "You know Eve, Jim, you have an amazing find there. It could make you very wealthy. But, and this is a 'big but'; you're going to have to get this thing verified before you can sell it. It could be a fake. Even though you've had it for eighty years someone could have fooled your Great grandfather."

Jim was stunned. "I hadn't thought of that."

"Who would do something like that and why?" asked Eve. Shilling turned to Eve, "Oh Eve, it happens all the time. Just think of P.T. Barnum and his famous Mermaid. Many, many of the items in his, so called "museum" were out and out lies and forgeries. Even his famous saying "there's one born every minute" wasn't really said by him!

They both started to laugh. Then Jim grew serious,

glancing at LeDuc to ensure he wasn't listening he said; "I guess you've got a good point David. But isn't LeDuc's verification good enough?"

David turned serious. "No, LeDuc is an expert in French historical items, but this is beyond his level. I'm not so sure LeDuc is the man for this job."

Jim thought that over for a moment. "I agree, just in the short time we've dealt with him I get the impression he's a...well, let's just say a bit over the top and leave it like that."

Eve leaned forward and lowered her voice as well, "I agree, LeDuc isn't my first choice. Do you have anyone you could recommend to validate this thing?"

"Well, all I can think of is a professor of French history I know over at the U," Shilling said, referring to the University of Michigan in Ann Arbor. "I'll call him tomorrow morning and set up an appointment for you."

They spent a few minutes discussing Dr. Bill Rousseau at the University; then they made the obligatory comments on the school's football and hockey teams, the upcoming Ohio game and other traditions of the area. Soon, fatigue began to creep into the room and it was clear everyone wanted to go home or at least to their hotel room. Eve mentioned it was late, and they all quickly agreed. Shortly thereafter the conclave began to break up. Shilling showed everyone out of his office and ante-room and said good-night.

Eve and Jim headed to the garage.

John Taylor went home to tell his girlfriend of his day's adventure.

Raymond LeDuc went to make a phone call.

Chapter 9

That Sunday afternoon, Jim and Eve drove home. Like most farmers Jim kept his hunting rifle and his shotguns locked in a tall metal cabinet known as a 'gun safe' in his basement. It was here that he placed the tube and its precious contents. They spent a nervous night knowing they had a possible fortune in the basement. They would feel much better once the items were stored in their safety deposit box at the bank. But first, they had to have these things authenticated. On Monday morning Eve took a vacation day and they drove to Ann Arbor to meet with Dr. Rousseau.

Fall is the best time of the year on the University of Michigan campus. The trees on central campus are bursting with colour. The "Diag," so named for two diagonal walkways crisscrossing a large square in the central campus park area is filled with students and various groups passing out fliers; everything from "Save the Planet" to "Stop the War." Banners screamed "Beat Ohio State" and still more solicited attendance at lectures by various experts on subjects as diverse as "Gay Health" to "America in a Changing Economic and Cultural Millennium." What Jim and Eve always found so interesting was how the local Young Democrats could pass out literature on one corner, the Young Republicans on the opposite, then the two meet for pizza at Pizza Bobs on State Street afterward. It truly was an eclectic place.

Dr. William Rousseau, the man Shilling had recommended, had agreed to see them late in the afternoon that Monday. Dr. Rousseau was an expert on French history and specialized in what he called the "transitional period" from King Louis XIV, through the end of the Bourbon Restoration and the fall of Louis-Philippe I. He had written several well-respected books and, as is increasingly the norm, had published many articles in various blogs and other web sites devoted to his particular area of expertise. They found his small office in the basement of Rackham Hall. The office, contrary to the image most have of a university professor, was neat and tidy with a pair of plain chairs facing a moderate sized desk. Behind him was a credenza with his computer monitor ensconced in a fairly good-sized bookcase. The three other walls were lined with bookcases as well.

Bill, as he preferred to be called, appeared to be near fifty years old and of average build with a salt and pepper beard and hair. They shook hands all-round and were directed to the two chairs. Bill listened closely to their story, stopping them only twice to ask a question and never interrupting the flow of the narrative. Finally, the story at its current end, he sat back in his chair and asked to see the tube and the Royal Patent.

Eve reached to the floor, picked up her large, oversized purse and pulled out, what appeared to be a cardboard tube. Removing the top she turned to Jim and waited. Jim, feeling a bit embarrassed by the procedure, removed a pair of white cotton gloves from his pocket and put them on. Simultaneously, Eve took a rolled up piece of cloth from her purse. Bill removed a few items from his otherwise neat desktop and Eve laid out the cloth. Jim slid the tube from within the cardboard onto the cloth. Then he removed a paper clip from his pocket, straightened it and opened one end of the tube as he'd been shown the night before. He then removed the leather scroll, placed the tube to the side and unrolled the Patent on the cloth.

Bill removed a large magnifying glass from his desk and said, "I'm impressed, you handled the document exactly as a museum curator would. Who showed you?"

"David Shilling, over at the antique auction. He said it would keep our skin oils off the leather," Jim replied.

Rousseau bent over the document and began to glass various portraits. "He's correct, very important to preserve this if it's authentic," he muttered, obviously deep in thought.

Several silent minutes passed. Rousseau occasionally muttered an approving comment, but largely stayed silent. After several minutes he walked to the bookcase across from his desk, searched for a moment, then removed two books.

Returning to his desk he put the books to one side, sat down and said, "First, let me say thank you for allowing me to examine such a wonderful find." Then, glancing at both Jim and Eve and sweeping his hand over the vellum document and tube he said, "Unfortunately, I am not the man that can authenticate these items." Jim could feel his shoulders sag. Before he could ask the obvious question Bill continued. "I would guess there is only one person that could properly do that in North America, maybe three or four in France. These pieces are truly extraordinary."

Jim and Eve glanced at each other. "Well, why is it so hard?" she asked. "I thought you'd just do, I don't know, maybe carbon 14 dating or something like that to establish the age, then maybe a comparison with similar works of the time and that would be that."

Bill looked at her and smiled. "That's actually very good. How did you come up with it?"

She smiled back. "I teach science, 7th grade. You've now got me at my limit of scientific expertise."

"I'd bet not," Bill said. "You're wrong, but not by much. We can't use carbon-14 dating. That process is helpful, but it will only put us in the general time period; probably within fifty to a hundred years. It's not nearly precise enough for this project. We do have a process somewhat similar to carbon-14 dating which will be helpful. And, we'll have to ensure this is not a contemporary forgery."

Bill paused and began to examine the Patent again. Almost as an afterthought he added, "No, for this project a chemical and dye analysis will have to be done on the ink and paint. That will give us the composition. The actual text and the paintings are also very important. The text will be examined for correct phrasing. The paintings will be examined to ensure they're identifying the correct people. The material itself will be examined using radioisotope analysis and other methods. Additionally, the tube will be examined; its age can be determined fairly closely by the ivory. The real trick will be doing this without harming the object."

"You said you can't do all that analysis correct?" asked Jim.

"Correct, I don't have the expertise for some of the testing. And, the royal family tree is not my forte. No, I would have to refer you to a colleague at the University of Montreal, Dr. Jean-Michelle Somme."

He then reached for the two books he'd previously retrieved. "Would you like a little context for these things? I may be able to add to your mystery, or take some of the mystery away, I'm not quite sure." He smiled and studied their faces.

"Yes!" "Certainly!" they both exclaimed.

"Well, first let me show you this picture. It's a rarely seen view of the royal seating area of the 'tribune royale'."

Jim clearly looked confused. Bill said, "The tribune royale is the area reserved for the King or royal sovereign in a cathedral. Very few cathedrals actually have one; the fifth chapel at Versailles is one of those few."

Bill walked to a small table in the corner and laid the open book on it. He tapped a picture and said, "Look at this."

It was a black and white picture of a series of cushioned chairs behind a wooden fence. They bent over the picture for a moment, then straightened, their confusion evident.

Bill explained, "This area is never visited by the public, no photographs are allowed and only scholars are permitted here. To the best of my knowledge, none has been given permission in thirty years. What is important in this photograph is the background. You see here?"

He used the handle of a small magnifying glass as a pointer and touched the image of a small altar to the side of the seats.

"This is the family altar. It's where the royals would go for private services, communion, contemplation, that sort of thing. To the side, you can't see it in this picture, is a confessional. I'm showing you this picture because of the ambry behind the communion table. The ambry is a storage area. Normally they only store the communion wafers, wine, chalice, and other items necessary for Holy Communion in an ambry. But, this one is different. See how large it is?"

Jim, being near sighted took off his glasses for a better look. Eve shouldered Jim aside, pulled her shoulder length honey-brown hair aside, took the proffered glass and adjusted the book for a better view. Jim, now standing to the side looked at Eve and grinned. "You goof," he said. "Ya snooze, ya lose," she shot back and laughed.

"Yeah, that is big," Eve said. "How come?"

"They need that much room to store the chalice and communion plate?" Jim asked.

"Actually, it's called a chalice and paten. And let's not forget the wine. But, even with the wine your eye is correct. That's a lot of space for those items."

"Well, why so much?" asked Eve.

"That, my friends...," Bill began with a satisfied sigh, "is an interesting story." With that lead-in all three resumed their seats.

"It seems the French monarchy is descended from the great warrior-king Charlemagne. Charlemagne conquered all of Europe from the English Channel and Atlantic coast almost to the Urals. At one time he held the title of King of the Franks, the King of the Lombards, and Emperor of the Romans. In short, he was a powerful guy, both politically and physically. He was unusually big and muscular for that period and, unfortunately, the swords of the day didn't fit him."

"How can a sword fit someone? I thought they were just a big, you know, a big knife," asked Eve.

"Oh, make no mistake, the fit of a sword is very important. A man's life depended on his sword. It must have the proper weight, balance point and length. If it doesn't then it's an inefficient tool. And, a sword is nothing if not a tool," replied Bill. "I'm not an expert in medieval weapons, but I've spoken with several that are and that's what they tell me. In any case, Charlemagne could not find a sword that fit him properly so he had one made. As it happened, when the sword was finished he entered into a period of great conquest. People credited the sword with remarkable powers and it began to take on a life of its own.

Eventually, the sword became so associated with Charlemagne and his successes that people began to see it as the source of his power. After his death subsequent Kings were measured against him. Naturally, his successors wanted to claim his legitimacy and his legacy. What better way to do that than become associated with his powerful sword? Therefore, at each coronation Charlemagne's sword was carried in front of the new King as a sign of that power and ancestry."

Bill paused, collected his thoughts and continued, "Charlemagne's sword is one of the most celebrated weapons in history. The sword is sung of in the oldest known piece of French literature, the Song of Roland. In that story the sword itself granted great power to Charlemagne and allowed him to avenge the defeat of some of his troops. The sword developed its own mystic, much like Excalibur in England. The sword was even believed to hold supernatural powers.

He paused again, "Does the sword hold supernatural power? I have no idea, but I do know that it became hugely important to the man. In one battle in southern France, Charlemagne had it ripped from his hand and he lost it. One of his knights, seeing the King without his sword searched the battlefield; during the battle no less, found the sword, killed the man that had it and returned it to his King.

"That sounds a bit nuts," said Jim.

"It does indeed, and probably was, but it did earn the man a great piece of land and ensured a town was named after the sword."

"They named a town after the sword? Not the guy that found it? Oh he got the short end of that deal," Jim laughed.

"Yes, they did name a town after the sword. It's why we now have the town of Joyeuse, France," Bill patiently explained.

"What, wait, I don't get it," Jim said. "He named a town "Happy" because a guy returned his sword?"

"Well, it does sound a little odd when you put it that way," Bill acknowledged with a grin. "But, the name of the sword is 'la Joyeuse,' they named the town after the sword."

"So how does the sword relate to this ambry?" Eve asked bringing Bill back to the original subject.

"Ah, well…this long area in the ambry is where the sword was kept between coronations." He again pointed with his pencil. "It is the symbol of the House of Bourbon even more than the fleur-de-lis. And, behind these smaller doors on either side were kept the instruments of the coronation called Regalia; the coronation crown and the individual crowns."

"What? Wait…what kind of crowns?" Eve asked.

Bill appreciated the question, "Another interesting thing…all Kings after Charlemagne were crowned with the crown Charlemagne himself wore. But, after the coronation, sometimes the same day, they switched to a crown made specifically for the new King. There are several good examples in the Louvre of these individual crowns. The crown of Charlemagne is also in the museum, it is known as the "Coronation Crown". Although, there is some dispute as to its authenticity among various scholars of that sort of thing."

Bill returned to the picture. Pausing to gather himself he said, "Here they kept the Royal Patents. You have a Royal Patent, but not just any Royal Patent. You have the Patent of the Dauphin of France. Royal Patents were rare even then. The royal family was considered to be *noblesse de epee* or *noblesse ancienne*. Both terms were used and they mean noble by the sword or simply traditional or old nobility. In any case, this type of nobility is handed down."

Jim and Eve were leaning forward. Bill had become the history professor he was and his excitement with their discovery was evident.

"A second type of nobility is for the newly noble. It's where the King confers nobility on someone. This is called "Noblesse de letters" and the letters literally mean a letter from the King saying this person is now a noble and confers the selected rank. That letter is called a Patent. Are you with me?" Bill stopped his lecture to ensure his students were following along.

"Got it" said Jim

"Wait, I don't." said Eve "If one type is by birth and the other is by a letter, then why would someone who is royal by birth need a letter?"

"Excellent question," Bill enthused.

"Teachers pet," Jim said in a mock stage whisper. They all had a laugh and Bill continued.

"You must remember, treaties and alliances were often made through marriage. In those cases, the old noble families of Europe wanted to know whom they were becoming allied to, and to whom they were becoming related to. There had to be some documentation. Thus, the invention of the Royal Patent. It didn't prove royalty, it documented relatives of the royal in question."

"Oh, that makes sense. You certainly wouldn't want your new sister-in-law to be the Queen you've been at war with for the past few years," Jim quipped.

"You joke," Bill said, "But you've got the point exactly. Remember, war is not always a military event, more often it is conducted via trade policies or religious activities. In those days France, Germany, Austria, the various nation-states like Venice and Naples, all of the European powers, were constantly struggling with one or another. Knowing who your friends were was important; knowing who your relatives were was even more important."

"This Patent is for Louis-Joseph, the oldest son of Louis XVI. Because he was the oldest, he was called The Dauphin. Dauphin was the traditional title for the son destined to be King." Rousseau paused to let that sink in.

Feeling that his point had been made he returned to his narrative. "There is an odd historical mystery that many scholars have pondered and no one has resolved. A few years ago a letter written by Charles Henri Sanson and sent to one of the revolutionary newspapers of the time was found in Paris. The letter was eventually sold at auction by Christie's auction house in London so I'm certain it was authenticated. Sanson, of course, was the High Executioner of France for the King, later for the revolutionary government."

In unison, both Jim and Eve, in a casual voice and wave of the hand said "Oh, of course...", then grinned.

Bill smiled and continued, enjoying this couple and their obvious happy union. "Sanson dropped the blade on the King himself in 1793. In this letter he claimed to be telling, quote, 'the exact truth of what happened'."

Bill looked closely at Jim and Eve. "Now, here's what makes this interesting. Sanson said that the King approached death with great calm and bravery and, just before he lay on the guillotine table he said 'Henri, Please do not touch Louis-Joseph'."

Bill smiled, "Now, here's the thing. France followed Salic law, which means that only the eldest male heir could assume the throne. History tells us that Louis XVI had four children. Marie-Therese, Louis-Joseph, Louis-Charles, and Sophie. Marie-Therese was obviously female and not a threat to the revolution. She survived the period known as "The Terror" when all those heads were rolling in Paris. Her younger sister Sophie died at eleven months of tuberculosis. The boys are why the story gets interesting."

Jim and Eve were thoroughly engaged. Both were staring hard at Rousseau's face as if to draw the words out. Much to their distress he paused. The break in the monolog seemed to hurt. He opened the other book on his desk and searched for a page, finally finding it he laid it on the desktop.

"This is a painting of Louis-Joseph. According to the news of the time, and royal proclamations, which were posted from one end of France to the other, he died of tuberculosis on the fourth of June, 1791. His younger brother, Louis-Charles assumed the role of Dauphin. Unfortunately for poor Louis-Charles, he did not escape the Terror and died in prison after suffering terrible abuse at the age of ten."

They looked up at him. He didn't say a word. Finally Eve said, "If Louis-Joeseph died on the fourth of June 1791..."

Jim interrupted, "…then why did his father ask the executioner not to touch him in 1793?"

"Exactly," said Rousseau.

Chapter 10

I

The Musée du Louvre in Paris is a world renowned treasure. The building itself was once the home of the French royal family. That was before Louis XIV decided he wanted to be away from the commoners in Paris and moved 18 miles away to the Château de Versailles.

The Louvre Museum contains nearly 35,000 objects from prehistory to the 19th century and covers an area of 652,000 square feet making it truly one of the largest museums in the world. Its historians and restoration specialists are among the elite in the world. Eight and a half million people visit this world treasure each year.

Running such a complex and well-respected institution requires the many specialized departments one would find associated with any large office building. There is housekeeping, food services, security, building maintenance and the rest of the routine functions. And, as with any leading museum, there are the expected research and technical departments such as art preservation, authentication, research and display staffs.

For many, the Art Acquisition Department is the premier department in the hierarchy of the institution. Headed by Professor Andre Rioux, it is this department that identifies and purchases art works for the museum's vast collections. Art Acquisition, in turn, is comprised of three branches: Frankish Art, Modern Art and the *crème de la crème*, the French Historical Art branch.

For reasons no one specifically remembers, within the French Historical Art branch a smaller sub branch, known as the Art Recovery section, is located. Little known outside the tight knit community of the stratospheric art world, the Art Recovery section's personnel are some of the best detectives in the world. This specialized group is charged with hunting artwork lost during the Nazi occupation, recovering works lost due to museum thievery and identifying art fraud.

The deputy director of the Art Acquisition Department

was a Monsieur Paul Marcil.   As a child Marcil had loved the
stories told by his father of the once great empire that was France.
He reveled in the medieval grandeur of the many kingdoms of the
Franks and celebrated the unification of France by Charlemagne.
His boyhood was built upon medieval knights. He dreamed of
adventure, treasure and heroic battles while on crusade.

Life didn't turn out exactly as the boy envisioned. His
father's history lessons and a failed attempt at law school, a failure
not wholly without cause due to his father's royalist political
teachings, led to five years in the French Foreign Legion. His
membership in that organization stemming from his birth in
Algeria just before the end of French colonial rule.

Marcil believed the country's leaders had failed to stop or
even control Arab immigration and the creeping takeover of his
country. Burqas in a French bistro or bakery were one thing,
seeing minarets desecrate the famous Paris skyline was simply too
much. He left the Legion after the minimum five years and
wandered from job to job, city to city and thus across France. He
was lost.

It was his interest in the past that led Marcil to a seemingly
odd choice of university studies. He selected the study of art and
art history at the Université de Paris. Here, the hardened, bitter ex-
soldier found comfort in the majestic art of the *Ancien Régime*. He
reveled in the glory that was then, took comfort in the power of
early France and came to hate the Revolution and the emperor it
spawned. He saw Napoleon as a disaster, a man who had failed to
maintain the glory of what had been and what had been won. His
worst offense being his defeat at Waterloo, making a return to the
monarchy impossible. Napoleon had suffered a righteous death on
a forgotten rock in the middle of the South Atlantic.

It was also here that the old associates and comrades of
his grandfather and his father found him. He was perfectly
educated for the job they had in mind. It didn't take long before
Marcil had been radicalized; soon thereafter he was a member of
the Action Françoise.

II

The organization Action Françoise, sometimes simply

known by the letters "AF", has been existence, in one form or another, since the French Revolution. In the beginning, 'organization' was too strong a word to describe the loose collection of deposed nobility trying to reverse the republican establishments created by the Assembly and institutionalized by the First Republic. There simply existed a loose confederation of nobles and supporters of the beheaded King who wished to see the restoration of the royal family.

This group became more serious in their efforts as Napoleon gradually increased his power. They quickly joined together becoming a powerful, though secret society in the heart of Paris. And, they fought Napoleon, hoping to usurp his empire. They were the source of inside intelligence to numerous European governments even as Napoleon's empire grew.

Eventually, their efforts were rewarded. When Napoleon was finally defeated the European powers restored the House of Bourbon to the throne. The monarchists were more than happy to assume the more lucrative positions in the new government. But, they overreached. Their greed was too much, crippling the economy of the newly restored kingdom. That and the fact that a monarchy no longer suited the French people proved decisive. Soon, Charles the Tenth showed his incompetence and was overthrown. This dealt a terrible blow to the organization whose members were increasing in wealth and power every day.

Seeing a true monarchy as no longer an option for France, the organization adopted a new strategy. Rather than the establishment of a formal monarchy, a curtain was to be drawn between those operating the levers of power, and those directing their operations. The AF would direct those operations. By the 1930's the AF had become quite adept at this behind the scenes manipulation of power. Maybe too adept, and once again they overreached. The AF considered becoming a legitimate political party. The chosen leader of this new party was Paul Marcil's grandfather, Monsieur Charles Maurras.

Charles Maurras is one of history's mystery men. Maurras was selected to lead the newly created legitimate political party established by the Council. Maurras was a "petit leader" of the AF, and certainly not a member of the inner circle, known as the Council de Governors. Instead, he became the public face of the organization in the 1930s. In this role he displayed that family trait he passed to his grandson, to wit: a hunger to be among the elite, when in fact he had neither the grooming nor the bloodlines.

Early in the war Maurras, caught up in the anti-government feelings of the time, proudly and publicly proclaimed the Nazi defeat of France to be a "divine surprise". This greatly angered the nationalist leaning Council. More ominously it angered the head of the Council, the Grand Duke of Orleans. In fact, it so angered the Grand Duke that Maurras was quietly cut off and isolated. The Council went one step further and dropped any support of its fledgling political party. The party's members, always kept in the dark about the Council and its activities, were allowed to fade away or be arrested. Eventually, Maurras was one of those to be arrested and jailed. Alone, abandoned and without friends he died in prison in 1952.

The AF, having relearned its lesson began to retreat deeper into the shadows. By the mid-1960s it was a forgotten organization, and that's the way it preferred things. As the AF returned to its core strategy of power manipulation it became increasingly apparent that its business plan was complicated and had a great number of moving parts. The AF needed to control the men who controlled power. That task requires an ability to quickly and permanently remove certain public servants and enforce discipline over others on a fairly routine and long-term basis. This reality drove a recruitment of first class men with skills not taught in the local university, but skills that Charles Maurras' grandson had gained in the Legion.

At first, Paul Marcil didn't know of the 'persuasive' side of the organization; he simply assumed the AF to be a political organization. Unaware of the family connection he was pleased that the AF fit nicely with the teachings of his grandfather and his father. He believed the government of Charles de Gaulle had imprisoned his grandfather without cause. He didn't believe the "Republic" was functioning at all. As proof he pointed out that de Gaulle, a military man, had been in charge of the government from 1944 until nearly his death. He didn't believe for one moment that de Gaulle had retired and "come back at the request of the people" in 1958. No, it was clear, de Gaulle had been a tyrant and a dictator who had killed his grandfather. The current French President was no better. Any fool knew a King was better than a tyrant. Kings passed their knowledge, wisdom and love for their people through their bloodlines. And so, the young, ex-Legionnaire secretly joined the same organization his grandfather and his father had served; the Action Françoise.

His service began by mirroring the work his father had done. This was mostly small tasks, such as delivering bundles of francs to journalists who had an interest or were sympathetic to a return of the monarchy. But, he had a gift and certain flair. His knowledge of French antiquity helped a great deal, and his military training hadn't been forgotten by the institution's leadership. Gently he was pulled into the more aggressive operations, all the while his public career was backed and aided by the AF.

This situation suited him. He moved from museum to museum, eventually landing a coveted position in the Louvre. Gradually he began to understand how the AF implemented decisions and influenced members of the government and clergy. Once this side of the equation became known he quickly decided this was the way he could move up the chain of command. He dreamed of sitting on the Council, his Uncle's fantasies of Kings and nobles blinded him to the reality. The operations side of the AF he assumed, was the short path to membership on the Council. It wasn't long before he began to employ his unique Legion-honed talents for the AF.

Marcil's ability to resolve "issues" quickly, quietly and thoroughly was unexcelled. He was particularly proud of his skillful employment of the "skiing accident." After all, it had actually increased safety on the ski slopes. Most skiers now wore helmets and he considered that to be a very good thing. The fact that it was a direct result of several high visibility members of government and high society crashing into trees and suffering fatal head wounds didn't bother him. It was an issue of the greater good. And, he had carried out the wishes of the Council efficiently and quietly. That too was a good thing.

As time went on, he grew to an age and stature where his work in the field became less important than his skillful management of certain intelligence activities of the organization. By the time he was fifty his cover life, as an art history expert, had landed him in the top echelon of the Louvre museum. This expertise in the Ancient Régime, his prior work for the Council, his skills and contacts combined, in his opinion, to warrant membership on the Council. Unfortunately, the reality of the royal system interfered. Marcil's non-royal blood eliminated his chances of ever becoming a Duke and a member of the Council.

And, here was the great dilemma of Marcil's life. He desperately wanted to be part of something bigger than himself, something that represented France's glory. But, that very thing kept him from obtaining his goal. He could not become part of the inner circle of the organization he so loved because he was not of royal blood. Merit had no impact on this. But, to Marcil, everything has its exception. And, if he could present something of incredible value to the Council de Governors of the Action Françoise then surely he would be welcomed, given a title and achieve his dream. The total absurdity of this line of thought never occurred to Paul Marcil.

III

The Art Acquisition Department's second mission, to authenticate ownership and pedigree of artwork and initiate recovery of stolen French artwork from around the world brings it into daily contact with Interpol and police forces across the globe. It therefore is possible to track and influence many of the investigations into art theft being conducted throughout Europe. And that was why the Action Françoise had worked so hard to place its own man in a high position in this particular branch. Paul Marcil was that man.

It was to Marcil that LeDuc was now speaking in rapid Marseilles' accented French. "No Monsieur Marcil, I do not know from where he got the Royal Patent. He said his Great grandfather found it during First World War and brought it back to the United States. No, he didn't say where he found it."

Marcil felt his initial elation slipping away. He found himself becoming angrier as the conversation continued, "Find out where the damn thing was found. We need some details." With that he hung up the phone.

Marcil went to his office cabinet and removed a bottle of cognac. He poured a small drink and studied the scene outside his window. Slowly his happiness returned. This could be it. Marcil had been searching for something like this for twenty years. If he could provide the Grand Duke with something truly extraordinary, matched with his past work for the Council, surely they would make him a royal. In the past twenty years he had chased several false leads; he'd searched for the Holy Grail, he'd searched for the Spear of Longinus, the real Sword of Charlemagne, relics of Joan of Arc and lessor historical treasures. But now, this was something real, something that had, for the first time, real physical evidence.

Marcil knew something that others did not. Because many of the museums in France reported to the Louvre, and those that didn't kept close contacts, he had information from around the country. His contacts with scholars all over France allowed him to assemble a bigger picture than the Council could see sitting in their tiny offices. He knew of sound academic research pointing to the possibility that the sword, La Joyese, and other royal treasures had been smuggled out of Paris during the French Revolution. This fit nicely with his own research. He suspected the royal sword on display in this very museum was a fake; and he had determined the Coronation Crown on display in the museum was not the original. Most importantly, he knew enough to keep this research off the radar of the museum's other department heads. If these Americans had really found a Royal Patent it was probable that it was somehow associated with the missing Regalia. If he could find out where the Patent came from maybe it would lead to the rest. This was his greatest chance to join the Council. It could not be mishandled.

Marcil stood at his desk, then walked to the window and looked out over the grounds. Action Françoise would owe him a tremendous debt of gratitude. They would solve the nobility problem by making him a noble. He began to fantasize about how he would be paid – Comté? Or only a baronie? He certainly expected an attractive sum would accompany the appointment, as it should, and did in the days of glory when the King not only granted nobility but also land. He expected and would deserve the same. Marcil shook himself; he had work to do. He had been hunting something like this for years, now he nearly had it.

Chapter 11

Eve and Jim had enjoyed their time with Bill Rousseau. He had even treated them to dinner at the Brown Jug, a campus restaurant named after a trophy passed between the University of Michigan and University of Minnesota football teams. Bill went over the French Revolution in some detail, making it sound like a novel rather than dry history. Jim and Eve began to know the main characters and found themselves rooting for one over the other. It was a sad, incredibly interesting and an ultimately tragic tale. While it had begun as an attempt to increase the welfare of the people, it degenerated rapidly.

Bill's description of the final, ugly convulsions of the revolution had them transfixed. The King pushed for war with Austria in an attempt to solidify support for the throne. It hadn't worked. War had indeed been declared, but the people did not rally around him as he had expected. Instead, prices for food and other goods were driven up and the plight of the people didn't improve. The situation continued to degenerate until a paramilitary coup occurred.

The waitress brought their food. Jim and Eve sat transfixed while Bill, between bites, brought the story to its climax. Eventually, the Jacobins, a radical revolutionary group, assumed control. Their leader, Maximilien Robespierre, from his seat on the Committee for Public Safety drove a radical, deadly period called The Great Terror. He dealt with opposition by beheading anyone associated with it. It was a real life horror movie. Soon, neighbors were turning on neighbors and family against each other. It was a miserable time to be French. The King was deposed, beheaded and counter revolutionary wars were fought, external wars were fought and a terrible death toll endured by the people of France. Bill ended the tale with a quick explanation of how the revolution had led directly to the dictatorship of Napoleon. It was a sad, but fascinating story.

Next, they discussed the necessary steps to validate their find, including the issue of going to Montreal. Jim and Eve were a bit nervous about the trip. Neither knew a great deal of the French language and the University of Montreal was primarily a French speaking institution. Bill did his best to calm those fears, having been to the University several times. He assured them that Dr. Somme was equally at home in English as she was in French.

After what seemed only a short time Jim ordered another pitcher of beer. The waitress delivered the beer and asked if there would be anything else. Jim checked his watch and was amazed to see that it was after midnight. They'd been talking for over three hours. "I'm sure glad this place is open all night." Jim said as he poured out the new pitcher. To his amazement, Eve didn't appear at all sleepy. "You're certainly a good story teller." She said to Bill as she sipped her glass.

"Well, there's one final thing..." Bill grew serious and locked eyes with Jim, then Eve. "...people will pay a lot of money for this." He pointed at Eve's oversized purse. "You'd better be careful with it. And, I wouldn't advertise that I had this thing laying around the house. You never know how far people will go to grab something of value, and this is worth a ton."

They spent the next week arranging a meeting with Professor Jean-Michelle Somme. Eve prepared extra lesson plans and then arranged for a substitute teacher. She made sure to do this early because she was very picky about who could substitute in her class. The next Wednesday evening they were back at the vets dropping Molly off. Shortly thereafter they were on the road, hoping to make London, Ontario for the night, then Montréal early on Thursday morning.

Chapter 12

I

Montreal is truly a beautiful city. Its downtown has a European flavor mixed with a high tech, modern urban landscape. Jim and Eve were intrigued with the city and anxious to do a little exploring, but first things first, they headed directly to the University. Bill had warned them of the rather odd positioning of the University. It ran along the length of the north side of two extremely large cemeteries, the Cimetire Notre-Dame-des-Neiges and the Mt. Royal cemetery. As they passed the first Jim said, "Ya gotta love a cemetery called Our Lady of the Snow". Eve smiled and said, "We don't live in Oklahoma anymore." Referring to Jim's last assignment at Tinker Air Force Base outside Oklahoma City and the oppressive heat of an Oklahoma summer. Using the cemeteries as a landmark, Jim circled the campus until they found their destination.

Dr. Somme was a member of the graduate school. Her office located in the Édouard-Montpetit Pavillon, took a bit of finding. Eventually Jim and Eve found their target and parked the Jeep. Soon they were at her closed door. Jim eyed Eve and asked, "Why do I feel like I'm going to see my professor with a late paper?" She smiled, "I don't know but I sure wish you'd knock, this hallway is cold." At that the door opened and a young man squeezed past looking none too happy. Jim pushed through the open door to stand face to face with a woman in her early forties, with an attractive figure and long dark hair matching her dark brown eyes. "Dr. Somme?" he asked.

She looked at him for a moment. His thin hair and gray temples ensuring he wasn't mistaken as a student. "Yes? Oh! You must be Mr. Crenshaw?" she said in flawless English. "Your wife did not come?" At that, Eve pushed the door completely open and said hello. Dr. Somme smiled and welcomed them both. Closing the door she escorted them though an outer office which was apparently shared with three other professors and into her comfortable personal office. She asked them to sit and then completed the more formal introductions. Jean, as she preferred to be called, quickly came to the point.

"So you believe you have a French Royal Patent and you want me to examine it? Royal Patents are very rare, none exist of the immediate royal family; only one is available to us of the second tier, that one being in Germany."

Jim nodded at this. "We've heard of it."

"There are several examples of lessor nobles from that period so we do have a good idea of the format and techniques for the fabrication of a Patent. But, now tell me the story of how you obtained this item," Jean said as she made herself comfortable in her office chair.

For the next thirty minutes she sat transfixed absorbing their story. Finally she asked for the tube, completed the white gloves ceremony and withdrew the Patent. Taking a large glass from her desk she moved it slowly in and out, focusing it and began to carefully examine the leather document. After several minutes she murmured, "This is amazing, if true this is the Patent of Louis-Joseph." Finally looking up at Jim and Eve she announced that it appeared to be correct, but she would need to run some fairly specific tests.

She then picked up the tube. She examined it carefully, paying particular attention to the engraving. After several moments she announced the tube would need further examination also. All told, she would need the objects for the next ten days.

Jim's surprise was evident. "You can't authenticate these today?"

"No, certainly not. The tests take several days to run. And, we'll need to schedule time on the machines. They're not here solely for my use you know," she patiently explained.

Jim and Eve were uncomfortable with letting the Patent out of their hands, but didn't see any choice and agreed to the loan of the objects. To this point Jean had been rather detached and, actually a bit aloof. Now, she dropped her guard, smiled and said, "You mentioned that Dr. Rousseau showed you a picture of the ambry where the Royal Patents were stored. Did he tell you that the ambry was ransacked sometime before the revolution?"

Jim and Eve did not see the significance. "No" said Jim, "but how is that relevant to authenticating this Patent?"

Jean eyed him closely, then continued, "It is extremely relevant, especially in light of what you may have here. You see, finding this specific Patent is more incredible than you may realize."

"How so?" asked Eve.

"It's a bit of a story. If I jump around please stop me and ask questions. You see, one cause of the French Revolution was the American Revolution!

"Oh, I've never heard that before," Eve exclaimed.

"Well, it seems that Mister Benjamin Franklin skillfully manipulated the French into siding with the Colonialists. It eventually cost France millions and millions of Francs. Add a few poor harvests in a row and the French people ended up broke, hungry and ripe for their own revolution," Jean said.

She leaned forward in her chair, her elbows on her desk and eyes intense. "Just a year after the Revolution France was struggling for its very life. The country was fighting a war on two sides and getting itself deeper and deeper in debt. One method of addressing the debt problem was to liquidate the treasures of the nobles and the church. To do that the new revolutionary government set up several 'committees'. These committees were to recover what they termed 'the people's treasures.' In truth, these committees simply ransacked the royal palaces and the holdings of the holy Catholic church."

Jean stood, returned to the file cabinet and, after a moment returned with several file folders. She began to spread several photos and photocopies across the top of the desk.

"These documents discuss this plundering of art works and other valuables from the nobles and churches," she said.

She continued to spread the papers in front of Jim and Eve. "The committee responsible was called 'the Committee for Restoration of Public Treasures'. The thefts or collections, depending upon your view, were confirmed by statements from two members of this Committee, given in trials for various crimes or affronts. Their testimony is found in trial records of the day." She began to point to various documents spread across the desk.

Jean checked her watch. "I'm going to have to run along to a meeting in a moment. But, these committee members also published their testimony in revolutionary newspapers, and they recorded very similar statements in their private diaries; so we place great credence in their truth. The records speak directly of the ransacking of the ambry that held this very Patent. They mention removal of King Louis XVI's crown and the Queen's jewels."

Again checking her watch she said, "Now, I must go, but let me give you this book and let's say we meet again tomorrow at..." She checked her desk calendar and said "...tomorrow will be difficult. Could we get together for dinner tonight instead?" Jim and Eve were delighted to accept the invitation and arrangements were soon made to meet that evening at a new restaurant on Côte de la Place d'Armes which had opened just the past month. Jean then escorted them to the office door, "Tonight then, 8 O'clock?"

II

Jim and Eve spent the rest of the afternoon exploring Montreal and shopping in the downtown area. Then they returned to their hotel, showered, changed and headed to the restaurant.

"Eve, I've got to admit I'm learning more about the French Revolution than I ever wanted to know," Jim complained as they walked to the restaurant.

"I thought you were the history buff?" she taunted.

"Mile wide and an inch deep," Jim said as they entered the candle lit building. They were escorted to their table and a few moments later Jean appeared wearing a fashionable dress and fur wrap. Conversation centered on where Jim and Eve had been stationed, which countries they had visited and when. Jean had lived in Europe for several years as well, and they shared stories of their trips throughout the continent.

At last Jean said, "Well, let's see. We were discussing French history when we parted this afternoon. I think I'd left off with the fact that the new French government was broke and ransacking the country for anything they could convert to cold hard cash."

"You had just told us about the ransacking of the Royal Ambry." Eve prodded.

"Yes, well...here things begin to get interesting." She paused, apparently for dramatic effect. "There has always been a bit of a mystery surrounding the French Royal Regalia. You see..."

"Excuse me" Eve interrupted, "What exactly is a Royal Regalia?"

"The Regalia are the signs of authority or right to the position. Traditionally things like a crown, a scepter, a throne, are collectively called the regalia." Jean patiently explained. "Royal regalia applies to kings and queens. The most famous are the British Crown Jewels, but regalia applies to the symbols of an office or station. Look at the President of the United States; the office has the Presidential Seal. Even a town mayor has a seal or the head chair at the town council meeting. These things are all regalia."

"Okay, got it." Eve nodded.

"So, the French Royal Regalia, since the Revolution, has always been a bit of a mystery. We know that before the revolution there were four items that played a key role in the coronation of any new French King. We know this from surviving official papers of the Church, as well as various diaries, and even from the examination of several paintings of different coronations." By this time they had completed their meal and Jim was wondering about the bill.

Jean continued her narrative. "The French were very Catholic and considered themselves to be, if not representatives, at least faithful servants of the Church. It was very important for them to have a direct tie to the Church. Therefore, the French kings were blessed by the French Cardinal as part of but prior to the actual coronation. For this the Holy Ampoule was used."

"And what is a Holy Ampoule?" Jim asked while trying to convert Canadian dollars to US in his head, finally giving up and simply handing his credit card to the waiter.

"Let me get that!" Jean nearly shouted.

"Too late Jean, I already did," Jim said with a smile.

Jean gave him a stern look then continued. "An ampoule is simply a container. Clovis the First was the first Frankish king to be baptized as a Christian. That occurred in about nine hundred, no one is certain of the exact year. It was said that the unction, or the physical act of the blessing, was performed using Holy Water contained in a Roman glass container alleged to have been found in the sarcophagus of Saint Remi. The container, or ampoule, was about 5 centimeters tall. Since the ampoule was associated with a saint it was almost by definition a Holy Relic imbibed with certain blessings."

"Wow, that's a great tradition. So, you're saying that the

Holy Ampoule is a piece of Royal Regalia?" Eve asked.

"Yes, it is," Jean replied. "And, now we move to the next piece. The French had a peculiar tradition of crowning the new king with a specific crown called the Charlemagne Coronation Crown. It was originally a simple gold crown, but over the years four large jeweled fleur-de-lis were affixed to the original piece. Immediately after the coronation this crown was removed and replaced with a personal crown. The personal crown was made specifically for the new king. But, the important one, the one that conferred the throne, was the Coronation Crown. So, while both crowns could be called Royal Regalia I want you to think only of the Charlemagne Coronation Crown."

"And that's because of what?" asked Jim.

"Ah…you like these historical mysteries don't you Jim?" Jean said with a smile. "Be patient, let's now talk about the coronation sword."

Jim interjected. "Actually, Jean, Bill told us a lot about the sword. He said it had been stored in the Ambry and that it was the actual sword of the real Charlemagne. He said all the subsequent kings used it to legitimize their reigns."

"Okay, perfect. Well then, in answer to your question, it's the same with the Crown. It conferred Charlemagne's image to the new king. So, we have discussed the three key items. The Holy Ampoule, the Charlemagne Coronation Crown, and the Sword of Charlemagne. But, we've not discussed the fourth…"

Her smile broadened and she looked from Jim to Eve. "How can you crown someone unless you know they're of royal blood?"

Jim smiled, "The Patent?"

"Absolutely. The fourth item is the Royale Patent. They were always kept together in the Ambry." Jean smiled, "So we have a mystery."

They spent the next half hour discussing the unique properties that made up the Royal Regalia. Finally, Eve observed it was very late. The three new friends agreed to meet again the next morning in Jean's office.

Chapter 13

I

"I need to know more about these two Americans!"
Marcil was becoming angry. He knew that a Royal Patent had been
found, but he didn't know how or where. He didn't know if the
Americans knew that the Patent was part of the Royal Regalia. All
he knew was that he didn't know much.

"Get in their house LeDuc, put a microphone in each of
the rooms. Search the place, maybe the fools left it laying out. Just
get me something or I'll have your manhood in Paris and the rest
of you at the bottom of the ocean. Do you understand me?"
Marcil growled into his phone.

LeDuc was not an exceptional man. He didn't consider
himself anything other than a deputy director of a museum. In
that he was wrong. Raymond LeDuc may not have had a classic
case of dissociative identity disorder, but he did possess two
personalities: one the mild mannered deputy academic, and on
occasion he was a cold-blooded killer. His friends in the Action
Françoise had recognized that trait long ago. And now he was
forever tied to that organization. How he'd gotten mixed up with
this Action Françoise idiot was only a distant memory. Now, here
he was years later with blood on his hands and unable to find a way
back to that simpler time. He hated Marcil. He hated being afraid.
He hated his other personality.

"Yes, Monsieur Marcil. We shall be hearing everything the
couple does and says." LeDuc thought about that for a brief
moment, then smiled in spite of his predicament. This might be
entertaining if nothing else. He hung up the phone and thought
over the instructions he'd been given. Bug their house? It was
madness. He didn't know how to bug a house. He only knew one
person in the United States he could ask to do this little favor and
the man was past his prime. This was not good, not good at all.
And, he'd have to stay here in this factory city even longer. Detroit
was no Paris. Finally, LeDuc left his hotel room and found the
elevator. Arriving at the ground floor he passed a small coffee bar
and approached the desk clerk. As he walked he glanced around

the lobby. Nothing unusual, no one knew him here and no one cared who he was.

"Good afternoon," he exclaimed. "I need to extend my stay a few more days."

II

Marcil hung up his desk phone with a crash. At least some phones could still be slammed. He thought for a moment, composed himself and decided it best to send a report to the Council. Surely they would be excited by the possible recover of such an important piece of Royal lineage.

He removed the tedious papers and reports lying on his desk pad. He then pulled a soft cloth from a desk drawer and dusted the desktop. Satisfied it was clean he removed a piece of thick, cream coloured stationary from his right desk drawer. Pulling open the drawer on the lower left, he removed a quill and ink well. The Council accepted only formal, old world penmanship, and only quill and ink was used. He dipped the quill in the ink well and began to write. His letter was addressed to the Action Françoise's Council de Governors. He struggled with the wording. It took two drafts and well over an hour, but he was finally pleased with the result. Occasionally, he paused and thought of how close he'd been to membership the last time, but there was always the issue of royal blood. This time surely....

III

Returning to his room LeDuc opened his smart phone, paged through the list of contacts and finally found the one man he knew in the United States. Touching the telephone number he listened as the phone rang. Claude Poteau had been a reliable and useful tool in the States for the past forty years. Now in his late sixties Claude was beginning to slow down, nevertheless, he was all that Ray had. The phone connected and LeDuc heard the cigarette-choked grunt of Claude Poteau.

"Eh? Oui, Qu'est-ce?"

"It's Ray, I need some work." The conversation went about as Ray figured it would: difficult, full of expletives and generally unsatisfying.

He disconnected the line and sat on his bed. How could he end his relationship with Marcil and the AF? He couldn't could he? Damn.

Chapter 14

Jim and Eve brought brioche and croissants and were seated once again in Jean's office.

"Last night after we left the restaurant I returned here to do a little additional research." Jean began. She had their attention. Jim and Eve immediately sat their brioche and café-au-lait on the table and stared at her.

"I have long held my suspicions. Last night I assembled my evidence; it is weak, and I have not published about this…yet. But, I believe I have discovered something very important."

They were sitting around Jean's small office table. Jean stood and crossed to a bookshelf behind her desk and, after a short search removed a large, slim volume. While walking back to the table she opened the index, dragged her finger down the page, simultaneously positioning herself between Jim and Eve's chairs. Then, with evident satisfaction she opened the text to a full page picture and laid it on the table between them.

"This is a painting of the coronation of Louie the sixteenth's father, Louis the fifteenth. Here you can see the blessing."

She placed her finger on the page. "Here you see the Cardinal making the sign of the Cross on Louis' forehead. That's the "unction".

Jim and Eve bent over the book.

"But look here in the Cardinal's hand." She moved her finger to the Cardinal's left hand. "Notice that the vial is held in a square receptacle made of gold?"

Jim glanced at Eve. She was as engrossed in this as he was. "Yes, and are those jewels on the square thing?" Eve asked.

"I think they are," said Jean. "Now, I want you to look here." She pointed to the altar behind the Cardinal. "See the crown? That's the Charlemagne Coronation Crown. See the four fleur-de-lis?" Both Jim and Eve were nodding their heads.

Jean then returned to her desk and picked up a large, atlas sized book. A ruler protruded from the top, evidently previously put there as a bookmark. She opened the book to the ruler and sat it on top of the first volume between Jim and Eve.

"Here is a painting of the coronation of Louis XIII." She pointed to a large painting of the King leaving the altar. He was proceeded by several young girls spreading flower pedals, four page boys carrying various objects, an armored knight holding a sword vertically with both hands, with the Cardinal and several priests leading the procession.

"I believe that is the Sword of Charlemagne." She said, her index finger stabbing the center of the page.

Jim was becoming increasingly confused. "Okay, I get all this Jean, but I just don't see what it has to do with our Patent?"

"A fair question." Jean replied. "Let me continue and it will be clear." At that she went to a file, pulled out a folder and extracted a CD. She inserted the CD into her computer, grabbed her 'cheaters', glanced at Eve and Jim and put on the glasses. After a moment she found what she was looking for.

"Here, here is a statement by the head of the royal guard at his trial for thievery."

"What did he steal?" Jim asked.

"Probably nothing. But many items that the Committee expected to find in the palace at Versailles were not there," Jean said. "Since they couldn't find these things they had to blame someone. This poor soul was blamed, given a fair trial and beheaded. Many scholars now believe that members of the Committee simply made off with these treasures."

Jim and Eve were now becoming absorbed with this story, much like when they had heard the first half of the tale from Bill Rousseau. Jean continued, "In any case, the guard related at his trial that the regalia as it was called always stayed with the Patents. These items were considered inseparable. That's because taken together they bestowed the throne to the next in line."

She eyed them closely. Jim and Eve stared back expectantly. Finally, she realized they had missed her point.

"The Patents were kept with the sword, coronation crown and the Holy Ampoule. Where one was there was the other. I have always been mystified at how the Louvre could have the Sword, the Ampoule and the Crown but not the Patent. The fact that you have what certainly appears to be the legitimate Royal Patent lends credence to research which questions the authenticity of the Regalia currently on display in the Louvre."

"There's more," said Dr. Somme. "There was a certain French General that was a favorite of King Louis XVI. Initially, he sided with his King and fought the revolution. At one point being wounded in the leg. We know this from his testimony at trial in 1794."

"Trial?" asked Eve.

"Yes," Jean said. "You see, General Nicolas Luckner switched sides. When the General Assembly was first called he supported the King. As things got out of control and the King was deposed, he publicly supported the revolution. About that time the remaining European monarchies realized this idea of the people running the government could spread."

"But what could they do?" Eve asked

"They declared war," said Jim. "She's talking about the Napoleonic wars."

"Not actually true," said Jean. "But very close. The period is called the French Revolutionary Wars. And, the war was perfect for General Luckner. He avoided the Committee for Public Safety, kept his head and helped the Army against the invasion. In 1791 he became a Marshal of France. The next year he became the Commander of the Army of the North. France did well and he was part of the reason. He had several victories. But, his luck turned. He suffered a terrible defeat, lost a lot of ground and eventually was removed from active command."

"All good things come to an end," grinned Jim.

Jean didn't even pause. "Things got worse for him. After his defeat Luckner was made generalissimo with orders to build a Reserve Army. That didn't work out well since the countryside had been picked clean of men and boys. There was no one left with which to build an Army. But, that didn't work as an excuse and he was eventually removed. He was getting on in years by this time; he was 71 or 72, something like that. In any case, he retired and went to Paris. Fate was still against him. The revolutionary group in power, called the Jacobins, didn't trust him and in less than a year he was arrested by the Revolutionary Tribunal. His trial went the same as all other trials of the day, and he was sentenced to death. He died on the guillotine in Paris in 1794."

"Wow," said Eve. "I should have taken more world history, I thought the French Revolution was just about 'Let them eat cake' and Napoleon, I didn't know about this other stuff."

"Now, here's the interesting thing. At his trial, a Colonel spoke against him. The Colonel said that in the early days of the Revolution he had been a Lieutenant under General Luckner. He had helped move several items of extreme value, a woman and a child out of the Château du Versailles during the opening days of the convention. It was in an ambush by members of one of the communes that the General was wounded in the leg."

Jim thought for a moment. "You think that is how the Patent got out of the Palace?"

"Yes, I do," said Professor Somme.

Jim and Eve glanced at each other. "This is all very interesting Jean, and probably very important to the historical record, but I thought we were trying to validate the Patent. What am I missing?" Jim was becoming increasingly curious about where Jean's long narrative was taking them.

"This all has to do with the Patent. But it's bigger than just the Patent." Jean's excitement could not be tamed. She returned to her bookshelf and removed a large catalog nearly three inches thick.

"This is the catalog of items held by the Louvre," she said as she flipped open to a specific page and laid the book between Jim and Eve. "This is the Coronation Crown in the Louvre museum." Then she uncovered the first book she had shown Jim and Eve. Placing her right index finger on the painting and her left index finger on the catalog she asked, "Do these look at all similar to you?"

Jim and Eve were dumbstruck. "They've got the wrong crown," Eve whispered.

Jean wasn't through. "Now look at this." She pulled the second text back to the edge of the table and next to Eve. "This is what the Louvre calls the Sword of Charlemagne. It doesn't look like this one does it?" she said as she pointed at the catalog. "They've got the wrong sword too."

What about the Ampoule?" Jim asked.

Jean's excitement was evident. "During the final crazy days of the Jacobins they trotted out the Holy Ampoule and destroyed it in public. They beat it with hammers. One piece was recovered and is now in the Louvre." Here she paused to add weight to what she was about to say. "Remember it was supposed to be made of Roman glass? Well, guess what…the one in the Louvre isn't."

Eve and Jim stared hard at Jean. "You're telling us they destroyed a fake?" Jim asked.

"Yes I am," Jean said with certainty.

The three of them looked at each other in silence. "So you think General Luckner removed the Royal Regalia and replaced it with fakes before the Revolution?" Jim asked.

"I do" Jean said emphatically. "And, because of whose Patent you have, I'll bet the child mentioned by the Colonel was the Dauphin."

Finally Jim said "So you think that because it takes all four of these items to crown a King that they were never separated. And, you think that someone, maybe this Luckner fellow, replaced the originals with fakes during the French Revolution?"

"Exactly," Jean said with relief. "It's the only explanation."

Eve studied Jean's face. Finally, she said, "That means one other thing. You believe that wherever Jim's Great grandfather found the Patent that's where the other items are too?"

"Exactly," Jean said with satisfaction.

Chapter 15

I

After a quick lunch, Jim and Eve thanked Jean for the education, reluctantly handed over the tube and said their goodbyes. Jean promised them a full report within two weeks. They all suspected it would be sooner since they were all excited about this find. The return drive from Montreal seemed to take forever. Seven hours later they had all the traveling they could take for the day. Eve spotted an acceptable hotel outside of Toronto and they quickly were checked in, unpacked, and in search of a nice restaurant. Eventually they settled on a small steak house.

Taking their seats in a booth Jim looked over the menu; put it down and began to examine the parking lot outside their window. Soon their food arrived and Eve attempted to make small talk. Jim only half heartily participated in the conversation and concentrated on his food. After the waiter took their plates he took off his ring, absently began to twirl in on his finger and returned his gaze to the parking lot.

"You've got something on your mind, and I'm guessing I'm not going to like it," she said.

Jim smiled. "Yeah, can't hide it from you. I'm pretty subtle that way."

"I've got a few years practice reading that face," she reminded him.

"Well, I've been thinking a lot about what we've seen and learned this past several days. Jean made some pretty startling claims. And, the conclusion is pretty awesome. If the Patent is part of the regalia, and the regalia is always together..."

"And Jean says they were," interjected Eve.

"I'm saying if they're always together, why wasn't the regalia found when my Great grandfather found the Patent?" Jim was now pointing his desert fork at Eve.

"Well, maybe he didn't look very hard. It was during a war. He might have been a little busy. And I hope that fork isn't loaded," Eve said with a smile and a bite of her cherry pie.

"I wonder if we can find exactly where he found the

Patent," Jim mused.

"How would we do that?"

"I don't know. That's what I've been thinking about this past hour or more. We would have to know where his unit was fighting and exactly where he was when he found the Patent. It's really impossible. I mean, he could have just been doing his laundry and there it was or he could have been digging a trench and discovered it. There's just no way that kind of thing would show up in some record."

After a moment of silence Eve said, "We know your great grandfather's unit right?"

"Yes," said Jim.

"Well, can't we find out where they fought? Wouldn't that tell us at least where he was?"

"No, history books only tell where the units were during major events. Sometimes they'll describe specific movements, but it rarely gets down to the unit level. It might help a little, but we wouldn't find a passage that said 'Oushel Crenshaw found an ivory tube beneath the big tree at the corner of this and that road' or anything like that," Jim explained. "The best a history book might say is this company attacked that town, but I'm not even sure it would get to that level of detail."

"Oh….that's not a big help is it?" She looked a bit crestfallen.

"No, not a big help, but not a bad idea," Jim said, "We should definitely read the battle history of the Red Arrow Division. It will at least give us an appreciation, and maybe a starting place."

"The Red Arrow Division? What's that?" Eve asked.

"That was the name of his division; well, the real name was the 32ed Infantry Division but they were known as the Red Arrow Division. The French called them 'Less Terribles'."

Eve laughed. "Your French accent is terrible! It's 'Les Terriblies'." Then, "Why the terribles?"

Jim grinned. "French isn't my strong point, ya got me. Anyway, apparently they were terrible, in a good way. They were never defeated, and they broke every German line they were sent against. Even the shoulder patch was changed, from a red arrow to a line shot through with a red arrow. I guess it's supposed to symbolize the fact that the 32nd Division penetrated every German line of defense that it faced during World War I. They were a pretty tough bunch of guys. I've read a little bit about them, and I'm pretty impressed."

"Well," Eve said, "I guess we're going to learn a whole bunch more about the Red Legged Division."

"Oh my God, RED AAROW Division," Jim cried.

"That's what I said." She quickly shot back and grinned.

II

Jim and Eve's driveway was fairly long and extended some one-hundred yards from the road to the house. On both sides sat corn fields so that, to an airplane overhead, the house, barn and equipment shed looked as if they sat on a small green island in the middle of a large yellow splash of corn. This year the weather had been just right. The corn stood eight feet tall and was a pleasant dry yellow colour. Their farm wasn't their primary source of income, more of a secondary source and an homage to the land they owned. Jim parked in the garage, went to the back of the Jeep and lifted the door. Eve opened the dog cage and put a leash on Molly. Meanwhile Jim opened the door to the house and walked in.

He immediately turned to punch his code into the house alarm then stopped. There was no beeping.

"Eve, we forgot to put the alarm on," he called. Then he thought about what he'd just said. Even if they had forgotten to put the alarm on it should have beeped. He examined the alarm pad. The face was dark, no lit number telling him the door to the garage was open. He closed the door and reset the alarm. Nothing.

"Eve, the alarm doesn't work," Jim called. "We'll have to get that fixed. I'll call the alarm company first thing tomorrow."

By this time Eve was in their bedroom and had placed the few things she'd bought in Montreal on the bed. She then unpacked her suitcase, putting the dirty clothes in the hamper and the clean cloths she'd not used back in their proper places. She stopped. Her bottom bureau drawer was slightly open. She couldn't remember leaving that drawer open, and it was not like her to leave things open. That, and an alarm not working, made her uneasy.

She went to the closet. Eve kept a neat closet, skirts, pants and blouses lined up. They were crowded to one end of the clothes rod. She turned to Jim's side of the closet, always a bit messier than her side. He'd left a pair of boots in the middle of the floor when they left, she remembered because she had stumbled over them on the way out and they'd had a word or two about his messy habits. He had made a show of standing them up beneath the hanging dress pants before they left. The boots were now lying on their sides next to his other shoes.

"Jim, come take a look at this." Jim could sense a bit of urgency in her voice. He hurried into the bedroom. Eve went to her bureau and pointed. The bottom drawer was open about a half inch. "I don't remember doing that," she said.

She then went to the closet. "My clothes aren't where I left them, and…" She pointed at his boots. "…didn't you stand those up over there?" she asked as she pointed.

Jim looked concerned, "Yeah, I'm pretty sure I did."

They began a search of the house. The first thing Eve checked was her jewelry. It all seemed to be there. Jim checked the garage, all his tools and power equipment was there.

Jim checked behind the back door. His .22 rifle was standing there. Like many farmers Jim kept the little rifle handy. Rats, woodchucks, coyotes and other critters are common on a farm and were not welcome.

They checked all the cabinets, several items were out of place, but nothing seemed to have been taken. They went upstairs. Their son now lived in the city. His room had been turned into a guest room and re-carpeted with a short pile carpet just two weeks ago. Eve had vacuumed the day before they left for Montreal. The nap of the carpet stood tall where the vacuum had lifted it. In the carpet they could see footsteps.

Eve looked at Jim. "I vacuumed in here before we left. Someone walked around this room."

They examined the rest of the upstairs. Nothing was missing.

They went downstairs. At this point Jim thought they may have surprised a thief. He was worried the intruder was in the basement. He stopped on the top step, went to the back door and grabbed the rifle. They descended the basement steps. The television was there. The bar in the corner looked undisturbed.

The laundry room looked normal. There was no one in the furnace room.

They opened the door to the utility room and turned on the light. Jim and Eve used the utility room as a sort of hobby room. She kept her spare quilting material in plastic bins in the corner. She also had several boxes of items she used at school in bins marked "Reading", "Math" or "Science". Jim kept his hunting and fishing equipment here. In the corner stood a gun safe. The safe was six feet tall, made of high-density steel and supposedly impervious to intrusion. That wasn't true. Someone had retrieved the torch from the barn and cut the hinges off of the safe door. It now lay on the floor in front of the safe. Inside, Jim's two hunting rifles and three shotguns stood proudly in their places. The drawers were all open, nothing was missing.

Chapter 16

I

The Michigan State Police force is a well-respected state organization. Its officers are considered professional, competent and generally held in high regard by the public. But, as is typical of public service organizations, it is chronically undermanned. In rural areas taking a report on a breaking and entering is low on the priority list.

Officer Ryan Harris arrived about two hours after Eve phoned the State Police post. He walked through the house with Jim and Eve. He examined the footprints in the carpet. Then began to try to find fingerprints. He dusted several glass surfaces with no success. He went to the basement and dusted the gun safe. Again, without success. Both he and Jim went to the barn where Jim kept his cutting torch. There were no surfaces likely to hold a fingerprint, but they did search the barn and the equipment shed. Nothing other than the torch had been moved. The intruder had left footprints in the dirt floor of both buildings. Officer Harris photographed them and made a plaster of Paris mold. He did not hold out much hope of finding the intruder however.

"Mr. Crenshaw, I would say someone definitely searched your house and barns looking for something," Harris said as they walked back to the house. "But, I can't imagine what it was they were looking for. And, I cannot explain why they would take the trouble to cut off the door of your gun safe and not remove the guns." He paused, stopped and looked at Jim. "You didn't keep anything in there that you shouldn't did you? Is there anything you haven't told me?"

Jim looked at the young trooper. "Officer Harris, you're exactly right to be asking that kind of question." Jim pulled his wallet out of his pocket and handed his retired military ID card to the man. "But, I spent most of my life serving this country honorably. I wouldn't disgrace myself now after all those years."

Ryan glanced at the I.D. card. His eyes widened a bit when he saw Jim was a retired, bird Colonel. "No sir, I bet you wouldn't," was all Harris said.

They opened the back door, and Eve insisted they sit at the table. She poured three cups of coffee and Ryan began filling out his paperwork. He started by asking the routine questions: when did you leave home, who knew you were going, full name and address, etcetera, etcetera. Finally, he said, "Do you have a home burglar alarm?"

"Yes, but the battery is dead. It's not working," Eve replied.

Jim leaned forward, "But….damn, I didn't think about this earlier. It should have beeped last week to tell us the battery was low. It didn't, I wonder…"

"The battery shouldn't have made a difference. Usually they're just back up for power outages. Let's take a look at that control panel," Officer Harris said.

The three of them went to the garage and Jim opened the control panel. He pressed in a code and attempted to arm the system. It didn't work. They checked the backup battery. Jim's voltage meter showed it fully charged.

Then they went to the exterior phone box on the wall outside the garage. There a series of new wires were attached to the phone cable. Officer Harris was the first to speak. "That looks like a very professional job." The telephone wire and alarm company cable were spliced. A nine-volt battery supplied power to a small black box with two wires attached to clips. The clips went to the alarm cable and the telephone cable. "Mr. and Mrs. Crenshaw, someone knew an awful lot about burglar systems; this thing has been by-passed."

Jim and Eve could only stare.

II

That evening was a tense one. Jim ensured all the doors and windows were locked. They tried to watch television, but couldn't get interested in any of their favorite shows. They tried a game of cards but that didn't last long. Finally Jim put voice to what they were both thinking. "Someone searched our house looking for something very specific."

"I know, and we both think we know what it is they were

looking for don't we?" Eve said.

"Do you remember what Bill Rousseau said to us?" Jim asked.

"No. Well, wait…didn't he say something about being careful?" Eve stared at Jim.

"Yup. He said people will pay a lot of money for the Patent and the tube. He said we'd better be careful with it." Jim put down his cards, scooped up the pile on the table and started to put them back in the box.

"Hey, I would have won you know." She objected, but it was just for show. "We didn't even have the tube here. Why would anyone be searching for it in our house?

"Well, they didn't know we didn't have it in the house. They probably thought they could snag it and sell it for a lot of money," Jim said.

They both grew quite. Finally, Eve said, "How are we going to find where your Great grandfather found the tube?"

"I'm not really certain, but I think I know where to start," he said. "I'm going to learn everything I can about my great grandfather and his unit."

"How do we do that? Can we get his records from the Veteran's Administration?" she asked.

"That's a great idea, but I don't think it will work. As I recall, all the World War I vets, or at least most of them, had their records destroyed in a fire sometime in the early seventies. No, I think this is going to be a library and internet search."

With that, Jim headed to his small office and the family computer.

Chapter 17

LeDuc was on the phone with what he had been told was 'a technical expert.' In this case the man might have been an expert with surveillance equipment and burglar systems, but he was not an expert at searching a house. Claude Poteau had failed him. He was simply too old, too sick and too lame. Poteau hadn't even done the job himself. He'd subcontracted the work to a young fool from someplace called "Hamtramck". My God, the kid wasn't even French. He was a Pollock!

"You fool," LeDuc hissed. The "Mr. Hyde" side of his personality was in full bloom. "Did you not see footprints in a freshly vacuumed carpet? How could you not think to look behind you? Are you blind?" LeDuc was just getting warmed up.

"Were you not told to make sure your visit was not discovered? Are you an idiot? Did you think they might overlook the door to a gun safe, with burned off hinges and LAYING ON THE FLOOR?" That last part in a thundering yell. "You ass! They know that someone wants the tube. They know its value and you warned them of its vulnerability! You fool!" LeDuc's blood was boiling now, and it spilled over with a string of oaths that would have made Satan himself proud.

Finally, his energy spent, LeDuc asked, "Did you get the microphones in place? Did you at least do that? Did you do one thing right?" LeDuc was satisfied with the answer. Conversations in the Crenshaw house were being recorded and saved to a computer hard drive. The computer was routed through an internet connection and could be monitored by simply logging into the server. He could monitor the house anytime, anyplace, from his smart phone or from his lap-top. This at least, had impressed him.

He pushed the 'end' button on his phone, hit speed dial and in a moment was talking to another 'technical expert', this one in Toronto. The world would soon be in need of a new recording "expert." Finishing that conversation, he put the phone on the table and thought about Poteau. The man had let him down. He'd done good work in the past, but now? Now, he was old, lazy, and a risk. He decided. LeDuc picked up his phone and hit redial.

Ridding the world of one extra idiot and an old man gave LeDuc no pleasure. It was merely a free service. Now he thought hard about the next phone call. LeDuc dreaded it, but it had to be done. He phoned Marcil. As expected Marcil erupted with a string of oaths of his own, matching LeDuc's in vehemence, violence and clearly winning in the creativity category. He would have to be careful of Marcil in the future LeDuc thought.

Marcil wanted the internet password so he too could listen to the American couple. LeDuc provided the necessary information and hung up. He began to think about his value to Marcil and wondered if he should return to France or find a nice beach in South America. Who could know?

Chapter 18

I

Over the next five days Jim immersed himself in World War I history. He spent hours at the library and even more time on the internet. He gradually became very familiar with the wartime unit of his Great grandfather. Oschel Crenshaw had joined the Michigan National Guard in 1915. The unit had been deployed on Mexican border duty during the pursuit of Poncho Villa. Later it was one of the first to sail to France to fight the Germans. After several large and bloody battles where it earned a distinguished war record the 32nd was charged with occupation of portions of Germany.

Jim found the reading interesting, even fascinating, but not helpful. He couldn't find details of any battles, only the role of the Division in larger campaigns. He still didn't have a clue as to where Oushel Crenshaw had found the tube.

The next Saturday Eve and Jim were scheduled to leave for his sister's house in Traverse City for the holiday weekend. They intended to stay for two days and return on Monday afternoon. But, before going Jim wanted to return the cushions for their yard furniture to the attic. "Seems like our little adventure started by me going up this ladder into that attic." He commented.

Eve smiled. "Yup, and it was what, a month ago? Feels like an awful long time ago now doesn't it."

She went back to rinsing off tools and patio furniture then stopped. "What did you say was in the soap box?" She asked, suddenly serious.

"Oh, some medals, a mess kit, a cigarette lighter, that's about it." Jim said as he ascended the ladder.

"No, you said there was more. And, I think you said there was a book. It was in your great grandfather's war stuff. Maybe there's something important in that book," Eve exclaimed, growing excited. "Let's take a look in there. Maybe something can help us out."

Jim went back to the attic and after several minutes of

shifting boxes and moving the Christmas decorations out of the way he found the Boraxo box. Clutching the box to his chest with one hand he carefully climbed down the ladder and carried it into the house. Finally he sat it on the kitchen island, took a beer from the refrigerator, then opened the box. There inside, under the knife, patches and other paraphernalia was a large, black leather bound book. Examining it closely he read, "The 32nd Division in the World War".

Quickly clearing away some paperwork from the kitchen table he laid the book flat and opened it. Together they scanned the index. The book was an homage, published by the state governments of Michigan and Wisconsin after the war and apparently presented to the surviving members of the Division on the anniversary of the Armistice Day, 1922. It contained a detailed history of the unit, its officers and men, a list of killed and wounded in action and a reproduction of after-action reports for each battle and skirmish fought by the Division. Commentary about the overall war and the unit's contribution at the moment of the report or series of reports was also provided. It was indeed an impressive record.

Soon Jim was engrossed in the history of the unit. It didn't matter to Eve, after ten minutes she was back on task. "Okay, we've got work to do," Eve prodded. "If we're going to be there by dark we'd better get this show on the road."

Reluctantly Jim agreed, put the book aside and began packing the Jeep. Soon, Molly was in her traveling cage, the suitcases and snacks were loaded and Eve was loading her pillow. In another twenty minutes they'd passed through town, stopped at the gas station and were entering the highway. Turning north on M23 they settled into a cruise. After little more than an hour they had reached I-75, passed Birch Run, Frankenmuth and Saginaw and had begun looking forward to their traditional stop for ice cream in Gaylord.

Jim's sister Sherrie lived in a traditional, northern Michigan fieldstone farmhouse situated on seventy-five acres just northwest of Traverse City. Jim's mother and father had purchased the property and moved there after Jim left home to attend the University. When Jim's parents had passed away Sherrie and her husband Gerry had moved into the house. Over several years they expanded and updated the house. It was now a beautiful, modern home and had been featured in several local "Parade of Homes" tours. Along with the home renovations Gerry had cleared more of the land and together he and Sherrie had turned the acreage into a cherry orchard. Now, they had a successful cherry farming business, supplying cherries to packinghouses and on-line customers.

Sherrie met them at the gate to the property with her big yellow Labrador at her side. After the usual hugs and kisses Jim gave Eve the keys and he and Sherrie watched the Jeep bounce up the driveway to the house. "We're going to fill those ruts in someday," Sherrie laughed. Jim put his arm around her and they walked to the house.

II

The next morning the four of them sat on the porch drinking their morning coffee and discussing the Patent, the French Revolution and their new friends Jean-Michelle Somme and Bill Rousseau. Eventually, the conversation turned to Jim and Sherrie's great grandfather. The family had a military background and Oushel Crenshaw was one of many who had served in the military. They both had heard a great deal about him as children. When Jim thought of those stories now, in the context of his own military training, he was certain the man had suffered from post-traumatic stress syndrome; he'd had a bit of a drinking problem and family stories often mentioned his frequent stops at various bars and pubs. He'd never been a violent or mean drunk, just occasionally "in his cups" as the saying went. Now, having read a detailed account of the man's wartime unit Jim was more convinced of it than ever.

"I wish I had known him," Jim said as they watched several wild turkey walk across the pasture. "I've no way of getting more information about him, there's no one left who really knew him. There's a lot I'd like to ask him about, not just about the Patent, but other things. What were people like? How did they do it? It's a terribly interesting and important time in history and so many know so little about it. I just wish I knew more."

"I've always been absolutely stunned by what they did and went through in that war," Sherrie said. "But you look at what they did in the years after the war and it's equally impressive. Remember Mom talking about the Great Depression and how people went without for so long? Our great grandparents and grandparents sure put up with a lot."

They all nodded and fell silent. After a few moments Sherrie said, "You know, I've got some of Grandma's things. Let's look through there. Maybe there's something in there of her father's."

Jim readily accepted and for the second time in as many days he was climbing a ladder into an attic. Unfortunately, two hours later all Jim had for his trouble were some of his great grandmother's dresses, some children's toys, photo albums and a bible spread out on the dining room table. And, a knot on his forehead where he'd hit it on a ceiling joist.

That evening Jim and Eve were in their room rehashing the day's events. It has been fun finding and looking over all the old things. And, they had found evidence of a family mystery. It seemed that a great aunt had run off with a lover at the age of twenty-three, never to be heard from again. Jim had found a picture of the wayward aunt in the bottom of a trunk containing the rest of their great grandmother's items. Gerry had promptly declared that he'd married into a disgraced family. Therefore both he and Eve should be excused from cooking and washing dishes for the next two days. Eve had promptly agreed, and the two of them then decided a trip into town was warranted. Sherrie and Jim were left to cooking and preparing the evening's barbeque.

But none of the newly discovered items had helped in finding the solution to the riddle of where the Patent had been discovered. Jim was becoming increasingly discouraged.

"Eve, I think we're stuck. There's nothing to tell us where to look. He fought from near Paris to the German border. There's no way we'll ever get this narrowed down."

"I know hon. I don't know how to help. But, really is it such a big deal? We do have the Patent. We know it's worth a lot. We're a heck of a lot better off than we were before this all started."

"Eve, it's not a money thing. It's family history, it's world history. This is important. We could be on to something that could change the historical record of an entire country. This is a big deal."

"I know babe, and don't give me that stuff about history. This is about your family…I wasn't born at night."

Jim started to laugh. "Oh my God, you never, ever, get sayings right. It's 'I was born at night, but it wasn't last night!'"

"Oh…," Eve said. Jim couldn't keep a straight face, and they both had a good laugh. Finally, knowing there was nothing more to say about the matter Jim went looking for something to read before going to bed. Leaving the bedroom he turned to his right and walked to the end of the hall. There on the opposite side of the staircase was a bookshelf. This part of the house was pretty much as Jim had remembered it from when his parents had lived here. He didn't think the books in that shelf had ever been changed.

Flipping on the hall light he began searching the bookshelf. A book entitled "Modern Bee Keeping" caught his eye. Pulling it down he laughed when he saw it had been published in 1958. Next he found several mysteries. His mother had belonged to a mystery reader book club many years ago. A new mystery had been sent each month. Next to the mysteries he found a book for the next several days, "Tarzan of the Apes" by Edgar Rice Burroughs. Removing the book, Jim noticed several smaller, thin books on the shelf above. Pulling out the first he was surprised to see it was a book of French phrases. It told how to ask directions, ask a few basic questions and contained a small amount of French geography and history. Jim was amazed to see it was published by the War Department, 1916. He was absolutely stunned to see the name "Oushel Crenshaw" written in pencil on the inside cover. Next to it was a small, weathered and ragged copy of the Bible, again the name of its owner was written inside. Immediately next to that was a small black leather bound book with no title.

Pulling down the small black book Jim found that it wasn't a book at all. Instead, it was a bound notebook. Its pages nothing but lined writing paper. He opened the inside front cover. Inside was a picture drawn in pencil. Someone with a lot of time, but not much talent had obviously drawn it. Opening to the first page he found a dozen or more French phrases, all in a messy stretched handwriting. Jim turned the book over and opened the back cover. At the top was the name "Lulu May Walters" then an address and a list of important information such as "first date", "birthday" and "favorite flower".

Jim's imagination fired. Not daring to guess what he had in his hands he sat down on the window seat. The book looked to be about a hundred pages or so. There were two cardboard dividers, the first at the one-third point, the second at the two-thirds point. Pausing a moment to gather his thoughts he opened to the second page of the book. It was a list of numbers and times. At the bottom of the page it listed track numbers. It was a list of train departures. The next several pages were crude pictures of people, boats and buildings. Then a block of blank pages had been folded over at the corner. The next page was a drawing of a machine gun. Each part was labeled. Following that was a page containing instructions for cleaning and servicing the weapon. The next few pages were blank, then a drawing or a map with arrows. A few small notes made Jim think it was notes for an attack on a fortified position. Following that were several blank pages, more drawings of houses, chickens and people. Then the first cardboard divider with a calendar for the year 1918 printed on the cardboard. Behind the divider the first page was labeled 17 April 1918 and it was full of handwriting, all in pencil. The second divider didn't divide anything. The handwriting simply continued on each page thereafter. The last ten or fifteen pages were blank.

Jim began to read. As he did his excitement began to grow. He'd found a diary. And, the more he read, the more excited he became. He'd found the diary of his great grandfather.

Chapter 19

I

Two days later Jim and Eve were back home, sitting on the porch and letting the sun sink behind the corn. Jim was reading the diary to Eve. Transfixed by the tale, they were transported back to a horrible time. It all seemed so real, made more so by the comments on day-to-day life. Jim's Great grandfather complained of bad food, no yarn to darn his socks, losing at cards. He spoke of the famous World War One trenches. In one section three pages were devoted to mud. His ancestor explained all the different types and uses of mud; how it deadened the noise of a shell. How it sucked in shells and made great showers when the shell exploded. How it stopped shrapnel and how it seeped into guns and trousers and food and cots and water barrels and wounds and on and on and on.

Two pages were devoted to the description of an observation balloon. They had set up anti-aircraft guns around the balloon and "aeroplanes" as he called them were constantly patrolling near the balloon. Several pages later there was one sentence: "The balloon was blown up today."

Sometimes the narrative was interrupted for several days; then a short list of friends killed, or maybe a story of how someone was lucky to have escaped death. Rarely was a battle described in detail, though sometimes a particular incident seemed to take on more than casual importance. The story changed subtly when a large battle was described as being heard off in the distance. The horizon flashed and artillery barked and boomed. The men all grew silent, many said prayers. They all expected orders to move forward to the attack on their own front but none came. The description went on for some time. It seemed Oschel had a difficult time sleeping that night.

The day after the battle in the distance the entry was very small. *"Army on the move."* was all it said. Several more entries were made which simply said the army had taken to the roads and began moving. Sore feet were now the problem and the topic of each night's entry. Whole pages were devoted to sore feet, drying socks and the best way to wrap feet before starting off in the morning. Food and supplies were a constant item of comment. Two pages were devoted to catching a chicken that had been spotted in a damaged chicken coop. Once there were three pages devoted to a French woman they had seen in a farmhouse as they marched past. The diary droned on, the sole topic being the daily observations of a man walking through a broken, war torn countryside.

Camp life seemed to be enjoyed. At least in comparison to life in the trenches described early in the diary. Hot meals were always commented on. It seemed they were served about every three days. A friend, who was only identified as Robert, was a noted barber in the unit.

After an hour, Eve said she needed to put some laundry in the washer and start supper. She disappeared into the house. Jim sat on the now dark porch, a cold cup of coffee on the floor next to him and read by the porch light. He read for another twenty minutes.

Suddenly Jim stopped. He called down the basement stairs, "Eve, I've got something. C'mer and listen to this."

She climbed the stairs. "This better be good. I've got things to do," she complained.

Jim looked at her and smiled. "Hon, you know I hate seeing you work so hard…." He began.

She cut him off "Yeah, yeah, I know, that's why you're staying up here where you can't see me, very funny. Now, what did you call me here for?" It was an old joke they'd been quoting at each other for years.

Jim got serious. "Okay, after you went in I kept reading. The diary went along just talking about routine things like food, cooking, one guy's birthday and stuff like that. Then, in mid-August it seems they caught up with the Germans. Apparently, the Germans were trying to reform a front and stabilize their lines. The commanders were trying to stop that and keep things from degenerating back to trench warfare. At least that's what the campfire generals were saying. Anyway, on August twenty-fifth he got into a battle near a little town called Chickery or something like that. Listen to this…" he said and began to read from the diary.

25 August 1918
Captain says we're to attack the town of Chehery
tomorrow. It's a pretty small town and we're hitting it with
four companies. I don't like where we're going. Captain
Walters put us on the right flank. That ain't the best thing.
It's closest to the main line of the Germans. If they come for
us we're sure to get in the thick of it.

27 August 1918
Chehery is took. But at a terrible cost. Captain
Walters is gone and so are many of those good boys. We
come through a woods in the middle of the night. It was
dark or nearly so but every once in a while the moon come
out so I could see the branches in front of me. Finally, we
come to a field. It was the prettiest field of grain you ever
saw with a big two-story barn by a creek and the town
laying just a ways beyond, at least that's what the word
was. They said that the Germans were in that town. After
waiting for a while at the edge of that field we finally
screwed up our nerve and started across. It was probably
an hour or less before sun up. We was crossing that field
all quiet and in fine fashion when all of a sudden every
artillery piece in the German army started to fire at us. The
gates of hell just plain opened up above us. I seen the
Captain just disappear in a red cloud. The boys was brave,
they run forward like good soldiers, but we was stopped by
that creek. Bombs and shells was bursting and the noise
was more than a man could stand. Me and John Turner
ducked into that barn pretty quick when them Huns started
firing their machine guns at us. John got killed a few
minutes later. A bullet come right through the wall. I dug in
the back of one of them stalls. Couldn't dig too deep
because I run into a pile of canvas. I got into that hole and
scooped hay and manure over me. I hid for the entire day,
didn't smell too good after that. Nearly got myself caught
by them Krauts. That night the rest of the 126th come and
rescued us. D Company was in terrible shape. We had a
lot of the boys git killed or wounded. Only about half of us
was walking that night. It was probably the scaredest I
been since gittin here in France. It was a terrible day.

Jim and Eve starred at each other. They had their clue.

II

LeDuc listened to the reading of the diary from his hotel room in Detroit's Renaissance Center. He smiled. This could be the ticket to a big payday. Marcil would be very happy. He pulled the ear buds out and turned off his laptop. He walked to his 72nd floor suite window. The view of Windsor Canada directly in front of him, and Belle Isle to his left was spectacular. He didn't see any of it. He knew what he had to do. He knew the potential payday, but he hated talking to that man. He wished he'd turned down that first little favor so many years ago. But, he was now a wealthy man; a wealthy man who lived in fear, but wealthy nevertheless. He sighed, "I guess all jobs have their unpleasantness," he said to the glass.

He then pulled his cell phone out of the holster on his belt. In minutes he had given Marcil the details.

A short time later Marcil disconnected the phone. This was an interesting development. It seemed the Americans were on to where the Patent had been found. At least they had a clue. That could lead the couple to the location of the Regalia. He thought this over a bit. A barn near Chehery. That didn't seem to be enough for anyone to find anything. He dismissed it. His issue now was to get the Patent from these two. Maybe then he'd look for a one-hundred year old barn near Chehery.

LeDuc looked at the dead cell phone. The boss had instructed him to keep a close eye on the Crenshaws and that he would do the rest. Whatever "the rest" meant. LeDuc did not know and didn't really want to know.

Chapter 20

Saturday morning Jim and Eve decided to eat breakfast at the diner in town. Several people greeted them when they walked in the front door. The local gossip was exchanged, discussions about the spring crops, markets, yields, sports, the availability and price of gas, seed and fertilizer for next year filled the next twenty minutes. It didn't take long and their order arrived. Eve began to tell Jim about an incident in her class at school. Jim tried to pay attention but she could tell his mind was elsewhere. Finally Eve said, "You're not listening. I know that look. It means you've got something up your sleeve. What are you thinking?"

"Do you think that barn is still there?"

"No way. I can't imagine it would have lasted nearly a hundred years and two world wars. And, I'll bet that little town is now a huge city and that whole area is all covered with concrete." She sipped her coffee and eyed Jim over the rim.

"You're probably right," he mused.

A moment later Jim waved down the waitress for more coffee. When she left he said, "Do you think we could find it?"

Eve seemed to think about that for a second or two and then said, "The city? Sure, we could find it. But so what? It's not like that barn will still be there. Jim, we're talking about events that happened in 1918. The odds of anything still being there are slim and none. You know that."

As they talked they became increasingly curious about the current population and size of the town. Returning to the house they hurried to the small office they had set up off the kitchen. Jim sat at the desk and logged onto their computer. They quickly found the right website and in short order were looking at an aerial view of the town of Chehery. Small was an understatement. The town was made up of approximately twenty buildings. Farmland ran right up to the back of many of the buildings. Several fields had barns in them. Two streams wound through the fields and what appeared to be several ditches. Any one of which could have been the creek in Oschel Crenshaw's diary.

"Doesn't look so bad," said Jim. "I just can't tell if these are one or two story barns, old or new or what. And, if one of those barns is it, well…"

Eve was silent. After a moment's hesitation she said, "Summer break is coming up. I've always wanted to see France. You really want to go check this out?"

He stared at her. "Are you nuts?" And then he smiled. "You read my mind again. Well, let me see how our savings account looks."

Chapter 21

The Duke of Orleans is the traditional title given to the oldest brother or, lacking a brother, oldest male cousin of the King. The Duchy is and always has been based in the city of Orleans. Located in central France, Orleans is a beautiful and historic city. It also rightly claims to be the site where the idea of the modern French nation was born. It was here in 1429 that Joan of Arc fought French Nobles and English soldiers alike to break the English siege of the city. Her victory was the beginning of her march to Sainthood…and the stake.

The city is the traditional home to the Duke of Orleans. Though, in truth, throughout history the Duke rarely actually lived in the city. It was from this line that the Orléanist claimants to the throne sprang. It was the Orléanists that had the support of the Action Françoise. In fact, the Orléanists had secured the backing of the AF well over a hundred and fifty years ago. In a brilliant bit of misdirection the AF had allowed the Unionists and the Legitimist lines of royalty to loudly and publicly state their case. As such, the Republicans had battled the two groups since the Reign of Terror. Initially beheading many, then simply denying them positions of power in government and industry. The Orléanists, except for that brief experiment prior to the Second World War had stayed in the shadows. Ultimately, using any means necessary the Unionists and the Legitimist were successfully pushed aside. They were not now, nor had they ever been, invited to participate as part of the Council de Governors.

Philippe Louis Palatine, the current and legitimate Duke of Orleans, was indeed widely known. He was not, however, the man known as the descendent of Prince Henri of Orléans, Count of Paris. That was a sham, probably one of the most successful cons in history. Palatine's bloodline ran back to Louis Philippe Joseph d'Orléans, Duke of Orleans at the beginning of the Revolution. Philippe, as he was more commonly known, had been an early supporter of the Revolution, seeing it as a way to supplant his cousin Louis XVI as King of France. He took the name "Philippe Égalité" and positioned himself as an alternative to Louie. Philippe was not blind however and when he fell out of favor with

Robespierre and the Committee for Public Safety he quietly disappeared. The Jacobin's couldn't stand for his escape and Philippe's brother was beheaded in his place.

Louis Palatine was the Chairman and CEO of Perpétuel Energy, the third largest producer of nuclear energy plants in the world. He was a man of uncompromising ambition with a dominating will. The Duke enjoyed his double life. His numerous appearances with the power elite of France were attributed to his many charities and his role as an industrialist. Very few people both inside and outside government knew that nearly everyone in a position of significant power in France owed their success, knowingly or unknowingly, to him and the Council de Governors.

The Council met in many different locations depending upon the urgency of the issue at hand. But, its preferred place of meeting was the Cathédrale Sainte-Croix d'Orléans. Its history as the church of Saint Joan d'Arc made it the obvious choice for the serious and important work of the Council. Unacknowledged, but just as important, was the fact that Orleans was over a hundred miles from the capital city's prying eyes.

Paul Marcil's position with the Louvre allowed him to travel throughout the country, and indeed throughout Europe, with little justification. A perfect circumstance when he needed to provide updates to the Council. Marcil didn't often meet directly with the Council. Which did nothing to shake his belief that he should be in attendance at each and every meeting. He performed an important function for the Council, and he was an important person at the Louvre. He had an important, long-term view of France. His opinions were important and deserved to be heard. He was important! This was a view not shared by the current Council members.

He had been invited to provide an update to the Council covering the Royal Regalia and his efforts at learning more about its location. He left Paris early in the afternoon, checked into his hotel, ate an early dinner, returned to the hotel, showered, changed into his finest silk suit and was now approaching the twin towers of the cathedral.

A man in a dark suit waived him into a parking space on Rue Jeanne d'Arc then walked away without saying a word. Marcil hurried across Place de L'Étape to the foot of the cathedral. He was here. He was with them. His pulse quickened and his palms began to sweat. He couldn't stop the feeling; the same sense of awe and fear he always felt when dealing with these men. This was power, and he wanted part of it. Marcil climbed the stairs to the tall, grand and massive doors, opened one and slipped in. Entering the sanctuary he dipped his hand in holy water and crossed himself. The irony of the gesture completely lost on him. This was, after all, a church. He proceeded down the central isle to the altar. A man wearing a very plain, but well-tailored dark suit, sat in the front row pew. As Marcil approached the man stood, blocking his way. Marcil handed the man his papers. The man typed Marcil's name into his cell phone. A moment later Marcil was waived toward a door leading to a small ante room.

Another man, in similar dark suit, stood next to a straight-backed, unpadded chair. His body at a slight angle, left shoulder pointed at Paul. He had his right hand inside his jacket. Marcil identified himself and handed over his papers once again. The man's hand relaxed under the jacket and Paul could hear metal slide against leather. The man then confirmed Paul's name on a small notebook and waived Marcil forward. He took three steps into the room, put his briefcase down and lifted his arms out to his side. He was quickly and expertly searched. The briefcase was then placed on a small table and opened. It too was quickly searched. This preamble completed, Marcil opened an elaborately carved door and descended to the cathedral's undercroft.

There, he found a small room. Again, a rather large man in a double-breasted suit was waiting for him. This man again searched Paul. This time the search was supplemented with a small metal detector. The guard then checked a pair of monitors mounted to the far wall. Hidden night vision cameras apparently fed one monitor, which displayed an eerie, greenish view of the outside front, back and each side of the cathedral. Monitor number two showed the area just outside the anteroom, the interior of the anteroom and the exterior of this room. After once more confirming Paul's identity against the names listed inside a large brown leather ledger, he was allowed inside the conference room attached to this small outer office. Before entering the room the man grabbed Paul's upper arm with a massive hand and reminded him to speak only when asked. The door opened and Marcil entered. The conference room was dominated by a large oblong table and lined with stone. There were no windows in this conference room.

The Council de Governors had been established prior to the actual creation of Action Françoise. Its original intent was to simply preserve, protect and hide current members of the nobility. Its membership suffered mightily during the Terror, and it quickly and harshly learned that its existence must be kept secret. Thereafter, an attempt was made to limit membership to the decedents of the original twelve French Dukes and of course the distant family of the King. This failed due to the loss of so many royals during the Terror. Ultimately, nine members of the nobility were selected and given Duchies by the Prince du Sang or "blood descendant of the King" and the stand-in King for the Council. Eventually, the Terror passed and a new evil took over the levers of power. The Council set about to destroy Napoleon. It joined forces with certain remnants of the ancient regime's nobliesse and formed the Action Françoise.

Marcil now faced the ten members of the Council. An eleventh chair, at the head of the table, and reserved for the Prince du Sang was vacant. The identity of the Prince du Sang was a closely held secret, known only to members of the Council. Marcil paused, gently inhaled and gathered his nerve. He eyed the men around the table each with their écuyer standing directly behind them. It was these squires that he feared the most. They were fanatical in their loyalty, first to the Prince du Sang and then to their respective Duke. It was they who actually made the nighttime visits. Each was armed and each very deadly.

Marcil took his position at the foot of the table. The members of the council studied him for a long minute. Finally, Marcil heard the word "Proceed."

He began by explaining who LeDuc was, his expertise and history with the AF. He spent some time describing the two Americans and their story of the great grandfather in the First World War. He explained about the antique show, LeDuc's role in that show, and the discovery of the Royal Patent. His confidence increasing, he paused to let the members digest his news. He could plainly see the level of interest was minimal. Inwardly he smiled. He was about to drop his bombshell. Marcil prolonged the delay by pouring a glass of water from the carafe in front of him. He then took a polite sip and began again. He explained that the Royal Patents were never seen without other treasures which were key to the monarchy. The heads of the members of the Council all came up immediately at this. They knew what this meant. Their interest was obvious.

"You mean you know where the Sword of Charlemagne is located?" the Duke of Bourbon asked.

"No, not exactly, but we have reason to believe we are coming close, and may in fact recover la Joyeuse, Monsieur le Duke," Marcil replied.

"Is the Coronation Crown found?" the Duke of Orleans quietly asked.

"Ahhh…no Monsieur le Duke, but we believe that….well, we have a clue as to…" Marcil could not organize his thoughts, he stammered. Slowly he regained control. Finally he began to explain where he was with regard to recovering the Patent and why he had failed in the first attempt. Finished, he bowed and turned to leave. Instead, a council member, known only as the Duke of Anjou, began to question him.

"What was your man doing? Was he installing a microphone or searching the home?" the Duke asked.

Marcil, unsure of where this question was leading, began to stammer. Before he could completely answer, the Duke of Brittany asked if he had given clear instructions. The Duke of Bourbon wanted to know why the Crenshaws had not been eliminated and the artifacts recovered already.

Marcil's stomach tightened. He had lost control of the conversation. The questions came at him too fast, and he wasn't allowed time to answer completely. He felt a bead of sweat release between his shoulder blades and roll down his spine. He did not have good answers. He had not practiced for this line of questions; he felt his credibility slipping away. The fool LeDuc in Michigan had completely failed to properly and secretly search and bug the Crenshaw's. Now he was paying the price for LeDuc's screw up.

Finally, the Duke of Orleans leaned forward, "Monsieur Marcil." The Duke's voice was smooth, calming, and it terrified Marcil. "I believe the Council would prefer if you returned with a better grasp of the situation. Do we make ourselves clear?"

This turned Marcil's body cold. He glanced around the table. Only dead stares returned his look. "Oui, I shall…..it shall…I will not fail you." Marcil sputtered.

He didn't notice the man approaching him from his left. Suddenly a large, powerful hand wrapped around his left bicep, lifted him from the chair and escorted him to the door. There, thankfully, his arm was released, and he was again in the stairwell.

What had happened? That was supposed to be a triumph, not a disgrace! Those people didn't know anything about the Sword or the royal artifacts fifty minutes ago! He found a small wooden chair and sat, head in his hands. After a few minutes he stood up, straightened his tie and walked to his car.

Chapter 22

Jim sat in the small office off the kitchen. He had a pile of paper on the desk and another on the floor. His method was fairly straight forward. He opened an envelope, read the bill, made out the check, subtracted it from his computerized checkbook, put the receipt in the proper file and put the opened envelop, sale inserts and other debris associated with paying bills next to his feet. Eventually, when there were no more bills needing his attention, he scooped up the pile of paper from the floor and forced it into his trash can. Two more handfuls of paper and the process was done for the month. "Finished, let's go for a walk!" he nearly shouted to Eve.

Eve put on her jacket, called Molly and met Jim at the door. They walked down the back steps and headed out to the barn. Jim showed Eve where he thought an owl had taken up residence. Then they walked behind the building and kicked a brush pile, hoping to get Molly started on a rabbit. It wasn't to be and they headed to the equipment shed. There, they stopped and watched several birds on a feeder they had installed the previous spring.

Jim stared past the pasture to their woods. "You know, we could clear about five acres out there and add it as pasture in about two years."

"I don't want to hire a bulldozer. I hate the way it looks when they're done," Eve said.

"We could cut the trees, fence it and put goats, then pigs on it," Jim mused.

"Does that really work?" Eve asked.

"Of course, it's the way they did it for hundreds of years," Jim replied.

Molly, nose to the ground, moved off in the direction of the barn. Eve ducked inside, grabbed a bucket of birdseed and filled the feeder there. Rejoining Jim they called Molly, who, contrary to her nature, came to them right away and they headed for the house. There they mounted the steps and sat in the two porch chairs. Molly went to her dish and nosily lapped up her water. After a few moments Jim finally said, "I've got a plan."

Eve looked at him. "About what?"

"France."

"Out with it, I'm getting older where I sit," she teased. He just shook his head and smiled.

"Okay, here it is. Jean is supposed to be in touch with us this week or next right?"

"Right"

"Well, I'm going to assume that she's going to tell us the Patent and the tube are the real deal. If she does, then I go down to the elevator and sell our crop in the field. We'll get less money, but we'll have a nice check in the bank by early next week. We use that money to go to France. We'll have to save a little extra over the winter for seed and fertilizer and what not, but we'll be okay. Let's check this thing out." Jim looked pleased with himself.

Eve looked at him; she'd become a pretty savvy farmer's wife and knew this was a hit at their budget. "We can afford this?"

He shrugged, "We'll be okay. It's not like we depend entirely on the farm."

"I knew we'd be going to France!" she exclaimed. They talked about France for a while, then about their college French classes as they watched the sunlight fade to night. Finally, they headed into the house to plan their trip.

CHAPTER 23

In the past, when Paul Marcil's ego had been abused by the Council he had retreated into his work at the Louvre. Here he was a man of influence and power, just as he should be with the Council. And, while the influence of the AF had been of considerable assistance it was not the sole reason he was where he was. He was not a stupid man. In fact, his academic record was stellar. Now, he approached his problem with the Americans and the Patents calmly, as any businessman would approach a large and expensive business proposition. It had become clear the Americans knew of the Royal Regalia, and they might be within reach of recovering it. He had elected to not have the Americans disposed of. He felt they would lead him to the remaining objects. But, it might be best if he had the Patent in his possession while the Americans searched for the remaining objects. His problem was how to get it and the tube.

Some problems have a solution so obvious that it is missed by most. This was one of those problems. After considerable thought Marcil decided upon the simplest solution he could conceive. He would simply ask the Crenshaw's for their treasure. He studied his desk clock while he rehearsed his speech. He always had trouble with the conversion of Paris time to United States time. Where did these people live? Was it the middle…what did they call it? Central? Was it Central Time or was it the first one…Washington Time, no…Eastern? Was it six hours? No, five…no, seven. He grew frustrated and finally decided now was good. He picked up the phone and called Jim and Eve Crenshaw.

Eve was grading papers at the kitchen table when the phone rang. "Mrs. Crenshaw" said a French accented voice.

"Yes?" Eve said.

"Madame, my name is Paul Marcil. I am deputy director of the Art Acquisition Department at the Musée du Louvre in Paris".

Eve suppressed her surprise; the Louvre in Paris was calling! "Good afternoon Mr. Marcil."

"Madame Crenshaw if I may take a few moments of your time. I hope I find you well today," Marcil said.

"I'm fine," Eve replied. "May I ask what this about?"

Marcil winced. "Why was it that Americans were so direct and impolite?" he thought. They had never mastered the art of a civilized conversation before they got right into business. "Madame, I am sorry to disturb your day, but it has come to my attention that you have a tremendously valuable and historical treasure of France in your possession."

"I'm sorry who is this?" Eve asked, her mind racing at what she'd just been asked.

"Madame, I assure you, I am whom I say. I am with the Musée du Louvre in Paris." He then proceeded to provide Eve with his office address, phone and fax numbers and other office specifics. He was doing his best to stay calm and eventually she accepted that she was, in fact, speaking to someone at the famous museum.

"Well…yes. We may have a valuable antique," Eve allowed. "If you don't mind, how did the Louvre find out? We just found out ourselves a few days ago."

"Madame, a Monsieur LeDuc was instrumental in the assessment of this treasure, was he not? You see, he is affiliated with the Louvre in a very real sense. He is the curator of a museum here in France. All of our museums coordinate their efforts to ensure our French history is respected and preserved," Marcil explained.

"I see. Well, yes, we have what Mr. LeDuc called a Patent and a tube of some sort that holds the Patent."

"I must ask you madam, how are you caring for this treasure now? You see it is important." Marcil didn't wait for an answer, "The Louvre considers this a treasure of France, and we intend to repatriate this important historical document."

'Intend?' What did he mean by 'intend'? Eve was trying to decide if she had just been threatened. "Oh boy, what if this guy filed a lawsuit?" she thought. "We could never afford the attorney's fees."

She hesitated before answering, "Mr. Marcil, my husband and I are very aware of the value of these items. We have taken the appropriate steps to make sure they are safe."

Marcil could sense she was becoming very careful, maybe a little afraid. He knew how to calm her fears. "Madame, we at the Louvre would like to offer you a significant amount of money for these items. But, we must insure they are indeed as Monsieur LeDuc believes."

Eve had been becoming nervous but the words "…a significant amount of money…" had her attention. Marcil continued, "So, you see, we would like for you to bring these items to our laboratories in Paris. We would of course provide you with the appropriate airplane ticket for both you and your husband and provide you with hotel accommodations. Would that be acceptable to you Madame Crenshaw?"

She was stunned. Take the Patent to Paris? "Well, yes, I think so, I mean, we could do that," Eve stammered.

"It is important, you see. We must verify these items as legitimate, no? We at the Louvre would need to perform tests to ensure the legitimacy of the items, you see?"

"Oh, yes, of course, yes, I understand completely," Eve said, not understanding completely at all.

"It is settled then," he said.

"Oh…well, okay, we can do that." She was still in a bit of shock.

"Then madam, I will have my assistant telephone to you to arrange your flights. I would hope to see you in Paris as soon as possible," Marcil crooned.

Eve hung up the phone. "This can't be happening," she thought. Then a big grin began to sneak on to her lips. Finally, she was actually laughing. "We're going to Paris France," she said to Molly.

Chapter 24

Two weeks later, on a cool Thursday evening, Jim and Eve began packing their bags for their trip. They had arranged a full day layover in Montreal, telling Marcil's assistant they were visiting a relative. The next evening they were to leave Detroit and fly to Montreal via Chicago which seemed odd to them both. Taking the diary and the history of the 32nd Jim wrapped them in a towel. Eve then packed them in her carry-on. Finished with the packing they went to the garage, called the dog, then they drove Molly to the neighbor's for the next ten days. The vet would charge too much to board her for that long.

They arrived in Montreal well after midnight, gathered their bags and found a taxi to the Hotel le Crystal. The next morning they met Professor Somme for breakfast in the expansive hotel restaurant. It was a warm reunion, and over eggs, bacon, toast and coffee Eve told her about the recent call from the Louvre. They then showed her the diary and described their research into the 32nd Division. Jean was fascinated by all the news and they spent several minutes discussing Paris, the Louvre, the First World War and Jim's Great Grand Father.

It was then Jean's turn to relate her news. She proudly proclaimed both the Patent and the tube as authentic and correct to their purported time. She then explained each and every test she and her team had run, the historical verifications done on each portrait on the Patent and the chemical analysis.

Coming to the end of her technical explanation she leaned across the table and in a low voice said, "There is something else." A large and revealing smile broke across her placid face. "The paint used is extraordinary."

"How so?" asked Jim, not exactly certain why Jean's voice had lowered.

"You see, a specific skill of all great painters was the mixing of their paints. After all, in the seventeen hundreds, one could not simply go to an art store and buy paint, could one? No. One had to make one's own." Jean had become a professor again.

"All the great painters had their own formulas. Each used different amounts of pigment, binder, thinner and extender in their formulas. In fact, many different things could be used for each pigment or other element of the paint." She paused and sipped her coffee.

"You see? No…?" She seemed a little disappointed. "It is important because each paint became a sort of fingerprint of the artist. Over the past several decades art historians have identified the recipes of all the great masters and many of the lesser known important artists of their era."

"I get it," Jim said.

"You can tell who painted the Patent can't you?" said Eve.

"You do not disappoint!" exclaimed Jean. "Yes! The paintings of portraits on the Patent and the decorations on the leather itself appear to be from the brush of one of the most celebrated painters of his day, Jacques-Louis David."

"Never heard of him," said Jim.

"I suspect not," Jean sighed. "He is considered a great master certainly, but he is equally known for being an anti-royalist and a member of the Committee for Public Safety." Her excitement was real.

"Wait, what? I'm not clear on this committee. Bill mentioned that. They beheaded people right?" Eve asked.

Jean smiled. "It is a period of European history not well known by many Europeans and even fewer Americans. The *Comité de salut public* was notorious," Jean said.

"Initially King Louis XVI intended to establish a constitutional monarchy similar to the model established in England. However, he was unsuccessful in managing the general assembly. It transformed into a National Assembly, which eventually became the National Convention. They struggled to create a republican government."

Jim and Eve listened intently. "Finally, unable to agree on the structure of the government the National Convention formed the 'Comité de salut public' to carry out the functions of government while they continued their work. The Committee of Public Safety became the de facto executive government in France. Remember this was during the time of the Revolutionary Wars."

Her voice dropped a bit, and she became more thoughtful as she talked. "Now, this is interesting because the Committee was originally set up to defend the new republic. That's the 'safety' part. They were to defend the new republic against all enemies.

Unfortunately, the saying "power corrupts and absolute power corrupts absolutely" was never truer. They quickly became a tyrannical bunch and lost all common sense. The committee was responsible for thousands of executions. Sometimes for infractions amounting to the absurd; women who complained the baker had no bread were considered anti-revolutionaries and beheaded. High-profile executions at the guillotine were routine. Anyone with even the most remote connection to wealth of any kind prior to the revolution was suspect. Frenchmen were executed for their alleged support of the monarchy or opposition to the Revolution. It is said nearly forty thousand went to the guillotine because of the Committee."

"Finding Jacques-Louis David painted the Patent may cause a change in our total understanding of the French Revolution. We will definitely dig deeper into his role in the Revolution. Was he in-fact a secret Royalist? Did he convert to the revolutionaries out of conviction or to save his neck?"

She sat back in her chair, pleased and excited. Her triumph evident, Jim could tell there were scholarly papers dancing in her head already.

Suddenly she leaned forward. "Obviously it is beyond question that these items are truly genuine."

Jim and Eve were stunned. The objects had been proven to be what they believed them to be and they were extremely important historical items. Jim and Eve were filled with a sense of gratitude they had not anticipated. Eve hugged Jean tightly. "Thank you," was all she could manage. Jim smiled, thanked Jean, then after a moment thanked her again; a moment later he stood up and hugged her. At that point they were all laughing.

CHAPTER 25

I

At 7:48 P.M. Air Canada flight 5946 departed Montreal for Paris, again via Chicago. Jim and Eve sat in first class, enjoyed the food, watched the movie, drank the free wine and slept in comfortable seats. The next morning they quickly cleared customs. Then, found the bus to the car rental lots and were on their way to the rental garage.

After a short wait in line they reached the clerk. There they showed their international drivers licenses and passports and were soon presented with a set of keys and a Paris map. A short exploration of the parking lot, and they soon found slot number 42 and their economy class Citroën. Jim stopped short. "Kinda small isn't it?" he said glancing at Eve.

"Hon, you know as well as I do, small cars are better in Europe. Now, quit complaining and take me to a hotel room in Paris!" Eve looked at him and grinned.

Twenty minutes later they were on their way to the hotel Britannique, a small boutique hotel with rooms reserved for them by Monsieur Marcil's assistant. They spent the rest of that day resting and touring Paris. They toured the Cathedrale Notre Dame de Paris and walked the West Bank. It was truly a magical day, topped only by a wonderful dinner at Le Voltaire.

"So what's the plan Mr. Bond?" asked Eve as she pushed a mushroom to the side of her plate.

"For this evening or tomorrow?" Jim asked with a grin.

"I know the plan for this evening," she said with a mischievous smile. "I'm curious about tomorrow."

"We meet with Marcil at what? Two O'clock?" he said. "I think we have to have him validate the Patent and the container. He needs to do that, and frankly, I don't know the law on this. Is it theirs? Is it ours? Can he just keep it? I think we need to see what he says." Jim didn't like the idea of the Louvre just taking what his great grandfather had found. It didn't seem fair. But then again, maybe it did belong to the people of France. "We probably should have hired a lawyer or something," Jim sighed. His fear of having the Louvre simply take the Patent and the tube by claiming it was theirs in the first place had been bubbling up about once an hour for the past week.

"Well, at least we get a free trip to Paris," Eve said with a satisfied smile.

"In any case, I think we check out of our hotel tomorrow morning. After we leave Marcil I think we should hit the road for Chehery. I'd like to start looking for the barn as soon as possible."

Eve finished the last bite of her Coquilles St. Jacques a` la Parisienne. "Works for me," she said with a smile. "Waiter, check please."

II

They arrived at the Louvre thirty minutes early for their meeting with the deputy director of the Art Acquisition Department. "The title must mean something to these folks," said Jim. "Did you see how everyone jumped to it when I mentioned the guy's name?"

"I sure did. You'd think we were going to see the Chief of Staff or something," Eve whispered. Jim smiled. She's always been a perfect military spouse.

A few moments later a portly man in a badly fitting suit approached them. "Madame and Monsieur Creen-shaw?" he said. They winced at the pronunciation, and answered in the affirmative. "Would you follow me to the Deputy Director's office please?" He said in fine English.

After several minutes of walking and one long staircase, upon which Jim thought their guide was going to breathe his last, the trio finally found a humble door with only the number '102' above it. The round man knocked and they entered an outer office. A pretty young secretary with a radiant smile greeted them. She said something in French to their guide, who promptly left, and then offered seats, coffee, juice or water to Jim and Eve. Her visitor comfort duties taken care of she then passed through an interior door to the inner office of the deputy director.

She returned seconds later, a bit flushed it seemed, and they were immediately shown into the inner office. For only being a deputy director, Paul Marcil had a grand office. Jim had seen the inside of a good number of high-ranking people's offices during his tours at the Pentagon and various headquarters, but this one was huge. From the window behind his desk the top of I. M. Pei's Pyramid could be seen. The desk looked large enough for a game of ping-pong. Opposite the desk was a large fireplace. In front of that sat two large couches, facing each other as if ready to duel. A beautiful, Louis XVI table stood between and to one side, it seemed to serve as referee. Marcil motioned for them to sit and took his place opposite them.

He began by offering them chocolates and a cup of coffee or tea. He then described the Louvre's many museums and displays. His conversation was practiced and polished. A trait which did nothing to ease Jim's wariness. The man knew how to schmooze. He promised them a private tour of the displays and the more private collections. Eventually, he got around to the business he had with them.

"Madame and Monsieur Creen-shaw," he said, completely missing Jim's involuntary wince.

"The Royal Patent and its container are without question an important part of French history." Marcil was warming to his speech.

"These items are extremely rare and represent the last legitimate heir to the throne of France. The artistic skill devoted to the fabrication of a Royal Patent is some of the finest of any age. Sadly, most of these art pieces were destroyed in the Revolution."

At this point Marcil's tone changed from conversational to businesslike. "We wish to display them in their legitimate place in the museum. I understand your claim to these pieces. And, in an attempt to avoid a long, costly and embarrassing legal battle which I'm assuring you, would not end in your favor, I wish to purchase them from you on behalf of the Louvre."

He cleared his throat and sat straighter on the couch. "We are prepared to offer five million dollars US for the container and the Patent. I am certain they would be purchased for much higher should they ever reach an auction. But, given our legitimate legal claims to these items I am also certain it would be many years before they did, if ever."

Jim and Eve glanced at each other. Eve suppressed a grin. "Well, sir…" Jim began. "I would, um, well; I think we'll have to discuss this."

"Of course, Monsieur Creen-shaw, of course. Now tell me, Monsieur Creen-shaw, your stay here in Paris is for how long, please?"

"We're not staying in Paris our entire trip," Jim replied.

"Oh, not staying in Paris?" He actually appeared physically injured.

"But sir, Paris is the most beautiful city in the world. We have the world's most important art. The food in Paris is without equal and our wine – ahhhhhh, our wine is…well, there is none better. Naturally, you would see some shows, no? And the Tower Eiffel, she is *incroyable*." Marcil was playing his part perfectly. He had always been proud of his ability to elicit information without the object of his questions realizing they were, in fact, being questioned.

"I intend to visit some World War One battle sites," said Jim. "My great grandfather's war so to speak."

"Oh, well that is perfectly understandable. It is regrettable that you will not spend time in our beautiful city….was your great grandfather in the Battle of the Somme?" Marcil asked innocently.

"No, no, that was of course, predominately English, and of course, nearly two years before the United States was in the war," Jim corrected. "No, he was in the Argonne area."

Marcil looked a bit embarrassed. "Oh yes, how foolish of me to forget my schoolboy history. What part of the Argonne did your grandfather, no…your GREAT grandfather fight in?

"Oh, he fought the entire way up to Germany. He was with the 32nd Infantry Division known as the Red Arrow Division. He was with them from the beginning, through the liberation of Sedan and marched into Germany itself." Jim proudly recounted.

"Ah, well, we owe your country a debt of gratitude I am sure," Marcil politely offered. "Now, to return to our business at hand. Five million dollars is, of course, a great deal of money. Before I can authorize the transfer of such sums, as I am sure you can understand, we will have to authenticate these items. May I ask when you intend to leave France?"

"We're only here for a week," Eve replied.

"A week? Oh Madame, that is much too short a time. There is, how do… there is too much to see, no? You should extend your stay certainly."

"I'm sorry. We would love to, but I have a seminar to

attend in one week," Eve politely insisted.

"Ah… *C'est dommage.* I am of course sure you will understand we will need to complete our studies of the Patent and its container. I will need you to give them to me so that our laboratories may begin work immediately. I am sure you would like to have your money before you leave, no?" Marcil said rather more firmly than Eve thought appropriate.

III

Having shown the Americans out of his office Marcil locked the door and contemplated the tube lying on his desk blotter. He thought it was beautiful. It was a light coffee brown with gold caps at each end. Crenshaw had shown him how to open one end. Its secret catch was a remarkable piece of machinery. The cap itself had delicate scrollwork engraved completely round. But, the true treasure was the piece of leather laid out next to the container. A Royal Patent, its colours still bright, its engraved leather surface as clean and clear as the day it had been painted. It was remarkable.

He carefully rolled the Patent into a scroll and placed it back inside the tube. Then, he removed a velvet bag from a credenza drawer and placed the tube inside. Having finished the housekeeping he rolled his chair back, slid the chair mat to one side and bent to a floor safe. He dialed the combination and placed the tube inside.

Marcil sat back in his chair. He glanced out the window, noticed the sky deepening in colour and thought about his time at University and art studies. After a moment, his worries and fears dealt with, he was ready. He made the phone call. On the first ring a voice answered, "Oui?" and Marcil gave the Council's representative an update on the Americans' visit. When Marcil came to the end and paused the voice at the other end asked, "*C'est fini?*" Marcil winced, answered yes, and the line went dead. A moment later he made another call, this time the roles were reversed and he was the superior.

CHAPTER 26

Claude "Le Couteau" Recheau snapped open his cell phone. He hated the damn thing. It was shrill, kept him on a leash, and its buttons were a pain in the ass to use. It was a necessary evil however because this one cell phone was his contact with his most prolific employer and the attendant future paydays.

"Oui," "The Knife" answered.

Recheau did not consider himself to be a small time hood. No, he considered himself to have reached the big time, and therefore he was due the appropriate respect. The past two years he'd stepped into some rather large commissions as a result of his work for the AF. He'd dealt with a Mexican drug lord who made the mistake of attempting to move cocaine into the village where the Duke of Burbon's granddaughter lived. A Mexican in France? The man was, emphasis on the word "was", a fool. And, he'd done other work for the Council; he'd "persuaded" two *députés* to vote on defense and budget bills as they properly should. His skillful use of a knife had provided him with a nickname he rather enjoyed, and which seemed to help his efforts in collecting various debts owed to the AF, and to himself. His routine employer was Monsieur Paul Marcil; and it was this never-ending source of funds that he was speaking to now

"I have two Americans I want you to follow. Just follow. Do you understand?" The tin voice came across the little speaker like a shrill girl.

"Oui, d'accord."

"Follow these two. Do not be discovered. They are looking for something. I do not know what. I do not know what it is contained in. I want to know where and when they go someplace. If they stop at a barn or start digging in a field, I want to know." Marcil's voice squeaked. "Do not bother them or stop them. But, if they discover something I want to know immediately."

"D'accord; where are they now?" hissed Recheau, thinking that he was being sent to follow two American fools. Dig in a field? What the hell kind of thing was Marcil wrapped up in now?"

Marcil gave him what details were available. Recheau

grabbed a small travel bag and quickly stuffed his gun cleaning kit, a change of clothes, his toiletries and several thousand Euros into the bag. Then, because a man in his business made deadly enemies, he placed several booby traps throughout the apartment. Satisfied, Recheau locked the door and walked to his garage. Selecting the most boring car there, a nine-year old, faded blue BMW, he set off to find the Americans.

Chapter 27

Having turned over the case containing the Patent and its container to Paul Marcil, Jim and Eve were anxious to be on the road. They intended to spend the evening in Chehery, but a review of their tour book made that seem problematic. Nevertheless, they elected to try their luck and see how far they could comfortably go. If they left now, they could avoid much of Paris' famous traffic.

Within the hour they entered the A4 toll road leading to the D764 highway. Eve closely monitored her cell phone GPS screen. She checking off each exit as they passed and compared them to the map and notes she had prepared. Having some experience with European driving they were not totally shocked by the speed and complexity of the trip. She expertly plotted their location on the map, keeping careful track of the upcoming exits and relayed to Jim the distance to their next turn or change.

Swinging into a long line at the tollbooth on the A4 Jim relaxed. "We're good from here," he said, more to himself than to Eve. She nodded and double-checked her map and notes and relaxed. Then, as was her habit, she began to examine the cars in the lines about them. Her goal was to guess their livelihood and determine if they were happy in life or not. Her guesses could never be confirmed, but she fancied that she was pretty good at the game. There was a funny old man in the battered car to the left, probably retired; and there a young couple that didn't look too happy; probably students. Over there a young girl, clearly supported by her parents, off on an adventure, and immediately behind her sat a young man on a motorcycle with shiny black road leathers, probably a store clerk.

She also examined the cars. They had lived in Italy for three years early in Jim's career, and in those days she rarely saw German cars. The roads were filled with Fiats and Alfa Romeos. Surrounding her now were Mercedes, Renaults, and BMWs. She noted several cars that looked new or sporty, including a Lamborghini. She couldn't help herself and smiled. She loved Europe, and the three years she and Jim had spent stationed in southern Italy had been one of the happiest times of her life.

Eventually they paid their toll and were speeding along.

Jim struggled to stay on course and out of the way of the aggressive French drivers. Eventually they joined the D764. After another thirty miles the road opened up, traffic thinned, and they were much more comfortable.

Twenty minutes later Jim said, "You know, it's odd, but there's a blue car back there that's been behind us since Paris. The rest of these jokers blow by us like we're standing still, but that guy seems to hang back."

Eve looked at Jim "I've noticed him too, every time I looked in the side mirror I'd see him all the way out of the city."

Just then they passed an exit. Instead of following along behind them the blue car left the highway. "Well, guess I spoke too soon," Jim said and soon the conversation lagged.

By early evening they had completed the drive to Charleville-Mezieres; a modest town near Sedan and the village of Chehery. They found an acceptable hotel, checked in then went in search of the evening's dinner. Eventually, they landed at a small restaurant with a large outdoor porch. They spent the evening sipping the local wine and watching the people.

Later, as they walked back to the hotel Jim noticed a blue BMW in the parking area of a small guest-house on the opposite side of the street. They stopped and Jim tried to focus on the car in the distance. "Eve, is that the car from this afternoon?" he asked. She stared hard at the car for a moment. The only light came from a distant street lamp and the light from the windows of a few businesses still open. "I can't be sure," she said.

They stood and studied the car for several minutes. "I can't be sure either," Jim acknowledged. He looked it over for several more minutes. Finally, unable to decide if it was or not, and not thinking the matter important in either case, they dismissed the BMW and finished their walk back to the hotel.

Chapter 28

Claude Recheau sat on an unpadded wooden chair facing a small wooden writing desk. Recheau had taken an upstairs room in what was advertised as a "Bed and Breakfast" in the center of the village. The building was old, the room small and the term "B&B" seemed overly grand. If asked he would describe the place as a boarding house.

He was not writing. Instead, he carefully pushed down the small lever on the top left side of his Beretta 9mm pistol. There were many guns used by professionals which were better and more accurate than this gun; he knew that. The German's Sig Sauers were great guns and their Glocks were good too. The Israeli IWI pistols were excellent. But, he simply liked this gun, it was an emotional attachment. The gun was simple, like things should be. And, it had a bit of weight to it, you knew you held a weapon when holding this gun. Plus, it was easy to clean; which was really the key to any firearm and something too many people did not do often enough he believed.

He removed the slide and barrel and sat them to one side. He then placed the frame on the table directly in front of himself and stood. Crossing the room to his overnight bag he removed a small leather case and returned to the writing desk. He opened the case and removed a cleaning rod, an orange bottle of solvent and a small bundle of cloth scraps held together with a rubber band. He removed the rubber band and inserted one piece of cloth into the slot at the tip of the cleaning rod. Then he opened the solvent, dipped the cloth tipped rod into the bottle and brought it to the bottleneck. There he rolled the tip against the side of the glass, squeezing the excess out of the cloth. Finished preparing the swab he inserted the rod down the barrel and pushed and pulled the rod through several times. Putting the barrel to one side he picked up the pistol frame. Just as he was beginning to enjoy this nightly ritual his phone rang. "Merde," he muttered as he put the pistol frame and rod down.

He opened the phone and hissed, "What?" He listened. "No, of course not." He endured another question then, "They are in a cheap, little hotel. And they went to a cheap, little restaurant, and ate cheap food. Then they sat there all evening drinking cheap wine and doing nothing."

He didn't have a hair trigger temper; he simply always was in a bad mood. After listening a few more moments his irritation growing he said, "Of course. Yes. Dammit, I know my instructions."

He then clicked off the cell phone, regretting the fact that it is impossible to slam a cell phone. Taking a breath he calmed himself and returned to the desk. He did not like being questioned. Of course, he hadn't been entirely truthful with his employer. He had been spotted. He was sure of that. But, realistically how could anyone follow an American who drove like an old woman on an empty and long highway? It was impossible. He knew the BMW would have to be replaced, and he intended to do that later this evening. But for now, he wanted to finish the evening's ritual; he would feel better when it was complete. Then he would solve the riddle of a new vehicle.

At 2 A.M. Recheau descended the stairs from his second floor room. He found the small kitchenette where the morning breakfast was prepared and escaped through the rear door, being careful to place a strip of tape over the catch so he could easily and quietly reenter the building. He walked to the street, turned left and then walked another four hundred feet. There, he again turned left and went to an alley that paralleled the street. Here he found the abused green Fiat he had spotted earlier that evening.

This car did not have the telltale red light blinking on the dash. There was a good chance it did not have an operating alarm system. He carefully examined the interior of the car. He was fairly certain there was no aftermarket alarm on this car. He removed a thin piece of metal from his coat and slipped it between the door glass and the frame. In a moment he'd caught the door locking mechanism. He pulled up. The jimmy easily unlatched the door. He paused. It was possible he'd misread the car. He removed several tools from his coat pocket. He arranged them all in his left hand where they were instantly available as soon as the door was open. One more time he carefully searched his surroundings for prying eyes. Then, he braced for the car alarm. Using his right hand, he opened the door and quickly sat in the driver's seat. No alarm sounded. He relaxed. Reaching into his other coat pocket he removed another tool. He quickly popped the ignition key cylinder out and in less than forty-five seconds had the car running.

He was a bit disappointed at the time, but in reality the car hadn't started when the motor first turned over; his time would have been shorter if it had. He drove a short way out of town to a small roadside café in Villers-Semeuse. The café was deserted, as he knew it would be, and he parked the car in the rear of the building. He then began the short five kilometer walk back to town, sure that in this countryside, at this time of night, no one would pass him on the road. He was correct.

Chapter 29

Jim and Eve ate a breakfast of coffee, bread and cheese in a small café just a quarter mile from their hotel. The morning was a bit cool and clouds were rolling in, but the walk to the café was pleasant. As they approached the building the blue BMW they had seen yesterday passed them headed out of town. Jim and Eve turned and watched it drive away. They discussed the car for the remainder of their walk, but the conversation quickly changed as they ate their breakfast. An hour later they were repacked and checked out of the hotel.

Over breakfast they had discussed their plan for finding the barn. Jim reviewed the brief description given in his Great grandfather's diary, "a two story" barn. Jim wasn't sure that description would be of much help. Most barns are two stories, a lower floor containing stalls and a drive bay where hay wagons came in, stopped, and were unloaded into the hay loft. He didn't know about European barns, but assumed they were essentially the same as American barns. They fulfilled the same roll after all.

"Their" barn lay on the outskirts of town. He hoped that would be an aid in his search, but couldn't be certain. The city or village could have grown around the barn by now. He assumed the town of 1918 could be seen from the barn given the diary's description. Also, his Great grandfather said they came "out of a woods" and across a field and there found the barn. So, there was a wooded area somewhere near the barn, at least there had been nearly a hundred years ago. Jim was afraid he had brought his wife on a bit of a wild goose chase when they should have been touring Paris.

They double-checked the map, then began the twenty-five kilometer drive to Chehery. Their route took them through Sedan, a town prominently mentioned in the diary. It was the goal of the allied drive during the battle in question. They could see parts of the town's magnificent castle from the road. Its bastions and drum towers prominent above the town skyline. Their plan, loosely formed, had something to do with finding all the roads into and out of Chehery and then driving those roads to find the right barn. It wasn't much of a plan, but it was all they could come up with.

Google Earth had not been as helpful as they had hoped in finding a two-story barn. It was all they had, and as Eve had said, it was more hope than plan.

Chehery is not a large village. There are six roadways leading in and out of the village. Jim and Eve drove carefully into the village, studying the buildings in fields and near houses as they approached the village. As Jim had guessed, all the barns seemed to be two stories. Well, at least Jim thought so. Every farmer had a stone barn. But, they couldn't tell if they met the definition of a one or two story barn. Each had what to Jim appeared to be a hay loft, but was the loft considered a second story or part of the normal barn structure. Why had Oushel Crenshaw remarked on it? There simply was nothing out of the ordinary with these barns. A small green Fiat passed them in the middle of town, stopped next to a small newsstand and the driver got out. Aside from that, no one was on the street. They drove through the village center and out the other side. Slowly they crept along the road looking at each farm. Nothing stood out.

For the next three hours they cruised the roads in and around the village. They examined each farm in the area. Newer barns, made of metal or brick were easily dismissed. But the older, stone barns were difficult to judge. The structures began to blur together, and nothing seemed to catch their eye.

They began to develop a routine. Jim would drive until an interesting barn was sighted, usually by Eve. Then, Jim would attempt to stop the car on the side of the road where a good view of the barn in question was afforded. Often this was more easily said than done; stonewalls, ditches, shrubs, no shoulders on the road or a host of other things made pulling off the road a difficult proposition. Once a car nearly collided with them after they had foolishly stopped just around the bend of a curve, hidden from traffic coming from behind. The driver yelled something at them as he braked hard and swerved around them. They were not sure what the man said, but it seemed angry and they were sure it was rude.

They ate lunch in the village center. Jim tried to explain their mission to the only other customer in the small café where they ate. The old man's hearing, Jim's French, or a combination of both doomed the conversation from the beginning. Their waiter was a young man who seemed to know a great deal about

American pop stars and very little about his own town's history. The rest of the day was spent driving every back road and path they could find.

By nightfall they were sitting in their room at what could only be described as a "rooming house slash bed and breakfast," French edition. Their hosts didn't speak any English, but insisted they sit in the garden and talk. After a shy beginning Eve's college French began to pay dividends, and they had a grand time talking to each other using a pocket dictionary and charades. They tried to ask about barns and the First World War, but the differences in language made it extremely difficult. The entire evening was a mental exercise, but did help them recall much of the language they'd both studied years ago. Too soon, the wine, cheese and bread ran out, everyone was tired anyway, and they all stumbled off to bed.

The next morning they decided to search the village itself before returning to Paris. The village was so small that their hosts had suggested they do so on foot. After several hours of walking from one end of the village to the other multiple times, they were dejected, tired and ready to return to their inn. Their hosts had suggested a visit to the town hall. It was there in a small courtyard behind the main building they came across an obelisk devoted to the American's of the 32nd Division. On the west side of the obelisk was an engraving thanking the men of the 32nd for liberating the village in 1918. Jim was thrilled. It showed they were in the right area at least. Engravings of flags and artillery pieces adorned the north and south sides of the monument. On the east side, highlighted by the morning sun, were the names of the twenty-six men killed in the attack.

"We're in the right spot. There's the proof," Jim said, a touch of despair in his voice. "Eve, if we were going to find the barn it would be right outside this town. Look, the battle occurred here. We can't find it. I think we've struck out on finding that barn hon."

"Maybe the town has a library or a town historian?" Eve mused, trying to remain hopeful. "We could see if there's any town records or news accounts or something like that. Maybe there's an old town map?"

Jim agreed it was worth a try and they continued their search. This time they were not only looking for evidence of his great grandfather's unit being in the area but also, hopefully, a library. An hour later, having seen every building in the village at least twice, they sat down on a bench and admitted defeat.

"Eve, we're done. There's nothing here. Maybe we ought to go back to Paris tomorrow and at least enjoy our last few days in France."

Eve looked at him, "Jim, we're not going to quit that easy, no we're not." She turned to him. "I don't need to see Paris on this trip. We can always come back. You don't need to worry about me hon; I don't think we're on a wild goose chase. I'm having fun. Besides we agreed to check this out, and we can't do it half-way."

Jim just smiled at her. "Okay, well, I just want to make sure you're not bored and you know, if you're not enjoying our trip...."

"Don't worry. We're doing exactly what we said we were going to do." She hugged him.

"Babe, I'm...., well, just thanks. I'm glad you're into this too," Jim whispered. Then, brightening up he said, "I do have one more thought. If we could talk to the mayor or someone on the village council they might have a bit of town history we could use."

"There ya go, we've got a plan. But, I do have one request. Let's go back to our room and let me soak my feet for a bit. Then let's go find the mayor."

"Great idea! My dogs are barkin' too!" Jim said with a laugh. Slowly they stood, each making comments about their sore feet and began to walk back to their room.

Suddenly, Jim stopped and grabbed Eve's arm. "Eve, what was the name of the Captain mentioned in the diary? The one killed by a mortar round?"

"I don't remember. Why?" she replied.

"I'm not certain. It should have jumped out at me when I looked at the monument. I just don't recall seeing it, so maybe I'm not remembering it right," Jim said.

"I really can't remember the Captain's name, but there was another guy mentioned. John something," she said. "The monument is just right over there." She pointed. "Why don't we go back to the monument and see if we can find the Captain's name?"

Despite their sore feet they nearly ran back to the

monument. Jim reverently read the names. "I see two Johns," Jim finally said. "I don't see any Captain listed. That's a little odd don't you think? I mean, it's pretty clear in the diary. The Captain was killed attacking this town."

"Give me a minute," Eve said. Turning toward her, he realized she hadn't been reading the names at all. Eve was pulling a small flyer off a kiosk on the street corner. Turning it over she took a pen from her purse and began to copy down all twenty-six names. The note was quickly folded and in her purse with the pen.

They spent the next thirty minutes examining the monument and exploring the little courtyard. Then, they attempted to enter the town hall. Jim pulled on the door handle, then realized the building was closed. A sign in the window seemed to say it was opened only when official business needed to be transacted. They reexamined the street corners since many corner buildings had small historical markers embedded in the walls. Ultimately, the obelisk in the courthouse backyard proved to be the only monument that listed any names, and it was the only one engraved in English.

Dejected, they slowly made their way back to their room. "Well," Eve said as she flung her purse onto the bed in their room, "maybe we can find something out about the Captain and John what's-his-name when we get to a computer."

After they had both freshened up from their day's work they decided to sit on the porch and relax. Before heading downstairs Jim pulled the diary out of the suitcase and hurried to catch up with Eve. When he arrived he found Eve sitting with a cat comfortably curled in her lap. It took Jim a few minutes to find the appropriate section.

"It's Captain Walters and a John Turner," Jim said.

Eve examined the list of names she had copied from the obelisk. "Neither one is here."

"I don't understand. How can that be?" Jim was becoming afraid that this was all a hoax. Just then their host appeared with a tray holding a pot of coffee, another of steamed milk, sugar, and cups. Jim fixed his café-au-lait and drank in silence. After several minutes he said, "I'll be right back."

Leaving Eve and her new friend the cat, Jim went upstairs and found the book his great grandfather had been keeping. He brought it down to the porch and resumed his seat.

"Remember that big, old book that was in the box in the attic? Here it is." He handed the book to Eve.

The book, printed shortly after the end of the war, was a history of the 32nd Division. Jim began at the back of the book, in a section called "Unit Heroes". It listed all those members of the unit killed in action. There were over two hundred names. Since the names were by unit, not alphabetical, it took him several minutes. Eventually, Jim found a Captain Walters and a Corporal John Turner. He then took the list of names Eve had copied from the obelisk and began to compare those names. After forty-five minutes he looked up, satisfied. They were all listed.

"I don't get it Jim. What happened to John Turner and Captain Walters? Why aren't they listed?

Jim was as confused as she was.

Chapter 30

Recheau was frustrated. He did not like simply following people. That was work for someone else. He was a highly skilled professional. He had been behind, in front, and beside these two Americans all day and for what? They'd driven around the countryside, only stopping the car to answer nature's call. He'd nearly crashed into the fools when the man stopped the car around the bend of a blind curve. They kept looking at barns, becoming excited at every barn they saw. First they'd drive past, then back up and study the barn. Sometimes they'd walk to the barn and around the barn. Once they found the owner of the barn who seemed as mystified as Claude as to why two damn fools would want to poke around his barn. What was so special about barns, barns, and more barns? They had walked around the village, first to one end, then back to the other. They'd sat. They'd walked. They'd gone back and forth to the same place two, three times. And the entire time Claude had watched them, staying out of sight. He deserved more money. These two were idiots and they were driving him insane.

Now Recheau was sitting in the front of the little Fiat watching the inn where the two fools were now. They were sitting on a porch with a *petit chat*. Recheau disliked cats. He took a last bite from a brioche and tossed the rest into the back seat. He wiped his hands on his pants, reached into his pocket and removed his cell phone. Another thing about modern life he did not like. Now, his employer wanted a report every night, sometimes every hour. The idea of being a professional and making his own decisions was out the damn window. He dialed and after a few moments heard a grunt.

"I followed them. No, they didn't find anything; they looked at barns." He frowned. "Yes damn-it they just looked at barns. They're back in the inn. They'll be looking at more shit-filled barns tomorrow for sure." He hung up and began thinking of how he could safely steal a different car in this little village tomorrow.

Paul Marcil smiled. Recheau was a crude son-of-a-bitch, but he was effective. The man always wanted to take action. He rarely knew what the appropriate action was, but he was ready for it. Men like Recheau were distasteful but, they were entertaining…and useful.

Marcil now turned his attention to the question of what the Crenshaws were doing looking at barns. They obviously knew that a barn played an important role in the finding of additional items, but they did not seem to know which barn. How would they know when they found the right one? He briefly thought about having Claude pick them up and getting that information from them. He decided that was simply a waste of time. After all, he'd then have to find the barn himself. No, it was better to have them continue to look. Recheau hadn't been spotted yet. At least he claimed that he hadn't. It was only a matter of time. The village was small and Claude was as much a stranger there as were the Americans. He thought about that for a moment longer then made his decision. Recheau was efficient at most tasks, but he was not an intelligent man. This job required a bit more. He picked up the desk phone and dialed.

Chapter 31

The next morning began much the same as the previous, a small breakfast, café and then a map review. Jim and Eve continued to search the countryside for a barn with a view of the town, across a field fronted by a wood. It was impossible. They'd seen every barn in the area…two, even three times. This was becoming hopeless.

Jim could now provide a dissertation on French barns. The *pan de bois* style was used. Every barn displayed the creativity of its builder, but most had a sort of Germanic style. Jim guessed it was from the proximity to Germany and the many cross border invasions, trade and family ties that had developed over the millenniums. Typically, the timber was visible on the upper level but not the bottom. Traditional full timber framing was also visible. The walls were filled in with anything from mud and straw, wattle and daub, or horsehair and gypsum. More recently built barns or recently renovated ones used bricks and concrete mortar.

They spoke with several farmers, always an adventure using Eve's limited French and their pocket dictionaries. They did manage to have a great time, were offered several lunches of wine and bread and generally enjoyed the day. But, by early evening they were forced to admit defeat. They returned to their inn, went to their room, kicked their shoes off and collapsed on the bed. After several minutes of silence Jim asked if Eve was ready to go to dinner. She didn't respond. He looked over to find her fast asleep.

Jim sat in the lounge chair reading the history of the 32nd. It was truly fascinating. The narrative had begun with their participation in the Texas campaign and the pursuit of Poncho Villa. Jim was now well into the history of the unit's campaign in France. Eve still slept on the bed. The evening light had faded, and he had only a small table lamp to read by. Suddenly he sat up in the chair. He had reached a passage describing the attack on Chehery.

The attack on Chehery was scheduled for 0700 on 26 August 1918. It was designed to be a frontal attack by the 126th Infantry Regiment under Colonel Joseph Westnedge. Companies A, B, D, and H were to attack from

the south and east of the town. The attack took place as
scheduled. Companies A and B attacked frontally after
thirty minutes of mortar bombardment. Captain Russell,
commanding Company A, led a charge across fifty yards of
open ground into withering enemy fire. Some casualties
were sustained in this attack, but the majority of the enemy
had already retreated to the interior of the village.
Company H, under Captain Davidson, attacked from the
east of the village and poured considerable amounts of
machine gun fire into enemy locations in support of Captain
Russell's attack.

Subsequently, Captain Davidson dislocated from the
eastern edge of the village, pivoted and entered the village
from the north. One H Company soldier performed the
extraordinary feat of single handedly capturing a large inn.
Private Donald Ross, of Owosso, Michigan, found a
staircase to the roof of the building and was able to enter
from the attic window. The enemy, not expecting an attack
from within their fortress, were taken by surprise. Private
Ross killed seven Germans within two minutes. After thirty
minutes of desperate fighting the small village was
liberated with the unfortunate loss of fourteen fine soldiers.

Jim looked around the room and wondered if he was in
the very building he had just read about. He sank back in his chair
and tried to imagine the events of nearly a hundred years ago. The
description of the battle was brief, the action obviously intense.
But, most importantly, his Great grandfather's unit, company D,
was mentioned. He was on to something. After a few moments
lost in thought Jim stood up from his chair. He took a blanket
from the closet and covered Eve, refilled his wine glass, and sat
back down in the chair.

Chapter 32

August, 1918

I

The D company commander was a well-liked man. He'd trained at Camp Custer with most of the men, had been with the unit in Texas, and was a native Michigander. Unlike most of the men, Captain Walters was not from Detroit or the surrounding area. He was from "Up North" near Charlevoix and both his accent and his knowledge of the woods bespoke that fact. Now Walters was kneeling beside a large oak tree, peering across a dark field in front of him.

"Sergeant Walkoski, where da hell is H Company?" he spat. It was more something to say rather than a request for Walkoski's input.

Walkoski was from Detroit and was considered to be 'a damn fine soldier' by his boss and his men. He'd been with the 32nd since it was formed with the boys from Wisconsin mixed in. He'd been to Texas after the Mexican, and he'd actually been one of the few who fired a weapon down there. Now, here he was trying to keep a Company of young scared kids alive. He hid his discomfort. If the Captain didn't know where they were how the hell was he expected to?

"I think they're just a bit to our south, sir," he said, not feeling very confident about his guess. He liked Captain Walters. The man knew his business. It was a rare thing for the Captain to ask a question like that. This march had turned bad shortly after dark. They'd been forced to march on the far side of a ridge lest their movement be heard or seen by enemy outposts. Then, after the Captain judged they had travelled the appropriate distance, they crested the hill and found a thick wood to their front. The dark sky and forest canopy made navigation extremely tricky. But, Walkoski was sure of one thing, if anyone could get them to the proper demarcation line it was this woodsman Captain of his.

Walters checked his retort at the 'I think' comment of his

Sergeant. Fact was, he wasn't sure either. The woods they'd come through in the darkness of the night had been longer and thicker than most in this war cursed land. It had also been wet, muddy and filled with vines that had turned him and everyone else in circles several times. Walking a straight line in that mess had been impossible. There had been a light rain all night, just enough to make everyone cold and miserable. Clouds overhead had blotted out the moon, and the darkness had covered them like coal dust. His compass only told him what direction North was, but not how far off course he'd actually gone. Now he stared hard across what obviously was a large field, the faint outline of the village was silhouetted against the lighter clouds. He suppressed a little smile. He'd actually found Chehery in the friggin' rain and dark.

Walters sent two men across the field to find out more. Then instructed Walkoski to check the men and have them relax for a few minutes. After fifteen minutes the two scouts returned. They reported the field to be over a hundred yards wide, no ditches or broken ground in the thing, just weeds, then the village. They'd have to cross the field. Hopefully the enemy wouldn't spot them at the half-way point, there would surely be hell to pay if they did.

"Pass the word. We're moving across this field into that village in five minutes. Tell the men to keep it quiet," Walters said.

Walkoski turned and hurried back to tell the men. He didn't like the feel of this. What time were the other companies going to attack? The troops moved up to the edge of the woods. He could hear men muttering; some said the "Our Father," others the 23rd Psalm. Returning to the Captain's side he asked about the other groups. "We're supposed to be first," was the only response he got.

After what seemed an hour, but was really only three minutes, the Captain stood up. Seeing the Captain stand Walkoski did likewise, then he kicked the man next to him and he too stood. Suddenly the entire edge of the woods came alive as ninety men got to their feet. Captain Walters began to walk across the field. Walkoski crossed himself and did likewise.

The troops walked steadily and quietly across the field. One man let out a low curse as he tripped on an unseen shrub, otherwise silence ruled. Clouds rolled overhead. They were ten yards out from the edge of the woods, then twenty. After two or three minutes they had crossed half the field. The darkness was beginning to pale in the east, but the sun wouldn't be up for another twenty minutes. They'd be in the village by then, and the light would be to their advantage. They just needed to get across this field. The clouds continued to race across the sky in the freshening wind.

II

The fate of the combat soldier often turns on something other than his own skill. A bullet hits or misses its target depending on the slightest gust of wind in the madness of a battle. A branch snaps under a boot, a message lost or untimely or any of a thousand other things can be the difference between life and death. But, the most uncontrollable and most pitiful circumstance is that created by a juxtaposition of natural phenomena and accident.

It was just as Captain Walters passed the forty-yard mark that one of the German soldiers felt the call of nature. The man stepped outside the building he was billeted in, walked across the back yard to the edge of the field and unbuttoned his trousers. He titled his head back and watched the clouds, backlit by the moon, race past. Just as he finished his business and was rebuttoning his trousers the clouds racing overhead parted, allowing moonlight to stream through the opening.

Unfortunately for Captain Walters and the men of D Company the moonbeams fell across them like light from a movie projector. Pale white soldiers were illuminated in the field in front of the German soldier. The man, terrified, forgot the remaining buttons and immediately ran to the large dinner bell on the side of the building. In a moment the bell rang out long, loud and shrill. The sound shattered the darkness. Men began to yell from the village, followed by yells from the field. Captain Walters screamed "C'mon boys!" and began to sprint. The soldiers of D Company followed suit, racing toward the village...exactly into the pre-targeted machine gun fire and falling mortar rounds of the fast reacting Germans.

Captain Walters led the charge. He went about ten steps when the first mortar round exploded. It fell at his feet, exploding as he hurdled the impacting round. He never knew what happened and disappeared in a mist of blood and tissue. Sergeant Walkoski saw what happened to his Captain, but didn't have time to react. A machine gun began clattering just at that moment, its operators focused on his stomach. Sergeant Walkoski was cut in half seconds later.

Private Oushel Crenshaw and two others were on the far right of the line as it moved forward. At the sound of the bell they began a sprint toward the village as did all their mates. Oushel glanced to his left and saw the rest of the company running with him. Then, to his horror a red mist appeared where Captain Walters had been. He could hear the clack-clack-clack of a single German machine gun. Oushel screamed and kept running. Fear washed over him. More machine guns joined the first. An explosion just behind knocked him to the ground. The man beside him didn't move. Oushel jumped up and continued to run. Suddenly there were no bullets zinging around him; he could see his friends falling but there was no sound. Crenshaw then realized a large barn stood between him and the village. A side door was open and directly in front of him. He dove through the door and landed on soft dirt. An instant later another man did the same and landed on Oushel.

Corporal John Turner looked at Oushel and said something. Oushel couldn't hear Turner even though he was less than a foot away. His ears now began to ring. The mortar explosion had temporarily deafened him. "What?" he yelled, trying to make himself heard over the explosions of the mortars and the clacking of the machine guns.

"We sure as hell got our hats handed to us out there Oush. You okay?" John yelled back.

Oushel just looked at him. Realizing what had happened John quickly searched Oushel for blood. Satisfied he wasn't hurt Turner crept to the far wall and looked out at the village. Oushel sat back against a door post. His uniform was wet. He couldn't tell if it was just wet from the march through the woods and run through the wet grass or was it blood? Maybe it was blood, he was in shock and John didn't want to tell him. He was going to die. He thought of his mother. His hearing began to return. Finally, he decided that nothing hurt so he mustn't be shot.

"I'm fine. You?" he yelled. John nodded that he was fine and went to the end of the barn. When he came back he cupped his hand over Oushel's ear. "We're about fifteen yards from the rest of the boys. There's a road and open pen between us and them. We can't cross it just yet."

The rest of D Company sprinted through the falling bombs and zipping bullets to the edge of the field. Clearing the field they crossed the road and nearly went headfirst into the heretofore unseen and unknown creek. Here they were stopped. The creek was flooded from the night's rain. They tried to hide in the tall grass along the edge of the creek, but grass does not stop bullets. To their right stood a barn which gave shelter from the gun fire on that flank, but an open piece of ground where the road turned and crossed a small wooden bridge prevented them from getting to the barn. They couldn't get to the village so they bunched up in small groups on the bank. Here the loss of Captain Walters was most acutely felt as the bunched up soldiers drew the fire of the Germans. Losses began to mount.

Behind them the road paralleled the stream and then bent away from the village. After the road bent left it paralleled a low hill. The hill was covered with trees. After what seemed like an hour, but in reality was only minutes, Sergeant Walacowski, only 22 years old from Hamtramck outside of Detroit began to organize the men. Crawling from group to group he got them dispersed. Then, he began a phased withdrawal toward the hill to their left. Slowly they began their escape. Nearly half their number were missing.

Corporal Turner stood next to the large barn doors, peering through a crack in the wood. Private Crenshaw at the other end of the barn watched the village. The gunfire was concentrated on the position of the company just twenty yards away. Fortunately the mortars hadn't found the range. Crenshaw spotted a group of Germans carrying a tripod and its machine gun attempting to circle the barn and flank them. He eased his rifle out of the window and fired four quick rounds. Two went down immediately. The other two turned around and sprinted for the village. Oushel took careful aim and stopped them both. After a moment the gunfire slackened as everyone assessed their positions.

Suddenly the ten men closest to the barn leapt to their feet and sprinted ten yards further away from the barn. Nearly simultaneously a Maschinengewehr clattered from the building nearest them. The aim was wild and cut across the wall of the barn, out across the field and followed the men as they ran. When they dove to the ground the streaks of death passed over them and down the line, failing to find anyone fool enough to take to their feet.

Oushel backed away from the window and began to tell Turner of his success stopping the machine gun crew. John Turner stood with his hand on his chest, blood oozed through his fingers. He looked horrified. Then he fell forward, no arms extending to break his fall.

Oushel choked back a tear and began to shake. He was going to die here and he knew it. He crawled to the body. John was dead, sure enough. What was he going to do now? John had always told him, John knew the answers. He crawled to the barn door and watched his mates move to the hill and woods. Each yard they crawled was one yard further from him. He began to feel desperately alone. He belly crawled to the far corner of the barn and into a stall. Moving to the back of the stall he sat with his back to the wall, his knees against his chest. His body began to shake. After a moment, the shaking reminded him of deer hunting as a boy. He'd sit in the winter woods, shivering in the cold, waiting for an unsuspecting whitetail. The thought brought a strange sense of normalcy, and he began regaining control of his nerves. Quickly he took stock of his situation. He knew the barn would be searched. He had to either get out of this place or hide. Rejoining the company was out of the question. The sun was up. No more hiding in the darkness. It was too far across open ground to run, and he couldn't get there without being seen. He'd have to hide.

He found a shovel hanging from the wall of the barn and began to dig. After two feet his shovel stuck in the dirt. He couldn't penetrate the soft ground. Panic swept through him. Dropping the shovel he began to scrape at the ground. Canvas. He found canvas at the bottom of the hole. He scraped the dirt off the object and pulled it out. He glanced at the cloth mass and tossed it over the wooden half wall into the adjacent stall. He went back to digging. After another foot of digging his shovel hit something hard. He dug along its length finding it to be fairly long.

A burst of gunfire erupted from outside the barn. Several explosions quickly followed. He quickly laid down in the hole checking it for size. It was a bit short, frantically he scraped more dirt out. Satisfied he put the shovel back in its hanger on the wall.

Then, sitting in the hole he pulled dirt and straw over his legs. He rubbed his filthy hands over his face and then dragged several large handfuls of straw over his stomach and chest. He laid back in his hole, pulled more straw over his face and wiggled deeper into the dirt. This would have to do. He settled into a long wait for life or death.

By eight o'clock that morning the fighting had stopped. Oushel fought to stay awake. He'd been up all day yesterday and marched all last night. Now he lay comfortably in soft dirt in a dark stall. He snored and knew the sound would give him away. As he lay there he imagined being home, a warm fire in the sitting room, his parents reading. He thought about his brothers and racing the carriage and team. He smiled when he thought about how mad his father had been when he saw how foamed up the horses were. His neighbors were walking up the drive toward the house; they were talking. What were they saying? It didn't make any sense. What were they yelling? He couldn't understand. No wait, it was a dream. He'd been asleep. Damn! There were Germans outside the barn. He listened. They opened the door. Silence. Then, a burst of excited words filled the air. How could those people do that? It was all one long word. It was a hundred syllables. Didn't they use commas and periods? They'd found John. Silence.

After several minutes he heard Germans speaking in a low voice. Along the central corridor at the far end were several doors. He heard them being banged open. The storage shed was searched. Then he could hear the grain door open. Next came the tack room. Finally, the stall doors were opened. Had he shut this stall door? Did it look different? He couldn't remember. They were in the next stall. He heard the door bang shut. Now his. He shut his eyes. He could feel the German standing over him. Any moment a bayonet would be shoved through him. He nearly sat up and surrendered. Someone called out from the opposite end of the barn. It was a name. They were looking for someone. From right above him he heard a yell back "Ya?" Then the stall door shut! They'd not seen him.

He started to breathe again. He listened to the Germans for a few more minutes. Maybe they were searching John's body? Were they going to search the barn again? Suddenly a torrent of screaming and yelling; must be a Sergeant. Do Sergeants yell in every army? He heard several voices saying "Jawohl" and more words. Yup, they were talking to the Sergeant, maybe an officer. What or whoever it was it didn't sound too happy. Someone was getting their ass chewed. Probably for something meaningless and stupid. After a few more minutes he thought he could hear them moving off.

Time passed. Oushel had to pee. He was hungry. His uniform, wet and warm last night was now wet, cold and scratchy. It must be midday. He thought about crawling to the corner and peeing. Suddenly gunfire broke out. Heavy weapons were being fired from the direction of the town, lighter ones from just beyond the barn. Off in the distance return fire could be heard. He could hear explosions near the woods and in the field they had crossed this morning. The firing got to be fairly close. He began to get scared again. The German line had fallen back. They set up near the barn; explosions and more machine gun fire from both sides of the barn. It grew more intense. It seemed to go on a long time. He was even more scared now than last night. Damn, he hoped artillery didn't open up on this barn. The sun was setting. Voices. He heard German voices. They seemed very excited. They were all around the barn. Then, lots of gunfire. It erupted from all sides of the barn, very close. Machine guns chattered. Bullets crashed through the barn. Streams of sunlight appeared in the dust. The gunfire wouldn't stop. The explosions continued. Some right next to the barn. Shit, he was going to get blown up right here in this barn. He let go. His pants were soaked. Then, impossibly, the gunfire and explosions became louder. More bullets smashed through the barn and the battle swept past. It was moving away. The sounds were closer to the village. Then in the distance, what was that? He heard Americans shouting. After an hour the shooting was much closer. It was Americans. They were cursing and shouting and surging around him. The Germans were gone.

He crawled out of his hole and stood up. He walked to the body of John Turner. John lay flat on his back. His hands were folded across his chest. The body had been searched, the pockets were all empty and turned out. Oushel's hands began to shake. He sat back on the dirt and began to cry. The barn door opened and three American doughboys walked in guns at the ready.

He was directed to a wagon near the brook where several

men were sitting at tables. Other men were hurrying to and fro and the whole group looked important. He didn't like being around officers but he'd been told to report to the Major so he did. The Major looked him over, looked at his pants. Oushel's embarrassment was evident. The Major didn't say a word. Instead he pulled a bag of tobacco out of his pocket, rolled a cigarette, then handed it to him. Oushel bent slightly to the offered match, took a long drag then stared at his hands. They were shaking uncontrollably. The Major poured a shot of whiskey.

"Sit down soldier. You look like you've had a long day." Oushel sat on an upturned ammo box. "Okay, tell me what happened."

When he was finished the Major asked a few questions. When Oushel finished answering he was told to get some chow. Now, he found himself sitting on a half log bench with a pedal powered grind wheel eating from a borrowed mess kit.

A man from Wisconsin was asking Oushel to tell his story. Reluctantly he was obliging. He came to the part about digging the hole in the stall then stopped. What was that canvas thing he'd tossed into the next stall? Now he didn't want to talk to this fellow. He wanted to see what he'd found in the stall. He summed up the rest of the story with a short, "Then you guys came." Standing, Oushel made excuses about finding his weapon and wandered over to the barn.

His rifle was near the corner under a pile of straw where he'd left it. Then he went to the stall next to where he'd spent the day. Searching the stall he finally found a small pile of canvas hidden in the shadow and picked it up. It was a knapsack. Its straps were rotted, the backpack itself having a large hole rotted in the bottom. Lifting the strap to unbuckle the knapsack it broke in two under the stress of that small call to duty. Inside he found black soil, rotting rags and a tube. The tube was about twenty inches long and nearly black with filth. It appeared to have a cap on each end. He twisted the caps, but neither would budge. Hearing his name called from outside he stuffed the tube in his inside coat pocket, picked up his rifle and rejoined the war.

III

Jim glanced up from his reading. Eve was still sleeping. The narrative was exciting. It was doubly so because he knew his great grandfather was part of this, and survived. He returned to the history of the 32nd.

A separate tragedy occurred with the mauling of D Company under Captain Walters. D Company, already depleted from its hard work the previous month, was to separate from H Company and move to the north some two thousand yards. There they were to pivot and attack from an offset northerly position. However, in the darkness Captain Walters became disoriented and moved his company against the village of Cheveuges some three kilometers north of the objective and behind enemy lines. Dawn came upon the Company as they crossed an open field to the village. Enemy artillery was brought down upon the exposed soldiers, killing eighteen men, including Captain Walters and injuring many more. The remaining soldiers were forced to battle through the afternoon before being located and relieved by the remainder of the 126th.

The book then began to discuss the occupation of the abandoned city of Sedan. Jim was stunned. This one paragraph was the clue he'd been missing. They'd been searching at the wrong village.

Chapter 33

The next morning they ate an early breakfast of coffee and toast. Eve, having not had supper the previous night, drank an extra cup of coffee and ate an extra roll. Jim teased her about a "minute on the lips, lifetime on the hips". She silently poked his stomach and said "…and what is it now, twenty pounds since you retired?" Jim smiled and agreed he needed to get back in the gym when they returned home.

After breakfast Jim unfolded the map on their table. The village of Cheveuges was only three miles to the north. They discussed their strategy for searching this town and its attending barns. Having learned their lesson about the town hall they decided to first search the village.

Forty-five minutes later they were parking the car on one of the few side streets Cheveuges had to offer. Moving the hundred yards to the north end of the village they began a systematic search to the south end. There was a small bronze plaque mounted on the corner of a large, official building dedicated to the young men killed liberating the village in 1918, but it didn't provide any details. Looking closely Jim found a small manufacturer's mark and could see that the plaque had been forged in 1954. At the town offices there was another monument. This one to the French partisan fighters who had fought the Germans in the Second World War. Jim and Eve took fifteen minutes to read the long citation, each using their pocket dictionary.

After walking about the village for the better part of two hours they returned to their car and began the road portion of their search. They selected a road leading to the south and began to follow it out of town. The town was very old and the buildings were of the traditional style, each half-timbered, with overhanging upper stories. Most were homes, many with a storage barn or business attached. A small pasture with twenty or thirty sheep edged up to the town. The pasture stretched nearly a hundred meters then came to what could only be described as a derelict classic, garish, United States Route 66 style gas station. The station was deserted. Its driveway filled with cracks, each one sprouting weeds of various types. The mechanic's garage sat to the left of a large, round office area constructed of glass bricks. The trim of the building and attendant concrete curbs once a bright blue, white and red was now faded and chipped. Two gas pumps, their faces gone and internal mechanical parts rusting in the weather, sat on a blue concrete island under a free standing roof that extended from the building, over the pumps and beyond, nearly to the road. Immediately past the gas station was a narrow strip of grass, then a large ditch with what appeared to be oil slicks on the water. A concrete bridge with low sides crossed the ditch. Just after the bridge the road tuned to the right and a large building with a collapsed northern wall stood near the curb as the street bent away. Behind the decrepit building was a small orchard of apple trees and then a vineyard. This clearly was the neglected end of town.

They continued over the bridge, turned right and then accelerated through the gentle left curve from 50 to 90 kilometers per hour. They drove completely to Cherhery. They looked at the same barns they had seen the day before. They drove back to Cheveuges and tried another road. Then they did the same thing, on different roads, again and again and again.

By mid-afternoon both Jim and Eve were tired. The car seats had turned to wood. They were bored with the French countryside. Patience with even the tiniest affront had long ago been lost, and they were starting to snipe at each other. They had approached four farmers and discussed their barns. None of these farmers were as friendly as the ones they'd spoken with the last two days. One had yelled in what some would call French, but it was probably a local dialect because to both Jim and Eve it sounded like it was half German. They ate their lunch in a terrible café, served by a rude Francophile who had no use for Americans and didn't appreciate a tourist's dollar, or in this case a tourist's Euro. They had two glasses of wine with lunch and now Eve was sleepy. The cheese they'd eaten at lunch didn't seem to sit well with Jim, who was getting angry at Eve because she kept falling asleep. After waking her up for the third time Jim decided to take one more look in the countryside to the southwest. If he struck out there he was calling it a day and returning to their inn in Chehery. Maybe they could salvage the evening.

They were exiting the village on the same road they had initially explored so many hours previous. Slowing, they passed the broken down gas station and approached the small bridge. This time, just before they crossed the bridge a flock of sheep, being driven to town from the opposite direction forced Jim to pull off the road onto the shoulder. "Damn these stinking animals." Jim muttered as he shut off the engine. This had happened a few times in the past three days. It had gone from being quaint to being a royal pain in the ass.

As they waited for the sheep to cross the bridge Eve dozed. Jim examined the orchard behind the half-collapsed building. He tried to decide what kind of apple tree he was looking at and daydreamed about planting his own orchard. Returning his gaze to the sheep he watched as the shepherd chased a small lamb. The animal waited until the shepherd was within ten feet, would bleat and run fifteen feet further away. The lamb was headed for the orchard behind the old building. Meanwhile, the rest of the herd had decided the grass around Jim and Eve's car was Grade A Choice and had surrounded the car.

The shepherd continued to chase the lamb and Jim went back to his daydreaming. He began to imagine what the collapsed building looked like when it was new. Slowly it dawned on him that this building was an old barn. This one was certainly different. It had an overhanging roof. Its internal structure was made of pillars, not timber frame. And, it looked like the roof was of tile. But, most importantly this building clearly was a two-story building, not a one story with a hayloft on top.

"Eve, I think we've found it," he whispered. She didn't move. He reached over and shook her. "Look" was all he said as he pointed out the window at the collapsing building just fifteen yards in front of their car.

Chapter 34

I

Claude Recheau could feel the blood pounding in his temples. He flung his cell phone across the car. The phone bounced off the seat, hit the door, rebounded and landed at his feet. Marcil was bringing in the Corsican. That murderous son-of-a-bitch was a lunatic and big trouble. At a minimum Claude would be splitting his fee. More than likely the bastard would try to slit his throat and take the entire commission. This was unprecedented. He was, after all, a professional. This was disrespect. If Marcil weren't so, so....so what? So...well connected. That's what it was. Marcil was a fool with connections, dangerous connections. This was a screwed up job anyway, following two simpletons around the countryside. Why not just snag the two Americans? He could have a little fun with the woman, maybe do that water trick with the man. He'd find out what they were doing for sure. Recheau thought the situation over. There was something more here. Something he hadn't been told. Whatever it was it meant a great deal to Marcil. He had one hope; maybe he could get this done before that bastard Corsican got here.

He sat in a Renault. Using a pair of military grade 22x50 binoculars he watched the fools by the side of the road. A flock of sheep had them surrounded. The sheep were shitting all around the car. That was funny; it must stink to high heaven in that rattrap car. The American woman seemed to be asleep. The man was daydreaming, and the sheep were shitting. It was boring as hell.

The man sat up straight, shook his wife and pointed. Another damned barn search. They were moving; now they were out of the car and walking toward the building with the collapsed roof. Claude sat back in his seat, pulled a pack of cigarettes out of his pocket and flicked his lighter. He thought about the Corsican. He thought about calling Marcil and telling him the Americans were wading in shit and searching another barn. Screw it. Action was better than following these fools. "I'll have to go visit that building with them," he thought; and he smiled for the first time in three days.

II

Jim and Eve approached the building. "Do you see how this one is different?" asked Jim. "This one has an overhanging second floor that's pronounced – see, look there," he said while pointing, his arm fully extended above his head.

"We've not seen tile roofs before either," said Eve.

"You're right, we haven't – good catch," agreed Jim.

They opened the building's double doors and peered inside. There was plenty of light as the north half of the building had collapsed and much of that part of the roof was missing. The barn had storage areas on both sides of a central hall that ran its length. In that central bay stood two old cars, one a Mercedes built in the early sixties Jim would guess and the other a Renault, also built in the sixties. "Stood" was actually a charitable term. Upon closer examination Jim saw that the two vehicles actually rested on concrete blocks; their wheels and tires removed. A small pile of pipes, old mufflers and other car parts lay to one side near a grain bin. At the far end of the barn, on the left was a sort of tool room. Then the building opened to the orchard beyond as the wall had collapsed around the corner post. The tool room's inner parts were on display as the roof above it had fallen when the exterior wall had collapsed. On the right, in seemingly good condition, were four horse stalls.

Jim fought down his growing excitement. "The diary says he hid in a stall." Jim pointed at the four stalls. "It doesn't say which one, but if it were me I'd have picked the one the farthest from the door. The last one. Let's check it out."

"Jim, there's a door at each end," Eve pointed out. "Okay, the one farthest from the road then." he shot back. Eve shrugged and squeezed his hand. "This is exciting," she said as they walked to the stall.

Jim pushed open the door to the last stall and looked around. The floor was hard dirt, scraps of straw were scattered about. Inside the stall stood an old oil drum, and several tires and rusting hand tools were scattered on the floor. They stepped into the stall and examined the floor and sidewalls. Nothing remarkable. They rolled the oil drum into the central corridor of the barn, pushed the tires out and then reexamined the floor of the stall. Again finding nothing unusual. They looked at each other.

"Tell you what…" Jim walked to the far corner and picked up a shovel. "If we can find a rake you rake the debris out of here then I'll dig a couple of test holes." Eve agreed, and they began to search the barn for tools. Eventually finding a garden rake they returned to the stall.

"I'll go down a couple of feet in nine holes, three on each side and three in the middle. If we don't find anything we'll do the next stall. If we still don't have anything we'll call it a day, go have supper and come back tomorrow. Sound like a deal?"

Eve looked at him and grinned. "You can count on me. Why, just this morning I was wondering if I'd get to dig holes in an old barn stall while I was vacationing in France. Nothing more I wanted to do!"

After forty-five minutes Jim had completed three holes down the middle of the stall. "Whew, this is taking longer than I thought," he huffed.

Eve had cleaned out the next stall and was beginning to clear the third. "There's a lot of old junk in this place. Why do people put all their cast off stuff in a barn? Just throw it away!" She was talking more to herself than Jim.

Jim completed the fifth hole, but was running out of places to move the dirt. Eve found a barn shovel and began filling in the dry holes.

"Ya know, you're pretty good with a shovel," Jim puffed as he lifted another shovel full of dirt.

"You sure know how to flatter a girl," Eve gasped as she drove her shovel into the pile of fresh dirt.

Jim was about to declare the sixth hole empty when his shovel hit a hollow sounding, apparently wooden, obstacle.

Both their heads snapped up, and they stared at each other. "What was that?" she said.

"I don't know, but it sounded good," Jim replied. In a flash Eve was by his side, and they began to dig with a vengeance. After only a few minutes they had what appeared to be an oblong box outlined in the dirt. Jim directed Eve to one end. Digging a bit further they were eventually able to push their shovels under the bottom edge of the box. After a moments rest they both began to pry the box out of the dirt. Two good pushes and the box broke free. Then they each pushed a hand into the dirt and, on the count of three, lifted the box out of the hole. As they lifted the box out of the hole they spotted a second, small square box underneath the first. Finding the first box surprisingly light they moved it to the center of the stall.

A second box took a bit more work as it was buried deeper. Ten minutes later they had it next to the first. A few moments later they'd convinced themselves there were no more boxes in the hole, and they sat down for a quick breather. Another search of the barn turned up a horse brush and they were soon on their knees in front of the boxes. Jim began with the larger box. He gently began to brush off the dirt. Occasionally he would tap gently with the side of the brush to breakup clumps of dirt. Finally, he exposed a once shinny wooden surface that appeared to have been lacquered. The lacquer had faded and clouded but it was clear it contained some sort of design. Three leather straps ran through guides around the box keeping it closed. Sweeping the front they found the three accompanying buckles. Eve looked at Jim. "Think this is what we've been looking for?"

He didn't answer. Instead, he examined the first buckle. He began to unbuckle the strap, one tug and the strap itself separated. They quickly pealed the remnants away from the box. The same thing happened with the other two. Jim glanced at Eve while taking a deep breath; she returned the look by holding up crossed fingers. With that, Jim lifted the cover of the box, and there inside was a medieval sword resting on a felt pillow. "Wow" was all they could say.

"It's wonderful!" exclaimed Eve. "That's got to be one of the neatest things!"

Jim sat back on his haunches and smiled. "This is really, really cool," he whispered. They looked over the sword in silence for a few moments.

Then Eve grew serious. "Hon, I gotta tell ya something." Jim noticed the change in her voice. This was certainly the wrong time to bring up something about the farm, bills or her health.

"What? What's the matter?" he asked worriedly.

"Babe, I gotta go to the bathroom." She looked grim. Her face set in stone. Jim could only stare. After a moment a grin crept onto her face and spread from ear to ear. Finally she was laughing at her own joke.

"Ahhh…you turkey! Now? We find a magnificent ancient sword and you've gotta go? You're a piece of work. Okay, well, just go around the back, no one will see. I'll wait to open the other one." Jim was laughing; she could always break the tension. She stood up and squeezed through the small opening at that end of the barn.

Jim carefully looked over the sword. After a moment he closed the box and moved it into the central corridor of the barn. There he found a shaft of light and sat the box down in it. He returned to the stall, picked up the other box and carried it to the corridor. Finding an old bucket he turned it upside down and sat on it. Carefully he cleaned the second box. There was a design on the surface of this box too. He tried to make it out, but the grime and faded surface was too much.

Sweeping the dirt away from his treasures he returned to the first box and opened it. Lifting the sword from the pillow he carefully examined the hilt, then the blade. Amazing. It did not appear as if any water or dirt had worked its way into the box. The sword did not show any rust. Its pommel was a bit dull and the leather wrapped grip was a bit off colour, but really, he couldn't find any damage.

Turning it over he examined the backside. The pillow had preserved the color of the leather wrapped around the pommel. It was clearly a working sword. He carefully ran his finger along the pommel and could feel an engraving underneath. It would require removal of the leather wrapping to examine. Jim dismissed that idea immediately. He then stood and held the sword in the sunlight. Its blade seemed to change colour in the light.

Chapter 35

"She's a beautiful weapon she is," a voice said from behind him. Jim spun around. There stood a large man with an even larger pistol in his hand. He pointed the pistol at Jim's forehead and, without a trace of emotion said "Monsieur Creen-shaw, où..., ahhhh..., where...is she your *épouse*...ah, ah...wife?"

"Who the hell are you?" Jim spat out. His mind raced. Was this the owner of the barn? If so, wow! This guy took trespassing pretty seriously. Why did he want Eve? Thought they outlawed guns in Europe? Why did the guy have a gun? It looked like the pistol he'd been issued in the Air Force, an M-9 Berretta. Should he tell him where Eve went? Could he take this guy in a fight? He looked pretty big.

Jim stared hard at the man trying to make out the features in the mixture of light rays and shadows caused by the collapsed portions of the barn. Where had he come from? Behind the large man were the double doors nearest the old cars. It was through these doors that the man had entered.

"That, she is not the issue now, no?" the man said.

The central corridor of the barn ran its entire length. On one side were the storage closets. The opposite side had the stalls and a workbench. Double wagon doors were at each end, allowing a drive through functionality. The side opposite the stalls had long ago caved in, but the wall structure of the lower level rooms on that side had prevented a complete collapse. There were, however, several large gaps in the wall as well as windows and cracks that allowed anyone outside that side of the barn to peer inside with relative anonymity. It was through one of these openings that Eve now watched.

"She had to go outside," Jim said.

"Where?" the man asked.

Jim thought that over a bit. If he told the man she went out where she actually did what would he do? If, on the other hand, he told this fellow that she went out the end where he had entered would he wonder why he'd not seen her? Was there an advantage to either answer? In the nanosecond that it took for these thoughts to cross Jim's mind he saw Eve slip through the door at the far end of the barn behind the man with the pistol. Her footsteps were silent on the packed smooth dirt as she carefully picked up a flat shovel and stepped between the two rusty old cars. There, she got to her hands and knees and looked along the ground under the car. She could see both Jim's shoes and the man's stylish loafers.

"She went out that way…" Jim pointed behind the gun, "and then around to the side. She had to go relieve herself."

The stranger smiled. "When one must…" he said. "Now, I want you to put that sword her back in her case, no? Then, you will close her up and walk to the doors….ah, ah…" he struggled to find the word. "In front me, no? Don't you try nothing stupid you and you might live to see tomorrow. You understand good?"

Jim knelt to the box and carefully placed the sword on the pillow. Then he closed the lid and positioned the awkward box under his arm. With his free hand he scooped up the second box.

"Allez, you… première…ahhhh…go…first you first." The stranger waved Jim toward the rusty cars with his pistol.

Jim slowly walked the length of the corridor. Approaching the two cars he moved to his left, keeping the cars on his right, and slightly increased his stride. He made a show of keeping the two boxes from hitting the car and the wall. As he reached the gap between the two automobiles he glanced down, being careful to move only his eyes and not his head. Eve had the shovel gripped like a baseball bat and was squatting on her heels. Jim took three more steps and then attempting to distract the man said, "So you want that sword? You can have it." Jim said this while gently turning his body to the left and stopping. This caused the man to perceive a threat from Jim and his eyes to follow Jim's movement.

Recheau smiled. He only needed a small excuse. He took a short step toward Jim. This caused him to step quickly past the gap between the cars. At that point Eve stood and stared directly at the back of his head. Silently she raised the shovel, being careful not to bump it against either of the two cars. She paused only a moment and then brought the flat of the shovel down on the top of the head of the stranger with as much strength as her five foot two inch frame could muster. He collapsed like a sack of potatoes. Jim was on him in a flash, grabbing the gun almost before it hit the dirt.

"Ou…that's gotta hurt," Jim said with a smile. "Nice job

babe!" and he leaned over and kissed her. "I thought I was in big trouble there for a second." Jim pushed the gun into his waistband.

"You know I've got your back babe!" she said with schoolgirl excitement. Then she and Jim dragged the stranger to the front of the Mercedes.

"Hon, take a quick look outside, make sure there aren't any more like this. I'll tie him up before he comes to."

"Is he going to be alright?" Eve asked, wondering if she'd hit their assailant a bit too hard.

The man's eyes seemed to be focused on the ceiling. Jim picked up a limp wrist and checked the pulse. It was there, strong and steady. Together they watched the pupils of his eyes expanding and contracting rapidly. Jim felt the back of the man's skull. "No depression in the bone, he'll live. We'd better get some rope and tie this joker up. Wonder who he is, and more importantly, why was he pointing a gun at us?"

Jim searched the barn and finally returned with a length of electrical wire. It wasn't enough to do a proper job but would have to do for now. He then tied the man's hands and sat him up against the Mercedes. Eve slipped outside of the barn and checked both sides. They seemed to be alone. She spotted Rechaud's car parked on the opposite side of the little bridge and decided to search it. Leaning back in the barn she told Jim of her discovery and that she would be back in a moment. He told her to be careful and began to search the man. After a few minutes Eve returned with the car's registration paperwork and a pair of binoculars.

"There was some half eaten food and a bunch of trash in the back seat. This guy's a real slob. The only other thing in the car was this set of spy-glasses. I figured we could check his ID against the registration."

"That's good thinking babe," Jim said as he rolled Rechaud's still limp body over on his face. "How's that dirt taste buddy?" Jim muttered as he searched for a wallet. Not finding one he rolled Rechaud to his back and checked his front jacket pocket. "Here," he handed a black wallet to Eve. She rifled through the wallet and soon found a driver's license for a 'Monsieur Andre Lefebvre'. The car was registered to a Madame Carolanne Crepeau, born in 1935.

Jim reached behind his back and pulled out the Berretta.

Pressing a lever with his thumb, he released the clip and caught it with his off hand. The clip was full. Pulling the slide back he ejected a shell from the chamber. "He wasn't fooling," Jim said, looking at Eve.

Jim sat back on his knees, thinking as he tucked the gun behind him. "Eve, we've got a problem. This guy's carrying a false I.D. And, he called me 'Monsieur Crenshaw'. He's not just some hood."

Eve was stunned. "How did he know our name?"

"That's the problem. I'm thinking we need to load those two boxes in the car and get out of here."

"Give me the gun. I'll watch this guy, you load the boxes," Eve commanded.

Jim reloaded the gun and handed it to her. Before he let go he met her eyes and said firmly, "If you're going to shoot, then shoot. Understand?"

She nodded and he turned back to the boxes. Then Jim stopped. "Why can't you load the boxes?"

"Hon, they might be heavy. And, they're pretty dirty." She looked at him and smiled. "Oh my God," Jim muttered and picked up the long box. A few minutes later Jim had both boxes in the trunk of the car.

"What do we do with this guy?" Eve asked.

Jim bent to look closer at the man. His eyes were fluttering open and closed. His breathing was steady.

"I think he's going to come around any minute," Jim whispered. "Let's see if we can find some more wire to tie him with."

Together they searched the barn again. This time checking every corner, cabinet and locker. Finally Eve found a rusted electrical fan. Stringing the cord out on the ground Jim raised a shovel over his head and slammed the blade down near the base of the fan, cutting the cord. They then doubled the tie on the man's hands.

Chapter 36

From the shadows of the abandoned gas station the Corsican watched the barn through his field glasses. He watched Claude Rechaud enter the barn and fully expected him to appear moments later marching the two Americans to his car. What he saw actually caused him to laugh. The little American woman, looking very much like a Saturday morning cartoon character, crept around the corner of the barn and into the same door Claude had just slipped through. A short time later she walked out of the barn and searched Claude's car. It couldn't be! Oh, this was good! The American couple had overpowered Rechaud! The Corsican couldn't stop laughing.

Soon the husband loaded two boxes into the trunk of his car and walked back inside the barn. The Corsican, never one to miss an opportunity, quickly slipped out of the gas station, sprinted across the small bridge and peered through the cracks in the barn wall. There was Claude, tied with an electrical wire.

The Corsican silently made his way to the rear of the barn. He paused, listened and then squeezed through a large gap next to the barn's corner post. The Americans and Claude were at the far end of a long hall. Twenty feet and two junk cars stood between him and his targets. As he watched the American raised his hands over his head and crashed a shovel down on something. Had he just killed Claude? It wasn't an issue; in fact, it did make things a bit easier. But still, it was a bit…well, odd.

"That should do it." The woman was saying.

"We'll call the police from some phone box on the way and have them come out here." The husband replied.

The police? Hadn't they just killed Claude? The Corsican began to creep to the back of the first old car. Bending low he looked underneath the cars to see Claude sitting on the ground, his hands tied behind him. He seemed to be coming around from a knock on the head. He was moaning softly with a few choice words in between moans. The Corsican suppressed a laugh.

"I wonder who this guy is?" the American asked his wife. In a moment he would be close enough. He would take all three.

He began to creep past the first car. Not fast enough. Before the Corsican could get to the front of the car they were out of the barn. The Corsican hurried to the door. He opened it a crack, just in time to see Jim close the driver's side door to their rented Citroën. A moment later they were headed in the direction of Cheveuges.

Closing the door he turned to the man on the ground. Rechaud recognized him and immediately stopped moaning. "What are you doing here you piece of shit," he spat.

"Claude, mon ami, you were careless." He whispered as he screwed a silencer on the end of a .32 caliber pistol.

Chapter 37

I

From Cheveuges to Paris would take several hours, and it was already late afternoon. Jim was not comfortable with trying to navigate at night, and they elected to postpone the trip until the next day. Instead, they decided to return to Chehery. Once there they found the side street with the village's sole inn. The owner, an elderly widow, recognized them from the night before and welcomed them as long lost friends. She then insisted they have coffee at a small pastry shop she was fond of. After taking their bags to the room Jim locked the car and its valuable cargo and they set off for the shop. The old woman spoke in rapid fire French while Jim and Eve desperately fanned their pocket dictionaries. All the while trying to keep an eye on where they were walking.

After an hour, trying but mostly failing to communicate, the old woman's patience had run out. She claimed a trip to the market was necessary and fled the shop. Jim and Eve settled into a comfortable silence. Finally, breaking the mood, Eve suggested they go over everything they knew. Maybe they could figure out who knew they were in Cheveuges and how the man with the gun knew their name. After thirty minutes of bending the truth to an unrecognizable series of events they gave up. It was hopeless. They met with a similar lack of success when they tried to figure out how they'd been followed let alone who had done it. Ten minutes later they paid their bill and began the short walk back to their inn.

"I'd like to get back to Paris first thing tomorrow. This feels like it's getting dangerous," Eve said as they walked along the early evening streets. "We've got what we came for, we think anyway."

Jim didn't reply immediately. After a few moments, more to himself than to Eve, he muttered, "I wonder what's in that other box."

"I'll bet it's a crown," Eve replied without hesitation. "Remember Jean mentioned some type of different crown used by the Kings. And some other type of relic, Holy Water or something. It would make sense if that sword is the one Bill Rousseau described. The Sword of Charlemagne he called it."

Jim looked at her and smiled. "I don't know why everyone says you're so dumb. I'll bet you're right. Let's check it out when we get back to the room."

II

"Marcil, sa moi." The Corsican was speeding to Sedan. He was staying at one of the finer hotels in the city, and he had a date with a nice young man this evening. He didn't intend to be late. "They have two boxes. Both are in the boot of their car. I do not know if they have opened both boxes. They have certainly opened the larger one. They know of the sword."

Marcil was furious at this news and began to shout. After a few moments the Corsican interrupted. "My friend, it is not so bad. They must return to Paris. I will find their hotel, recover your items and ensure they never leave the city."

This did not placate Marcil. "But mon ami tonight is impossible." Already the Corsican could see his plans for the evening were unraveling. "But Marcil, how will I know where they are staying tonight." He listened intently, finally, concealing his anger he agreed. "D'accord....Claude followed them last night did he not? I will find them." Marcil had stopped shouting and was more understandable. "Good, that is probably where they went tonight. I'll pay them a visit, retrieve your property and tomorrow we shall have a nice dinner, n'est pas?"

It worked. Marcil was calmer. He had stopped making ludicrous demands. He was thinking again. Finally, satisfied that Marcil was comfortable with his plan the Corsican relaxed and ensured that Marcil didn't take him completely for granted. "Oh, and Marcil, I would appreciate it very much if you would send flowers to Claude's service. He met an untimely end early this evening."

The Corsican's thumb flicked a button on his steering wheel. The call ended. His evening in Sedan was ruined. He was not happy.

III

The Corsican drove slowly through the center of Chehery. He spotted the restaurants, the police station sign on the village hall and just one block off the main street what appeared to be a short residential street that had metamorphosed into a series of small shops. The first building in the line was an ancient two-story home that had been converted into the village's only inn. Parked in the driveway stood the American's rented Citroën. He smiled. It really had been too easy.

Behind the old building, for the length of the street, ran a dirt alleyway. Here the trash barrels and owner's vehicles were parked. Stopping his car in the dirt alley behind the inn he examined the building. Seeing no one he slipped into the tiny backyard of the building. Opening the back door he entered the kitchen. Quietly moving across the kitchen he came to a door equipped with spring loaded swing hinges. Here he faced the largest risk. He paused, pulled his pistol from its holster and screwed on the long silencer. Then, slowly pushing the door open he stepped into the next room. It was a large dining room with an ancient wooden table. The room's walls were covered with equally ancient, slightly browning wallpaper depicting a hunting scene. On his far right another door marked with a brass plaque that said "Privé." It had to be to the owner's suite. He pushed the door open and checked the two small rooms. Empty.

The front foyer of the house had been converted to a lobby, with a large roll top desk serving as the proprietor's work station. Swinging the ledger around he quickly reviewed the most recent entries. Business was slow. It appeared there were four rooms upstairs. Only one room was occupied tonight - by a Mr. and Mrs. Crenshaw.

Jim and Eve's room was a modest affair. A double bed sat against the west wall. The door to the room opened directly across from the bed on the east wall. Entering the room, just to the left of the door stood a small wash basin. On the right, and covered from view when the door opened sat a lounge chair with lamppost. It was in this chair that the Corsican decided to wait. He sat down, pulled a magazine from the table and began to read, his silenced pistol on the arm of the chair.

Chapter 38

I

It had been a cool evening and Jim and Eve were glad to be back at the inn. The owner wasn't back yet, probably afraid she'd be obligated to attempt to talk to them again. Jim was sure she spoke French with a heavy German influence since both he and Eve could make out only every fourth or fifth word. Or maybe she was partially deaf. Or maybe their French really was that bad, and everyone until now had simply been nice to them. But the fact remained, they hadn't struggled with the language nearly as much before today.

As he unlocked the door Eve asked Jim if he thought either of the names in the wallet were real. Jim stepped into the room, tossed the room key on the bed and began to shut the door behind Eve. "I don't know, but I sure wish we knew who he was."

"His name was Claude Rechaud; and he worked for the same man I do," the Corsican said as the door closed revealing him sitting in the cushioned chair.

Jim and Eve both jumped at the sound of an unexpected voice. Spinning around they spotted the end of a pistol barrel only a few feet from Jim's chest.

"Who the hell are you?" Jim cried.

"Ah, let us simply say I am a man interested in history, just as you are." The Corsican replied. "I do hope our mutual interests are profitable. But first, Monsieur and Madame, before we talk, I need a slight favor."

"I don't do favors for thugs," Jim replied through clenched teeth.

"Sir, it is nothing really. But, I believe you took a weapon from my associate, Monsieur Claude Recheau? As you know, guns can be very dangerous. I need to know where that weapon is now. Think carefully how you answer sir. A mistake would be disastrous for you…and your wife."

Jim began to see the situation could spin out of control rapidly. Besides surely the man had searched the room. "The gun is in the night stand. Now, what do you want?"

The man continued as if this were a totally normal occurrence. "Very good. A wise place to keep it. Now, s'il vous plaît, I believe you have two items that my associates believe would be more properly employed in their care. As I recall, they are in the boot of your car."

Jim glanced at Eve. Another mystery. Who was this man, and how did he know about the boxes? The man continued, "We are going to go quietly downstairs and unlock your car. I should be very grateful if you would then transfer them to my car."

Eve stared at the dark skinned, smiling, youngish man. He was pointing a small gleaming chrome pistol with a long tube, it could only be a silencer, at them. He was as casual and calm as a man walking his dog. He wore double pleated pin stripped pants, a dark, what appeared to be, silk shirt and a fashionable leather jacket. She glanced at Jim. "What's going on here? Are you the police? We want to speak to the police. Do you understand?" Eve insisted.

"Madame, we will not be speaking to the police." He said very matter-of-factly, neither he, nor the pistol moving.

"Then I guess the question is who are you, and who do you work for?" Jim replied instantly, also not moving.

"I am, what you would call, an independent contractor. It is my job to…I guess one would say, ensure corporate success in a dynamic business environment." Again, a big smile. "Now, please follow my instructions without fail, and we will not have, ah…we will not have a failed business relationship." At that he smiled again, seemingly pleased with his corny business analogies.

The man stood, grew serious and opened the door. "After you Madame," he said looking at Eve.

The three of them descended the stairs. Jim fervently prayed the old woman hadn't returned to her inn yet. He could only see a tragic outcome if she had. They reached the dining room. The man quickly checked the owner's salon, the kitchen and then peeked out each of the room's windows. Finding no one, he waived Jim and Eve forward. They exited the rear of the building and proceeded to their rental car.

In a fashion that could only be described as overly polite the man gave instructions for the car to be unlocked. The two boxes were to be picked up and carried to a chocolate brown

Mercedes S parked in the alley. Doing exactly as directed, Jim and Eve placed the boxes on the ground next to the Mercedes. The man pushed a button on his key fob, and the vehicle's trunk popped open. Directing Jim to a small storage bin inside the trunk he asked Jim to remove the tool bag. Inside the bag was a folded plastic bag provided for wrapping a flat tire. Jim was directed to line the trunk with the bag. Once satisfied he ordered Jim and Eve to place the two boxes on top of the plastic.

With a great show of politeness, the stranger asked Jim to sit on the ground with his hands on his head. He apologized for soiling Jim's pants. He removed a length of rope from his trunk and tied Eve's hands behind her, asking several times if they were too tight, and ensuring he did not cut off the circulation to her hands. He then helped her get into the backseat of the car. He tied Jim's hands the same way and then helped him to his feet. In what Jim considered an incredibly strange idiosyncrasy, the man then took a brush from the trunk and brushed the dirt from Jim's pants. Returning the brush to the trunk he then assisted Jim in getting into the car as well. Jim slid into the back seat and looked at Eve, "Who is this guy? He's a friggin' neat freak! What the hell is going on?" Eve simply shrugged her shoulders, her eye's wide with fear.

Using his key fob the dark skinned stranger locked the car doors. "Why did he just lock us in here?" Eve asked more to hear her voice than expecting an answer and kept her eyes following the man as he walked to their car. The stranger reached the rear of the Citroën and removed the keys from the trunk lock where they had been left. He then got in the driver's seat and backed out of the driveway.

"He's gone! Help me untie this rope!" Jim turned his back to Eve.

"Hon, how the hell can I do that? My hands are tied too!"

"Turn your back to my back and…I'll try to untie your hands by feel."

"That only works on TV."

"No, no, it will work, go ahead…."

She cut him off. "Jim, never mind…there he is."

The stranger had simply driven around the house and was now coasting past them. He drove to the end of the alley, parked the Citroën behind a dumpster and was now walking toward them.

In a moment he was opening the door to the car. The stranger slid into the butter brown leather seats and started the engine. He backed the car slightly and then shifted to drive, turned hard left and drove out of the small town.

In a few moments they were on the road and headed south. "I never thought I'd ride in a Mercedes S, and I sure as hell didn't expect to be riding in one with my hands tied behind my back!" Jim whispered to Eve. She looked at him. For a moment he got the "Are you nuts?" look, then fear returned. She went back to staring at the back of their driver's head. The car simply glided over the road as they drove in the direction of Cheveuges. A moment later the car's Bluetooth phone system activated. The man answered, "Oui," and a burst of rapid fire French filled the Mercedes. The driver listened and replied in equally fast French.

Jim looked at Eve. She listened intently and whispered, "Something about objects and the Americans. I think he used the word 'mort,' but I don't know about the rest. It's too fast."

Jim didn't like that. 'Mort' meant dead in just about any language. The remainder of the ride was in silence. Jim and Eve didn't try to whisper, and the driver hadn't spoken since the phone call. After thirty minutes or so they arrived at a small cottage. The building seemed old as did most of the buildings in this part of France Jim thought. Again, with great care, the dark skinned man helped Eve and Jim out of the car and escorted them into the cottage.

The building had probably seen more than enough history. Its exterior walls were fabricated from fieldstone, and its floors were wooden planks. The planks just over the threshold were well worn from years of grinding boots and shoes. The exterior door opened into a small, but what in happier circumstances could only be called a 'friendly' kitchen. It didn't feel friendly now.

II

As Jim and Eve looked around the kitchen he asked them to take seats at the table. Then he sat down across from them. Not saying anything he removed a knife from his pocket, opened the blade and began to clean under his fingernails. Finished with his left hand he switched the knife and began on his right hand. Without looking up he said, "Monsieur e Madame, I am only going to ask questions once." He finished with his right hand. Then, again without looking up, he carefully placed the knife on the table and sat back in his chair. After a moment he reached out a long slender finger and gently tapped the backside of the blade. The knife swung round, perfectly aligning with the lines in the tablecloth. Without looking up from his examination of the knife and the tablecloth he said, "I expect complete truth. You cannot fail me in your answers, no? We will be truthful with each other one hundred percent, no? If we are not, our business relationship must, of necessity, be altered. You understand?"

Jim and Eve were scared. Eve looked pale, absolutely gray thought Jim. He began to wonder if they were going to see the next day. Thinking there was nothing to lose Jim decided to try to confuse and delay the man with the knife.

"Before you ask us any questions, let me ask you what the hell is going on? That fella Eve smoked in the barn, who was he? And why did you point a gun at us and tie us up? What the hell is this all about?"

Jim was trying hard to delay whatever came next. He figured his best bet was to go on the offensive. At least he thought he could get a conversation going. He'd been taught that if taken hostage get the hostage takers to talk. He figured that his questions could start that ball rolling. It was a poor attempt.

"You are in possession of a certain French historical artifact, non? A tube containing a document," the man announced.

"Yeah...well...yeah, we used to be, but now it's at the Louvre in Paris. They're authenticating it," Eve offered.

"It is? Well, that is unfortunate. Tell me, you found a sword. What do you know about this sword?"

"We don't know anything. We didn't even know we were going to find a sword. I do know I wish I had that sword in my hand right now!" Jim said.

"Now, now, Mr. Creen-shaw, you don't...."

"Hey, how do you know my name? That other man knew my name too. What's going on here? I'd like to see the American Council or the local police please." Jim knew this sounded ridiculous, but figured it would keep the man talking.

"It is no matter how I know your name Mr. Creen-shaw," the man smoothly retorted.

"Wait...You know my name, and I don't know yours.

And, why can't you people say CREN SHAW?" asked Jim, grabbing for his delaying tactics again.

"Oh, forgive me....Mr. Creen-shaw, as I said, you don't know..."

"No, no, it's CREN, not CREEN; CREN, say it, CREN SHAW." Jim said.

Eve looked at Jim. "He's out of his mind," she thought.

"Creen"

"NO, CREN!" Jim did his best to sound offended.

"Oui, Okay, okay. CREN shaw, is that it? Now, Mr. Creen...Mr. Crenshaw why did you dig up the two boxes?" the man asked, only now a little taken aback.

"I want to speak to the police," Jim pressed.

"Sir, clearly you understand that is not going to happen. Now, please, tell me how you came to discover the two boxes." The stranger had not yet completely regained his composure.

"We didn't know there were two boxes. We just read that there was something in the stall so we dug." Jim switched tactics, figuring he'd give as much as he could without giving anything of value; although he didn't have a clue what he had of value that the man wanted. After all, he already had the two boxes.

"I didn't, I mean we didn't know what was in there. But, it was a just a lark."

The man looked confused. "A lark? A singing bird?"

"No, you know, a lark, just something like an adventure. We read about this place in my great grandfather's diary and figured we'd go see what was there."

"So you know nothing of what you found?" the man asked.

"NO! Except that we found a sword; and I wish I had it in my hands now!" Jim allowed his voice to get loud and emotional. "That's it."

The man studied them. They were clearly just a couple of middle-aged tourists. What was Marcil thinking? He stood up. "Please come with me."

"Where to?" Jim demanded.

"Sir, I do not negotiate, and I do believe that you need to begin to cooperate. My patience is coming to an end. Things could look bad for you very quickly...or for Mrs. Creen...Crenshaw." The man looked at Eve very seriously.

Jim felt the blood drain from his face. He glanced at Eve. Her eyes were on the Corsican. She didn't look afraid. She looked mad. Jim weighed the options. Seeing that they really had no choice he finally said, "Alright, lead on."

The Corsican smiled. "I like your spirit Mr. Crenshaw. But, no, you and your wife need to move through that door." He then directed them to a narrow staircase and up the steps to the second floor. There, he escorted them into a small bedroom. Backing to the door he smiled, turned and walked out of the room. Jim winced when the Corsican locked the door from the outside.

"What is going on?" Eve whispered.

"I wish I knew," Jim replied, then shouted, "Hey, you can't leave us tied up in here! HEY!"

"Hon...hon....HON!" Eve said, gradually elevating her voice. "Please shut up...I think it's better that he's out there and not in here."

Jim thought about that for a moment and couldn't deny the wisdom of what Eve had just said. With that, Jim and Eve began trying to figure out how to untie their ropes.

Chapter 39

Paul Marcil walked through the Renaissance Masters section of the Louvre. His assistant was telling him about a minor Normandy painter's work found in Argentina which, in his worthless opinion, the museum should acquire. Apparently this painting had been spirited away by some minor Nazi thief when the bastard had fled to South America. It did have a good story Marcil admitted to himself, but the artist was, in truth, not very good and not very important. He was about to tell his assistant to forget the painting when his cell phone vibrated. Marcil, grateful for the interruption, waved the assistant away and placed the phone to his ear.

The report was better than he could have hoped. He sat down on one of the benches near The Sabine Woman by Delacroix. He could barely conceal his excitement. His backup man had performed admirably, as he always did. It seemed this little pair of Americans had provided him with the most precious French artifacts in the history of the Kingdom. He certainly would be made a Royal now. He was going to be catapulted to the top rung of the Action Françoise and he would be a wealthy and secure man for the remainder of his life. He heard the Corsican, but didn't listen to him. Would he be a Duke? Certainly he would be made a Count, at the minimum a Baron. He thought about what kind of castle he should live in, of course he would buy a castle. And the Duchesse? Ahhhh, she would be a trophy... The Corsican was asking if he was there. Of course he was. And the man should speak with more respect!

The question now was what to do about the two Americans. The Corsican didn't know if they'd opened the second box. He didn't think they'd had as they'd not mentioned it when he'd questioned them. He had been wise not to open it in front of them, but unfortunately they had seen the contents of the first. That caused some issues. If they told anyone about the sword, and someone figured out exactly which sword it was then its value would, by necessity, be lessened. That was only natural. The sword would become a hunted object. The Council would have to take extraordinary measures to protect it. If, on the other hand, they were not allowed to tell anyone...well, that was an entirely different story.

The question was one of risk and reward. A great many people knew of the Crenshaw's discovery of the Royal Patent. It had even made its way to the American newspapers in Detroit. Many people surely knew these two had come to Paris, even to see him. Of course, not many knew they had actually completed that visit, and no one in the museum knew what they had brought. At least he didn't think they did. He was fairly certain that no one working for the Louvre read the Detroit Free Press! He wasn't sure who knew they had left Paris to search for other items associated with the Royal Patent. But, certainly there had to be someone, if no other than the car rental company's staff. There was the matter of the two professors the Crenshaw's had spoken with. They must have discussed the possibility of additional items when they visited the American professor at the University. He couldn't be certain, but it was only logical. Most disturbing was the fact that they had spent several days speaking with many, many people in and around Cherhery. No, their disappearance could not be completed simply. He thought this all over and then told the man on the phone that he needed to consult with his associates. He would provide additional instructions shortly. With that, he disconnected his phone and rejoined that blathering fool of an assistant.

Chapter 40

Jim and Eve were surprised when, about ten o'clock that evening the door of the room opened. They were made to sit on the floor opposite the door. Then they were presented with a teacart. On its top were several different cheeses, meats, and fruits. A bottle of wine and glasses were visible on the bottom shelf of the wheeled cart. The dark skinned man untied Eve's hands, said "Bon appétit," turned around, left the room and closed and locked the door.

They looked at each other. Stunned was the word, but it didn't accurately portray how surprised they were. Eve quickly untied Jim's hands. They held each other for a moment. "I'm scared Jim," was all Eve could say.

They searched the room for anything that could assist in their escape. Nothing. They listened at the door; only the faint sound of the television downstairs could be heard. They examined the bed, the armoire, and the small chest of drawers. Nothing. Eve went to the window and peered out. There was nothing but a small field, with a stand of trees on the other side.

They hadn't eaten since lunch so they quickly gave up their search of the room and descended on the cart. They ate in silence. An hour passed. The light bulb had been removed from the one overhead lamp. Dusk had long ago crept into night. The man came to the door and knocked. Jim hesitated then answered with a simple, "Yes?"

"You should please to sit on the floor. On the opposite wall of course please."

"Yes, now what?" Jim answered a moment later.

The man entered, his pistol tucked into his belt. He threw a blanket on the bed, took the cart and left. Silence returned. The only light in the room came from the keyhole in the door. Eventually, they fell asleep.

The next morning Eve and Jim were awake at dawn. They carefully listened at the door. Nothing. The television was still on in another part of the house. Jim got to his knees and tried to look under the door, but that view didn't extend as far as he'd hoped. He then tried to look through the keyhole. Being an old fashioned, skeleton key lock this met with some success. He was able to see into the room opposite and part of the staircase. It was like peering through a straw but it did work. He could hear the television. Had it been on all night? Their antagonist was not in view.

Eve went to the door, leaned over Jim who was still looking through the lock and put her ear against it. Then she tried the other walls. "I don't hear anything except the TV," she whispered. Jim shrugged. Then he looked up at her and said, "Pound on the door." He put his eye back to the lock. She made a fist and began to hit the door. After several blows she gave a funny jump, "Ouuu.....that one hurt." She said as she rubbed the outside edge of her hand. Jim continued to watch through the keyhole. Nothing.

After ten minutes and no response, Jim decided to pound on the door. After five sharp raps he went back to the keyhole. Nothing. He then announced he was going to break down the door. He prepared to ram the door with his shoulder then stopped. He examined the doorframe. "Hon...this isn't like on TV. This frame is heavy duty. I don't think I can do it." He began to look around the room. "I'll take the bed apart and we can use it to batter down the door."

She looked at him. "Hon, why don't we just break that window and go out that way?"

He looked at the window. He looked at the bed. "We didn't think of that last night?"

"No" she said.

"You have got to be kidding me," he said, more to himself than to her.

They peered out the window. Only a small yard surrounded the house, at least on this side. Then a field of grass gave way to a small wooded area. Jim tried the window. He couldn't open it. Several coats of paint insured this window wasn't going to be opened without a toolbox full of knives, screwdrivers and crowbars. He stepped to one side of the window, back flat against the wall, and tried to look along the outside wall of the house. Nothing. He went to the other side of the window and did the same. Nothing. Eve stripped the blanket off the bed and gave it to him. He wrapped his hand several times, stepped to the side of the window, wound up and hit the window as hard as he could.

Immediate pain shot up his forearm. "DAMN that hurt! God I hope I didn't break my arm. DAMMMMNNNN that hurt." Jim gripped his arm. After a few moments he stopped pacing around the room.

They sat on the bed. Several seconds passed in frustrated silence. Then, without a word, Eve went to the door and looked out the keyhole. Nothing.

The question was how to break the window. They examined the bedroom again. Finally, Jim pointed at the bureau. They had already searched it and found it empty, but now they attempted to remove the drawers. Eventually, they found the catch and successfully removed the middle drawer. Eve went to the keyhole and peered out. Nothing moved. The television was still on. She gave a thumbs-up to Jim. He picked up the drawer and slammed it into the window. The glass exploded outward. He quickly looked at Eve. She peered through the keyhole. Nothing.

He broke out the rest of the glass from the frame. Eve had already tied the blanket to the bed. He tossed it out the window, climbed through and slid down the blanket. Jumping the last several feet to the ground. Walking next to the wall he went to the front of the building and checked for signs of their antagonist. Then he went to the back of the house. No sign of the man or his car. Returning to the room window he motioned for Eve to climb out. After a pause she summoned her strength and was sliding down the blanket. After a few feet she lost her grip, choked back a scream and landed on Jim who was trying to catch her. "You could have waited until I got your feet, I could'a let you down easy," Jim complained.

"Sorry. I lost my grip," Eve had a lot more to say, but kept quiet.

Staying close to the side of the house they circled the building, nothing. The Mercedes was gone. They went to the front door. It was unlocked. They crept into the house. Silently, carefully, they searched the bottom floor. No one was there. They were alone.

Jim looked at Eve. "We've got to get out of here, NOW." With that Jim took Eve's hand, dashed out the kitchen door and began to run toward the field. They made the field and kept running. Finally they had crossed the field and entered the small wood. Here, Jim slowed. They slid behind a large beech tree, turned and watched the house. They didn't see anyone.

"Why are we running? That guy is gone," Eve gasped.

"How do we know he's not driving back down the road right now?" Jim puffed.

Eve's eyes opened a bit wider. "Okay, I'll buy that, but now what? We can't stay in this little woods forever, and I can see through it anyway. We'll be spotted in a heartbeat."

Jim walked to the edge of the woods nearest the road. Keeping a tree between himself and the road he checked as far as he could see. Nothing. Where had their captor gone? Suppose the man had only left for a brief time. Surely they'd be in danger if he returned and found them missing.

Chapter 41

The Corsican's car fairly flew over the French countryside. His conversation with Marcil hadn't gone as he'd wished. It made no sense to leave two people alive that had seen his face and could identify him and his automobile. He'd made that point to Marcil. It did no good. Marcil had insisted the danger was less if he left them alone. He'd fully expected to kill them last evening. Had he known that Marcil didn't want the man and woman dead he wouldn't have allowed his face to be seen. This was a terrible breach of etiquette on the part of the stupid Frenchman. But, the commission was considerable and customer satisfaction was what he prided himself on. Therefore, he'd put a large amount of antihistamine into their wine and cheese. It was just enough to ensure they slept soundly when they did fall asleep. He didn't want them to have any suspicion of the drugging.

He'd slipped out of the house shortly after three that morning. Sadly, he'd have to get rid of the car. He should have done that before he left Cheveuges. But, the odds were on his side. Being caught now in this car was simply an unlikely proposition. The chance of a police notification for a stolen car was much greater. After all, the number of steps required were greater. The Americans had to get out of the house, get to the police, establish their credibility, provide an accurate description of the car, and then the police bureaucrats had to establish a watch for the car. But, even with all that it would be done, and it probably would be done within twenty-four hours. Not an issue, tomorrow this car would be a smoking wreck.

The two hundred fifty kilometer drive back to Paris was a pleasant ride. He arrived in the early morning, took a short nap, ate a small meal, showered changed clothes and he was a new man. Removing the sword from its box he took several pictures. Then, he wrapped a sheet of white paper around the pommel and made a rubbing of the piece all around. Naturally the leather wrapping showed, but so too did the underlying crosshatched engraving. He then carefully replaced the sword in its box. Opening the smaller box he was stunned to find a relatively plain crown with four fleur-de-lis extending upward from a modest gold band. Again he took several pictures of the piece; then replaced it in the box.

Moving to his in-home office he sat down at the computer. There he downloaded the pictures from the camera to his computer and hit 'print'. In a few seconds the printer provided high quality photo prints to his outstretched hand. Placing these in a folder, along with the rubbing, he scooped up the two boxes and carried them down to his car.

Shortly after lunch he drove to the Louvre, parking in the underground employee and VIP parking garage. There he transferred the large box containing the sword to the trunk of Marcil's BMW 750i. Returning to his own car he removed the smaller box, wrapped his coat over it, and headed to the elevator. In less than five minutes he was shown into Marcil's inner office.

Chapter 42

I

"What do we do now?" whispered Eve.

"We've got to get back to town and our car," Jim whispered back. "But we've got to be careful that he doesn't see us walking on the road. And I don't think we need to be whispering."

"Any suggestions on how to get to town and the police while a psychopath is looking for us?" asked Eve in a normal voice.

"Okay, we….well, we….I think we…I don't know hon. I'm not a Special Forces guy. I'm a retired logistics guy." Jim's frustration was boiling to the surface. "Okay, here's an idea. We stay in the woods, close to the edge and parallel the road. We'll be out of sight and not get lost. Maybe we can sneak back to town that way."

"Alright, sounds like a plan. Let's do it." Eve sounded perfectly confident in Jim's idea. Jim took his eyes off the house and looked at her. "We're going to have to be very careful on this; and if he comes, you run as fast and as far away from me as you can, got it?"

Eve met his gaze. "Not going to happen, but sounded good hon. Now let's go."

The wood they were in was little more than a stand of trees between two fields. It provided only meager concealment, but they considered some better than none. They turned and slipped out the back, keeping the trees between themselves and the house where they'd been kept. Finding the road they paralleled it, staying just inside of the edge of the wood and out of sight as much as possible. Finally, they came to a fence line with trees growing right up to the road. Here they crept closer and waited. After forty-five minutes Jim heard a tractor approaching. Hiding behind a tree he waited and watched. After determining the farmer to be exactly that, a farmer, he stepped into the road and waved his arms. The man, slightly taken aback, stopped the tractor and began a loud and excited speech in French. Apparently, he was upset with Jim for stepping in front of his tractor. His manner changed when

Eve stepped into the road, and a few moments later he agreed to deliver them to Cheveuges.

Their anxiety grew as the tractor chugged toward town. Once the man stopped, dismounted, and examined a field of grass; determining if it was ready for cutting and bailing. The man causally walked across the field while Jim and Eve attempted to hide behind the tractor whenever a vehicle approached on the little road. Eventually they arrived back in town and began a search for their rental car. It was not in the alley where their abductor had left it. The old woman at their inn took fifteen minutes to explain that she had no knowledge of it or its location. A fast walk around the small village didn't locate the vehicle. Finally, in desperation they elected to go to the police.

A sign on the front of the town hall directed police department visitors to the rear of the building. They rounded the building and there, in the police parking lot, sat their car.

"What do we tell the cops?" Jim asked.

"What do you mean? We tell them that some nut pointed a gun at us in that barn and another nut kidnapped us!" Eve nearly shouted.

"Well, let's think this over," Jim replied.

"Think it over? What's to think over? There's a couple of nut jobs out there pointing guns at people," she insisted.

"Hon, the problem is that the police will ask us why somebody was pointing a gun at us. Then they'll eventually find out we were digging in the barn looking for some of the most important and valuable items in the history of France. I think that will raise a few eyebrows. I'm sure someone will be upset that we didn't notify the authorities we were looking for the Sword of Charlemagne, only one of the biggest deals in French history and culture. We don't have an answer for that. We might be charged with trying to steal the things or something."

"What, who cares? Why is that a big deal? And, we did tell someone. Remember we went to the Louvre? We told them!"

"Yes, we told them about the Royal Patent, but we didn't say anything about the sword or anything else," he paused. "We might be charged with some law that says we should have reported searching for antiques or something. Maybe we were trespassing in that barn?"

"Are you telling me we're criminals? We didn't do anything

wrong! We're the ones that had a gun pointed at us and got kidnapped." She was getting excited.

"Actually, yeah, I guess I am. All I'm saying is we'll be better off not to mention the gun and the kidnapping. Let's just say we were picked up by a friendly stranger and spent the night in Chehery. We walked back early this morning and are just picking up our car now."

Eve didn't like it, but they told the tale to the policeman at the desk. He didn't blink, fined them twenty Euros, and twenty minutes later they were standing next to the now liberated Citroën. A stop at the pastry shop for a quick breakfast, and they were headed back to Paris. They drove in silence, stunned by the events of the last forty-eight hours. Eventually Eve asked, "What do we do now?" The question hung in the air.

After a moment's thought Jim slowly said, "OK, where are we….let's start from the beginning. My great grandfather found the Royal Patent. Jean said that the Patents were always kept with the Sword of Charlemagne and other items. I think we found that sword. She also said that a coronation crown might be with the sword. I'll bet that was what was in the other box."

Eve thought for a second then said, "Agreed. But, we don't have any of them now and the chances of getting any of them back are pretty slim. Let's not forget two guys pointed guns at us; one left the other after I smacked him on the head." Eve looked at Jim who merely shrugged.

She continued, "And, the other kidnapped us and tied us up in some old house then disappeared. This is all very weird."

They thought for several minutes. Finally Eve broke the silence, "In fact, I have no idea where to even start. What do we do?"

Jim shook his head, "I don't know." Neither said a word for the next ten minutes.

"Well, we've got the Patent and the tube," Jim said.

"No, the Louvre has them." She corrected him, "and, there's no guarantee that they're not going to just keep them. The way our luck is going they're going to say that the items really belong to France, and all we get is a thanks, get outta the country and don't let the door hit you on the rear end."

He thought about that for a moment. Then, he looked at his petite wife. For the first time since they'd walked into their room to find a mad man and a gun he smiled at her. "You're getting fired up."

She looked at him and grinned, "Damn straight."

They both grew quiet. Jim passed a few slower cars on the highway. Eventually he said, "Seriously, you've got a point. They could just keep everything and kick us out of the country I guess. Hopefully they're not that cold, but it is possible. In the meantime, let's think about getting the boxes back. Any ideas?"

"Get them back? All I can think to do is report what's happened to the Louvre," Eve said slowly. "They'll know we're telling the truth, and they'll see that what we've done makes sense. The thing is I just didn't like that guy, he seemed a bit, well, odd."

"Really? The guy we met with? Hervey or something like that? He seemed a bit stuffy but alright to me," Jim said, checking his rear view mirror for the umpteenth time.

"Hervey? Not even close. It was Marcil." Eve said, looking at Jim with a grin. "You're really bad with names."

"Yeah, so you've said. Anyway, he's alright. And, I think your idea of talking to him sounds like a decent idea…it makes sense anyway. I'm just not sure it will get us any closer to the boxes. The only good thing is that it does get the authorities looking for them. And, at a minimum it gives the French government a chance to save its historical treasures from some crook that probably doesn't know what he has. And, it gives us a good chance of staying out of trouble, which strongly influences my vote, as they say. Let's do it."

"Jim, it's not that big of help to the police."

"How so?" Jim asked.

"We've still got the same problem. We don't know how to find the boxes so we don't know how to help the police or whoever the Louvre puts on this."

"Yeah, I guess that's true, well…wait, no…no…it's not. We know two important things. We know what the guy that grabbed us looks like and we know about his car," Jim said.

"We know he was dark skinned, dark eyes, and dark hair," Eve replied.

Jim looked at her. "That's the best you've got? That's the entire male population of every country on the Mediterranean."

"Who knew I was going to have to draw a picture of the man pointing a gun at me!" She shot back, not amused at the sarcasm.

"I'm just sayin'..." After a moment Jim continued, "He was wearing a nice suite. And, he was about, what? Maybe a hundred fifty, hundred sixty pounds?"

"A suit? It wasn't a suit. It was a nice pair of pants and a leather jacket," she said then lapsed into thought. A few minutes later she said, "And, now that you mention it, he was in pretty good shape." Eve grinned at him.

"Hey, hey, stay focused here," Jim said with a smile.

"Knew I'd get you with that."

"Okay, so, he wore nice clothes, was a buck sixty, didn't have any meat on his bones..." Jim glanced at Eve with a grin. "...was about five foot six would you say? Anything else? Any marks on his face that you saw?"

She thought for a while. "No, I'm not good at this. I was looking more at that gun than him. That was a silver pistol with the biggest barrel in the world. That's all I've got."

Jim shook his head. "Yeah, I know. He had a few days of beard so if there were scars or marks they would have had to be pretty big. But, we can do better on the car. That thing would stand out anyplace. It was a new, dark brown Mercedes S with a light brown interior."

"And it was a leather interior," she added.

"Did you get the license plate when we put the boxes in the trunk?" he asked.

"No...well, I don't remember. It was something like, it started with two "As" because I thought of Alcoholics Anonymous, so it was AA then some numbers and letters." Eve sounded sure of herself.

Jim tried to picture the car. He just couldn't get it. Finally he said, "Okay, let's go with the AA. Now, look at all the plates on the cars we pass, they're all two letters, three numbers then two more letters. Maybe that will jog our memories." He thought for a few miles. "I think the numbers were 278 or 298, but I'm not certain. And, I can't remember the last letters at all. But, the stripe on both sides was blue, I'm sure of that." They discussed the license plate for a few more minutes, but didn't make any progress. Eventually, they both became lost in their thoughts.

They drove in silence for the next ten minutes, each rehashing the events of the past twenty-four hours. Finally, Jim glanced at Eve, "Do you think it was really the Coronation Crown in the little box?"

"I have no idea," she said, turning in her seat. "That sword was pretty neat though. Do you think it was the really the sword Charlemagne used? That would be something. The box had to contain the Coronation Crown; there's no other explanation."

They toyed with license plates for the next several miles. They couldn't be sure. All they had was the AA and the 278 or 298. Even the numbers were suspect. They couldn't be certain they had those right. Finally, they gave up and drove the remainder of the trip back to Paris in silence, each lost in thought.

II

It was late afternoon as they approached the city's outskirts. As a precaution they elected to spend the night in a cheap hotel outside the city center. Dinner was at a small restaurant in the town of Saint-Maurice.

As they waited for their order to arrive Eve began to talk about the Louvre. Finally, she got around to what was really on her mind. "Jim, when that guy Marcil first talked to me on the phone back home, I didn't like him."

"Not liking him isn't a reason not to go tell him what we've been up to," Jim said as he took a sip of his wine.

"No, not liking him isn't the right words. I didn't trust him. He sounded pretty determined to get that tube and Patent from us. I don't know, It's just that, well…Jim, do you trust the guy," she asked.

"I don't see any reason not to," Jim replied. "He's a bit of a bureaucrat, but he's not done anything to us. And, he did buy us the tickets to get here. Why wouldn't I?"

"I'm not sure. There's just something there," Eve said. "Something about him. I don't know, maybe it's the way he was aloof and the way he demanded we leave the tube with him when we met him in his office. Or, maybe it was from the first time I spoke to him on the phone. He seemed to get under my skin then. He said that they intended to….um, what was it? Repatriate, yeah, repatriate was the word he used. He was going to repatriate the tube and the Patent. It was as if it was a done deal. There was some sort of implied threat if we didn't hand the things over. I got a little leery of him. And, when I was about ready to hang up on him he offered to buy the tube and Patent; said he'd have to authenticate them first and offered us the trip over here for that purpose. That's how we got here. I guess I was so shocked by the money and the trip I forgot I was getting upset with the guy."

"That doesn't sound too terrible Eve. They need to authenticate items in the Museum. I'll bet they get hundreds of fakes every year. Sounds to me like the guy was just doing his job."

Just then the waiter arrived with their food. The conversation lagged as they ate a wonderful dinner of stuffed trout and sautéed vegetables. After several minutes and between mouthfuls, Jim asked, "You really got a bad feeling about the guy huh?"

"Jim, I don't know. I just feel like there was something else going on," Eve replied. "I can't put my finger on it but he didn't have the right approach. It just seems to me that a big museum would be much less demanding and more polite when they call someone out of the blue."

"Okay, I understand. Tomorrow we'll get to the Louvre in the early afternoon. It'll be nap time for most of these Europeans. We'll keep a sharp lookout for anything odd he says or does."

"Honey, you're thinking of the Med, places like Spain and Italy. I don't think they take a siesta here." They had a good laugh and left the restaurant. The remainder of the evening was spent at a small jazz club just off the central hub of Saint-Maurice.

Chapter 43

The traffic on Avenue du General-Lemonnier was extremely heavy as they approached the massive museum. "I wonder what's going on today." Eve said, not expecting an answer.

"Something big, looks like a street art festival or something like that. Guaranteed there's no parking available," Jim observed.

They turned into the underground parking entrance, and stopped at the booth. A large sign reading "Parking Garage Full" in a dozen languages hung from a saw horse. Jim swore and shifted into reverse, anticipating a long afternoon attempting to find a place to park and a long walk to and from the car.

Just then an attendant exited the booth. Eve frantically waived him down. In her best French she explained they were there to see Paul Marcil, deputy director of the Art Acquisition Department. The man was impressed by the name and assumed these must be important people. He ducked back into the booth and reemerged with a visitor's pass. Handing the pass to Jim he directed them to the employee and official guest parking area. The guest parking spaces were nearly full and Jim and Eve were forced to park at the far end of the allocated area. Finding a space in the middle of the row Jim quickly parked and they walked to an elevator. Pausing before pushing the button for the main floor he looked at Eve. "Into the lion's den," he said with absolutely no trace of a smile.

The elevator quickly delivered them to the main floor. From there it was a short walk to the administrative section of the Louvre. Stepping off the elevator they faced a uniformed guard. They explained the purpose of their visit. The guard, speaking flawless English, escorted them to the administrative areas and asked them to take a seat in the small waiting area. He then phoned Paul Marcil's secretary.

After a short conversation he hung up the phone, shot a smile in their direction and informed them that Mr. Marcil would see them momentarily. A few moments later a pretty young woman approached the guard, who pointed at them. She walked to Jim and Eve and announced she was there to escort them to Mr. Marcil's office. They followed their guide along a majestic hallway,

their escort providing them with a running narrative of the
paintings they passed, the occasional sculpture or artifact.
Eventually, they completed the maze and were standing once again
outside of Room 102.

"I hope he's not going to be too upset," Eve muttered.

"I hope we don't get tossed out of the country or in jail."
Jim replied.

They entered the suite of offices and were quickly shown
into Marcil's inner office. They sat on one of the sofas and
admired the Louis XIV furniture around the room. The secretary
again offered them coffee and the laborious small talk began.
Marcil seemed excited about a fundraiser for the Louvre that was
being held that night in conjunction with a new exhibit that he had
helped put together. He spent several minutes explaining the art
pieces which were to be included and the anticipated guest list.

After several minutes of this Jim decided to take the
plunge and explained everything that had happened to them since
they last saw the deputy director. Marcil listened intently, his face
grew red and Eve noticed that his collar seemed to be getting
tighter as Jim continued with their story. Finally, unable to stay
silent, his face now blotched with crimson but clearly striving
mightily to remain the picture of a French gentleman he said,
"Excuse me, may I ask why you did not tell me of your interest in
the Sword of Charlemagne and the coronation crown? These are
extremely important and valuable items."

The anger in Marcil's face and voice was barely concealed.
The voice had remained level in volume, had not quivered, nor
cracked. It simply got its question out. It was a question that Jim
didn't have a great answer for, merely an adequate one. He claimed
he knew nothing of the artifacts and was only retracing his Great
grandfather's steps. He thought his story sounded plausible, but
improbable. Marcil wasn't to be put off. "You realize this may be
theft of French property and you may be held liable?"

"What!" Eve exploded, "…we didn't steal anything. In
fact, we've found national treasures that…." Jim reached over and
put a hand on her arm. She snapped around to look in his face,
not happy being interrupted just as she was winding up for a
tornadic argument with Marcil.

"Sir," Jim said evenly, "you and I both know we didn't steal
anything. And, you know the police are not going to prosecute us.

I suggest we return to the business of finding the sword and the other item. I'm guessing, but I'll bet that box held something just, or nearly, as important and valuable."

Marcil gritted his teeth and pressed on, Jim's analysis not seeming to budge his thinking in the least. "Because of your failure to bring this to the attention of the authorities...to my attention, they may now be lost!" He seemed to be fighting down an eruption. Jim could see his neck muscles tensing and a vein on his forehead seemed to be standing out. Marcil stood up and returned to his chair behind the desk.

"Madame e Monsieur, do you realize what my role is here at the museum?" he asked. His voice had become hard, cold and calculating.

"Well, we thought you were responsible for collecting French made art," said Eve, starting to sense this was going to go on for awhile.

"You are correct, but there is more to that role than one would think. As part of those responsibilities it is my duty to pursue thieves who have removed valuable and historic art work from our country." Marcil was sitting back in his chair now. "And, I prosecute those responsible for such thefts. Do I make myself clear?"

Jim felt a hole opening in his stomach. He glanced at Eve. "Damn, I wish I'd let her at 'em," he thought. Eve was becoming gray again. "Well, we didn't take anything so there's nothing to prosecute us for," he said.

Marcil continued. "You may not have removed anything, but you are responsible for one of the greatest losses of French history since the Revolution." He sat forward and glared at them. "Now, I must decide whether you simply were foolish Americans or had evil intent, no?"

Jim interrupted him, "We really didn't know what we would find. Actually, we didn't expect to find anything. This was really more of retracing the steps of my Great grandfather than actually looking for lost treasure." It was the best Jim could do, even though it did sound a bit hollow.

Marcil stared at Jim. Seconds ticked by. No one spoke. Jim began to feel like he was caught in a box and didn't know how to get out. Finally, Marcil leaned forward on his elbows. "Excuse me," he said, picking up his phone. A burst of rapid fire French filled the room. In a moment a young man entered the office. Marcil stood, "Renee, take these two Americans to the security department. Take their full statement and have it stamped. When they are finished show them to their vehicle." To Jim and Eve he said, "As an officer of the law of the sovereign nation of France I order you to go home. After you are finished here you should find the next flight to the United States. Do I make myself clear?" Not waiting for a response he continued, "I will be notifying the law enforcement agencies of my country. Do not interfere with my country's history or its efforts to recover lost artifacts again. Additionally, you are forbidden from ever entering the Louvre again. Good day."

The young man named Renee lightly placed his hand on Jim's shoulder signaling that it was time to leave. Jim and Eve stood and began to walk out of the office. "Hey, what about the Royal Patent, we found that and it belongs to us," Eve said.

"Madame, it belongs to France," Marcil shot back, his head never looking up.

"So, you were able to authenticate the Patent and the tube?" Jim asked.

"Yes," said Marcil curtly, glancing at Jim.

"How?" asked Jim, not willing to be led out of the office just yet.

Marcil slammed his pen down. "We did an analysis of the document using fairly sophisticated techniques. Why is that of interest?" he nearly shouted.

"Oh, it's just that Eve is a science teacher. Did you find anything unusual about it?" Jim replied.

"No, nothing!" Marcil snapped.

"What did you think of the portraits?" Jim insisted. "Was there anything unusual about them?"

"They were accurate in every way. Now please, I have work to do," Marcil replied now looking at Jim.

Eve's eyebrows shot up. "You didn't notice anything about...."

"Well, we're sorry for the inconvenience and apologize to you and to France," Jim said, deliberately cutting her off. Jim glanced at Eve.

She looked at him angrily. She didn't like to be cut off, and this was the second time in the past few minutes. Then, she realized he had done it with purpose. "Goodbye sir," she said.

Marcil wasn't looking. His head was down and he had returned to his paperwork.

Chapter 44

I

Renee escorted them to the elevator. They rode to the top floors of the building in silence, Eve and Jim occasionally stealing a nervous glance at the other. Exiting the elevator on the top floor they were lead through a series of inner offices and cubicles. Eventually reaching an office door marked "SÉCURITÉ." They were escorted inside by another man, separated and placed in small interrogation rooms. Each room was equipped with a single table, a hard, straight back chair on each side and a tape recorder.

After a thirty-minute wait two men identifying themselves as detectives of the Louvre entered the room with Eve and began to question her. Much to her surprise the questioning didn't take long. In thirty minutes they were finished. They stood, said something to each other, then to her, none of which she understood and again left her alone in the small room.

Over an hour later Jim's questioning was also complete. They were allowed to rejoin each other and shown to a hard bench with a view of a bulletin board and drinking fountain. Twenty minutes later an officer appeared holding two folders. "Come with me," was all the officer said.

They were escorted to the desk of an older woman. The desk was piled with paper, a clearing had been made in the middle of the mess. Various pictures, souvenirs, perfume bottles and make-up containers decorated the edges and a shelf above the desk. The officer gave her the two folders. She studied the contents for a moment then looked at Eve and said "Madame Creenshaw?" Eve winced and said, "Yes". The woman then looked at Jim, "Monsieur Creenshaw?" Jim glanced at Eve, "Oui," he said.

She ordered them to raise their right hands. When they didn't move she muttered, then grabbed Eve's arm and raised it to the proper position. Turning to Jim she said, *"Comme ça"* and pointed at Eve. Jim did as he was told. Then she spoke rapidly in French. Finishing her speech she stared at them expectantly.

Neither knew what she said. Finally, in an exasperated voice she asked "*Oui ou Non?*" Jim and Eve both said "Oui". At that the woman reached into her lap drawer and removed a pen and pointed it at Eve. "*Approuvez.*" Eve took the pen and signed the document. The woman then did the same with Jim.

She then removed a stamp pad and a large wooden stamp from her desk drawer. She opened the stamp pad and with a small wind up pounded the stamp into the pad and then crashed the stamp onto their statements. Jim glanced at Eve. Neither mentioned that they were unable to read a single word.

Taking Eve gently by the elbow Renee escorted them to the elevator. The doors opened and they entered. Renee leaned in, pushed the button for the basement parking garage, said "*Au revoir*" and retreated to the hallway. The doors closed and Jim looked at Eve. "I've had better days," he said.

"Me too." Then, between gritted teeth she whispered, "I knew we couldn't trust that jerk." They rode the rest of the way to the garage in silence. They had been in the Louvre for over three hours; both Jim and Eve were tired, hungry, and mad.

II

The elevator stopped on the lower level of the parking garage. A burst of cool air rushed in as the doors opened. They exited, turned right and began walking to their car. Glancing around to ensure no one was near, Eve turned on Jim. Fire shot from her eyes as she stopped and stretched to her full five feet two inches. "Hey, by the way, I hate it when you cut me off! Don't do that. I don't do that to you. It's rude. You're not the boss. I get to have my say. Jim that's just...."

"Eve, hon, Eve.... Eve, I'm sorry, but what are you talking about?" Eve's explosion surprised him.

"In Marcil's office. He was lying to us, and I was going to let him have it."

"Hon, listen to me a second." Jim was trying to keep his voice down. "Did you hear what he said?"

"Of course I heard what he said. I was right there."

"When I asked him if there was anything unusual about the paintings on the Patent?" Jim whispered.

"Yes, he said there was nothing unusual and that the portraits were accurate in every way. And so what, you still don't cut...."

"Eve! Listen to what you just said." Jim and Eve were stopped in the garage facing each other.

"What do you mean 'listen to what I just said'; I heard what I said; I said it!" The more Eve talked the angrier she got.

"You said that he said there was nothing unusual about the portraits," Jim said evenly.

"Yeah..." Eve's voice began to show signs of doubt.

"Exactly," Jim replied.

"What do you mean 'Exactly'?" Eve allowed a trace of frustration into her voice.

Jim glanced around and began slowly walking to the car. "I thought you were on to him in there. Remember, Bill said there was only one lab in North America that had the equipment and the people to do the authentication. That was Jean's lab in Montreal. But, in Europe there were three or four or something like that. Anyway, the Louvre was one of them." Jim was picking up steam and now having a hard time keeping his voice to a whisper. Eve could tell his mind was racing.

"When Jean told us about the Patent do you remember how excited she was? She claimed the paint was unique, and she had identified the specific person who painted the document. She was going to change history because the guy was originally on the side of the revolutionaries and here he was painting the Patent for the Royal family. She said if her lab could do that kind of analysis then certainly the Louvre could. Remember all that?"

"Yeah, but I still don't get what you're driving at," Eve said, a touch of impatience edging closer to daylight.

"Well, if the Louvre could identify the actual painter that did the work, why didn't they?" Jim asked.

Eve thought about that a minute. "I'll be damned. You're right! What the hell?" Eve exclaimed, all anger at Jim gone.

"Exactly! Why did the entire Louvre laboratory staff, in the finest museum art laboratory in the world, not find anything exceptional about the paint; yet, Jean Somme at the University of Montreal called the paint extraordinary and potentially history changing?" Jim was on a roll now.

"Because I was right!" Eve exclaimed. "The guy's a

dirtball."

"I think that's it exactly!" Jim agreed. Eve smiled "Okay, you're forgiven," and hugged Jim.

Just then they reached their car. Jim fished the car keys out of his pocket, unlocked Eve's door and opened it for her. Then he went around and got behind the steering wheel. The car started on the first turn of the key and Jim checked his rear view mirror to ensure the path behind was clear. Slowly a brown Mercedes S crept past the rear of the car. Jim froze. Eve began to say something, and he motioned for her to be quiet. She didn't understand and began again. "Shhhhh…." Jim hissed as he watched it wind through the parking garage and exit to the street. Eve sat back in her chair and crossed her arms. Jim could tell she was mad as hell.

Chapter 45

Marcil held the two statements of Jim and Eve while looking out of his window over the interior courtyard. These two were causing him problems. He wanted to be rid of them. He didn't have a reason, but his instincts told him it was necessary. Unfortunately, it all came back to risk; they had told too many people of their trip to Chehery, to Paris and to see him. It would be too messy. It was better to just get them out of the country. He was sure he'd done that. They were sufficiently intimidated now; they wouldn't stay long. He thought about that. He couldn't kill them while they were in France, but when they returned to their home, ah, that was a different story. That decision made he returned his thoughts to the Regalia. He needed to get the sword, the crown, the Patent and anything else those boxes held out of Paris. He walked to his desk, opened the lower left door and revealed a small shredding machine. He fed the reports into the machine. There was a loose end that needed to be cauterized. He picked up his cell phone, hit speed dial and called the Corsican. There were two Louvre detectives now destined to have terrible automobile accidents.

Finished with his cell phone he reached for the desk phone. Hitting the intercom he told his secretary he was not to be disturbed and hung up. Then he went to the office door and turned the lock. Next, he opened the floor safe and removed the small box which had been delivered less than an hour ago. The box itself was not overly large, nor heavy. He carried the box to his desktop and sat down. The box was beautiful. The Corsican had cleaned it and now an ornate engraving of the fleur-de-lis outlined with what appeared to be gold could clearly be seen. The wood itself appeared to be a dark exotic, but he wasn't prepared to guess what type without a more scientific analysis. Carefully opening the hasp he lifted the lid.

He allowed himself a moment to marvel at what he found. There sat a gold crown with four royal fleur-de-lis standing from the band. The crown rested on a dark purple pillow. Tassels hung from each corner and the pillow was fringed with gold ribbon which was used to tie the crown to the pillow. Forcing himself back into the role of the trained art historian he was he began a careful examination using his magnifying glass. After five minutes he'd gone over the box, crown and pillow in detail. Satisfied he untied the ribbons and removed the crown.

He spun in his chair and sat the crown on the credenza behind. Then, returning to the box, he removed the pillow. Under the pillow was an intricate rococo carving of the Crucifixion. Carefully examining the carving he quickly realized it hid a false bottom. Once more using the magnifying glass he found a release disguised as the Shield of Longinus. Pressing the shield he released the false bottom.

Marcil's hands began to tremble. What additional treasure had he been given? Sitting back in his chair he took a deep breath and, regaining his composure he removed the false bottom to reveal another thin purple pillow. It took a moment for his brain to process what he found. A heavy gold chain was affixed to a large oval gold necklace. Jewels alternating with rubies sparkled from the circular edge. In the center was a small, very dark green or black bottle no more than two inches high and half as wide affixed with wire to a square of what appeared to his educated eye to be ivory.

Could this be the Holy Ampoule? But, hadn't it been destroyed by the revolutionaries in 1793? He pondered this mystery for a moment. Turning to his computer he brought up "Holy Ampoule" and confirmed its destruction. But what was this? Then it became obvious. He had in his possession the Sword of Charlemagne, he was certain it was the authentic item; he knew the sword on display in the Museum was not. He had this Crown, which he hadn't proven, but strongly believed to be authentic. He had the Royal Patent. These items were all for the coronation ceremony. There was only one key item left and that lay before him. History was wrong! This must be the authentic Holy Ampoule.

Checking his excitement he carefully examined the necklace. It was beautiful. It seemed he could feel its power. There were no obvious signs that it was a fake. Laying it aside he removed the pillow underneath and examined the box again. No new treasures jumped out at him. He spun round and laid the necklace next to the crown. Returning to his computer he began a painstaking comparison of the crown with various artists' depictions. After twenty minutes he'd made a preliminary confirmation by comparing subtle details of the item on his credenza with the crown depicted in three different contemporary paintings of royal coronations.

Closing his computer he pushed it to the far edge of his desk. He then removed the blotter from the top of the desk and leaned it against the wall behind his chair. Walking to the bookshelf in the corner he took down a picture of his wife. Turning the frame over he removed the back, picture and glass. Returning to his desk he laid the glass in the center of the desk. Next, he placed the crown on the glass. Reaching into his pocket he removed a small pocket-knife and began to scrap the inside of the band until a small pile of gold flecks formed on the glass. Standing, he returned the pocketknife to his pocket and walked to a cabinet built into a wall bookshelf. There, he removed a small bottle of hydrochloric acid. Using an eyedropper he placed a small amount of the acid on the shavings. As he watched the reaction he began to smile. The metal was nearly pure gold.

He returned the crown to the box. He picked up the glass, took it to his private rest room and washed it. Then performed the same test on the necklace. It too was nearly pure gold. Next he examined the ampoule. He didn't have the instruments to determine if this truly was Roman glass, but a careful examination of the thing strongly suggested it was. At least it held the appropriate visual clues.

The evidence was overwhelming. He was convinced these items were real. After a moment's celebration and a glass of Cuvée cognac he replaced his desk blotter and took out his quill and special paper. A detailed report was due.

Chapter 46

I

"Don't ever shush me again!" Eve spat.

"Did you see that?" Jim was staring at the garage ramp in disbelief.

"See what?" asked Eve, oblivious to the traffic in the garage.

"That was the Mercedes! That guy was talking on his cell phone and drove right by here," Jim was nearly yelling.

"What? No, I didn't see it. You sure? Where, where did he go? Are you sure?" Eve had gone from tired and ready to fight to fully alert and ready for action.

"Okay, now, let's think about this. Should we follow that car? I'm not sure... What do you think?" Jim was trying to put together a plan; he wasn't really asking for Eve's opinion. He was simply talking out loud. Eve had plenty of experience with this little oddity in Jim's personality. She never resented it, but she never failed to give her opinion either.

"I say let's go to the police," Eve began.

"Except that they'd arrest us," Jim replied.

"There is that. Okay, look, Jim, if we follow this guy it's like a dog chasing a car. What's he going to do when he catches it?" She said, pleased that she'd used the idiom properly. "If we follow the car what happens if we catch it? We're in deep trouble – he's got a gun and we don't."

"I'll tell you what we do," said Jim "We make sure we don't catch him, and we make sure he doesn't see us. Then we report where he goes to the police." Jim looked at her, "I don't have a better plan."

Gradually Eve began to nod her head. "Let's do it," she said.

Jim put the car in gear. They exited the garage and stopped at the street. "Left or Right?" he asked. She sat up straighter in the seat and looked to the right. He did the same and looked left. "I don't see him," she said.

"Me either. Guess! We've got to move!" Jim cried, exasperation in his voice.

"Okay, turn left," she exclaimed.

They turned left and Jim accelerated. After three blocks Eve cried out, "I got 'em! He's about five cars ahead."

"I don't see it, what lane?" Jim fired back.

"Middle lane," she replied as she pulled a Paris street map from the glove compartment. A second later Jim shouted, "OKAY, I see him!" and swung the car into the middle lane, leaving five cars between himself and the Mercedes.

"Don't get too far behind." Eve's voice sounded tense.

"I can't get too close he'll see me."

"No, you're too far away!"

"I'm fine."

"What happens if a light turns red between us and him? You'll lose him. You need to get closer," she insisted.

"Eve, I'm telling you we're fine. If we get too close he'll see us and then we're hosed," Jim replied.

"That light's turning! Hurry! Hurry!" she shouted.

Jim couldn't accelerate in the traffic. The light turned red as the Mercedes shot through the intersection. "SEE I TOLD YOU!" Eve shouted.

"Hon, hon, it's okay the light at the next block is red. I can see him. We'll catch back up." He was trying to remain calm.

"Look! He turned right at the next light. You're going to lose him!" She was nearly hanging out of the window.

"Eve, relax. We're not going to lose him. I've got this," Jim assured her. For the next ten minutes they were able to follow the Mercedes, always keeping three to five cars between themselves and the object of the chase. The Corsican kept generally southwest, finally joining highway D533. Shortly after passing the village of Bievres the Mercedes exited the highway on Rue de Bievres, passed the traffic circle and continued west on D36. Now, half way to Chevreuse, signs indicating roadwork ahead began to appear.

II

"Oh boy, we're in trouble here." No sooner had Jim finished his sentence than traffic began to slow. Soon it had slowed to a near stop, and the road necked down to one lane with oncoming traffic on the shoulder. This turned into a happy circumstance as it allowed Jim and Eve to stay less than a hundred yards behind the Mercedes and still keep several cars directly between them. Then the road closed in even further. A flagman stopped traffic every few moments, allowing oncoming traffic use of the road for thirty seconds or so. Then the process reversed. Just as Jim approached the flagman he waved his flag to stop. Eve's heart sank. Jim swore, pounded the steering wheel and together they watched the brown Mercedes speed off into the French countryside.

"Now what?" asked Eve.

"I have no idea," Jim replied as they cleared the flagman. They were in solid countryside now, fields on the north side of the road and woods on the south. Each field was bordered with a small hedgerow, line of trees or sometimes just a wire fence. They drove as fast as Jim felt safe, first cresting a hill then swooping down and cresting another. It didn't seem to matter. There was always a slower car to be passed. By now the Mercedes was out of sight. Jim tried to reassure both himself and Eve that they had not lost the quarry. They hadn't yet passed a crossroad but he knew they would. They had to catch a glimpse of the brown luxury car soon or this little drive was for nothing.

Suddenly, a tower of black smoke rose from a small wooded area several hundred yards to their front. They instinctively slowed. When the car pulled parallel with the smoke they spotted a two-track dirt path leading between two rows of hedges and trees in the direction of the woods. Casting a glance at Eve and receiving a nod in response, Jim slowed and turned.

The term 'road' was overly kind. They were on a two-tracked path. Each track made by the tires of vehicles driving back and forth, grass growing between each path. Creeping slowly along the two-track path Jim became more and more worried about being ambushed here.

III

Finally, he stopped the car. "Look hon, this is dangerous." Jim had opened his door. "Someone could be in the woods and ambush us as we pass. We'd never see them. I'm going to walk ahead, see what's there. I'll come right back."

She stared hard at Jim. "That's the worse plan I've ever heard," she said.

"Yeah, let's hope it works," he replied. Leaning over and giving Eve a quick kiss he slipped out of the car and gently closed the door. Moving to the edge of the two-track path he began to walk forward.

Eve did not like this. She was alone; her husband was off trying to be a stealth warrior and neither of them had any idea where the man in the Mercedes was. After several minutes she decided that it would be better if she were in the driver's seat. Lifting the armrest she slid out of her seat and across. Thankfully Jim hadn't taken the keys out of habit. She adjusted the seat and mirrors then sat back and tried to be patient. It wasn't working. She watched the two-track road carefully. Nothing, no movement, not even the tree leaves were rustling. The smoke of whatever was burning up there still billowed above her head. She could smell the burning rubber. It must be close.

This was taking longer than she liked. It was time for an executive decision. She started the car, pulled the shift lever and slowly began to roll forward. The soft dirt in each track muffled the sound of the tires. It was a new car, the engine quiet. She sat up straight in the seat trying to see further along the two-track.

Chapter 47

Jim had slipped off the path and was in the shallow woods between the path and a field. After just a few moments the car was out of sight. He was alone. His pace was slow; each step taken with great precision. He carefully checked the ground with each foot placement. He made certain to not break any branches and avoided dry leaves as much as possible. The stillness of the afternoon weighed him down, slowed his movements. Not even a bird sang. He wasn't wearing the right kind of shoes. He could feel the heat from the ground leaking through the soles of his loafers. He was fairly confident in his quiet approach, but was trusting to luck that if anyone was ahead, he'd see them first. Moving carefully forward he came to a small clearing. On the other side of the clearing the two-track picked up again. This wooded two-track and path completely crossed a large field. Suddenly he realized he was in the tractor traverse; this was how the farmers moved equipment from one field to another without running over crop. The clearing was where trucks or trailers were parked waiting for harvested grain to be transferred from the field equipment. At the far side of the clearing sat a brown Mercedes S, engulfed in flames. He didn't see anyone near the vehicle.

Jim instantly realized the danger. Only two possibilities existed, neither of them very good. The man was in that car dead or about to be and his killer or killers were in the near vicinity or, the man was alive and maybe watching him right now.

Quickly deciding that discretion was the better part of valor Jim stopped and turned to go back to Eve and the car. "Excuse me Monsieur Creenshaw. Why are you leaving in such a hurry?" The question exploded like a grenade in the silence. It was the Corsican. Jim turned back to the clearing and there stood a medium built man with bright blue hair, a nose-ring, tattooed face and wearing a skin-tight black shirt. Next to him was the owner of the voice.

Neither the Corsican nor the blue haired kid made an impression on Jim. Instead, he was focused on the pistol pointed directly at his chest. "Did you want to join us for our little bonfire? We were just leaving but I am certain that if you want to stay we can arrange that." That comment sent the blue haired kid into a nervous laughter. The Corsican didn't even crack a smile. "I'd rather not," was all Jim could muster.

Chapter 48

Eve winced as a branch scraped the side of the car. "There goes the security deposit on this rental," she thought. The two-track had a very slight bend with branches and leaves overflowing into the path at this point. At the bend the branches obstructed her view. She slowly crept round the brush. On the far side the trail straightened out once more. She could see nearly thirty yards straight ahead, but nothing to the sides.

The two assailants motioned Jim out of his hiding place to the center of the clearing. "I think it rather rude of you to be spying on us," said the Corsican. "Had I known you were coming I would have brought – what do you call them? Hamboogers." The blue haired kid thought this was tremendously funny. "Unfortunately, we do not have time for one of your cook-outs, no? So, I believe it is time we put a stop to your spying and allow me to go about my business." At that he reached to his young partner and pulled a length of rope from the man's coat pocket. Grabbing Jim's elbows the Corsican stepped behind and began to loop the rope around Jim's arms.

The Citroën gently ghosted its nose out of the woods. Eve spotted the three men at the center of a clearing, some twenty yards away. The first man was their kidnapper! Across from him stood a strange man, no…make that a strange boy with blue hair! Between them was her Jim. It took only a moment, but Eve reacted like a woman possessed. She mashed the accelerator petal to the floor.

The car seemed to squat for a moment then leap forward as the front-end shocks were compressed under the sudden acceleration then released. The car engine roared, dirt sprayed the sides of the little car as she centered the nearest assailant in her sights. The men all turned in unison as the previously overlooked vehicle bore down on them. It only took a moment. Eve shot across the clearing, hitting the Corsican square in the middle of his hip and flipping him up and off the side of the car. His gun flew out of his hand, sailed straight up, banged off the top of the car and was deflected into the long grass. The man/boy/thug, having caught the danger just a bit earlier dove out of Eve's path to the right, rolled in the grass, came up on his feet and sprinted to the

Corsican. Jim, his hands not yet tied had deftly side-stepped the on-rushing Citroën. The car stopped and Eve opened the door.

"Oh my God, did I hit that man? Is he all right?" Eve didn't have a mean bone in her body and her genuine concern was evident.

"Eve, he's fine! Get back in. Let's get out of here!" Jim was running to the passenger side of the car. The Corsican was up and both he and blue boy were frantically searching for his gun. Eve wasn't slow. She instantly recognized that maybe she hadn't hit him hard enough and she was back in the car in a second. An instant later Eve and Jim were speeding around the clearing, dirt flying and heading for the path they had just traveled.

In mere moments they had cleared the woods, found highway D36 and were on their way to Paris. In the distance they could hear the distinctive sounds of a European emergency services siren. They turned toward Paris and proceeded calmly on their way. A few moments later a fire truck raced past them. Jim watched the truck disappear in the rear view mirror, turned to Eve and assured her that no one was following them.

They came to the road repair bottleneck and successfully passed through it. Neither was able to put into words the feelings of fear and confusion they were experiencing. Finally, they reached N118. Before entering the highway Eve pulled to the side of the road and parked. Turning to Jim, her voice cracking she said, "You idiot, you could have been killed!"

"I'm sorry hon. It sort of seemed like a good idea at the time," he said with a sympathetic smile.

"Oh Jim, how lame, 'sounded like a good idea'? You sound like an airman basic," her voice a sob mixed with a laugh.

They sat there for a few moments in silence. "Thank you hon, that was a close one. I'm sorry I scared you." She leaned her forehead against his. "Jim, don't ever do something that stupid again. I put up with 27 years of deployments and separations and late nights. I don't need you getting hurt now." Jim couldn't tell if she was more mad than relieved but figured he was in enough trouble that he'd better not ask.

After a few moments silence Jim whispered, "We're missing something. What was that brown car doing at the Louvre? Why take it out into the sticks and burn it?"

Eve had regained her composure and was now getting out

of the driver's door. She walked around to the passenger side. "Good questions. I have no idea what the answers are. But, I do know this. I'm not driving in Paris. Push over."

Chapter 49

Arriving in the center of Paris they quickly selected a new hotel, parked and entered the lobby. A small line had formed at the desk and they took up station directly behind a British businessman. After a few moments a second hotel desk clerk arrived and soon both the businessman and Jim were being helped. Completing the check-in process the man folded his receipt, pushed it into his pocket and walked through the lobby; Jim and Eve right behind. Soon they were approaching the elevators, at that moment the man's cell phone rang. He stopped, placed his hotel key on the lobby table, answered his phone and, holding the phone with his shoulder attempted to remove several documents from his briefcase. It was a bad plan. The phone began to slip; instinctively the man's right hand went from the briefcase to the phone. This caused a loss of grip on the briefcase and it crashed to the floor spreading paper about the lobby floor. Eve immediately bent to assist him in picking the papers up.

It was a spur of the moment decision. Jim saw his chance and deftly picked up the man's room key and replaced it with his own. Moments later Jim, Eve and the Brit were loading into the elevator. When the man left Jim turned to Eve and said, "I'm probably getting paranoid but have you noticed how many people seem to know our name, where we're staying or what we're doing?"

She nodded and Jim held up the room key. "I switched keys with the British guy."

Eve smiled and took the key from Jim. "That, sir, was a great idea."

An hour later, having showered and changed clothes Eve was ready for dinner. Jim, pleased with his James Bond switch of the room key was hungry too. They exited the hotel's side door and walked toward the Louvre. After a short walk they were seated in a pleasant café next to a window overlooking the Rue du Rivoli, just a few hundred yards from the parking garage entrance to the Louvre.

Dinner was wonderful, and they lingered over a bottle of wine and basket of French bread. They discussed the day's events and rehashed their adventure. Jim took a sip of his wine then leaned forward, "Remember what we were talking about before we saw that Mercedes drive by?"

"Yeah, we were talking about you cutting me off in Marcil's office."

"No Eve, we were past that. We were talking about how, if Jean's lab found the formula for the paintings why didn't the most famous art laboratory in the world?"

"Yeah, I know. I just wanted to remind you about cutting me off," Eve smiled. "Anyway, maybe the Louvre made a mistake? Or, maybe Jean was wrong?"

"Somehow I doubt that. Remember, we're talking about the most famous museum in the world. I just find it very hard to believe that they would miss something like that. In fact, ya know, I wonder. Let's….What time is it in Montreal?"

"Jim, you know I'm not good at that. Let's see. When we lived in Italy it was six hours earlier in Italy than at home. No, wait, people called us in the middle of the night so it was six hours later. But, France is an hour or two different than we were… I'm not sure, about four hours I think.

"I think we're good, let's call Jean." Jim said.

It was just after 4 P.M. in Montreal. Jean had just finished teaching her one required undergraduate class and was walking to her office when her cell phone rang. Eve briefly ran through the events of the past few days, lightly passing over the men with the guns. Then, almost casually, she asked if there was a chance that Jean had made a mistake or if Jean's lab was better than the one at the Louvre.

"Oh, no, absolutely not…" Jean stated emphatically. "First, I didn't make any mistakes and second, sadly, my lab isn't as well equipped as the Louvre's lab. But, think about it, they have significantly greater funding. They've purchased the finest spectrometers, ion radiation detection equipment; even some of the world's best electron microscopes. Why? Are you hinting that they disagreed with my findings? There's no way. We're dead on. I supervised the tests and we ran them multiple times." Jean began to become excited. "No way were we off on those tests." She was emphatic by this time.

"No, no, nothing like that," Eve said doing her best to downplay the question and even to her own ear it sounded hollow. Eve then attempted to steer the conversation to small talk and finally was able to gracefully end the call.

She turned to face Jim. "It doesn't seem as if there's any realistic way the Louvre missed the paint recipe thing," she said putting the phone back in her purse. "Something is really odd here."

"That means somebody is playing a game. Which, also means that I think someone is trying to steal our tube and Patent. And, that's a pretty valuable pair of items that I don't think we should just give up on." Eve could see Jim was getting angry.

"I still think we could go to the police," she murmured, knowing it was an idea that was dead on delivery.

"Eve, you and I both know, we'll never see those things again if we do that. And, Marcil said he was going to notify every law enforcement office in the country. What if he did? Who are they going to believe? Him or us? We'd be in jail or tossed out of the country in a heartbeat. Face it babe, we're screwed. We can't go to the police."

She looked hard at Jim. Then she decided she'd had enough of guns, kidnappers and Royal Patents. "I don't want to think about this junk any more. I want to be a tourist. I want to see Paris," she said.

Jim thought about the danger, about a courteous killer, and decided the odds of him finding them while they were being totally random tourists was very small. "I agree. Let's see Paris at night from the Eiffel Tower."

Chapter 50

Early the next morning Jim and Eve sat in the salon of the hotel and sipped their coffee. Last night's optimism had given way to this morning's depression. Eve was trying to feel good about the adventure they'd experienced and failing miserably. Jim was becoming more and more depressed that they'd not been able to recover the sword and other items, and the fact that it now appeared he'd lost the Royal Patent as well. To add to their concerns, they were feeling the pressure of their airline return tickets. Their return flight to the States left in three days, and they really hadn't solved anything, instead they'd found more questions than answers.

"Okay," Jim said after twenty minutes of near silence, "I'm starting to have some serious questions about our buddy Paul Marcil. He's got to be working both sides of the street."

"I'm not sure I understand what that scene in his office was all about yesterday. Why so rude. He's already holding all the cards," Eve observed.

"Well, that's a good question, but I was wondering why Marcil lied to us about the painting on the Patent?" Jim asked.

Eve looked up from her croissant. She stared off into space, thought for a moment and said, "I don't think the lab techs at the Louvre missed that. They're supposed to be the best."

"I agree. They didn't missed anything," answered Jim. "I don't think he knew about the original artist and the paint and the identification via recipes because he didn't really get the thing authenticated. He couldn't."

"Oh Jim, that's a pretty big leap," Eve cautioned. "Does it make any sense for him to tell us he had it authenticated and not really do so? What good is that?" Eve was doing her best to play Devil's advocate.

"Hear me out…" Jim insisted. "I think he didn't want others in the Louvre to know what he had. I think he offered us five million bucks to get us to give him the Patent and container. I think he knew that the sword of Charlemagne, the Coronation Crown and the Holy Ampule all traveled together. Bill and Jean aren't the only French Revolution experts around you know. And, since we found a piece, he knew the rest were probably in the same place. So, he had some goon follow us. But, those two guys didn't like each other. That's why when you conked the first one on the head the second one didn't fix him up or try to get him in the car. He left him there. In fact, that first guy acted like he was all alone. He may not have even known about the second. Maybe there are two groups trying to get the sword and the other stuff? Or, maybe the boss sent a second guy to check up on the first?"

"Oh Jim, you're becoming quite the conspiracy theorist, aren't you? We don't have any evidence to support that. How could you prove any of it, even if it were true?" she insisted.

"And," Jim continued "...remember the blue car that we saw on the drive to Cherhery?" Eve nodded her head. "We both commented on it being odd that it was behind us for most of the trip." She again nodded her head affirmatively; then took a bite of her croissant.

"Did you tell anyone where we were going after we left Paris?" Jim still hadn't moved his fork.

"No, I was with you the entire time." She spoke slowly, thinking over her answer.

"But that doesn't mean that I didn't tell someone. And, I think I did." Jim said thinking through what he was about to say.

"I don't remember you telling anyone where we were going." Eve offered her support.

"Remember when we met with Marcil? He got me talking about what we were going to do while his laboratory validated the Patent. I told him we were going to go look at some of the battlefields where my Great grandfather fought. I told him what division he fought with...and, I specifically mentioned the town of Sedan. Well, we were only a few miles short of Sedan when we were at Cherhery and Cheveuges," Jim explained. "It wouldn't take a lot of research to show that the 32nd was busy in those towns too."

"I have kind of wondered who the skinny guy was calling when we were in the car. It sounded like he was reporting in or something like that," Eve offered.

"Exactly, he was reporting to his boss. And, just how did not one, but two people know where we were and that we were after something worth a ton of coin? You know who I think that boss is? Paul Marcil!" Jim was becoming even more sure of himself.

"I must admit, you're putting together a pretty sound case, but it's all circumstantial. We don't have any real proof." Eve was trying to be responsible and rational, but Jim could tell he was winning her over.

"Then here's my final argument," Jim said defiantly. "Yesterday, what was that all about? We explained everything to him. We discover something they haven't found in over two hundred years, and we get treated like dirt. What happened to his offer to buy the Patent and the container? The five million? Gone. I'm sure he lied about that too." Jim was getting excited. "Oh, and what about the odd circumstance of the same car, driven by the same lunatic that kidnapped us, driving around in the parking garage under the very building where Marcil works?" Jim sat back in his chair looking very sure of himself.

Eve thought for a moment. "Okay, assuming you're right on all that, why go out and burn the car?"

"They were dumping the car because we had seen it and could probably identify it to the police. It's the only tie between the skinny kidnapper guy and Marcil." Jim was pleased with himself. He put his fork down, folded his arms and looked very serious.

Eve looked at him, noticed the very serious look on his face then smiled. "You could pull off that tough guy pose if you didn't have so much gray over your ears."

Jim started to laugh. "Seriously hon, Marcil's a bad guy. I'm sure of it."

She studied Jim's face. "All right, I agree. But what do we do now?"

"I didn't say I had all the answers. I just have the sight picture. We're going to have to think this over a bit.

They left the rest of their breakfast on the table and walked out to the street. Paris street life was fully awake and the sights were straight from a movie. Eve looked at Jim. "You do know how to show a girl a good time," she said with a grin.

They began to walk toward Notre Dame Cathedral when Jim stopped and grabbed Eve's arm. "I've got an idea. Look, we're pretty sure Marcil's behind our little misadventure in Cherhery and Cheveuges right? We think he's the boss that fancy kidnapper guy was phoning. So, if that guy delivered the sword and the other stuff to Marcil, and it looks like he did; then I think the delivery was at the museum. That's why we saw his car in the garage. That means he's got to move the boxes out of the museum maybe even the Patent. We need to follow Marcil. He's got to move the stuff and I'll bet it's tonight."

"You and your following people! What are we going to do? Jump a man with a gun, tie him up and point the sword at his heart?" Eve was not liking this new adventure one bit. "Why not just go to the cops now?"

"Hon, Marcil has contacts in the police. We don't know who or how many. If we approach the wrong guy or the wrong detective is assigned to the case we're in deep trouble. Knowing Marcil, he'd have us in jail for months."

"Okay, that's a good reason. But why follow Marcil? He had all last night to get rid of the sword and the other box. Why didn't he move the stuff out then?"

"Because he was lazy, there was that festival and too many people on the street, because the Mercedes had just delivered it, because we were there that afternoon, because all the investigative staff was looking into us and our story, because…hell, I don't know…" Jim paused, then brightened.

"Wait, yes I do. Of course he couldn't move it last night. The Louvre had that charity event and the opening of a new display that he put together. He was too busy. I'll bet he hobnobbed with the movers and shakers of the Paris art world all night. Remember he was pretty proud of that event when he told us all about it. Look hon, all I can say is let's hope he didn't. It's our only chance. Besides, we've been to cathedrals before, this one's just the same."

She laughed, "Oh, I'm sure that will go over big with the Paris Chamber of Commerce tourist guy."

"Eve, you know I'm right. We've got to follow him and get that sword and our Patent back." Jim was getting serious again.

"Well, it's a plan. I'm not saying it's a good one, but it's a plan."

"…not exactly, but I'm putting one together," Jim said with a smile.

"I'm not going to like this I can tell," she replied.

They began walking back to their hotel. Suddenly Eve stopped. "Jim," she said. Jim immediately noticed the sober tone of her voice and turned to her. "If they burned the car because we had seen it and could describe it to the police…don't they have to get rid of us too?"

Chapter 51

That evening the Council met to hear Marcil's report. The écuyer of the Duke of Orleans finished reading the five-page document, bowed curtly and assumed his position behind the head of the table. The council was no longer formed into a committee of the whole. The Duke of Orleans had assumed his position in the chair reserved for the Prince du Sang. He did not believe there would ever be a formal, recognized King of France again, but that did not alter the fact that indeed, one existed. These items would deliver the continuity with the past that he represented. They discussed Marcil's report. The Americans would soon be gone, back to some state no one ever had heard of, then disposed of. Why did all Americans believe everyone in the world knew the location of each of their many states? He sighed deeply. The detectives would be dealt with. The story was therefore contained.

They moved on to Marcil himself. He was not well liked; his past carried a certain, what? A certain odor was the best way to describe it. But, he was.....useful. It was a question of degree; was he of more use than liability? His current position did put him in place to make exactly these types of finds. And yet, what use were they really? His efforts had not paid great returns on the money they had invested in him. He had high aspirations. Something which could lead to problems in the future. They knew he aspired to sit at this very table, which of course was impossible. The Council began to discuss the pros and cons of the issue. It was a short conversation; Marcil would not become a royal or even a noble. This one, spectacular find did warrant a reward. But, there needed to be a pattern of such benefits to the Action Française to grant anything like a nobility. They would grant him a few hundred thousand Euros. That was more than sufficient and if it was not, he could be dealt with in other ways. The Prince du Sang approved the expenditure. But, he wasn't so sure. Marcil could become much like his uncle, more a burden than an asset. In any case, after this he would bear watching.

Next on the agenda were the promotions in the Army. Certain members of the Senate did not approve of some of the selections. This must be changed. Then there was the silly issue of this President's mistress and her modeling. This was unacceptable. She would have to be dealt with. A nomination of a Frenchman to the Presidency of the International Monetary Fund was approaching. They would have to choose someone for that. Members of the Government wanted to trim the nuclear industry. That too needed to be changed. There were too many men here whose wealth depended in part on this industry. It would simply be too expensive. A member of the opposition was gaining popularity and had decided to campaign for the Presidency. He was unacceptable and would soon be accused of raping a hotel maid. Palatine sighed. This would be a long, but profitable night.

Chapter 52

I

The Corsican's Paris flat occupied the entire top floor of a four-story walk-up three blocks off the Champs-Elysees. This morning he sat on a small balcony overlooking the street. The ice pack on his hip had turned to a room temperature wet rag an hour ago. His hip hurt and sported a large multi-coloured bruise, but he didn't notice the pain. His demitasse of espresso was untouched and cold. He was deep in dark thoughts. Marcil hadn't wanted anything to happen to the Americans. He'd demanded the Corsican not harm them. That had been a mistake. They should have been killed in Cherhery and none of this would be an issue. He'd left two people alive who could describe him. He had not done that before, and he had argued the point with Marcil. An argument he ceded. That too had been a mistake.

He had attempted to disassociate himself from the car. That hadn't gone well at all. The Americans had stumbled into the scene just as his lover arrived to take him back to Paris. This entire job, simple as it had been, was mismanaged from the beginning. No more. The Americans were on to something. He didn't know how much they knew, but they'd followed him yesterday; which meant they knew enough.

He'd never completely disregarded his customer's wishes in matters such as this but, frankly, sometimes the customer is wrong. Now, it didn't really matter what Marcil thought. He could be identified. His lover could be identified, which meant, sadly, that it had been necessary to dispose of him. Business risk was accumulating. The two Americans represented that risk if they remained alive. He made up his mind. He was going to take care of this issue today. Now, it was simply a matter of tracking down the two fools and making their disappearance look like a Paris street crime.

He would begin with the license plate of their car. He'd noticed the rental car at the barn, a low-end Citroën C3 Picasso. How could they drive across the country in such an uncomfortable vehicle? He shuddered at the thought. Nevertheless, they had done it and now that was the vehicle he had to find. Once he found that, he would have their hotel.

II

The word gendarme derives from *gens d'armes*, meaning men-at-arms. These armored soldiers had supplanted the armored knight as medieval society had faded. By the fifteenth century the men-at-arms had become a fixture of French society; their roll had been defined and solidified. They came from the nobility just as a medieval knight. They provided their own armor, horses and other equipment just as a knight. But, now they were organized and attached to a formal, semi-permanent army as part of the French cavalry. They had been organized into a fearsome unit, and the French heavy cavalry had become a superior weapon of war.

But it was not simply a military necessity that the gens d'armes had filled. Certainly, they filled a legitimate need for power on the battlefield. For that the kingdom had been grateful. Equally important the gens d'armes provided an honorable, well-paid lifestyle for the second sons of landed Nobility. These men were without inheritance, but were educated and well trained. They could not take a job and they had few assets. It simply would not do to have them running about without means of support and no means to maintain their honor. That was a certain route to disruption and possible overthrow of the system.

In time, heavy cavalry became a thing of the past as gunpowder replaced swords and lances. The roll of these men changed to one of protecting internal routes of travel from gangs, thieves and pirates. They became a sort of nascent national police force. Eventually this role was formalized and the new organization was charged with formal police powers and entitled "Le Maréchaussée", or the Constabulary. This remnant of the Ancien Régime could not be allowed to stand unchanged by the leaders of the French Revolution, and it was renamed the *"Gendarmerie."*

Today, its role has evolved. No longer charged with simply the protection of rivers and roads it now took the French lead in the pursuit, detention and defeat of terrorists and other extremely violent criminals. The Gendarmerie has become an extremely efficient paramilitary organization and is one of the premier policing organizations in the world. It was to this unlikely organization that the Corsican now turned.

It always helps to maintain contact with old friends he thought. Especially when those friends like to gamble, are not very good at it and happen to be members of the Gendarmerie.

The Gendarmes had recently succeeded in fielding a new computer system that tied together police logs, traffic enforcement, security, licensing, and other law enforcement databases in Europe. Using this system, the Gendarmes could check traffic tickets issued in the smallest village as well as access Interpol to review the most complex investigations. Thus, if one has a friend from one's days in the Foreign Legion, one has, depending upon the strength of the friendship, access to every French city's police computers. These databases were not the object of the Corsican's desire however. The hotel registry was. In Paris, as in the rest of France and most European countries, it is mandatory when checking into a hotel to register one's passport and complete a vehicle registration. This registry, also recently computerized and now tied to the police information mining system, has become a powerful tool in locating and preventing criminal and terrorist acts across France. Few were as skilled at the use of this new computerized tool than the Gendarmerie's Chief of Data Management in the city of Tours.

The Corsican enjoyed the early morning. The air didn't have the taste of car exhaust…yet. The sun seemed brighter and the sky bluer. He sat on a park bench and watched the traffic on the river Seine. He finished his coffee, ate the last of his brioche and made his phone call. Half an hour later his smart phone vibrated. Glancing at it he allowed himself a small smile. He had the name of the Americans' hotel. He stood, messaged his hip just a bit and began walking. It was still early, and it would take less than twenty minutes to reach the hotel. He would take them in the garage. A short ride to the countryside and he would be done with this little task by noon. He planned on spending the remainder of the day touring the Versailles palace. Later he had a plane to catch.

Precisely twenty minutes later he was strolling the hotel parking lot. After a short search he'd found what he was looking for. A large BMW, with an equally large trunk, perfectly positioned for watching the Citroën.

High-end BMW's are not the average thief's first choice. The doors are difficult to open. Its keys are electronically verified. A 'slim jim' is rarely successful. Instead, it takes a bit of skill, an electronic universal key and the use of specialized lock picking tools to open their door. Fortunately, he had all of the above.

Acting as if he had the proper key he removed a set of jigglers from his coat pocket, inserted one in the driver's door lock and scraped the bottom of the cylinder. This he did while manipulating the electronic key. In a moment he was sitting behind the steering wheel and had begun his wait. It would be bad luck for the owner of the BMW to come for his car just now. But, these things happen in life, and in death.

The morning stretched into midday. The garage was mostly empty. Most had checked-out of the hotel earlier that morning and no one could check-in until midafternoon. Hunger was his biggest distraction. He had been hungry before, infinitely hungrier than this. It wasn't an issue. He was more bored than anything. He was supposed to be enjoying a visit to Versailles today; instead, here he sat.

An hour later, a motorcycle, its driver wearing a full facemask and black leathers, with a boy riding behind in similar gear, rolled into the garage. The Corsican slouched lower in the front seat of the beamer. The motorcycle circled the parking garage once and returned. It slowed and abruptly turned down the row of cars across from him, stopping in-front of the Citroën! What was this? The boy got off, waved at the driver of the bike and, using a key, opened the door of the car. In a second the two were leaving the garage! Damn!

Cursing for allowing himself to be surprised he frantically searched his pockets for his electronic universal key. It took a moment to find. He had the key and the jigglers and set to work on the ignition. These cars were even more difficult to start than they were to unlock. It took him a full ninety seconds to start the engine. He backed out of the parking space and sped to the exit of the garage. There he looked left and then right, his quarry was no-where in sight. He turned left. Jim and Eve had turned right.

Chapter 53

The BMW F800 ST motorcycle is a well-balanced, euro cruiser. Its rider sits centered over the bike, feet directly below the seat; unlike an American cruiser with its laid back, 'easy-rider' mystique. This one was well handled, leaning into turns and accelerating out with a bit of panache. The bike sped northwest. Eventually it passed the Republic subway station then leaned through a sharp left followed by an equally quick right onto the Boulevard Saint-Martin. Passing several small boutiques the bike slowed. Eventually finding the appropriate shop the driver braked hard, rolled the bike between two cars, parked and hurried into the shop. A few moments later the driver returned, stuffed a package into the hard side touring case then backed the bike into the street and sped off; a Citroën C3 in close pursuit. Eventually, Saint-Martin turned into Montmartre. At Rue de Richelieu they turned left and accelerated. Three blocks later they were at the Louvre.

Circling to the left around the museum the bike eventually came to the underground parking garage. It stopped fifty feet short of the entrance. The driver dismounted and removed his helmet. Then, unsnapping the right saddlebag he removed a small plastic bag and walked to the Citroën.

"You know the plan?" "Got it," came the reply.

"I tested the radios in the shop, they're good. Use the ear plug, it has a microphone about six inches lower on the cord, it plugs into the radio here." He pointed as he talked. Jim handed Eve a small two-way radio. "You'll still have to push the button to talk, and let up on it to receive, but it's still easier like this, especially if you're in traffic. Got the map?"

Eve looked at him, "I've got the map, and I know how to use the radio. I'm just scared they'll catch you."

Jim leaned down and kissed her. "They're not going to get me. Don't worry about that." A car honked behind the Citroën. He kissed her again then returned to the bike. A few moments later he was entering the underground Louvre parking garage.

He parked the bike in the public area and locked his helmet in place. He removed the jacket and rolled it into a tight ball. Then, he took a backpack and a set of binoculars from the saddlebags; replacing them with the jacket. Next came a small brightly colored package from the other side. This he sat on the garage floor. Squatting next to the motorcycle he pretended to be working on the motor. Instead, he carefully scanned the garage to find any video cameras. There were three, two facing the entrance, the third in the general direction of the internal ramp leading to the lower parking level. Picking up the backpack and the small package Jim walked to the employee section and again carefully checked for cameras. He didn't see any, but that didn't mean they weren't there.

Squaring his shoulders and taking a deep breath Jim walked into the employee parking area as if he owned the entire museum. As he walked he flashed back to an afternoon as a student at the United States Air Force's Air War College. The irony struck him. The instructors had moderated a debate on the implications of George Jacques Danton's famous saying "Audacity, more audacity, always audacity." Funny, he never thought he'd be a living test of a leader of the French Revolution's favorite maxim, but here he was. Keeping an even pace he scanned for video cameras. There was only one and it pointed at the exit. He crossed to the far end of the parking garage and found a spot between two cars where he could sit with his back against the wall and still see the elevator doors.

Jim removed the package from his pack and blew up a beach toy. Putting the air pillow on the pavement he sat down. Perfect. He then removed the binoculars and checked the garage. No one. He pushed transmit on the radio and spoke into it. Eve immediately responded. She was sitting at the café across the street, the car at the curb in front of her. Again, perfect. He settled in to wait.

Chapter 54

I

Paul Marcil could not be a happier man. His day had been spent receiving congratulations on a tremendously successful fundraiser the previous evening. He had been the center of attention. He'd rubbed elbows with the elite of Paris. This, plus his recent chairing of a major new art exhibit were highlights in his "normal" life that he truly appreciated. His training in art and art history had been successful and vindicated. Even more gratifying and definitely more enriching, he now had four of the rarest, most valuable historical and artistic items in the history of France locked in his office.

That thought gave him pause. He smiled. He estimated their worth in the thirty to fifty million euro range. Of course, there would be authentication issues, but he felt reasonably certain these could be dealt with; the preponderance of the evidence seemed to support his belief that these were the real thing. The coronation crown, even melted to a lump of gold, was worth a small fortune. He had no idea of the value of the Holy Ampoule, but the gold, rubies and jewels making up the necklace were certainly worth several million. The Patent and its tube would sell conservatively for something north of five million; but the *piece de resistance* was the sword of Charlemagne. He could only fantasize about its value.

Hitler had tried to find the sword, believing it held great power and would make him invincible. The French Kings had paraded it at their coronation as a symbol of their power. He tried to imagine a value. It was impossible. He had an item that was priceless. When he presented it and the other items to the Council they would have to welcome him to the table. Surely he would be made a nobleman. This was his chance to have real power. He was going to be well taken care of.

II

At 5 PM the museum offices closed for the day. Office workers streamed out of the elevator. Jim hadn't thought about this. He'd assumed that Marcil would come to the garage well before the office workers and day shift personnel went home for the day. That didn't appear to be the case. A young woman approached his hiding spot. She got into the car to his immediate right and started the engine. Jim quickly crawled around the front bumper of the car to his left. The girl pulled out of the slot and drove away. Fortunately, Jim was in deep shadow.

A prudent man would standup, join the crowd and leave right now he thought. He stayed. Binoculars centered on the elevator doors. Thirty minutes passed. Another fifteen. Eve was calling. What was the status? Status? Zero, nil, nothing that was the status. Jim was bored, stiff and sore.

Finally! Marcil stepped off the elevator. He carried a backpack and had what appeared to be a cloth shopping bag. He must have the Patent in one of those bags. Marcil walked the length of the parking garage until he was parallel with Jim. The taillights of a large, luxury sedan began to flash on and off, its horn sounding in rhythm with the lights. The car was two rows in front of Jim. Jim quickly glassed the license plate. Then the trunk popped open. Marcil glanced around to ensure he was alone and then placed the book bag and shopping bag in the trunk. Taking a last look he slammed the lid shut.

Jim placed the helmet on his head and, remembering to act like he belonged, calmly walked out of the shadows toward his motorcycle. Glancing sideways at the vehicle he identified it as a Renault Latitude. Marcil was now getting into the car. In a moment the motor was running.

Jim found the bike, took his seat and keyed the microphone. "Eve, it's a Renault Latitude, that's the big one. It's dark blue or black. I'm not sure because of the light in here. I think he's got everything in the trunk."

"Okay, I'm ready," she replied.

The Renault backed out of its slot and Jim started the bike. Raising the visor and keying the radio at the same time Jim whispered, "Here he comes."

The car rolled to the exit, paused and then joined the

traffic on Rue de Rivoli. Eve had timed her departure perfectly. She placed the Citroën three cars behind the Renault and matched his speed. Jim waited thirty seconds, exited the garage and accelerated to catch his wife and his target. "I'm three behind him," she said into the microphone. They traveled through the city for ten minutes like this. Approaching the traffic circle at the Arc De Triomphe, Jim again accelerated. He passed Eve and settled into a spot just one car length behind Marcil. Eve turned onto Avenue Victor Hugo and parked. Moments later Jim's voice shouted in her ear, "He's taking Pelouse de la Muette."

"What? Wait." Eve studied her map. "I can't find that. What the heck is that? Your French is terrible." Eve exclaimed. "Spell it."

"Spell it? Eve, I'm on a friggin' motorcycle; I don't know how to spell French." Jim sounded exasperated over a radio.

"Eve, never mind! It's the A13, it's the per-pen-frique extra something.

She studied the map. There it was the A13 or Peripherique Exterieur. "It's the Peripherique Exterior. I've got it." She shouted into the microphone. She pulled on to the street and raced to intersect her husband.

Jim decelerated. He was on a highway now. The advantage was that he could legitimately stay fairly close without passing his prey. The disadvantage was the he was very visible to every driver on the highway, including Marcil. Suddenly his ear piece barked, "I'm just entering the A13 where are you?" "Just passed exit four," Jim replied. "Okay, I'm at exit two," came the welcome response. Eve accelerated again, hoping there were no Paris policemen in the vicinity. A few moments later she swung her car behind Jim's motorcycle and matched his speed. The Renault then left the road at exit 5 and joined the D182. Jim spotted a hill and slowed the bike. Eve passed him and assumed his position two cars behind their target.

When the Renault and the Citroën crested the hill he braked to a stop on the side of the road. He dismounted and quickly removed his black leather jacket. He opened the left touring case and removed a red windbreaker. He then stuffed the jacket into the case and removed his helmet. He clamped the helmet in its lock and pulled wraparound sunglasses and a small cap out of the other case. Jim put them on, turning the cap backward so it wouldn't blow off in the wind then remounted the bike and sped after Eve and the Renault.

Jim spotted the Citroën as they neared Versailles. Accelerating hard he caught the quick moving but unintended procession and settled into a cruise some two-hundred feet behind her. There were two cars between Eve and Marcil, and to Jim's relief he didn't believe they had been spotted – at least not yet. After several minutes like this Jim again accelerated and passed Eve and then the first car. He was now just one car behind Marcil. Here he settled into a gentle cruise. He keyed his microphone and shouted over the wind, "Eve, drop back about a mile so you're out of sight." She slowly decelerated and soon was a distant spot in Jim's rearview mirrors. Jim followed for another few minutes then spotted a sign whose meaning was clear in any language, an outline of an airplane with the words "Toussus-le-Noble" underneath. He immediately keyed his radio "Eve, I think he's headed to Too-sus lay noble airport." She winced at the terrible French then picked up the map and held it against the steering wheel. Repeatedly glancing down at the map then up at the road she searched for the airport. It took her a moment, but finally she spotted it. "Okay, I've got it, do you want me to go there?" "Yes!" came the reply.

Chapter 55

Toussus-le-Noble airport is one of a series of regional airports which ring Paris. The two parallel runways, known by their respective compass heading and differentiated with a Left or Right are perfectly capable of handling most large commercial aircraft. However, there is no need as Charles De Gaulle Airport handles the vast majority of those flights. As a result, the airport plays host to a number of private jets belonging to the rich and famous, various Fortune 500 companies, the French government, medical and emergency services aircraft. But, because flying in Europe is significantly more expensive than in the United States the airport is generally quiet. It was especially quiet now in the early evening as all the airport workers had left for the day.

The Renault turned into the long airport drive. Jim, not wanting to be spotted, drove past the airport road and stopped behind a bank of shrubs which hid him from view. Marcil drove to a parking area across from the airport's small general aviation terminal. The parking lot was sparsely filled. A delivery van was parked at the far rear of the lot and five identical Fiats were parked all together in a middle row, a numbered sign in front of each. They must be rental cars Jim thought. In the front row was a Jaguar XJ. Marcil parked next to the Jag. Using the binoculars Jim watched him exit his car and walk into the terminal.

Just then Eve's panicked voice exploded in his ear, "Jim, I missed the exit! I've got to turn around. Where are you?" Jim explained the layout of the airport and the entrance road to the terminal. "Eve, he's going to fly outta here. You'd better hurry."

Suddenly, Marcil and another man walked out of the building to the Renault. Jim studied the new man carefully. It was their kidnapper! They walked toward the car. Its lights flashed as it was unlocked. As they rounded the rear of the vehicle the trunk lid popped open. Marcil lifted the backpack out of the trunk and put it on. He then picked up a black box and paused to wait for his companion. The well-dressed man had gone to the rear door of the four door sedan and pulled a long black box from the backseat. He quickly put it under one arm and closed the door. "That's the sword," Jim said out loud. The two men then walked into the terminal.

Jim's shoulders slumped. These two were going to fly away with a treasure of immeasurable value, and he was powerless to stop it. Jim wasn't certain what to do, but he did know that nothing good was going to come from just sitting on a motionless motorcycle waiting for an airplane to take off with what he now considered to be his and Eve's treasure. He started the bike and rode to the parking lot. There, he parked the motorcycle out of sight on the far side of the delivery van. Jim carefully stepped to the front of the van and began to watch the terminal through the van's passenger window and out the windshield. The time had given him a chance to relax a bit and begin to think over his next step. And that was the issue. What to do now?

A moment later the doors of the terminal building opened and their dapper kidnapper exited. He walked to his Jag, opened the trunk and removed a suitcase and suit carrier. The timing couldn't have been worse. Looking up, he froze as Eve drove the Citroën past the front doors of the terminal and into the far entrance of the parking lot. She didn't see the man at his car, her attention was focused on the terminal's front doors. She turned into the parking lot, drove past the rental cars and parked one row from where Jim now stood, unobserved by the van. The Corsican smiled, replaced his suitcase and suit carrier and walked toward the Citroën. Eve place the car in park and opened her door. Looking up she spotted the man and instantly recognized him. Fearing Eve would panic Jim quickly keyed his radio. She'd forgotten she wore the radio and she jumped when Jim's voice barked in her ear. "Eve, stay calm, keep talking to this guy and keep his back to me. Do you understand?"

The Corsican stopped ten feet from the car. "Mrs. Creenshaw how are you?" he said with a smile.

The Corsican had approached directly from his car. Jim couldn't think of worse luck. But, before he could radio Eve it became apparent she'd figured the angles already. Slowly she began to talk, all the while edging around in a wide circle. "Perfect, good girl," Jim thought. "I thought Jim told you its Crenshaw, not Creen-shaw," Eve shot back.

"Ah, how forgetful of me. Well, I'm certainly pleased that we've met once again. Tell me, Mrs Creen, ah…there I go…forgive me please. Tell me, Mrs. Crenshaw, tell me where your husband is right now would you please?" She continued to creep to her left, around the car, forcing him to turn to meet her gaze. Finally, his back was to Jim.

"I'm not telling you anything," Eve retorted. "Oh, how's your side? Understand you were in a bit of an accident?" Eve was going into her attack mode. "Hope your hip isn't bruised too badly." Jim couldn't believe it; she was taunting him! She had stopped with the car between herself and her antagonist. She was perfect; the taunts kept coming.

Jim started to creep across the parking lot; he was now twenty feet behind the man. His soft soled shoes were silent on the pavement and the Corsican's attention was on Eve. "Mrs. Crenshaw…" the Corsican spoke as he removed a silencer from his jacket pocket with his left hand. "…sarcasm does not become you. Now, I must again tell you that honesty is the only acceptable answer to my questions." He removed a pistol from under his jacket and placed the silencer at the end of the barrel. He paused before turning it onto the threads of the barrel. "You see Mrs. Crenshaw, it is very painful to have ones knees shot by a pistol. And, of course, it causes one to limp the rest of their life. You do not want this tragic fate to befall you, no?" His voice remained steady. Eve could feel the blood drain from her face.

Try as she might she was having problems staying composed. This latest threat didn't help. "No one is shooting my knees!" Eve nearly yelled.

The Corsican had the silencer on the threaded end of the barrel. He began to turn the silencer, tightening it down the threads and onto the barrel. Jim figured this was as vulnerable as the man would get, and he broke into a run. "Sort of like sacking the quarterback," thought Jim as he launched himself at the man's shoulders. He hit the Corsican high, driving him to the pavement and bouncing the side of his face on the blacktop. His gun hand hit the pavement. The pistol bounced once and slid under the car. Jim continued over the back of the Corsican and landed in a heap between the man and the Citroën.

Both the Corsican and Jim were up and facing each other immediately. "Ah…Mr. Creen-shaw, there you are." The man said slowly as he went into a classic *Savate* fighting crouch and began to circle Jim. "Ouch, you look terrible, that skinned up face has got to hurt," Jim replied.

The two men circled each other. After a moment the Corsican moved a step closer. Jim fought down his fear. A detached, other world voice spoke inside his head, "I've got him by a couple of inches and maybe thirty or forty pounds." They continued to circle. "Who am I trying to kid? I'm not really trained for hand to hand combat. I'm going to get my ass kicked. This is going to hurt."

The Corsican inched closer. He shifted his weight to his left leg and began a circle type kick. He didn't perform the move smoothly, his bruised hip prevented that.

"That son-of-a-bitch is going to try to kick me!" Jim thought. He was right. The Corsican's right leg shot out in the classic French kickboxing roundhouse style kick. Jim, anticipating the move had his left arm up. The man's shin crashed into Jim's elbow, shooting pain up the arm, but doing no permanent damage. The leg bounced off Jim's elbow and crashed into his ribs. Jim thought he heard a rib crack. Instinctively, Jim dropped his arm over the leg and pinned it to his side, leaving the Corsican on one leg.

The Corsican now had two choices. He could attempt to punch Jim in the face or jump and kick Jim with his other leg. He began to try the latter move. Jim, not knowing what he was supposed to do next, did what came instinctively. He hung on to the man's leg with his left arm and punched the smaller man in the nose with his right. Jim heard a distinctive crunch and then blood spurted from the man's broken nose. Suddenly, as the man reflexively raised his hands to protect his face Jim remembered watching Chuck Norris movies. He raised his right arm over his head and brought his elbow down on the pinned knee as hard as he could. A scream of pain erupted from the Corsican and he collapsed. Jim let go of the now limp leg and kicked the down man as hard as he could in the stomach. The Corsican, dazed, hurting and certainly not expecting any of this tried to get up; he rolled to his stomach and quickly got to his hands and knees. Jim had by this time completely lost control of himself. Seeing another opportunity he kicked the man's face as hard as he could. The Corsican's head snapped back, a tooth flew across the parking lot and he rolled over. Jim began kicking the man repeatedly in the face and body. Eve, having grabbed the gun from under the car screamed, "Jim stop, you're going to kill him. JIM STOP!"

The second yell penetrated Jim's now manic world. He snapped out of his trance. He stopped his kick in midair and looked at the man on the ground. His first reaction was horror. He'd nearly killed a man and didn't realize what he was doing. The man's face was a mass of blood and his nose was bent to one side. He lay on his side in a fetal position trying to protect his body and head. His beautiful suit was bloodied and torn.

Jim glanced at Eve. "Are you alright?" he asked, still in a bit of a daze. She nodded yes and handed Jim the pistol. Before anything more could be said the distinctive winding sound of a jet engine filled the air. Then, a "poof" as the engine lit and a scream as the pilot advanced and retracted the throttle. Quickly it settled into a steady jet engine drone.

They turned in the direction of the terminal, looked past it to the idling jet, and there was Marcil running up the steps of the doorway ladder wearing the backpack and carrying the two boxes. He turned, scanned the tarmac and the terminal for his companion and, not seeing him, lifted the door into place. Immediately the plane began to taxi.

Jim looked at Eve. The sound of the aircraft had snapped him back to reality. She appeared pretty calm, considering, and seemed to be in control of her emotions. "Eve, keep a gun on this jerk. Call the US Embassy, ask to speak to the military liaison. You've got to get them here immediately."

"How can I do that?" She asked.

"I don't know...make up a story. Tell him that your husband is a retired Colonel, with a top secrete clearance and is being kidnapped by a terrorist; tell them there's a bomb, just something! See the letters on the side of the airplane? Those are the same as the numbers on airplanes back home. Tell them those letters. Tell them where we are and to get the police here fast. Also, tell them to get an Embassy person here pronto. Got it?"

Eve nodded, "What are you going to do."

"Make sure that plane doesn't take off!" Jim yelled as he sprinted toward the motorcycle.

Chapter 56

Jim raced the bike across the parking lot and toward the terminal. The airplane, a twin engine Cessna Citation, pivoted on its right main wheel and began to taxi forward. In a moment it left the ramp and turned right on the parallel taxiway. Jim sped out of the parking lot toward the terminal building, spotted a small drive encircling the terminal building and turned onto it. The drive went to the front of the terminal and past the building's front doors. There he skidded to a halt. A fence separated him from the active airfield; there was no way to get through it in time. He could feel his chance passing. He raced past the terminal keeping the Citation in view to his left and accelerated down the hanger access road. Between each building was that damned fence. He continued past the third hanger. Their luck finally swung his way. A groundskeeper had just opened the gate to the airfield and was about to drive his lawn mower through. Jim gunned the motorcycle, jumped the curb and raced through the gate past the irate groundskeeper. He then rolled in the power and the BMW leapt forward.

Fortunately, the near runway was being resurfaced and was therefore closed. The jet had by now reached the end of the taxiway, turned left and continued past runway 25-Left toward runway 25-Right.

European airspace is strictly controlled. Aircraft have a very narrow window of time in which to take off. No early or late departures are allowed. This, combined with the necessary preflight inspection and cross-check procedures brought the business jet to a halt before its pilots pushed in the throttles and accelerated down the runway. Jim knew it was only a moment's stop. He was now at a loss. He had no idea how to stop that jet.

That was it; just stop the jet! Jim hadn't been a pilot in the Air Force; he'd been one of the thousands of people responsible for keeping airplanes flying. However, he did know a great deal about jet engines. The one overriding thing about jet engines is that they absolutely hate anything other than air being sucked inside. A tool, bird or anything of even negligible size entering the engine would strike several of the whirling turbine blades and cause extensive damage in the process. The picture was very similar to a lawnmower blade after its owner has run the machine over a large rock. A small item could do such extensive damage that the engine would require a complete overhaul. He simply needed to throw something in the engine!

Jim raced ahead of the airplane. As he passed it he could see Paul Marcil's face framed in the window behind the wing. He stopped the motorcycle at the end of the runway and dismounted. The airplane began to turn on to the runway. He only had seconds. The Citations' engines protrude from the fuselage just in front of the tail assembly. Jim ran to the side of the aircraft behind the wing. He could feel the air being sucked from around him up and into the engine. He threw his radio at the engine intake. It fell short, hit the side of the airplane, caught in the inflow of air, bounced off the bottom of the engine and smashed on the pavement. The engines began to increase their scream; the pilot was going to release the breaks any moment. The sound of the engine deafened him. His chest pulsed as the sound waves literally beat him.

Paul Marcil stared down at him from the window just over his head. His snicker had broken into an unconcealed grin. Jim searched for something else to throw at the engine. Then it hit him; he took off the jacket, waded it into a ball and threw. The river of air being sucked into the engine immediately grabbed the windbreaker. It spread out from the tightly wadded ball, briefly took the shape of a man with his arms spread wide and disappeared into the jet intake.

Almost at once the engine's sound frequency changed, a puff of smoke exploded from the rear then streaks of red began to appear in the exhaust of the engine. At the same time loud noises occurred and then an even louder bang as a hole appeared in the side of the engine nacelle. A turbine blade had separated and been launched through the side of engine. The screaming engine began to die; the pilot had shut it down. In contrast, the opposite engine began to scream louder, the brakes were released. For a moment Jim thought the pilot was going to attempt a take-off on only one engine. Disappointment washed over him. But the pilot, knowing one engine may be on fire and about to explode chose to turn back to the taxiway.

Jim raced back to the hangers. He exited the same gate,

then sped to the parking lot. There, he found Eve sitting on the trunk of one of the rental cars. The Corsican sat with his feet straight out in front of him some ten feet in front of her. Eve had the Corsican's gun in both hands, elbows on her knees and the gun leveled at the man. She began to get off the car and go to Jim when he called from the bike. "Don't take your eyes off that man!" The Corsican stared at Jim, one eye completely closed, his face bloodied and bruised. He couldn't go anyplace if he were sitting here alone. It was clear he had a concussion. Eve settled back on the car and refocused on the Corsican.

Jim parked the bike next to their rental car. Before he could dismount Eve said, "I called the Embassy. They said they'd have people here in about thirty minutes. Are you okay?" She spoke without looking away from the Corsican.

"I'm fine, but thirty minutes? Damn. We've got a problem." Jim was nearly yelling. "Marcil is on that plane, and if he comes off with a gun or there's more than just him on that thing we're in for some big time trouble." Jim took his belt off and circled the Corsican. He had the man put his arms behind his back, then cinched the belt tightly around the elbows. Jim then pulled the smaller man to his feet. A push and a shove and the Corsican was staggering to the middle of the parking lot. Jim sat the Corsican down and told him to kick off his shoes. Jim quickly removed the shoelaces and tied them together. He then pushed the Corsican's back against a street lamp. Looping the shoelace around the belt, then light pole he tied the man to the lamp, finishing with a square knot. Jim then ran back to Eve.

"We can't let these two get away. We've got to delay them until the Embassy or the police get here. That will hold him for a little bit, but it will only take a good hard pull to break the laces. Now, let's go." They ran back to the Citroën and drove to the delivery truck. "Hide behind this truck until the cops get here," Jim insisted. Then he moved the car to the opposite corner.

Chapter 57

Pistol in hand, an absolutely furious Paul Marcil ran out of the front door of the terminal. Glancing quickly around the parking lot he immediately spotted the Corsican. He jogged to the man and knelt to untie him. "Don't touch him!" Jim shouted as he stepped from behind the Citroën. Marcil looked up to see the Corsican's gun leveled at him. "I'm pretty good with a pistol. I don't think you want to find out how good," Jim shouted.

Marcil dove behind the street lamp, rolled and fired. Jim heard the bullet whine over his head and ducked behind the car. "Shit, he just shot at me!" Jim heard himself say.

Marcil, keeping the streetlamp and its concrete base between them quickly untied the Corsican. The man tried to stand up; it didn't work. He sagged back against the lamppost and slid to the ground. Jim, despite the danger he now found himself in, couldn't suppress a grin. At that point Marcil made a dash for the rental cars. Jim leveled his gun but hesitated. Shooting at targets or hunting was one thing. Shooting at a real person was another. Marcil was behind the first Fiat before Jim could fire.

An eerie silence broke out. Jim kept the Citroën between himself and Marcil. After three or four minutes of mere glimpses of his prey Jim decided he had a better chance if he were at the near end of the rental cars. He only needed a few moments to reach the spot.

Seeing Marcil peek up over the top of the first rental car Jim snapped off two shots, then dashed for the opposite end of the line of rental cars. Marcil returned fire but both men had missed their marks.

Eve began to silently cry. She could see both Jim and Marcil by stretching up and looking through the windows of the truck. She was certain that Jim was going to be killed. Suddenly Jim fired his gun, stood up and ran from behind their Citroën to the far rental car. He was getting closer to Marcil. Was he nuts? At this point fear was overcome by anger. What the hell was Jim thinking? She crept to the front of the van and peaked around the corner. Marcil had his back to her and was about forty feet away. The line of five rental cars were all that separated him from Jim.

Jim looked through the windows of the five Fiats. He could see Marcil, but a bullet couldn't pass through all those windows and find its mark. Jim moved to his right. Marcil watched Jim and slid to his own right. Stalemate. "Perfect" thought Jim, "…all I have to do is wait for the police."

Marcil evidently thought the same thing. He moved to his left and peered along the front bumpers of the cars. Jim looked back. Marcil fired. The shot missed wide left, but forced Jim behind the Fiat. Marcil stood up and started for his own car. Jim fired once, missed. Marcil thought better of the long open space and dove back behind the Fiats. Quickly getting to his feet he looked down the line of cars for Jim, didn't see him and ran to the trunk end of the car, stopped and peeked around the corner. No Jim. Turning rapidly he went back to the front of the car and looked for Jim on that end. Nothing. Marcil then got to his knees and peered under the cars. Nothing. Puzzled he returned to the bumper; again nothing. Panic was setting in. He whirled and went to the front. Then stood to look along the tops of the cars.

Eve took advantage of Marcil's preoccupation with finding Jim. She sprinted across the parking lot, coming to the last five feet she screamed at the top of her lungs and launched herself at Marcil's back. Landing with her legs on both sides of his hips she wrapped them around and crossed her feet. Her left arm went around his neck and she grabbed her wrist and pulled. Marcil was thrown forward, bounced off the Fiat and spun round. Eve stayed on his back like a rodeo rider. Jim, who had been hiding behind the rear wheel of the Fiat to confuse Marcil saw what had happened, swore and sprinted toward the bucking bronco that was Marcil. Seeing Jim sprinting at him Marcil attempted to level the gun but a thumb in his eye destroyed his aim. The shot went wild. Eve now bit his ear and Marcil screamed in pain. Jim rounded the corner of the last Fiat and put his shoulder into Marcil's stomach, knocking all three of them to the ground. Eve's grip never lessened. Another cry of pain as she drove her thumb into his eye once more. Jim was on his knees and grabbed Marcil's gun arm. Marcil screamed again as his wrist was bent backwards. He let go of the gun. Jim rolled away, grabbed the gun and was on his feet.

"EVE! Eve, okay, let him go!" Jim yelled, holding the pistol at Marcil's head. Slowly she released her grip and crawled away. Marcil rolled to all fours. Eve, now standing, kicked him in his butt as hard as she could. Jim looked at her astonished, then grinned.

Marcil began to stand up. "Don't temp me Marcil!" Jim shouted. The man sank to the parking lot and slowly raised his hands over his head.

Eve limped the few feet to Jim. "Are you hurt?" he asked as he wrapped one arm around her. "No…" she whispered, "…but I might have broken my toe when I kicked him."

Moments later the whine of sirens could be heard, then the blue lights of the French police. Two police cars and a white sedan raced into the airport. A United States Army Colonel approached as Jim and Eve waved both hands over their heads. "Mrs. Crenshaw?" he asked.

"Yes, and this is my husband, Col. Crenshaw. Thank you so much."

Chapter 58

The Secretary finished reading the motion, and the board members voted their approval. The men all stood and began filtering out of the room. A few lingered for the usual side conversations but essentially the thing was done; a small turbine parts manufacturer would shortly be absorbed by Perpétuel Energy. Several of the members offered their congratulations to the CEO. In fact, they were offering their thanks. This acquisition would significantly reduce operating costs, thus increasing their bonuses. Louis Palatine shook their hands and slapped their backs. But he did not linger; his real job, for running the Action Française was a job as well as a duty waited.

In short order he was whisked to a waiting limousine and taken to the airport. A Dassault 2000S was waiting. In less than an hour the airplane landed. His driver arrived as the aircraft steps gently touched the tarmac. In twenty minutes they were at the Cathédrale Sainte-Croix d'Orleans. He was early.

The Duke of Orleans, Prince du Sang and true King of France listened to the report of the écuyer. He had taken his seat as Duke. They were arrayed in the Committee of the Whole to listen to the report and to debate the next course of action. He couldn't believe that two simple Americans had actually won a fight against trained killers. Despite himself he smiled at the thought. To see Marcil and the Corsican now would be priceless. Somehow it was fitting; the two men were some of the most egotistical individuals he knew. Snapping his thoughts back to the matter at hand he listened carefully to the comments of his brothers on the Council. As usual, the group was split. Could these people never see the obvious? The debate raged; silence the Americans or drop the matter.

After ten minutes he stood, the room grew still. He walked to his chair at the head of the table. The Prince du Sang surveyed the room. "Mes amis," he began, "...our purpose is to ensure our people are ruled well. We need the respect of the people to accomplish this goal, n'est pas?" The Council members all nodded in agreement. "In this case our royal belongings have been returned to us, have they not?" The Duke of Normandy quickly objected, "Sire, they have not, our…your Royale Regalia has not been returned. They are now out of reach inside the Musée du Louvre."

"This is true mon ami, but, are the Regalia not now located in a most secure and noble location? Where would you have them? The people of France can now view them, appreciate them and dream. Our American friends have done us a great service. They have found and returned our property. Do not worry. The Regalia is available for our use when the time comes. We have other friends in the Musée du Louvre." He surveyed the table. Slowly heads began to nod.

"There is one other thing. We have on several occasions debated the usefulness of Monsieur Marcil, have we not?" Heads nodded around the table. "The man is crude at best and a liability at worst. He has had visions of joining this Council for some time. There is, in all honesty my friends, simply no foreseeable way for that to happen."

He surveyed the table. Some here did have a tie to Marcil, but he suspected those ties were not strong.

"Once Marcil realizes this he likely will turn on the hand that feeds him." Again the heads around the table nodded. "The Americans, they have rid us of an inconvenience, no?"

The Council members thought this over. The Duke of Bourbon finally spoke. "Our Prince is correct. We have a responsibility to France and her people. And, we have been rid of a loose cannon, a man whom we could never trust. A man who always wanted more, a peasant." One by one the realization of this simple truth crept around the table. The Council members nodded.

"Then I believe we have reached an agreement, no?" The Prince du Sang raised his hand. He looked first to his right, then left and made the sign of the Cross.

Chapter 59

Jim's new combine rolled steadily across the nearly frozen ground. The big red machine cut the corn stalks off at their knees while picking and shucking the cobs. It then sprayed the mast out behind. He loved this combine. It had a good cabin heater, it started up on the first turn of the key, it was easy to use and didn't take a lot of maintenance; what more could a man ask for?

He thought about Paul Marcil. The man had been stealing art from France for the past ten years. He'd headed a group of killers, art thieves and blackmailers with tentacles all across the country. It seemed impossible, but the French *Police Nationale* had solved more than two dozen crimes after questioning him. They had faced two professional killers and a madman. It was a miracle they had both survived. The French government had been grateful, extremely grateful. That, combined with the gratitude of the Louvre and he and Eve would not need to worry about the price of corn anytime soon.

In short order the last rows of standing corn were down. He unloaded the crop into a grain wagon. Hopping into the seat of his tractor, he pulled it to a small silo next to the barn. The corn wouldn't stay there too long, the market seemed to be moving in his direction, and he'd sell within a month.

He put the combine and the wagon in the equipment shed. The tractor went to the barn. Returning to the combine he spent the next hour cleaning, changing filters, greasing bearings and the other general work required to put the machine up for the winter. Then, for the next forty-five minutes he did the same with his tractor. He was certain he wouldn't be running these machines until the spring.

Stuffing his hands deep into his pockets and hunching his shoulders against the wind Jim left the barn. The snow wasn't deep, only an inch or two lay on the nearly frozen ground. He walked across the backyard to the house, knocked the snow off his boots on the bottom step then climbed the five steps to the porch. There, he turned and looked at his fields. With the corn down he could see the woods behind the house and the neighbor's fields on both sides of his. He preferred the summer when all he could see was his own fields and pasture. It was dusk, the wind was cold and the sky a metal gray. He opened the door and went inside.

"Are you done?" Eve called.

"Yup, everything is cleaned up and ready for the winter. That new combine is great, and nothing beats a heated cab."

She brought him a cup of coffee as he took off his boots. "Got the tickets…" she said, "…plane leaves next Friday."

"You know hon; at first I didn't like the idea, but a winter house in Key West. You're brilliant."

Postscript

Philippe Louis Palatine, Chairman and CEO of Perpétuel Energy, Duke of Orleans, Prince du Sang, and rightful King of France walked slowly along the sidewalk on the east side of the *Musée du Louvre*. In his hand he held a small package. Inside the package, a solid gold replica of the Sword of Charlemagne. The box was nearly a foot long and weighed over a pound. He stopped and stared at the museum for a long moment.

"Merci beaucoup," he whispered.

After a short walk he finally stepped to his limousine. A middle aged man, with salt and pepper hair held the door. "Have this delivered for me if you would Henri."

The man glanced at the package. "Sir, there is no address."

"Ah, yes, mail it to Jim and Eve Crenshaw, someplace in the United States. Michigan, I believe."

END

About the Author

HJ Gaudreau is a retired Air Force Colonel. Originally from Michigan, he currently lives with his wife Eve and beagle, Molly, in Oklahoma. They have one son, living very near to his Uncle Gerry and Aunt Sherrie.

The house is for sale and they hope to soon move home to northern Michigan.

SAMPLE HJ GAUDREAU'S NEXT NOVEL

THE COLLINGWOOD LEGACY

Only the treasure in an old smuggler's boat can save a business empire

Madness turns to murder

Follow Jim as he races to save his wife from a killer

Please enjoy the first seven chapters of H J Gaudreau's next thriller

Learn the truth behind the Royal Regalia, the Purple Gang and the Collingwood murders at:

www.HJGaudreau.com

THE
COLLINGWOOD
LEGACY

AVAILABLE NOW!

Chapter 1

Detroit, September 1931

Anna Lademan ran an iron along the length of a man's long sleeve shirt. Not satisfied with the result she sat the iron on its end and picked up a tall glass bottle with a yellow Vernor's label and a cork sprinkler head. She gave the bottle a shake and scattered small droplets of water along the sleeve. Again taking up her iron she finished the sleeve, placed the shirt on a hanger, and hung it next to a dozen similar shirts. After a quick glance at the remaining baskets of laundry she placed her hands on her hips, bent backward, chin to the ceiling and sighed. At five cents a shirt she could not afford to rest, but she had earned a quick stretch.

Anna then took a woman's floral dress from her basket and began to spread it on her ironing board. She did this with a bit of nostalgia. Her wedding dress had been a pretty flowered dress like this one. They had met in late winter, 1916. Her husband Abell had been a big man, with a full head of red hair and a broad back. He was also a romantic; he loved flowers and the spring. He had insisted they marry when the earth was new, crops were in the ground, and flowers were blooming. So, in the spring of 1918, two weeks after Anna turned nineteen they married. He died the next November.

She always thought that ironic, so many people were celebrating the end of the Great War, and her husband, who had fought in it hadn't been there. Abell had gone off to war in January 1917. By the February of 1918 he was home, one leg left behind in France, but home. She had her man and they would be all right. Then came the Spanish flu. Abell left in the morning for his job at the post office, that night he came home with a cough, by evening he couldn't stand, and he died before morning. The speed of his death had always troubled Anna. She hadn't had time to tell him how much he meant to her, about their unborn child, to make plans. He hadn't seen his boy, didn't know how much his son looked like him; never tussled his hair. Anna's eyes began to tear.

In what seemed like the Almighty's ploy to drag her from the depths of depression a crash sounded from the small living room behind her. An instant later Anna's pride and joy, her son Ezra, exploded into the kitchen.

"David told me he needs help selling newspapers today," the boy announced.

There had been another murder; one of the Licavoli Squad had been gunned down by the Purple Gang. The Times had run an 'extra' edition.

"He said I'd get two cents for every paper I sold."

"How much does David get?" Anna asked with a knowing smile.

"He keeps three cents. He said it's because he's the official representative of the Times and he's responsible. Come on Ma, I can get us a half bushel of apples if I sell twenty-five papers."

Anna smiled a mother's smile and nodded at her boy. "Give me a kiss," she said and Ezra was out the door.

The fall of 1931 was cold and rainy. Today was no exception. David Puginwitz stood outside the Collingwood Manor apartment building and called to the pedestrians on either side of the street. In the last hour he had sold only five newspapers, and the day was turning old. David pulled his collar up and shoved his hands deeper into his pockets. It worked for a moment but the strap of his newspaper bag slid off his small shoulder and the bag fell to the wet sidewalk.

Worried the newspapers would be ruined, David uttered a curse he'd learned from his father, removed his hands from his coat pockets and hiked the strap back to his shoulder. He then blew on his clenched fists and jammed them back into his pockets. If he hunched his shoulder the bag held its position. Sadly, to David's never ending annoyance, the moment he relaxed his shoulder it fell to the sidewalk and the process was repeated.

As David pulled the newspaper bag to his shoulder for what seemed the fiftieth time he heard his friend Ezra's voice. The two boys greeted each other and immediately fell into a detailed discussion of their mutual obsession, the Detroit Tigers. David was a master of recalling the details of each of the summer's games. And, what he didn't remember he could invent. Ezra was a walking almanac of baseball statistics. Today, the conversation quickly turned to how bad this season had been and which players their team needed to replace. After a few minutes of baseball David pulled the newspaper bag from his shoulder and handed it to Ezra.

"I'm going inside to get warm. Don't let the bag get wet. I can't sell a wet newspaper."

David got all of two steps when Ezra suddenly exclaimed, "I almost forgot! Look what I've got!"

With that, Ezra pulled a tin from his coat pocket and opened it. Inside lay a small stack of baseball trading cards; several packs of cigarettes lay on top of the cards, candy wrapped in foil peeked from between cards. Ezra put the newspaper bag on the sidewalk, causing David to grimace and handed one of the cigarette packs to David.

David examined the pack of Sweet Caporal cigarettes. "What do I want with these? I don't smoke. And I ain't startin' now. Ma says it makes your teeth fall out."

"Geeze, I know that. But, turn it over," Ezra said with a proud grin.

David did as he was told. To his delight on the back of the package was the prettiest Ty Cobb trading card he'd ever seen. "Holy smokes! This is great!" he explained. All thoughts of a warm stove disappeared. Immediately David began offering combinations of his cards in trade for one of the new Ty Cobb cards. A brief argument over the value of various cards, new cards versus old cards, gum cards versus dry goods cards, a round of potential deals in which both boys tried to dump hated Yankee players on the other and soon a deal was struck. A few minutes later David was examining his new card when the possibility that Ezra had stolen the cigarettes crossed his mind.

"Where'd you get the cigarette packs Ezra?" David said with newly found suspicion. "If you lifted them and my

Ma finds out..."

"I didn't steal nothin'!" Ezra then began to explain how Mr. Kacrozowski left two cartons of cigarettes and four shirts at his house. He was coming to the part about how a drunken Mr. Kaczorowski tried to grab his mother, and what she had called Mr. Kacrozowski when she hit him on the head with a frying pan, when a new, black four-door Chrysler coasted to a stop in front of the building. Instinctively, both boys ceased their chatter.

The front passenger door opened and a man with a dark gray tweed overcoat stepped to the curb. He took a moment to study the street. His glance passed over the boys, then both sides of the street in each direction. Finally, he studied the windows of the nearby buildings. Satisfied, he nodded in the direction of the car. Two men climbed out of the back seat. One reflexively skimmed his hand over his hip and said, "I didn't bring my gun."

The other glanced at him, "I told ya, ya don't bring guns to a meeting like this." Walking around to the trunk of the car he removed a brown briefcase. The three men gathered on the curb. The driver shut off the engine, got out and walked around the front of the car. As if on command the three men, in matching strides, approached the steps to the building. Their shoes making a rhythmic 'smack...smack...smack' on the wet concrete as they approached the boys. The driver hurried around the car and ran to catch up.

Ezra knew something about the street. These guys were going to take his baseball cards and maybe shake down David for his paper money. Realizing it was too late to slip the tin back in his pocket he pushed it to the bottom of the newspaper bag. Then he stepped behind David.

The three men swept past the two boys without looking at them. The driver, now only a step or two behind, turned and flipped a silver dollar in their direction. "You kids! Keep an eye on my car," he snarled. Ezra tried to catch the coin and missed. The man stopped. The coin rang off the step and rolled to the sidewalk.

"C'mon Sol!" one barked, and the men entered the apartment building.

Chapter 2

Harry Keywell stood silently at the window of Collingwood Manor, apartment 211 and watched the street. After ten minutes he finally said, "They're here."

Irving Milberg and Ray Bernstein both joined Harry at the window. Harry Fleisher remained sitting on the couch.

"I don't have any argument with Sol," Irving said.

"I don't want a witness," Harry replied.

"Look, Sol's alright. We leave him alone," Ray announced.

Fleisher stood up, "You sure about that Ray? I hope Sol doesn't bite us on the ass."

A moment later Keywell answered the door. Joe Lebowitz, Hymie Paul and Izzy 'The Rat' Sutker walked in. An awkward silence filled the room. Finally Bernstein broke the tension. "Boys, take a seat," he said and pointed to an oversized couch and easy chair.

Ray's eyes focused on the briefcase. Maybe this would go alright. Harry turned on Izzy Sutker, "I think we all know what this is about," he said.

"Sure Harry, we know we owe you some money..."

"Not just some, you owe us a lot of money Izzy."

"You know we're good for it" Sutker continued.

"I've heard that before," Ray said from across the room. "You've promised, and you've promised. You came to us and asked for a loan and I gave it to you. It makes me look like a fool. But the worst thing is that you idiots went and tried to cut us out of the business. Then you guys had the moxie to ask for another loan..."

"And we damned well gave it to you," Milberg cut in. Ray glanced at Milberg, then continued, "Now you're telling us you need more time. We already gave you more time. After all that, you tell us you can't pay."

"What is this?" Harry demanded.

Hymie Paul concentrated on Harry's every move. He

glanced at Milberg and Bernstein then his partners Izzy Sutker and Joe Lebowitz. Finally he said, "I think we can work something out." He patted the case. "I've got half of your money right here. It'll take us a little time, but we should have the rest of the money to you in three months."

Keywell erupted, "Half? You come here with half? What the hell do you think this is?"

Almost imperceptibly Ray shook his head no.

Fleisher put his hands out as if to pat the air. "Boys, let's all be calm. Look, let's not get worked up about this. I've got some cold beer in the basement. I'll go get us some and we'll work out some terms." The decision had been made. Ray, Irv and Harry Keywell all glanced at each other.

"Yeah, I think you're right," Ray said.

Fleisher walked out into the hall and headed for the street. The car would be idling in back in three minutes.

"We need it all," Irv said a moment later.

Harry Keywell moved to the next window, his hand slipped inside his jacket and gripped his pistol.

"Look, we ain't got that much, we're lucky to have this," Hymie's throat had tightened; his voice was almost a squeal.

Irv grinned, "I don't think you understand. We employ you, we give you a good territory, and you knock over our runs, you don't pay your debts, you steal from us!"

Irv's voice was getting louder, he took a breath then very slowly he said, "We…need…our…money…NOW." His fist slammed onto the table.

Lebowitz glanced at his two partners. "Look, Irv, I understand. We'll get you the rest. But it will take time, we'll need a month."

Milberg looked at Keywell and shrugged, "Seems like an awful long time don't you think?"

Keywell pulled his gun, "Times up."

David stooped to pick up the silver dollar. Ezra had failed to catch it when Sol had tossed the coin. "Those guys look like gangsters, Ezra. We've got real life gangsters right here!"

Ezra was staring at the door where the men had disappeared. David sat down on the wet step, Ezra joined him. Still shaken neither boy said anything. After a few moments Ezra stood up and announced, "I'm going home."

"What! You can't leave. Neither can I. That guy gave us a dollar to watch his car. That's a lot of money. If we leave he'll come back and get us. We have to stay right here." David was older and so he must be smarter. Ezra sat back on the step.

"I think those guys were the Purple Gang," David said a few minutes later. "There was a story about them in the paper last week. I saw their picture. They're famous."

Suddenly a series of pops could be heard from a long distance away. Both boys jumped to their feet, eyes searching the street as they turned a slow circle. Another round of gunfire and this time the two friends could identify the location of the sound, as one they turned and looked to the second floor. A moment later the building's front door burst open and the driver of the car ran out carrying a brown briefcase. Taking the stairs two at a time he collided with Ezra and David knocking the boys over and falling to the sidewalk. The case flew from his hand scattering several bundles of cash on the sidewalk. The case slid across the sidewalk and under the big car.

"What the...," David cried. Ezra slid across the sidewalk and came to rest against the Chrysler.

"Gimme that," Sol Levine shouted at Ezra as he jumped to his feet. Sol grabbed the newspaper bag and pulled. The boy was jerked forward and fell to the sidewalk, landing on the side of his face with a yell. Sol dragged the bag from the boy's grasp. Then he scooped up the bundles of cash laying on the sidewalk and stuffed them into the bag. After a quick glance at the door of the building he ran to the Chrysler. In a moment the engine roared and the car was turning the corner onto Grand Boulevard.

Seconds later three men tumbled from the door of

the apartment building, each man carrying a pistol. They ran down the stairs, past Ezra and David and into the center of the street. The three men turned in circles looking for the car. It was too late. One man spotted the briefcase laying on the curb. He picked it up, looked inside then threw it back on the street.

"The little shit! He took it all!" the man yelled.

"Ray, I'm gonna kill that little S.O.B.," another whispered.

The three men then walked back into the building. It was as if David and Ezra were invisible. Ezra dabbed his bloody nose and began to cry.

Chapter 3

Detroit was an ethnic melting pot. Poles, Czechs, Germans, French, Italians, and Jews. Each had their own gang. But the meanest and easily the most feared was a gang founded by four Jewish Russian immigrants, the Bernstein brothers, Abe, Joe, Raymond and Izzy. The boys began their life of crime with simple street jobs; muggings, purse snatching and "smash and grab" robberies. They quickly progressed to shaking down local merchants. Legend had it that the gang got its name after hitting a meat market. "Those boys are rotten, purple like the color of rotten meat," the shopkeeper supposedly said. The name stuck.

The country should have seen the rise and violence the eighteenth amendment to the Constitution would bring. Michigan had instituted its own version of Prohibition, the Damon Act, a year earlier with disastrous results.

With the Damon Act's implementation the manufacture and distribution of alcohol became illegal everywhere in the state. Within months "rum running" was the fastest growing profession in the Motor City. As one newspaper complained, "the average citizen can make a year's wages in one month by becoming a gangster or bootlegger."

After every arrest the rumrunners invented an even more ingenious method for smuggling and distributing booze. The police tried to stop the flow of liquor to no avail. The money, the resources of the gangs, the corruption and the intimidation was too much. Liquor flowed from Windsor Canada across the Detroit River and into the fourth largest city in quantities no one could imagine.

The Purples knew a golden opportunity when they saw one. Soon they were the most powerful and feared gang in Detroit. Seventy-five percent of the illegal liquor coming into the United States from Canada came through Detroit. Its twenty-eight mile long Detroit River was just a mile from Canada and dotted with thousands of coves, boat yards, nooks and crannies - it was a smuggler's dream.

At first, the Purples tried to keep the Detroit river front to themselves. It was an impossible task. There were too many rivals; the Purples couldn't kill them all. But, they could impose a territorial system. Nothing moved along the docks of Detroit without the permission of the Purples. If it did, a savage lesson was taught. The Purples employed the new Thompson submachine gun as their business card. The 'Chopper' could cut a man in half in the blink of an eye. It ensured their rivals knew who had done the shooting and it left an impression.

The Purples dominated the Detroit underworld for years. No one went to jail. No one talked. The Purple Gang simply owned the police and killed anyone who complained. Business was business. The Detroit underworld flourished; the East Side Gang, "Singing Sam" Catalanotte, Chester "Big Chet" La Mare and the rest were, for the moment, happy with the arrangement.

The Purple Gang's lock on the waterfront and bootlegging couldn't last. The fall of 1931 saw an unprecedented opportunity for the competition. The American Legion was having its national convention in Detroit and the demand for liquor would surpass even the Purple's capacity to supply it. Now rivals from all over the country were slipping into the city. Worse yet, some of the gang's own associates began to moonlight. This didn't go unnoticed by the Bernstein brothers.

Foremost among the moonlighters were three new members of the 'Third Avenue Navy'. The Navy was part of the smuggling operation of the Purple Gang. Equipped with some of the fastest boats produced on the Great Lakes and armed with Thompson submachine guns the Navy made the run across the Lake and stopped others from making the same trip. The Navy's running fights with the U.S. Coast Guard were big news and widely reported.

The Navy was a major part of the supply side of the Purple Gang's operation. It was highly paid work, members were lost as a result of the work and to arrest. New members were recruited continuously. With the coming convention the Navy had to increase its size. New recruits were brought in without proper vetting. Hymie Paul, Isadore "Izzy" Sutker, and Joe Lebowitz were three of those new recruits.

That summer, in a show of supreme stupidity the three began diverting portions of each run. The lightened loads were not unnoticed, but good fortune smiled on the three double-crossers. A negotiation was taking place with the North Side Gang of Chicago. The Gang was losing its power in Chicago and the Purples were exploring ways of moving in on Al Capone's Chicago Outfit. A partnership seemed possible. The Purples simply didn't have the time to devote to these relatively small losses.

Unable to stand prosperity the three made another incredibly bad decision. They decided to start 'making book'. They set the odds, took bets from all comers, including the opposition, and counted on the betters to lose. The scheme should have worked, but the boys were swimming with the sharks.

A great pastime of the day was motor boat racing. Different categories of boats from sail to yacht, professional and amateur, were raced on the Detroit River to the delight of the populace. One of the more popular races was the "Gentleman's Motor Yacht" race, and the most famous of those racers was the "Volstead Act," a 34 foot locally built Chris-Craft.

Not knowing the monthly river races were fixed Sutker, Paul and Lebowitz bet big on the "Volstead Act." Unfortunately, they lost to members of Detroit's Italian East Side Gang. The East Side Gang, with its heavy New York connections and Sicilian pedigree was not in the habit of overlooking debts. To say that losing a bet to the East Side Gang was bad business was like saying Babe Ruth was just a ball player. It didn't come close to describing the reality.

Hymie and the boys knew of only one way out. Trading on their association with the rest of the Purple Gang they bought a hundred gallons of Canadian booze on credit. They then watered down the whiskey and sold it, undercutting the Purples' price for the same watered down booze. It didn't cover the debt, but the boys figured to make the rest up through their gambling operation.

The big score, and their only hope of salvation, was the boat races. Hymie and his friends only succeeded in proving that stupid really can strike the same spot twice. They again set odds on a river race, again the race was fixed, and again they lost big to the East Side Gang.

Forgetting the "First Rule of Holes", the boys didn't stop digging. Since the scheme had worked before they again approached their associates in the Purple Gang and again made a deal. A hundred gallons of Canadian whiskey were purchased, all on credit. Again they diluted the stock and undersold the market. It was one time too many for the Bernstein brothers. Hymie and the boys had forgotten they were cutting into the Purple's trade. To make matters worse, they didn't make enough money on the watered down booze. They couldn't pay back the Purples and they couldn't pay off the East Side Gang. They had succeeded in provoking not one, but two of the most powerful criminal organizations in the United States. Paul, Sutker, and Lebowitz were already dead and had simply been waiting for the Purples to tell them.

Chapter 4

April – This Year

Herman James Crenshaw preferred to be called "Jim". It never became an issue, but this morning a new teller at the bank had insisted he show two forms of identification. Ordinarily this wouldn't bother Jim; in fact, he was a big believer of better safe than sorry, but in this instance the young man knew Jim personally. Not only that, but Jim was putting money into his checking account, not taking it out.

He knew everyone in town, they knew him. Jim had umpired the kid's Little League games and coached his pee-wee basketball team. He knew it was "procedure," but knowing everyone was why he'd returned to a small town and not retired in D.C. or Boston or some other big city. Plus, the whole idea of showing two forms of identification to put money INTO his account struck him as absurd. Jim didn't care who put money into his account; he just didn't want anyone taking it out.

Leaving the building he shook his head, smiled and started his truck. He had two more stops on his morning errands. He needed to stop at the dollar store and pick up five packs of suckers, five packs of number 2 pencils and a pack of colored paper. Apparently, Eve's kids had earned a reward of a sucker and had also broken, stolen or sharpened to extinction the five packs of pencils he bought two weeks ago. Computers and the internet hadn't made pencils obsolete, at least in Eve's classroom. Next was a quick stop at the combination feed and seed store and grain elevator office to check on the price of fertilizer. Here he parked his truck in front of the building, rolled both the passenger and driver's windows up to the two-thirds position and got out. His dog Molly watched him walk away from the truck with sad eyes, gave one bark, then curled up in Jim's seat to wait for his return.

April was a wonderful time of year, the snow was gone, there was always the chance of a tee shirt and shorts day, opening day of baseball season proved the Union would last at least another year, and best of all those fields around the house just looked anxious to get to work. Jim had planted corn the last three years and was beginning to think this might be a year for soybeans. Crop rotation was something he should pay attention to he knew, but he hadn't owned the farm long enough for it to matter. Now, for some reason he couldn't explain, it mattered.

Jim had retired from the Air Force just six years ago. He'd worked for a defense contractor for a little while, found that to be an experience similar to a root canal without Novocain and quit. Four years ago he and his wife Eve had purchased their little sixty-acre farm. They'd taken a year to build a cottage style home, a barn and equipment shed and then planted their first crop. Jim grimaced as he recalled that first year. He termed that year's crop a "learning experience." Eve called it a disaster. Since then Jim had learned about seed depth, acid balance, seed spacing, nitrogen requirements, soil types, nematodes, a multitude of bugs, various fungi, and a host of other things that he'd never thought of before. He loved it.

Returning to the farm Jim parked the pickup in front of the garage, opened the truck door and moved aside as Molly rushed to be the first to the house. Jim walked to the rear of the truck, grabbed an armful of bags and headed for the house. Placing the bags on the kitchen table he filled Molly's water bowl, stood, then noticed the light on the telephone answering machine. Pushing "Play" he heard the welcome voice of his sister, Sherrie.

Chapter 5

The light turned red and Sol Levine braked the car to a stop. He checked the rear-view mirror for what must have been the fiftieth time. He had just witnessed three men murdered. He was on the edge of panic. What had he been thinking? In the confusion of the murders he'd grabbed the briefcase and run. He'd taken money from the Purple Gang; it was a death sentence.

His forehead was covered with sweat. He took off his brown fedora and wiped the hatband with his handkerchief. His hands were shaking. Sol had to get out of Detroit, he knew that, he just didn't know how. He checked the rear-view mirror again.

Sol had circled Detroit twice trying to decide what to do. Evening had turned to night; night was becoming morning. No one was behind him…for now. There would be. He thought he spotted a familiar Packard. Frantically he pressed the accelerator. Sol came to Jefferson Avenue and smashed the brake, attempted to downshift and missed the gear. The transmission gave a loud clatter and rattled the shift lever in his hand. He found third gear and accelerated as he turned left on Jefferson to parallel the Detroit River. He had to calm down.

Sol took a deep breath. He passed Owens Park, then Memorial Park. Suddenly Sol was inspired. He'd worked for Izzy Sutker before. A couple of times he'd helped Izzy unload booze at a boathouse just down the street. Once, Izzy had taken him on a run to Canada. They'd crossed at night, loaded the booze on the boat and come back all in one night. He'd made fifty bucks for one night's work. The more he thought about it the better Sol liked his idea. What better place to hide out than in the Purples own boathouse?

He slowed when he came to the Detroit Water Works building. A little further and he'd found a small dirt path, more a driveway than a side street. The big Chrysler crept silently down the small two-lane path, coasting to a stop at the water's edge. Sol turned the lights of the car off and carefully studied his rear-view mirrors. Nothing moved. No one had followed him. Sol had never owned a gun, he wished he did now. This was not a totally safe place, but it was the only place he was sure they wouldn't be looking.

He stepped down from the car and allowed his eyes to adjust to the darkness. After a moment he was calm, well, as calm as he could be right now. Sol carefully examined his surroundings. He was alone. No, maybe not. Maybe they were waiting for him. He couldn't decide. He stood next to the open door, engine running. Again Sol checked his surroundings. No one was here. He was almost sure. He bent into the car to shut off the engine. If someone was going to grab him it was going to be now. With a grimace Sol turned the key. The engine died. He listened to the night. A horn blared in the distance. Street noise filtered down between the warehouses and garages along Jefferson. Against Windsor's lights he could see a working boat making its way toward Lake Huron. Sol relaxed just a little.

Nervously Sol fingered the newspaper bag. He glanced left, then right, took a deep breath and sprinted across the parking lot to a small boathouse and slipped inside. Happy that he hadn't been gunned down before he reached the door Sol sat down on the floor and caught his breath. He started a nervous laugh. After a few minutes he stood up, cracked the door open, and peered into the night. Nothing moved.

Sol turned and groped his way across the building. Eventually outstretched hands found a workbench. Reaching into his pocket he found a match box. Fishing one out he gripped it in his fist and flicked his thumbnail against the match head. It flared and Sol tried to get his bearings. Quickly the match burned down; he struck another. He fixed the layout of the building in his mind and began to work his way to the end of a long workbench. There, he searched the wall.

It took a minute, but soon Sol found what he was

looking for. He struck another match, turned up the wick in an oil lantern and a quiet light illuminated the inside of the building. Across from the bench, resting peacefully at its moorings sat a beautiful Chris-Craft cruiser.

Sol didn't pause to admire the boat. Taking a small step stool from its hook Sol placed it on the edge of the dock. A moment later he was aboard the boat and opening the door to the small cabin below. There he slid into the cabin booth and emptied the newspaper bag on the table. Out fell a small tin, several newspapers and packs of money.

Sol was amazed. The sight of the money didn't erase stupid, but it did make Sol brave. He quickly counted the cash, twenty packs of hundreds. Twenty thousand dollars per pack, four hundred thousand dollars. He grinned. This was the big score. Sol would be sitting pretty the rest of his life, all he had to do was grab his girl and get out of town. He could easily get lost in Canada somewhere. He'd always heard that Toronto was a pretty town, maybe Montreal…the possibilities were nearly endless.

Sol picked up the tin. It was a Blue Bird caramel container. Opening the top he shook out the contents. A pile of baseball cards, a few coins, several packs of cigarettes and a handful of caramels. He grinned, unwrapped a caramel and stuffed it into his mouth; this was perfect. Sol pocketed the coins, some of the caramels and two packs of cigarettes. He scooped the rest back into the tin. Pressing the cover onto the can he shoved it into the bottom of the newspaper bag. Still this was serious business. He had to think.

Gradually the grin returned. Sol got up from the bench seat and made his way to the boat's forward cabin. Here he removed a board from the floor to expose a small compartment. This compartment extended forward three feet and was specifically built to hold five cases of Canadian whiskey. Sol had loaded this very compartment when he'd gone on the trip with Izzy. Normally, no one would find it. But Sol knew that his friends were also his enemies and they knew about the compartment as well as he did.

Leaving the boat and returning to the workbench Sol

took a few moments to find the tools he needed. He tied on a carpenter's apron, shoved the tools he'd selected in the apron and hurried back to the cruiser. Feeling better about his chances by the moment Sol sprinted up the small foot stool and bounced onto the cruiser's deck. Moving into the cabin, he pushed the compartment cover out of his way and lay on the floor. Then, turning on his back Sol wedged himself into the whiskey compartment. He lay there for a moment, head and shoulders in the compartment, heels on the deck. The edge of the compartment cut into the small of his back. Reaching with his right hand he grabbed the lantern and sat it on the floor of the compartment above his left shoulder. Now he had light. Removing a screwdriver from the carpenter's apron he reached above his head deep into the compartment and began removing the brass screws which held the end board. After a few minutes he had all eight out and was able to pull the board away from its frame. Sol then took the canvas newspaper bag, wrapped it in newspapers, and wedged it into the bilge of the cruiser. Forty minutes later he had replaced the end board and painted a fresh coat of shellac over the entire compartment. No one would find any evidence of his handiwork.

He crawled out of the hole, stood and rubbed his lower back. Then Sol took a bottle of Windsor Canadian from behind the captain's seat and sat down at the settee. A grin began to grow; Sol lifted the bottle, toasted the now dead "Captain" Izzy and took a long pull. He imagined his girl Dolly in the finest Chicago fashions; she'd look just like Gretta Garbo. He pictured her leaning on a long bar and whispering, "Give me a whiskey, ginger ale on the side, and don't be stingy, baby." Just like Garbo herself.

He'd get himself a new suit and look just like Cagney. He had it planned. The grin broaden to a smile, things were looking up. Sol killed the light and went to the front of the boathouse. A narrow walkway extended along the wall to the opening and around the side of the building. It allowed operation of a large, garage-like door into the boathouse. Sol could just squeeze around the wall without falling in the river.

Sol liked this, it allowed him to see the surrounding area from a place no one would suspect. He studied the shadows between the buildings, the light was low, the morning sun was just peeking over Windsor. Satisfied that no one was watching Sol jumped to the shore then sprinted to the Chrysler. Starting the car Sol grinned again. "Who knows? Maybe Dolly Eleanor Grongoski would even become an honest woman," he thought.

Chapter 6

Dolly Grongoski was not a shy wallflower. Raised on the poor, sandy soil of northern Michigan she was used to long days, hard work and hard people. Small, just five foot four inches tall and skinny, too skinny by her own standards, she had left the farm for a job in Detroit the day she turned eighteen. That was just under a year ago. She'd fallen in with hard people and lived a hard life, but she was proud of the fact that never, not once, had any of them been able to take advantage of her. She could out think them, and she wasn't afraid of a fight.

The one bright spot in the past year had been Sol. She didn't love him, he wasn't very smart and he could never make it on a farm back home, but he had a kind heart and he gave her lots of things and spent money on her when he had it. It was a good deal for both of them; she only worried about getting pregnant.

But Sol was not her dream. Dolly intended to be someone, she did not want to end up like her mother or cousins. Spending the rest of her life ironing someone else's shirts or feeding chickens was not her idea of a life. She would be a nurse or a school teacher or a secretary to some big executive.

To add color to the dream Dolly liked to take the bus all the way out to Ann Arbor on her days off. That's where she was this morning. She would walk across the University campus and pretend she was a student. She would sit on the benches, admire the clothes the girls wore, and dream about having something more than a tenth grade education.

At noon Dolly began to get hungry. She used the engineering building's archway to leave the campus and made her way south on University Avenue. Soon she came to the East Quadrangle dormitory. She waited until several students were entering the building and joined the crowd. A blond haired boy politely held the door and Dolly was in.

Carefully she explored the building. It only took a few minutes and she'd found what she had come for, the cafeteria line. The line moved steadily along and Dolly closely watched the process at the door. A student sitting on a stool fought off boredom while checking each person's University identification card. Several of the students claimed they had forgotten their ID card or had otherwise lost it. The ID checker then consulted a list, found the name, then passed the offending party into the land of food and ice cream. Satisfied, Dolly gave up her position in line.

A few minutes later she was again outside the building's main entrance. She waited until one of the school's few women students approached, then leaned against a light post and began to cry. The young woman immediately came to her aid.

"Hi...ahhhh....are you all right?" she asked.

"Nooooo." Dolly moaned. "I just broke up with my boyfriend, and I want to go home." She tucked her chin down to her chest and gave a few silent sobs.

"Oh honey, that's tough." The girl put a hand on Dolly's shoulder. "We've all been through it. Maybe you should go back to your room and lay down."

"No, I can't, I've got to go to class," Dolly sobbed.

"Well, you can't go to class crying like this. Come on, I'll walk you back to your room." The girl gently took Dolly's elbow.

"Thank you," Dolly said and let herself be led along. After a few steps, in her most pitiful voice, Dolly said, "What's your name?"

"I'm Mary Ellen Bennett. What's yours?"

"I'm Debbie Williams." A few steps later Dolly shook herself, stood to her maximum height and in her most confident voice announced. "Oh, I'm alright. I'm not going to let him ruin my life. I really should go to class, it'll be fine."

Mary Ellen smiled, "That's the spirit. You'll have another boyfriend in no time, you'll see."

Mary Ellen didn't take a great deal of convincing and

soon she went on her way. Dolly waited until the girl was out of sight then slipped back into the dormitory and rejoined the line for the cafeteria.

It wasn't such a pleasant day for Sol. He was on a frantic search for her. Nervously watching his rearview mirror Sol visited the diner where Dolly worked, checked her apartment and searched her favorite stores. The afternoon was slipping away and, afraid to return to his own shabby room, Sol took up residence in a bar on Fort Street. There he began calling her boarding house phone every thirty minutes.

At six that evening Dolly was back in Detroit climbing the stairs to her flat when Mrs. Boardman, the boarding house owner, stopped her.

"Dolly, a man's been looking for you. Wouldn't say his name. I don't approve of men in the building miss. You know the rules."

Dolly thought a moment, decided it had to be Sol, then examined the exceedingly large woman. Using her most charming smile Dolly said, "He's my cousin, I'm sure this is about my mother. She's very sick you know."

The woman eyed Dolly. "I'm sure," she said, then slammed her door.

Shortly after Dolly had closed her apartment door the phone at the end of the hall rang. It was answered by one of the building's tenants. Seconds later the loud cry, "Dolly, ya got a lover on the line," careened through the house. A minute later Dolly was talking to Sol.

"Dolly, babe, where ya been?" he didn't wait for an answer. "Never mind, I've got some big news. We've hit the big time baby. I need to pick you up. I'll be there in ten minutes. Meet me in back of the building." And, before Dolly could argue Sol had hung up.

They drove to Grosse Pointe just to get out of the city and let Sol explain what he had seen and done. Dolly at first panicked. She wanted out of the car and intended to run as far from Sol as she could. She was no fool and knew what happened to people who crossed the Purples.

It took a while, but eventually he convinced her to

calm down. When he did, Dolly began to think the situation over very carefully. Sol said he had a lot of money, more than a lot. And he wasn't lying. He was too scared to be lying, she could tell. She asked a few questions and slowly it came to her. This was legit. Dolly was convinced; this was their chance for a big score and to get out of Detroit.

They ate an early dinner in Hamtramck, then headed to the river. Dolly insisted on stopping at her apartment for a change of clothes and to pick up some keepsakes she'd brought from home. Then they headed to Sol's apartment.

Chapter 7

Sol rented a room above a small meat market. Mr. Spadoff went home for the day at six, the market was closed, lights off. They circled the block twice. Sol was careful to keep his speed up and tried not to draw attention to the car. Nothing moved, no one sat in some dark car. It looked normal.

On the third trip past the store they slowed to a crawl and Dolly peered through the windows inside the market. A small red glow flared in the back behind the meat counter. Dolly spotted the cigarette just as Sol began to brake, intending to park next to the front door. "GO, GO, GO!!" she yelled.

Sol stepped on the gas and the Chrysler lurched forward, caught its wind and sped off. The door of the meat market burst open and two men ran out. By the time they reached their car Sol and Dolly were ghosts in the night.

Thirty minutes later, certain they'd not been followed, Sol turned off Jefferson Avenue and coasted to a stop ten yards from the boathouse. Sol moved Dolly's two bags from the car to the Chris-Craft.

"We're all set doll. I just need one thing. Run up there to the market and get me a razor and some blades would ya? A man's gotta look presentable when we get to Canada."

"Where's the market?" Dolly asked.

Sol walked Dolly to the door and pointed. "Around that shed, up the hill, between those two warehouses and down the street to the corner." Dolly agreed and was on her way.

Sol watched Dolly as she rounded the small tool shed and walked to the alley leading to the street. "She's got a great ass," he said to himself. He then turned and headed into the boathouse. Sol boarded the Chris-Craft and quickly checked the forward liquor hole. No one had tampered with it; the money was safe. He jumped to the side of the boathouse and grabbed a hose connected to two fifty-five gallon drums. The drums were on an elevated stand and gravity fed the hose. It took twenty minutes to fill the fuel tanks. When he had finished Sol checked his watch, muttered "Damn, bet she got lost. Where the hell is she?" Unfortunately, it was a question that Sol would never have answered.

THE COLLINGWOOD LEGACY

Available Now!

Find out more about HJGaudreau
and the stories behind the story at

www.HJGaudreau.com

www.ingramcontent.com/pod-product-compliance
Lightning Source LLC
Chambersburg PA
CBHW021952170626
46808CB00001B/118